180° MAGNETIC

SUICIDE SAIL

JIM SCHOENDALLER
JEANNE C. STEIN

JAMES SCHOENDALLER PUBLISHING

180 Degrees Magnetic - Suicide Sail

Copyright © 2021 by Jim Schoendaller

ISBN - 979-8-9904650-4-6

James Schoendaller Publishing

Cover design and illustrations by Leslie Waara

ACKNOWLEDGMENTS

Whereas this final book of the trilogy took a significant effort, especially the ending, there are several individuals that I wish to recognize.

My wife Amy and daughter Natalie - A giant "Thank You" for your patience, understanding, and encouragement. Writing a trilogy is a long process and your support never faltered.

Jeanne C. Stein - Another giant "Thank You" for investing your time and writing mastery. Making sure there was nothing hanging in the final book of the trilogy presented unexpected challenges. Like you say, "Writing is 10 percent writing and 90 percent rewriting." That couldn't have been more true this time.

Deanne Conte, mom #2 - Thank you for your feedback and support.

I wish to thank my self-publishing support group - Stuart Smith, Avant Studios; Deborah Dove, editor; and Leslie Waara for the artwork.

I wish to thank my subject matter experts for their valuable assistance - Jim Cook, the founder of the Victoria Sailing School; Cmdr Nicole Schwegman and Lt. Taija Griffin, US Pacific Fleet, Naval Surface Force, Public Affairs Office.

I am also grateful to my beta-readers for reading the entire manuscript and providing their honest feedback (sometimes too honest - lol) - My wife Amy (my toughest critic - lol); Steve Bohn, sailing and ballroom dancing friend; Leslie Hock, neighbor and sailor; Phil Stein, Jeanne's wonderful husband.

Jim Schoendaller

When we started this project, Jim came to me with a manuscript years in the making. I can't tell you how complemented I was that he wanted to share his work with me. Now we have not only completed one book, but three! I can only take credit for helping him in the creative process. The ideas and sailing expertise are all his. His love of the sea is infectious, it comes through on every page.

Jim mentioned all his contacts who added to the accuracy of the book—to that I want to add my thanks as well. And to Amy, Jim's wife, and Natalie my unofficial goddaughter and tennis partner, thank you for letting me be a part of your family. To my own husband, Phil, and daughter, Jeanette who have always encouraged me to spread my writing wings, know that I couldn't do it without you.

Jeanne C. Stein

A Nautical Glossary can be found at the end of this book to aid
in your navigation through *Suicide Sail*.

I stared at the approaching fog in disbelief. How could Pat, my best friend, be doing this to me? Not only to me, but to Reid, Charles, Jane, Vee, Bev, Candy, Dreamgirl, and Marta —all of us aboard *The Aquaholic*? Did she really plan to use the technology she'd gotten from the aliens to send us back twenty-five thousand seven hundred years into the past? I felt rooted in place, unable to speak or move.

But Reid Adams, my lover and former sailing instructor, didn't stare. He sprang into action, immediately heading for the helm of *The Aquaholic*. The engines were running since we had been rafted to *The Lady Anne*, and Reid wasted not one second in shifting from idle to forward and quickly accelerating.

I realized what he was doing, but I also knew that even

with the catamaran's speed, we couldn't outrun the aliens' fog. Before I could remind him of that, he began giving orders.

"Vee," Reid said. "Divide everybody into pairs."

Since Vee was *The Aquaholic's* captain, I wondered if there would be an argument about who was in charge and should be giving orders. There wasn't. Vee moved to where she could see Reid clearly. "What are your orders?" she asked.

"Send one pair to disconnect the main and starting batteries, the starting batteries now and the main batteries the instant I shut down the engines," Reid said. He spoke calmly but loudly enough to be heard over the rumble of the engines.

Vee acknowledged by nodding.

"Next, one pair needs to lock down the shipping screws on all of the compasses."

Vee nodded again.

"One pair needs to remove the batteries from the portable radios and all but one of the flashlights. Don't worry about any phones or handheld GPS units. Do those last."

"Is that it?" Vee asked.

"Have someone close the valves on the propane tanks," Reid replied. "Get Charles and Jane to help." Then he looked at me and added, "Jot down our current GPS position."

After I noted our position in the log, I climbed up to the helm and sat beside Reid. I knew we couldn't outrun the fog. I also knew we couldn't stay topside once the fog overtook us. Exposed to the elements, we'd never survive the trip through the aliens' electromagnetic time portal.

I watched as the fog got closer, coming at us from the side.

But Reid wasn't watching the fog. His eyes were locked on *The Lady Anne.*

She was maybe two hundred yards in front of us and headed away. Her sails were down, so she had to be motoring.

"What are you doing?" I asked. I had been through the time portal before, twice actually, and going through it again didn't scare me all that much. I knew I could survive it.

It was the reason why this was happening that made me angry—furious really. Pat Taylor had jumped to the conclusion that Reid and I and the others on board *The Aquaholic* were leaving her alone to face the CIA over the disappearance of a Navy ship, *The USS Fields.*

She had convinced herself Reid was in love with Dreamgirl and that Dreamgirl and I were both having a relationship with him, much the same way Pat, Reid, and I had bonded on *The Lady Anne.* In her mind, we were running off together. Reid had never been given a chance to explain. Rather than confront him directly, she decided to send us all back in time.

And to make matters worse, she was using the alien technology that I had warned her against. I knew that having access to that kind of power might corrupt her. But she kept harping at me that it was necessary for self-defense. I finally gave in and she successfully lobbied the aliens for the ability to initiate the time portal with a simple device she had made using portable radios and foil-wrapped antennas.

The fog was maybe fifty yards away now and closing in fast. Vee had told the others what needed to be done. I couldn't see anybody from where I was seated.

"Tracy," Reid said. "Go below and try and establish communication with the aliens. See if they'll stop the time portal."

As I climbed down from the helm, Vee approached, carrying some tools. I figured she was going to fix the helm compass so the needle wouldn't break off when we went through the portal.

"What are they doing?" Reid shouted. I looked back at him, then followed his gaze to *The Lady Anne*. Her wake indicated she had changed course. Now she appeared to be slowing.

The fog was closing in, but we were quickly gaining on *The Lady Anne*. I wondered what in the hell Pat was doing. I mean, why would she let us catch her?

CHAPTER 2

A few seconds later, the fog overtook us. I could no longer see *The Lady Anne*, or much else for that matter, but based on my last look, we were bearing right down on top of her.

Reid shut down the engines and then helped Vee lock down the main compass. The fog encased us like a soft, wet blanket. We now had close to zero visibility. I put my palm directly in front of my face. I could barely see it, but I could hear water rushing past the hulls. From my experience docking a boat under power, I knew our momentum would carry us quite a ways. I silently hoped we wouldn't crash into *The Lady Anne*.

Keeping one hand up and out, I moved slowly, baby steps. When I bumped into the cockpit table, I turned right and headed forward. The main salon couldn't be more than a few feet away.

Somebody ran into me from behind. I jumped and nearly fell over. Whoever hit me roughly grabbed my arm and helped me stand.

"Sorry, but I can't see."

It was Reid.

"Neither can I," Vee added. It sounded like she was behind him. Reid put his hand on my shoulder and told me to keep going.

I saw a faint light ahead and cautiously made my way toward it. When I entered the main salon, I saw a figure holding a flashlight. It was Charles. He offered his hand and pulled me closer to him. Reid followed me. Vee followed Reid, sliding the door closed behind her.

The misty fog had entered the salon, but it wasn't as heavy as outside. I watched as Bev entered the salon from the forward side. "I closed the door to the foredeck," she announced.

"I've got the portholes and hatches closed in the starboard hull," Candy said. "And the batteries on that side are now disconnected."

"Same for the port hull," Dreamgirl added.

I looked at our other two passengers, Jane and Marta. They were seated at the salon table. A small pile of disassembled radios and flashlights was in front of them. Jane was putting stuff into small baggies, keeping everything together so it could be reassembled later. "Almost done here," Jane said, not looking up for more than a second.

Reid went over and picked up the pieces of a disassembled flashlight. He quickly reassembled it, tested it, and then handed it to me. "Take this, go below, and do what I asked." I noticed Bev and Candy looking at me, but they didn't say anything. Neither did I.

I took the light and went belowdecks into the starboard side hull and into the aft cabin, telling myself the back of the boat was safer than the front, just in case we did smash into *The Lady Anne*.

It was dark and I could no longer hear water rushing past the hulls. I figured we had stopped. The cabin was eerily quiet. The air was moist and heavy. I lay down on the bed, switched off the flashlight, and closed my eyes.

I used to have to get drunk to contact the aliens. But Pat and I had been given a new way to establish contact that didn't involve alcohol. All I had to do was relax. Relax and focus on telling the aliens I needed to communicate.

From my two previous journeys through the time portal, I figured I had about ten minutes before the fog dissipated and the light show began. During the light show, ozone would form and intensify until its odor was nearly overpowering.

I inhaled deeply through my nose. I didn't smell anything.

I reminded myself that static electricity would follow the ozone. The static electricity would be with us as we entered the archway that would become the time portal. The portal would make a painfully loud humming noise. Then I would blackout and wake up in the past—twenty-five thousand seven hundred years in the past.

I exhaled and relaxed some more. I began counting backwards from ten. I counted nine and relaxed my eyes and face. Then I relaxed my head, neck, and shoulders, working my way down my body, relaxing each part as I counted down.

I chanced another sniff. Still no ozone. I continued to force myself to relax, knowing that everyone topside was counting on me to communicate with the aliens and stop the time portal process.

"Don't think about what you can't do," I silently told myself. "Focus on relaxing; you're almost there."

I reached three and pictured that number in my mind. I saw a large three, black and red. My body felt relaxed, totally relaxed. Head to toe.

"This is Tracy calling the aliens. I need to talk to you. This is urgent."

I waited a few moments and repeated my thoughts. When the aliens made contact, I'd "hear" them in my mind, then I could ask them to stop the process. I repeated my message again, projecting it into my mind, concentrating on the singular thought of talking to the aliens.

My body was relaxed, my mind was focused. My breathing was relaxed. "This should be working," I told myself.

"This is Tracy. We need to talk. Can you hear me?" I kept mentally projecting those three short thoughts. There was no response.

I felt myself sink into the bed. "Keep relaxing," I told myself. "You can do this. This is Tracy Palmer calling the aliens. Are you there?"

When I smelled ozone, I had a bad feeling that either the aliens weren't "hearing me," or they didn't want to "talk."

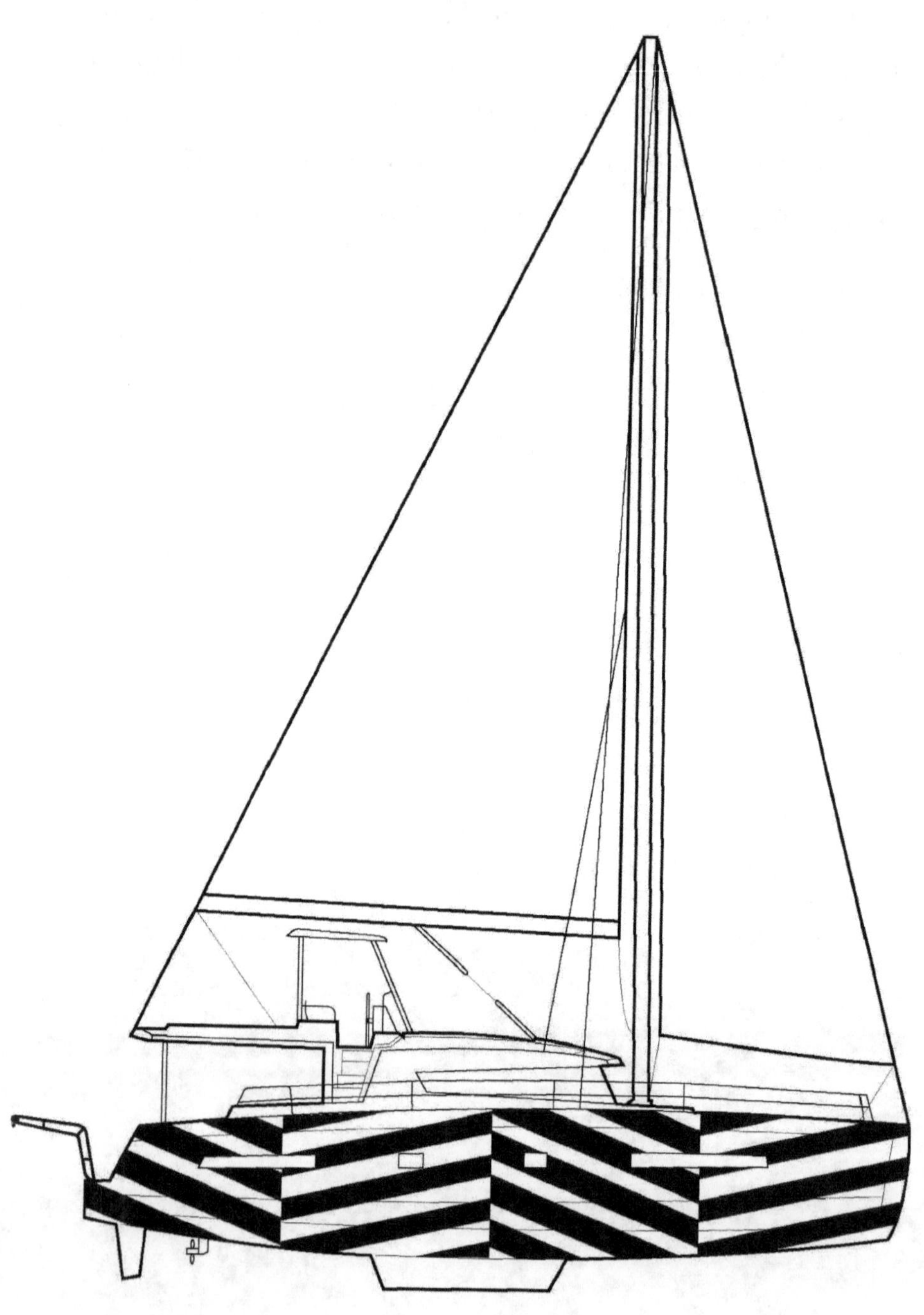

THE AQUAHOLIC
VESSEL OVERVIEW
NOT TO SCALE

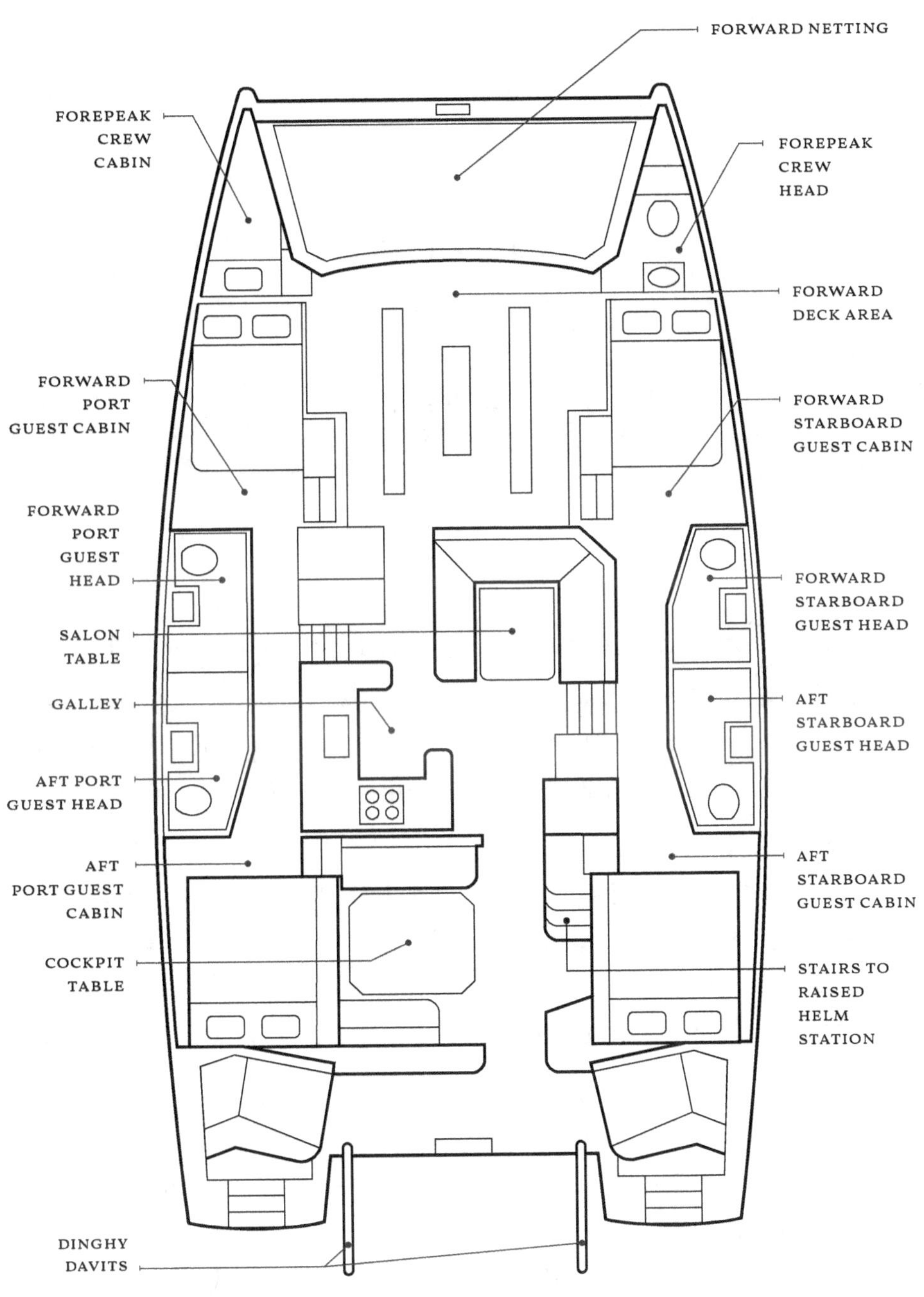

THE AQUAHOLIC
CABIN LAYOUT
NOT TO SCALE

CHAPTER 3

My concentration was broken by a light knock on the cabin door. I tried not to listen, tried to focus on communicating, but between the knocking and the ozone smell, my attempt to establish communications with the aliens had ended.

I opened my eyes. It wasn't as dark as before and, without needing the flashlight, I could see the cabin door. The knocking persisted.

"It's unlocked," I said, a little annoyed that whoever was knocking had interrupted my thoughts.

"No, it isn't," Reid answered.

"Shit," I thought. "I must have locked it by mistake."

"Hang on," I said, getting up.

Reid was standing there. He looked concerned. Maybe he was irritated that I had locked the door. Maybe he could tell from my expression I had been unsuccessful. When he told me the archway had appeared, I knew that he knew my attempt had been futile.

"I told the others what to expect," he said softly, squeezing my hand. "With the exception of Marta, you and I are the only ones aboard who have gone back in time."

"Are they okay with what's about to happen?" I asked, squeezing his hand back. "Did you explain it to them?"

He smiled. "They aren't thrilled about getting overpowered by the stench of ozone, then getting shocked, followed by potential hearing damage from a loud hum before finally passing out, but since you weren't able to stop the alien process, there isn't much they can do except pair up and wait to wake up on the other side."

For a split second I thought Reid was blaming me for what was happening. He had said since you weren't able to stop the process. I looked into his eyes. The look he gave me in return told me I had imagined any blame. His expression told me his remark was innocent.

"Will some of the others be joining us?" I asked.

Reid closed the door behind him. "It's just us in here. Charles and Jane are forward, and the others are in the other hull, split two and three."

"Is Jane okay?"

"She's remembering how Marta, Elouise, Pat, and I looked after our earlier rescue mission," Reid replied, smiling. "The crazy hair, light bruising, and killer headaches."

The cabin was illuminated by a metallic gray light from

outside. I knew that everything alive onboard was now being sterilized.

I looked at Reid. He was glowing silver. So were my hands. The silver light subsided and was replaced by bright flashes of colored lights. The ozone smell got stronger. We lay down on the bed. "Wind your watch," he told me.

I glanced out the porthole. Different colors of light were everywhere, flashing and shooting about.

Sparks were drawn to the flashlight and I quickly disassembled it and pushed it away. There was a lot of electricity jumping around all over. No matter how we contorted our bodies, we were constantly getting shocked. I tried to take Reid's hand but I could "feel" the electricity flowing between us and had to let go.

The light grew brighter, forcing me to close my eyes. I heard hissing sounds outside, getting louder. My body began to twitch. The sound became thunderous, almost unbearable. "I should have brought earplugs," I told myself.

"Wish my earplugs weren't onboard *The Lady Anne*," Reid yelled, echoing my thoughts. I almost smiled. We'd had the same thought. But we hadn't had much time to prepare and didn't have anything to lessen the pain of the noise.

I pressed my hands over my ears. It didn't help much. I wondered how Buster had fared when he went through this. Dogs have such sensitive hearing. Pat had really good hearing too, better than mine. If I was in pain from the sound, I knew it had to be worse for her.

But it wasn't happening to Buster or to Pat. They were both aboard *The Lady Anne*, not *The Aquaholic*. But thanks to Pat, my eardrums were close to shattering.

CHAPTER 4

I woke up with a doozy of a headache. It felt like my skull was cracked. The daylight pouring into the cabin hurt my eyes, so I closed them. I felt for Reid, but the bed was empty. I tried rubbing my temples, but my arms were sore. Hell, everything was sore. Going through the time portal was not for the faint of heart.

I heard the cabin door open, so I forced my eyes open. It was Jane. "Are you awake?" she asked.

I nodded. Her hair was standing on end, but I didn't comment. I knew mine was too. Another souvenir from the portal.

"Take these," she said, handing me three Tylenol and half a bottle of water. "Reid's advice. Everyone else is conscious but pretty beat-up. Take your time and come topside when you feel able."

I heard the engines start. Their rumble didn't help my headache. Wobbly, I stood up and looked in the mirror. My hair was a total mess, sticking straight up. "That's one way to get taller," I joked to myself.

I made my way topside. I didn't see Reid nor Vee, but everyone else was there, either seated at the salon table or leaning against the galley counters.

Bev had stuffed her hair under her Bacardi cap. The rest of the women had crazy, poofy hair, like mine. "You look like we feel," Candy greeted.

Charles didn't have a hair problem, but he had a lot of dark bruises on his arms. Looking at me, he asked, "So are we in a parallel dimension or have we gone back in time? I never got a definitive answer before, and now I insist that you tell me—tell us—the truth."

I blinked and my mind raced. Shit. Should I tell them or not? If I lied, Jane would likely figure out the time period we were in when she saw some fish or birds that were supposed to be extinct. Being a former museum curator, it wouldn't take her very long at all once we saw something besides ocean and sky. But if I told the truth, would me breaking my promise piss the aliens off to the point they'd never return us to our time?

I looked around for Reid. He was at the stern, watching to make sure the engines were cycling coolant water properly.

I went over to him. "Charles wants the truth," I said softly.

Reid knew what I was referring to. When we'd embarked

on a rescue mission earlier, we'd said we were going to a parallel dimension, not that we'd gone back in time.

Reid nodded, but didn't make eye contact. "I'll tell him," he said. "You go and try to make contact with the aliens again."

Charles looked surprised when I walked past him. Without saying a word or acknowledging his gaze, I made my way below.

I heard Reid speaking, but once I closed the cabin door, it was quiet. I lay down on the bed and tried to make contact again. Despite a gallant effort, I got no response. I debated getting drunk and trying, but talked myself out of it. If they weren't hearing me sober and relaxed, the way we had agreed to communicate, why did I think going back to getting drunk would work?

After close to thirty minutes, I returned topside. To Reid's questioning glance, I simply shook my head. He smiled and then went to the helm and shut down the engines.

Almost immediately, Vee objected. "We need engine power so we can recharge everything," she said.

Bev added, "And we need hot water so we can get cleaned up."

I agreed with Bev as I desperately needed a hot shower. So did the rest of the women. Only Jane remained silent.

Reid held out his hands, stopping the women's pleas. "We are going to conserve fuel until we know our status with the aliens," Reid retorted. "We'll need it if they don't return us."

"Who put you in charge?" Vee snapped, raising her voice. Evidently the detente was over.

Reid spoke quietly. "Until, and if, Tracy can get the aliens to return us to our time, what fuel is onboard is all we have. That means no wasting fuel or propane."

She looked at him. We all did. But then Vee zeroed in on me. Coming very close, she said, "Do it. Tell the aliens to return us."

"It doesn't work that way," I said. "I've already tried twice —unsuccessfully. They aren't answering me." I pressed the palms of my hands against my eyes. "I'll try again later, but I've got to get rid of this headache first."

Vee was glaring at me, but Reid told her to chill.

"There are only two people on the planet that can ask the aliens to return us," he said. "One of them sent us back in time. The other is standing right here." He looked at me. "So you need to relax and be patient."

Jane made her way aft, looked around a bit, and then said, "Nothing looks any different."

"I was thinking that myself," Charles added, moving nearer to her.

"It will," Reid answered. "It will."

Candy came up to stand beside me. "I thought you and Pat were the best of friends."

I shrugged. "So did I," I answered.

"I'm surprised at Pat's actions," Charles said. "I never would have expected her to snap like that."

I shrugged again. "Me neither."

I tried not to show how upset I was with Pat. Getting mad wasn't going to change anything. Alien technology had sent us here. It would take alien technology to send us back. I didn't really want the pressure of being the only one aboard who could communicate with the aliens, but I told myself, it is what it is.

I got another bottle of water and told them I was going below to try again and to please be patient and quiet.

CHAPTER 5

Two more attempts failed. When I finally returned topside, it was a relief to find everybody busy cleaning up *The Aquaholic* instead of waiting to question me.

Jane was boiling water. Marta, Candy, and Dreamgirl were swabbing the decks. Charles was placing the solar showers in the sun. Vee and Reid were looking at a chart. Bev was working on the main compass, loosening the shipping screw so it would work.

Bev stopped what she was doing and asked if I had been successful. Her tone was calm. If she was mad, she was concealing it well. I shook my head.

"Maybe you can try again later," she said. I nodded and she went back to work on the compass.

I went over to see what Reid and Vee were doing. Reid

asked me the same question Bev had. He got the same answer. His reaction wasn't one of disappointment, so that was good.

They had plotted our position based on the coordinates I had obtained when the fog showed up. They agreed we were approximately one hundred thirty-five miles southeast of the big island of Hawaii. From there, numerous smaller Hawaiian Islands dotted the water to the west for miles.

"This is the closest landfall," Reid said, pointing. Vee said she thought we could be there by tomorrow if the wind held.

She then directed Bev, Candy, and Dreamgirl to stop what they were doing and check what condition the sails were in.

Charles came over and reported the solar showers were filled and heating. "You shouldn't have lied to me, to us, about time travel," he said, looking at me and sounding more annoyed than pissed.

"We weren't supposed to tell anybody," I replied. "I'm sure Reid explained that."

He looked down at the chart. Reid pointed to our position. Charles didn't say anything right away; he just kept staring at the chart. Finally he looked at me and said, "I normally have a serious trust issue with people who have proven themselves liars."

I swallowed.

He paused.

I was worried. Losing his trust would be disastrous.

Then he smiled and said, "But in this case, I understand. I'll make an exception."

I exhaled, feeling very relieved.

Reid motioned Jane over and showed her where he thought we were. "What sort of condition were these islands in twenty-five thousand seven hundred years ago?"

She took a moment before answering, squinting a little at the chart. "The Hawaiian Islands are part of a much older volcanic chain, so there might still be volcanic activity."

"If there were volcanoes erupting, it might be unsafe to go there," I thought.

"How about fresh water or food?" Reid asked.

"Maybe," she replied. "In limited quantities."

I had visions of scrambling over rocks and lava flows, chasing lizards. Or perhaps picking berries and then wondering if they were edible. We found Caribbean islands in the past weren't very lush or tropical. I figured the Hawaiian Islands were even less so.

Marta got some more hot water from the stove for her bucket. Then she set it down and said, "So what about that Navy ship?"

We looked at her. I had forgotten about *The USS Fields* until now.

"Approximately where was *The USS Fields* when Pat sent it back in time?" Charles asked.

Vee opened the log and found the coordinates of our naval encounter. Reid quickly plotted them. Based on his calculations, *The USS Fields* was about one hundred fifteen miles away, assuming it hadn't moved after going through the portal.

Bev joined us. "Our sails are charred but usable for a while," she reported.

Vee acknowledged with a nod and told her to prepare to set sail for Hawaii. After a moment's work with the chart, Reid gave her a heading.

"We're liable to run into that Navy ship," Marta stated. "Won't they head for the nearest land as well?"

"Drifting around out here isn't very productive," Vee replied. "I don't see a lot of other options. Do you, Reid?"

He looked at the chart and shook his head. "Hawaii is pretty much our only choice. What do you think, Tracy?"

I was surprised he asked me. I didn't have an immediate answer. Until I was able to make contact with the aliens, there didn't seem to be a lot of options besides heading for the nearest land. But if Marta was right and *The USS Fields* had headed for Hawaii, there might be a problem.

I was sure they thought the portal was the product of a nuclear war and they might believe they were the only people alive on the planet. How would they react seeing one of the last two ships they had encountered before the fog? What would I do if it were me? I wouldn't be very friendly.

"We should set sail for Hawaii, but keep a lookout for *The USS Fields*," I finally responded.

CHAPTER 6

We got underway and set course for Hawaii. Almost immediately, there was a problem. Vee assumed she was still *The Aquaholic's* captain. Reid thought he should be the captain since he had experience sailing in the past.

After a little back and forth, Reid and Vee were still at an impasse. Bev suggested we vote. It was pretty easy to guess how a vote would turn out.

I tried to lobby for Reid to be the captain and felt I was making progress with getting Charles to agree. But neither Vee nor Bev backed down. Finally, Reid graciously let it go, agreeing that Vee could remain captain.

Vee asked Reid to make a watch schedule for her approval. He got started immediately. She then asked Jane, Candy, and me to take a complete inventory of all stores on board.

She told Dreamgirl and Marta to finish cleaning the vessel.

She wanted them to clean up the dead bugs belowdecks at their first opportunity. Jane was appalled at her daughter's housekeeping. Reid explained that bugs onboard, especially in the tropics, were pretty much a given.

What he didn't mention was the alien connection—that they wouldn't allow a life form from the future to potentially interfere with the evolutionary process on Earth.

Vee said that when the solar showers were moderately warm, we could take breaks long enough to clean up. She was very nice about giving orders. As much as I wanted Reid to be the captain, I conceded that Vee was well qualified and had the disposition for the job.

During inventory, Reid caught up to us and helped with the counting. He casually asked Jane who discovered Hawaii.

"James Cook. The explorer arrived in seventeen seventy-eight," she replied almost instantly.

"Who discovered the Hawaiian Islands before him?" Reid asked. Now I was curious, wondering why he wanted to know.

Without hesitation she replied, "The Spanish Captain Villalobos saw them in fifteen forty-two."

"And before him?"

"The Polynesians discovered and settled them about four hundred CE."

"What's CE?" I asked, never having heard the term.

She patiently explained that CE, or Common Era, and AD were the same.

She added, "Samoa was settled about 800 BC, but it's about two thousand-six hundred miles southwest of Hawaii."

Reid didn't have any more questions for the former *Jeopardy* champion.

When I got a moment, I quietly asked him why he wanted to know all that stuff about who discovered Hawaii. He whispered that if we were spotted by Polynesians, one of two things were likely. The first was that we might be mistaken for gods, lower case *g*.

"And the second?" I asked, whispering back.

The way he looked at me made me sure I wasn't going to like his answer. "The second reaction would be taking us for a warring tribe and attacking."

My heart began pounding. Getting attacked by Polynesians didn't sound good. Not good at all. Then Reid smiled and added, "But we're twenty-five thousand years ahead of the Polynesians, so we don't have a thing to worry about."

His reassurance was sincere but I told myself to keep an eye out for outrigger canoes whenever I had the watch.

The three of us finished taking inventory. Had we been this close to Hawaii in our time, none of us would have been concerned. But we weren't in our time, and I knew that when we told Vee what was onboard, she wasn't going to like it.

I let Candy report what we had, figuring if Vee got exasperated with the messenger, it wouldn't be me.

The Aquaholic had two two-hundred-gallon diesel fuel tanks. If we filled them with all of the extra diesel in the spare cans, the tanks would be a little over half full. It was the same for our propane supply—a little over half.

However, there were almost thirty gallons of gasoline for

the outboard motor or the portable generator. That was enough for several fillings.

Candy reported we had fourteen fresh eggs, bread making ingredients, onions, Spam, lemons, a little string cheese, some frozen meat, and a good supply of cans, bags, and boxes from Costco and PriceSmart. We also had the bucket of freeze-dried emergency food Reid had gotten from Tommy Kraft back in Bermuda.

The water maker was working and our bottled water supply was good, but the liquor supply onboard was nearly exhausted. Toiletries and first aid supplies were solid. We also had a good supply of fishing gear.

The last thing she reported was that the basil plant was dead. That didn't surprise me, as I knew the aliens didn't want twenty-first-century plants, like bugs, alive in this time.

"Use the perishable items first and don't waste anything," Vee told us. Her comment was sound but predictable.

While looking in all of the storage compartments, I found the spare bags that Reid, Pat, Charles, Mo, Gert, and I had placed onboard back in Bermuda. I had forgotten about packing three days' worth of clothing and toiletries onboard *The Aquaholic* in case the crews got switched.

Finding the stash of extra clothing would make trying to borrow clothes unnecessary. Taking that find as a sign of good luck, I excused myself to try and make contact with the aliens again. Reid wished me luck. So did Vee.

I found a quiet cabin and began relaxing. It didn't take very long before I was totally relaxed.

"This is Tracy Palmer calling the aliens. We need to talk. Do you 'hear me?'" I thought, trying hard to focus on only projecting those thoughts.

My eyes were closed. I relaxed a little bit more and repeated my thoughts.

We are listening.

I "heard" their reply in my thoughts.

"Would you please return us to our time?" There was no reply so I repeated my thought.

No.

I "heard" their simple response quite clearly. I couldn't believe they had said no. I had really expected a different answer. I needed to ask them why they wouldn't return us, but before I could concentrate on that question, I "heard" something else I hadn't expected:

Connection terminated.

I tried to reestablish contact, but new thoughts about being stuck in the past took over and I couldn't concentrate. I felt my breathing increase, and my feeling of calmness and peace suddenly evaporated.

My eyes opened. I could feel my heart beating faster. My body was limp. I raised up slowly. I had failed. My eyes began to tear.

After a moment of looking around an empty cabin, I returned topside.

"Are you crying?" Jane asked the instant she saw me. "That's not a good sign."

Reid moved close, followed by Vee and Charles.

I wiped away a tear. "I failed," I stammered, wiping away another tear.

"Failed to make contact or failed to get the aliens to return us to our time?" Charles asked.

"Oh, I made contact all right," I replied, taking the tissue that Jane offered.

"And?" Reid asked. His voice was soothing, but I felt like lava inside. My thoughts were churning. I recalled how much weight Mo and Gert had lost after their few months trapped in the past. Had we not showed up and rescued them, they would have died a slow death by malnutrition.

I recalled how evil Captain Rick had become, never really accepting he was stuck in the past and taking his anger out on his victims.

Reid squeezed my hand, interrupting the flow of negative thoughts and images.

"They said no," I replied, letting go of his hand to blot away more tears.

"Good try," Vee said. "At least we know where we stand."

I looked at her. She wasn't smiling, but if she was angry that I had failed, her face didn't show it.

By now everyone had gathered around the salon except for Bev, who I assumed was at the helm. Their eyes held a million questions, but they didn't say anything. I wondered if they were in shock too.

"What exactly did they say?" Charles finally spoke, breaking the uncomfortable silence.

I sniffled, used a new tissue, and then answered. "I asked if they would please return us to our time and they said no. Just no. Then they terminated the connection." I began crying again but managed to say, "We're stuck here."

"Did they explain why?" Charles asked.

I shook my head.

Jane took me by the shoulder and steered me toward the table so I could sit down. I felt embarrassed for crying in front of everybody. Vee went to the helm, presumably to tell Bev what she had missed.

Candy, Dreamgirl, and Marta had moved away and were whispering. No doubt they were talking about me and how I had failed everyone.

A wave of depression washed over me, enveloping me with a dizzying sadness. Faces in the salon began blurring. The pressure of knowing I'd failed at the one chance we had of being returned to our time came crashing down. I closed my eyes, wondering if I was going to pass out.

Vee startled me when she shouted, "We've got company."

Everybody jumped at her outburst.

I looked around but couldn't see anything but my shipmates.

Then I heard it. The distinctive sound of a helicopter.

CHAPTER 8

Everybody scrambled outside, where they had a clear view of the sky. I followed Reid forward. Sure enough, there was a helicopter heading right for us.

"That has to be from *The USS Fields*," Reid said.

I had been so intent watching the helicopter that I failed to notice that Candy had come forward with us. "Unless you're wrong about us being sent back in time," she said, "I agree with Reid. There's only one place that chopper could have come from."

Vee joined us too, with her binoculars. After she looked at the helicopter, she panned the horizon. "Go ask Bev if there's anything on the radar," she told Candy. "And when that chopper leaves, tell me what course it takes."

We watched as the helicopter got closer. It circled us three times, descending a little each time, until on the third pass I was sure they could see our faces; they were that close. Then it flew away. If Reid and Candy were right, it would be heading back to report to *The USS Fields*. Regardless, the helicopter had no doubt radioed our position. I was sure the Navy ship was already plotting a course toward us.

I didn't want to get blasted before having a chance to talk. I thought of a phrase I could make using signal flags. It had to be short, effective, and couldn't repeat letters. I got one and grinned, telling Reid we should use the signal flags and spell out NO FIRE AT US.

"That's perfect," he said. "Except *The Lady Anne* has the whole set of signal flags; *The Aquaholic* doesn't."

"Oh yeah," I managed, feeling suddenly stupid for getting the boats' flags mixed up.

"Angie does have a happy hour flag though." Reid smiled, sensing my dejection. "Maybe we should fly that and invite them over for cocktails?"

"We can have Dreamgirl wear a bikini and invite them aboard *The USS Cleavage*," I joked. Dreamgirl had gotten her nickname after a one-night stand. I thought it very complimentary. I wondered if Reid or anyone else had ever called me that.

He smiled. Vee gave me a disapproving look but didn't comment.

Vee noted the direction helicopter was heading when it left and went below to see how far Candy had gotten in plotting a course on the chart. She beckoned Reid and me to follow.

Based on *The USS Field's* position when Pat sent it into the fog, we all agreed that it would have most likely set course for Hawaii, probably Oahu, since that's where Pearl Harbor was. Using the direction of the helicopter today and our proposed route to Hawaii, Vee noted where the two course lines intersected. Comparing the two positions, she guessed *The USS Fields* was at least sixty miles away, give or take.

Marta appeared suddenly to summon us topside. We followed her to find Bev peering up at the mainsail.

"We've got a problem," she announced, pointing at a tear that was forming.

Vee looked the sail up and down and then shook her head.

"Between the stress of the electrical discharges and the turbulence caused by that fucking helicopter getting so close, the mainsail has had it."

I snapped my fingers. "Didn't *The Aquaholic* get new sails in Panama?" I asked.

Candy grinned. "I'll get them."

Curiously, she didn't head below but headed forward. Marta followed her.

"Just get the mainsail," Vee shouted. "The Navy ship isn't that far away so we're going to have to do this quickly."

Then she looked at Reid. "That sail needs to be changed. We can do it manually while under sail or we can motor into the wind and change it. I know you insist on sailing, but I propose we use the motor, and while it's running, we keep charging electronics, run the water maker, and make hot water. Will that be acceptable?"

He nodded and answered, "Yes. Thank you for asking."

She smiled.

Candy and Marta returned carrying the new sail. In response to my questioning looks, Bev clarified that the fore-peak cabin was being used for storage. We had forgotten to inventory those two forepeak compartments. I asked Jane if she'd mind updating our inventory list. She agreed to. Charles offered to help and the two of them went forward.

Vee and Marta went below to get things charging while the engines were running. She reminded Bev to keep an eye on the radar. I was anxious knowing *The USS Fields* was on its way to intercept us, but there wasn't anything that could be done.

I watched as Reid, Candy, and Dreamgirl changed the sail. The old one was burned everywhere that it had been near metal. The heavily blackened areas easily crumbled when touched. I was surprised it lasted this long.

I went forward and checked the jib. The part I could reach was blackened and fragile like the mainsail. I motioned for Bev and showed her the jib's condition. She reported it to Vee, who instructed Candy to change that sail when they were finished with the main.

Finally, we got the sails replaced and resumed course. Vee looked at Reid and then shut down the engines. Marta had already sneaked a shower, so Vee told everyone else they could clean up while we had hot water but to conserve, conserve, conserve.

I accepted. So did everyone else except Reid and Charles. They were happy to use the solar showers. If they wanted to be macho, it was fine with me, but I wasn't going to pass up an opportunity for a real shower.

CHAPTER 9

Less than one hour later, the showering was finished. All hands were topside. It was the fastest shower I had ever taken, but I was clean and wearing fresh clothes. I felt human again. I wondered how long it would take the Navy ship to show up; the radar was still clear.

Jane reported that she and Charles had checked the forepeak cabins. They were full of trash bags. I smiled. I wondered where Angie had been keeping her trash. Jane mentioned they saw two unopened bottles of Bloody Mary mix, several gallon jugs of drinking water, some leftover Coca-Cola from the canal transit, and some extra dock lines. The forepeak head had extra bars of soap, some extra toilet paper, and a stack of beach towels.

They also checked the coolers. The small one was empty.

The larger one contained two large blocks of ice and one bag of cubes, kept frozen by dry ice.

Reid was taking a turn at the helm when he suddenly called out, "Dolphins ahead."

We all scrambled forward. There were several large, black dolphins straight ahead. Jane got the binoculars and, after a few moments of observation, reported she didn't think they were dolphins. She thought they were melon-headed whales.

Charles took a look and confirmed Jane was right. I could tell he was impressed she had known.

I had never heard of a melon-headed whale, but they didn't look very big and didn't sound dangerous.

We sailed right through them. I hoped they would surf in our bow wake, but they didn't. They did look like a dolphin except they were bigger and had a bulge on their head. They were either black or perhaps dark gray.

Vee got her phone and took some video. I didn't have the heart to tell her that if the aliens did return us to our time, her phone would have to be destroyed.

Thirty minutes later, we found some more melon-headed whales. There were just a few, and then a few more, and then a few hundred came into view. Before long, there might have been a thousand of them, swimming in all directions.

A few of the smaller ones did surf our wake, which was cool. Everyone whose phone was charged starting taking video. Again I didn't say anything about their phones being destroyed to get rid of any evidence of time travel.

The sheer numbers of these small whales was very impressive. I should have been worried about getting rammed, but the majority of the whales were keeping their distance and didn't seem at all threatening.

Charles told us how he and his late wife had sailed the waters around Hawaii quite extensively and seen melon-headed whales numerous times. He had never seen this many all together, and he usually couldn't get this close as the whales were skittish around boats.

I took over the helm so Reid could take a break and watch the whale's antics. *The Aquaholic* sailed fast, faster than *The Lady Anne*. Her new sails were working perfectly. We were moving fast but weren't heeled much, if any.

Since the GPS didn't work, I had to steer by compass. The needle was very sensitive and moved at the slightest turn of the wheel. I did my best, compensating a few degrees plus, then minus but overall, holding our course.

Just as I was really enjoying my turn at the helm, I happened to glance at the radar. There was a blip heading steadily toward us.

It had to be the Navy destroyer. When I announced the radar contact, the mood onboard immediately changed from light to tense.

Vee, Bev, and Reid all looked at the radar. The blip held steady. At twenty-two miles, the ship wasn't visible to us, even with binoculars, but it was visible to the radar.

"What are we going to do?" I asked, trying hard to keep my voice from quivering.

"We can't outrun them and we can't hide from their radar

or another helicopter," Vee stated. "So we should hold our course and see what they do."

Her response was logical and reasonable.

"What do you think they'll do?" Jane asked.

That was a good question. I waited to hear the answer.

When Vee didn't answer right away, Bev did. "Their ship sustained more damage than we did going through the time portal since it's a steel vessel."

That made sense.

Bev continued. "Their captain would have assumed he had been attacked. He would have sounded 'battle stations.'"

Again, that seemed likely.

Then Vee continued. "Once their captain had determined the extent of damage to his vessel and been apprised of any injuries to his crew, he would have tried to make satellite contact with command to figure out what happened."

Bev took over. "But since there isn't anyone here to answer, he would have been unable to make any contact."

"If I was him, I would have sent a helicopter to Hawaii for reconnaissance," Candy added. "I would want to know the status of the military bases there."

"Exactly what I would have done," Vee said.

"But twenty-five thousand and seven hundred years ago, the Hawaiian Islands would have been uninhabited," Jane said.

"So when his helicopter confirms that, the captain is going to have to listen to the government agents he has aboard," Candy chimed excitedly.

"And those agents—Agents Hill and Washington—will promote their time travel theory," Bev said, rechecking the radar.

"Not having any better ideas, the captain will have to at least consider the possibility that those men are right," Candy said.

"And if he finally accepts that he might actually have been sent back in time, when one of the vessels suspected of knowing something about time travel is spotted by his helicopter, he would immediately investigate," Reid said. "He'd have no choice."

Knowing they were pretty close with their prediction of the Navy captain's behavior, I excused myself below.

"Where are you going?" Dreamgirl asked.

"I need to make a phone call."

CHAPTER 10

I went below. I needed to ask for alien help.

When that Navy ship showed up, they'd either sink us or take us prisoner and demand answers. Neither of those options was acceptable.

My thoughts whirled in my head like leaves in a storm. Since the aliens said no to me once, there was a good chance they would again. But without alien help, we'd have to face the wrath, or desperation, of the Navy captain by ourselves.

So what exactly did I want the aliens to do?

"Get us the hell out of here," I said aloud. "Send the fog back and return us to our time before *The USS Fields* arrives."

What would I do if they said no again?

I blinked a few times, not sure what to do. And then I had an idea. It just came out of nowhere. I mulled it back and forth in my mind but it wasn't going away. Perhaps there was a chance.

I went into an empty cabin and lay down on the bed. I began relaxing. I wasn't sure how long it took, but I was able to make contact with the aliens.

We're listening.

I "heard" their answer clearly in my mind.

I concentrated on the following thought. "I'm not going to ask to be returned to our time because I know we must face the consequences of our actions."

I repeated that message, thinking slowly and clearly.

What are you going to ask us?

Their reply resonated directly into my mind.

"To prevent my friend Pat Taylor from sending anyone else back in time, please disable the technology you gave her access to." My request was simple and straightforward. I mentally repeated it.

I had succeeded in making contact and I had said what I wanted to say. I told the aliens thank you. Then I stopped the communication by opening my eyes and sitting up.

I was alone in the cabin. My thoughts were my own. My head was clear. By simply waking up from my relaxed state, I had effectively stopped the communication.

I returned topside. "Did you make contact?" Charles asked. He and Jane were in the salon. Everyone else was watching *The USS Fields* closing on us.

I moved to where I could see. That ship was coming fast and looked pretty intimidating.

"I did," I replied, not turning to face Charles.

"Are your alien friends going to return us to our time before that destroyer gets here?" Jane asked.

"I didn't ask for that," I replied.

My answer took Charles by surprise. He and Jane didn't speak, but I could guess what the next question would be.

Sure enough, Charles cleared his throat and asked, "What did you ask?"

"I asked them to disable the alien technology Pat was using to send vessels back through time."

"That's it? That's all you asked?" Charles's normally cool demeanor had changed. I could hear the disappointment in his voice.

I turned and looked at him. He probably thought I was the dumbest blonde he had ever met. I looked at Jane. She looked at Charles. They both had the same bewildered look.

"They already said 'no' once, so if I would have asked the same question, I would have gotten the same answer," I replied, trying to sound confident. "So I asked a different question, a request to stop Pat from sending anyone else back here."

"What did they say?" he asked, looking closely at me.

"I don't know. I stopped the communication before they replied," I answered, smiling. "I didn't want to drag out the communication. I kept it short and simple. I can't risk the aliens thinking I'm pestering them. When I make contact again, I don't want them to ignore me. Especially if we get in trouble with the Navy ship."

I could see that Charles was thinking of what to say next when the engines started. A moment later, *The Aquaholic* turned into the wind.

Candy made her way toward us.

"What's going on?" I asked.

"Vee ordered the mainsail furled," she replied.

I could see the jib was already furled. "So we're stopping?" I asked, already knowing the answer.

Candy nodded.

"Why don't we just heave to?" I asked.

"Catamarans don't do that very well," she replied.

Bev walked past.

"Do you suppose they'll fire at us?" As soon as I had asked the question, I was sorry I had. If she answered "yes," I feared I might start crying in front of everyone. I waited for the answer.

Bev shook her head. "They won't fire unless they consider us an imminent threat."

I felt relieved. No way could they consider us an "imminent threat." Then I saw the way everyone was looking toward the ship. I turned too.

"But their main five-inch gun is aimed in our direction," she said, her voice cold.

I watched her, hoping she would smile or at least grin. She didn't.

CHAPTER 11

Dreamgirl came over. "Those little whales are leaving," she announced. She looked disappointed. A naval destroyer had its guns pointed at us and she was worried about Jane's melon-headed whales leaving the area. I wasn't sure what to think of that.

Reid came over next. "I don't see any fog, so I assume it didn't go well with the aliens." Before I could answer, Charles mentioned how I hadn't even asked for their help.

I hoped Reid wouldn't jump to conclusions before I had a chance to explain myself, but he surprised me by saying, "I trust Tracy with my life. Whatever she did or didn't ask, I'm confident it was the right decision."

The engines were shut down and *The Aquaholic* began to slow.

Vee came over. She looked concerned. My heart was

racing, but she was amazingly calm, considering a massive warship was only a few hundred yards away.

"We'll be right back," she said, motioning Candy, Bev, and Dreamgirl to follow her below. Marta went with them.

Jane, Charles, and Reid looked at me. I fidgeted, looking back and forth. I excused myself below. I had to pee.

When I returned topside, Vee and her group weren't to be seen. I moved alongside Reid and watched as the destroyer lowered its dinghy.

"What are we going to do?" Jane asked. I was glad to hear that she sounded rattled. I was hoping I wasn't the only one getting more scared by the minute.

"If the captain had a helicopter check out Hawaii, and if he listened to the CIA and NSA agents aboard his ship or read any report they made, his only viable option will be to talk to us, or more specifically, you," Reid answered, looking at me.

The last thing I wanted was to be interrogated by the freaked-out captain of a Navy destroyer. "I don't like where this is going," I said. "What am I going to tell them?"

"Tell them the truth," Reid answered. "They'll figure it out anyway, like Mo and Pat did."

Vee returned topside, followed closely by Marta. Vee had changed into her nautical white uniform. Marta was wearing sweats. "Probably slipped them on over her spandex," I thought. Candy and Bev came up a few minutes later, followed by Dreamgirl. They too had changed into their uniforms.

The Navy's dinghy approached. I saw two sailors and the same lieutenant from before. There wasn't anyone else aboard.

"Request permission to come aboard," the lieutenant hailed. He sounded friendly. I was thankful there were no agents with him.

"Permission granted," Vee replied, directing Candy and Bev to the stern to assist them. I moved slowly behind Reid. I wanted to hide. I knew they would want to talk to me sooner or later, probably sooner.

The sailor in the bow moved away from the machine gun and threw us a line. Candy pulled them in close and tied them off. The lieutenant stepped aboard.

"Nice uniforms," he said, sounding sincere, not sarcastic.

"We thought them appropriate," Bev responded.

"Our chopper didn't see the other sailboat in the vicinity," the lieutenant said. "Are they okay?"

Again, he sounded sincere, but I noticed he had changed the subject.

"I appreciate the small talk lieutenant, really I do," Vee replied, looking directly at him. "But why don't we cut to the chase. What do you want?"

He didn't flinch but instead removed a small piece of paper from his trouser pocket. He slowly unfolded it and then read it aloud. "Captain Murphy insists that Patricia Taylor, Tracy Palmer, Reid Adams, Morrie Morris, Gertrude Kohler, and Angie Pepper join him and his senior officers aboard *The USS Fields,* immediately."

He then looked at Reid. Tilting his head slightly, he saw

me standing behind Reid. He smiled a little before looking at each woman. "Are the others below?" he finally asked.

"Tracy and I are here. The others you mentioned are on the other vessel, *The Lady Anne*, and it's not available right now," Reid responded.

"Then I will escort you two for the short ride back," he said.

Charles moved in front of Reid. "We are United States citizens aboard a US flagged vessel in international waters. None of us are going anywhere with you. Thank you but no thank you." His voice was firm.

The lieutenant stared at Charles. His expression indicated he didn't like that answer. After a few seconds, he straightened his hat and said, "You know I could come back with a VBSS team . . ." His voice trailed.

"What's that?" I whispered in Reid's ear.

He leaned his head back. "VBSS stands for visit, board, search, and seizure."

His last word, seizure, was pretty frightening.

Bev moved close to him. The lieutenant didn't react. I noticed then that he didn't appear to be armed. "Don't threaten us," she said. "Go get your captain and join us at the cockpit table. Your dinghy can keep him covered. He can bring a few of his officers or department heads with him, however, leave the CIA and NSA agents on your ship."

"I'll answer your questions," Reid spoke.

"So will I," I added, moving alongside Reid, relieved that we might be able to talk to their captain on our turf.

The lieutenant didn't immediately respond. He tilted his head slightly and alternated looking between me and Reid, with an occasional glance toward Bev and Vee.

I waited, hoping that Charles wouldn't say anything to antagonize him. Finally, the lieutenant nodded his head and said, "That may be a reasonable compromise. I'll let you know if your terms are accepted."

CHAPTER 12

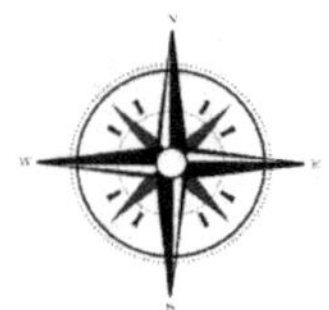

The lieutenant returned to his dinghy, and Candy shoved him off. The dinghy motored slowly away at first, but then quickly accelerated and raced away.

"How will we know if their captain accepts our offer to talk here?" I asked. I kind of doubted he would leave the safety of his ship. I figured he'd send an underling or a junior officer or someone like that.

Bev gave me a strange look. "Just watch who comes back in the dinghy," she said. Her tone was borderline condescending, as if she were explaining something to a small child.

I knew that a few officers returning in the dinghy was a good sign but that a bunch of armed sailors was bad. I also didn't especially like Bev's tone. Anyway, I was still too tense to be offended.

While we waited, Jane offered to make sandwiches.

Nobody was hungry. I, for one, was way too keyed up to eat lunch.

Instead of making lunch, Jane just got the container of cookies. There weren't enough cookies for everybody to get their own, so she broke them in half. I remembered Vee's crew saying they didn't eat carbs, but I noticed they didn't pass on their half-cookie.

I was eyeing the remaining half-cookies when Candy pointed and said, "The dinghy is returning."

I immediately got scared. Reid must have noticed because he came over and held my hand. "We'll get through this," he said softly. "Just answer their questions. Remember, they're just as scared as you are. Their entire world has just been turned upside down and their manuals and procedures weren't written for being sent back through time by aliens."

The dinghy came over and, as before, Candy helped them secure their line. I took a seat at the cockpit table. Reid sat next to me. Charles sat next to him. Vee sat on my other side. The rest of our crew moved aside so the Navy people could join us.

I recognized Colonel Wolf and the lieutenant from before. I couldn't determine the rank of the other three. "Which one is the captain?" I whispered to Reid.

"The one in the middle," he whispered back.

The man in the middle was in his late forties or early fifties. He was slender and clean-shaven. I guessed him to be five foot eight or nine. He was wearing a wedding ring. He was also carrying a pistol.

I glanced at the others. The only one that wasn't armed was the lieutenant. "They've all got guns," I whispered.

"They're just being cautious," Vee whispered back. "Don't worry. Getting shot is the least of our worries."

She smiled to help me relax. It didn't work.

The man in the middle introduced himself. "Captain Sean Murphy, *USS Fields*." He sounded friendly enough.

The other two we didn't know were the chief engineer and the communications officer. They introduced themselves.

We then took turns introducing ourselves. When I said who I was, I noticed the captain took a long look. I figured he had been told by the CIA agent that I was the one who could speak to aliens. That thought made me even more fearful.

After introductions, Captain Murphy motioned the dinghy away. Candy untied it and it backed away, maybe fifty feet or so. Then it just waited off the stern, drifting with us. Thankfully, its machine gun wasn't aimed at us, at least not now.

The two Navy officers slid around the table. The captain sat on the end. The lieutenant and Colonel Wolf stayed on the stern, out of the way.

There was a lot of glancing about between everyone but nobody said anything. It was awkwardly quiet. Finally, Jane moved closer and placed the container of cookies on the table, directly in front of Captain Murphy. "Would you like a cookie?" she offered.

He smiled and took one, then pushed the container in

front of his men. The communications officer took one; the engineering officer didn't.

After they ate their cookies, Jane offered to get them some water. They thanked her but graciously declined. She offered the cookies to Colonel Wolf and the lieutenant. They each took one. Marta took the last three.

"Now that we've observed the niceties, I have some questions for Ms. Palmer," Captain Murphy said, removing his hat and placing it on the table in front of him.

I swallowed.

"It has come to my attention that the CIA, and others, strongly believe that you are able to communicate with an alien species. Is that correct?"

CHAPTER 13

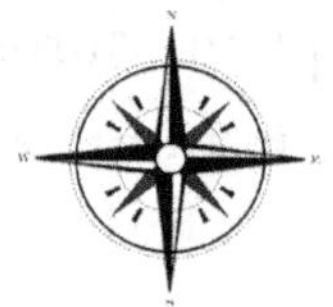

Knowing everyone was looking at me, I swallowed. "Sometimes I can," I answered, looking directly at Captain Murphy.

"Before you explain how, I have a more basic question." I waited, my breathing quickening.

"Why is an alien species on our planet?" he asked, leaning forward and tilting his head.

For whatever reason, I suddenly had a vivid recollection of talking to the image of the "little green man" alien the first time I was sent back in time. I remember asking that very question. I clearly remembered the alien's answer. "They study the evolution of planetary life over the span of time," I responded.

"For what purpose?" Captain Murphy asked. He sounded more concerned than curious.

"They are here to study and observe us," I replied.

"And what has an alien species learned about us?" the engineering officer asked. His tone was a bit sarcastic.

Again I remembered asking that very question. I smiled and repeated the alien's answer. "That our species generally acts without considering consequences."

Everyone listened intently while I explained how Pat, Reid, and I had been sent back in time for taking video of the alien's ship. I told them the aliens suppressed evidence documenting their existence. I told them the aliens used relocation through time as they had no offensive weapons.

Colonel Wolf moved closer. "So that's what happened to you and *The Lady Anne* when she disappeared between the Turks and Caicos and the Bahamas," he said.

I nodded.

"Captain, are you buying this time travel story?" the chief engineer asked.

"It would explain what the reconnaissance team found when they flew over what they agreed was the big island of Hawaii," Captain Murphy replied.

"What did they find?" Reid asked.

"A mostly barren island with minimal vegetation," Captain Murphy replied.

"And no sign of any roads, buildings, or any civilization either, I'd wager," Reid added, sounding confident.

"The helicopter didn't land, but like I said, the crew reported the island was pretty barren."

"Was there evidence of recent volcanic activity?" Jane asked.

"They reported blackened lava flows and saw some smoke but kept their distance," the captain answered.

The chief engineer was shaking his head. It was obvious to me that he was skeptical. He noticed me looking at him and said, "So we've really been transported back in time to the same general area, but twenty-five thousand years in the past?"

Before I could answer, Reid beat me to it. "According to Mo Morris, who was also sent back in time, we've been sent back twenty-five thousand seven hundred years, more or less."

"Calculated how exactly?" the engineer asked.

"Mo was a space scientist for NASA and he based his calculations on the positions of the constellations," Reid answered. "He had a sextant, a nautical almanac, an accurate timepiece, and he was able to adjust his mathematical calculations to arrive at the approximate year."

"That would explain why we've been unable to make contact with anyone," the communications officer added, looking both dejected and relieved.

"How did you get back last time?" Colonel Wolf asked, moving closer. He was looking at me. One by one, the captain and his two officers turned to look at me too.

I swallowed again. "It's complicated, but basically I asked the aliens to return us and they finally agreed to do so."

"Are you going to ask the aliens to return you again?" Captain Murphy asked. If he was anxious, his voice was calm and his tone didn't convey it.

"Yeah. I did that already, but they said no," I replied, looking at Captain Murphy.

"You said the aliens are here to study and observe us. Is that correct?" Captain Murphy asked.

I nodded.

"So why did they attack my ship without warning? That doesn't jibe with study or observe."

I fidgeted. "They didn't attack your ship. They relocated it back in time," I replied, trying to keep calm.

"I've got three dead sailors and dozens of injuries, some of them pretty severe," Captain Murphy said. His tone had noticeably changed. I swallowed and blinked.

I had no idea that anyone would die going through the portal. I wondered what they died of. I wondered if Pat had any idea that people had died because of her action. If she did find out somehow, would she have any remorse?

"What kind of injuries?" Reid asked.

Captain Murphy looked directly at him, paused a second, and then answered. "Mostly severe burns caused by close contact with strong electrical fields."

That made sense. Sailors in a metal compartment on a metal ship would have trouble getting away from anything metal. Electricity would be everywhere. Not getting shocked would be impossible. I was curious what the three had died from, but I didn't ask. I hoped nobody else would ask either.

It suddenly got very quiet around the table. The three officers glanced back and forth at each other and then at me, but all three remained silent.

I wasn't sure what to say. I kept waiting for Charles, Reid, Vee, or someone else to say something, but nobody was talking. Colonel Wolf scratched his chin, and I was sure he was going to speak, but he didn't.

"I'm sorry about the casualties," I finally said, needing to say something to break the awkward silence. "But it really isn't the aliens' fault. If it's anyone's fault, it's mine."

That got everyone's attention.

CHAPTER 14

"It's not your fault," Bev said quickly. "It's Pat's. She's the one that initiated the time portal."

"I should have stopped her from getting access to that kind of power," I replied.

"So you just admitted that you're responsible for the deaths of our shipmates?" the engineering officer asked.

I blinked.

"She's admitting no such thing," Charles said. The forcefulness of his reply startled me.

"Don't even think about going there," Reid hissed.

The engineering officer leaned away. He looked surprised that his comment had gotten such swift pushback.

Captain Murphy raised both hands. As it got quiet, he rose. I watched, wondering what he was going to say.

He placed his hat on his head and then spoke. "I am not

blaming anyone for the deaths or injuries to my crew. My chief concern is how to return my men to their families."

He didn't sound mad, and for a second, I felt a little relief.

He continued. "Since only the aliens have the power to return my ship, I implore you to ask them again."

He was looking at me, and the momentary relief I had just experienced was quickly replaced by apprehension. My breathing increased, and I could feel my heart hammering in my chest.

"Our crew will get burned and shocked again if we have to go through that confounded electrical portal," the engineering officer said. "There may be additional deaths from electrocution and severe burns."

Captain Murphy shot him a stern look. "Now that we know what to expect, we can take precautions to insulate ourselves."

I wasn't sure how you'd insulate yourself when going through an electromagnetic portal surrounded by metal, but I didn't say anything.

Captain Murphy sat back down. I watched as he exhaled. When he looked directly at me, I knew what he was going to ask.

"Ms. Palmer, would you try to get the alien species you can communicate with to at least return my crew to their time? As captain, I'm willing to stay here, in the past, with *The USS Fields,* but I must implore you to see if you can get my crew returned."

"That's a good angle," I thought. "At least he's not selfish.

Kind of reminds me of me." I had said the same thing to the aliens. That I'd be willing to stay in the past if my friends could be returned.

Based on how this whole discussion could have gone, with their engineering officer wanting to blame me for the deaths of three sailors, maybe more, I was eager to accept his terms.

"I'll see what I can do," I said.

"Do you need a radio or something?" the communications officer asked.

He sounded sincere, almost sweet. "Nope, just a quiet cabin and as much time as it takes," I replied, waiting as Charles and then Reid slid out of my way.

As I headed inside, I noticed Reid returning to the cockpit table. He sat down and said, "While Tracy is gone, I'll do my best to answer any remaining questions that you may have."

I made my way below. I wasn't sure if the aliens would return the sailors aboard *The USS Fields* if their captain offered to stay behind. But his offer was unselfish, and the aliens seemed to like that quality.

I closed my eyes, began relaxing, and concentrated on making contact with the aliens. Surprisingly, communication was established fairly quickly. My first question was if they had disabled the time portal device so Pat couldn't send anyone else back through time. They responded that they had.

Before I could ask about the possibility of returning the crew of *The USS Fields*, the aliens told me that Pat was headed down a path they had witnessed before. They called it "the path of bad choices."

They explained that Pat was using a problem-solving process they showed her for personal gain. The aliens were adamant that Pat be stopped. I wasn't sure exactly what Pat had done, and the aliens wouldn't elaborate, but I offered to stop her if the aliens returned me and my shipmates back to our time.

The aliens said there would be consequences for Pat's misuse of the time portal. I held my breath, wondering if they were going to show me images of Pat being incinerated or something equally gruesome.

Thankfully, they didn't. But they did tell me that in order for me and those aboard *The Aquaholic* to be returned, there was a condition. We would have to return to the Bermuda Triangle. It was only from there that they would return us.

Sensing an opportunity, I asked, "What about the crew of the Navy ship?"

They didn't reply.

I quickly added that the ship's captain had offered to stay behind.

Still no reply.

I used their pause to pursue another subject. "Thank you for the plans for the plastic magnet. It is my intent to go forward with production and begin removing plastic refuse from the earth's oceans as soon as possible." I let a beat go by. "That is, after I take care of whatever problems Pat is causing."

The aliens remained silent. I repeated my question about returning the crew of the Navy ship.

No.

"But why?" I asked, already knowing what the answer would be.

It is statistically impossible for that many humans to keep quiet about what has happened.

"But three of their crew were killed when their ship went through the portal," I stated. "And they have numerous injured sailors, innocent sailors."

Loss of life is always unfortunate.

"What if they accompany us to the Bermuda Triangle?" I asked. "Can the Navy ship be returned then?"

Their answer was swift and clear.

Those onboard when this vessel was sent through the portal can be returned when you reach the area known as the Bermuda Triangle. No one else. No other vessel. Use the time to reflect on Pat Taylor's consequences for her actions. Connection terminated until you reach the Bermuda Triangle.

CHAPTER 15

"Shit," I thought as I lay there, eyes closed. "That Navy captain isn't going to like that answer."

I was glad the aliens were going to return those of us aboard *The Aquaholic* but wondered why they insisted we go back to the Bermuda Triangle.

I mean, how bad had Pat been? What kind of a path of "bad choices" was she following?

I opened my eyes. I was alone. I took a few minutes to think about what I was going to tell the others.

Reid wanted me to tell the truth. I wondered if a lie would be better. I mean, if Captain Murphy was told neither he nor his crew would be returned to their time, how would he react?

Blast us?

Arrest us and lock us up in the brig?

Reprovision us and wish us well on our journey?

Ask if we would take his injured men with us?

I doubted he'd spare any food or fuel once he accepted being twenty-five thousand seven hundred years in the past. I wasn't sure about anything else.

I wasn't particularly keen on sailing all the way back to the Caribbean. I mean, we had just come from there, and it had taken weeks.

But if that was the only way to get back, we didn't have any alternatives.

"Oh crap," I said aloud. "The Panama Canal hasn't been constructed yet. We'll have to go all the way around South America."

Maybe that wouldn't be so bad. Perhaps I could persuade my shipmates to stop at the Galapagos Islands this time. I still wanted to see them, and they were on the way. So was Easter Island. When we were going along Chile's coast, maybe I'd get a chance to see some condors. After we rounded Cape Horn and reached Brazil, maybe we could take a day trip and see the Amazon.

But what about Pincus and Onion being ashore somewhere in Costa Rica? "That won't be a problem," I said to myself. "I'll just remind Reid and Vee to stay well clear of that area."

It would be the same for the East Coast of the United States where that other ship, the one that had kidnapped Elouise and Marta, had run aground. We would just have to stay well offshore.

I knew *The Aquaholic* had been reinforced to sail from

Bermuda to Hawaii. If she had been having problems, Vee certainly would have said something.

We had three possible captains: Vee, Bev, and Reid. Charles, with his experience, was qualified too. I was sure I could sail as well as Candy and Dreamgirl. Between us, we had a lot of sailing experience. I also knew how to catch fish. I was sure Jane and Marta could manage galley duties.

"It might be fun," I thought. "Reid and Charles aboard a boat full of attractive, single women. Talk about every man's fantasy."

I wondered if Reid would finally agree to a three-way with me and Dreamgirl, or possibly one of the others. I smiled at how Charles would feel. I knew he missed his late wife, but I also knew he had made an outlandish orgy wager the night he played poker with Pat. Would he be able to control his sexual urges aboard a boat full of sexy women?

I was certain the men would enjoy themselves.

An old saying came to mind. *If life hands you a lemon, make lemonade.*

The Aquaholic sailed fast. We had a water maker. I could catch fish. If Marta wanted a workout, she could reel them in. Jane could play her violin and serve as a living "Google," answering all of our questions. Reid could cook and tell us lame jokes. He could also satisfy my needs. I could see to it that our watch schedules overlapped.

Once we made it to where the aliens wanted us, we would be returned to our time. I could go and find Pat. Being so close, she had likely taken *The Lady Anne* to Hawaii. If she remained there and she really liked Hawaii, she was staying in Charles's compound. If not, chances were good that she would have flown back to Colorado.

Regardless, I was sure I could find her and see what kind of trouble she was causing. Then I'd just fix it. After, I could keep my promise to clean up the earth's oceans and get the plastic magnet built and working.

But first things first.

I got up, exhaled a couple of times, and headed topside.

CHAPTER 16

Reid met me in the salon. "You were below quite a while," he said slightly above a whisper. "How did it go?"

Before I could answer, the engineering officer spotted me and called out, "She's back."

I turned to see him standing near the cockpit table. As he motioned me toward him, Vee came down from the helm. Captain Murphy was behind her.

I heard a noise behind me and turned. Colonel Wolf, Bev, and Charles entered the salon from the foredeck.

As I moved toward the engineering officer, I saw Jane, the lieutenant, Candy, and Dreamgirl standing on the stern.

Reid motioned me to slide in around the cockpit table and then followed. Vee took a seat next to me, and Captain

Murphy slid in next to her. Everyone else stood where they could see and hear.

"Were you able to make contact?" Reid asked.

I nodded.

"Are they going to help us?" he asked.

"Sort of," I replied.

"Meaning what exactly?" Vee asked.

I swallowed and tensed up. I wasn't sure how the aliens' condition to sail back to the Bermuda Triangle would be received. I also feared what Captain Murphy might do when told his men would have to stay in the past.

"Go ahead," Captain Murphy said. "Tell us what kind of alien help we can and can't expect." His voice was calm. I hoped it would stay that way.

I looked directly at him. "They have agreed to return *The Aquaholic* and her crew to our time."

"That's good," Reid said, looking at me and then the others.

"If . . ." I began.

Reid looked at me. I wasn't sure he really wanted to know what I had to add.

"If what?" Bev said loudly, startling me.

I turned to look at her. I could feel everyone watching me.

"If we sail back to the Bermuda Triangle."

Bev looked down and shook her head. So did Vee. Even Reid looked dejected.

"What about my officers and crew?" Captain Murphy

asked. "*The USS Fields* doesn't have the range your sailboat does."

I made eye contact but hesitated. Reid must have sensed I had bad news because he squeezed my hand. Captain Murphy looked straight at me, waiting.

"The aliens won't return you or your vessel," I finally said, averting my eyes. I didn't want to see his reaction. I felt bad, knowing all of those sailors had wives, girlfriends, or family that would be haunted by unanswered questions about *The USS Fields'* mysterious disappearance at sea.

Captain Murphy glanced at his officers and then looked back at me. "Did the aliens give any reason?" he asked. If he was incensed, he didn't sound it.

"Yes," I said. "They said it was impossible for all of you to keep quiet about being transported back in time. 'Statistically impossible' I believe were their exact words."

I watched for his reaction. He stared right back at me. It had gotten quiet.

Charles moved close and sat next to Reid. "So if I heard you correctly, the aliens will return us to our time but not the Navy ship or its crew."

I nodded.

Charles continued. "But for us to be returned, we have to reach the Bermuda Triangle."

I nodded again.

"And even if *The USS Fields* was somehow able to accompany us all the way back to the Bermuda Triangle, the aliens still won't return them, fearing loose lips will sink ships, so to speak."

I hadn't heard that expression in a long time, but it was pretty accurate. I nodded again.

"This is fucking nuts," Bev exclaimed.

I turned my head. I had heard her quite clearly but hadn't expected a response like that.

"Excuse me?" I said, looking right at her.

"Sailing *The Aquaholic* back to the Bermuda Triangle is an impossible condition," she replied.

"Why?" I asked. "We just came from there."

"Because it's a suicide sail."

CHAPTER 17

Her words hit me like a brick. I froze. I didn't understand why she had called it that. Before I could ask any questions, Bev sat down next to Captain Murphy. He looked surprised.

"Since you're stuck here, can I stay with you on your ship?"

That was the second thing she had said that I hadn't expected. While I was trying to figure out why, Candy moved near Bev.

"Me too," Candy said, looking at Captain Murphy. "I want to stay with your ship."

Just as Bev's words "suicide sail" repeated in my head, Dreamgirl raised her hand and stated, rather loudly, that she wanted to join Bev and Candy onboard *The USS Fields* as well.

I was stunned and speechless. Thoughts invaded my head

from all directions. Why were they so eager to jump ship? Didn't they want to get back to our time? How bad could sailing back to the Bermuda Triangle be? We had come this far with no problems, at least none since we had gotten rid of Pincus and his associates. All we had to do was reverse course. It would be an adventure we couldn't tell anyone about but one we would never forget. Was I missing something? Why in the hell were all three of them so spooked?

Reid interrupted my onslaught of thoughts when he said, "Tracy, will you please ask the aliens to reconsider?"

I blinked and looked at him. I wondered what I had said that was getting this kind of a negative reaction.

"Yes," Vee added. "Would you please see if there is an alternative way for us to get returned?"

"Her too," I thought.

I closed my eyes for a second and took a deep breath. I opened my eyes, exhaled, and then told them that the aliens had terminated further communications until we reached the Bermuda Triangle.

"This just gets better," Bev moaned, clearly exasperated. She glared at me for a fraction of an instant.

Then she turned to face Captain Murphy. "How about it?" she said sweetly. "Can my friends and I go with you?"

Before he could answer, I said what had just entered my mind. "Anyone else want to stay here in the past?" I asked, looking directly at Reid, then Vee, followed by Charles, then Marta, and lastly Jane.

None of them said anything. They glanced around but

remained silent. Answering my question must have been harder than I expected. Sailing back to the Bermuda Triangle didn't seem like that big of a deal.

"We've got plenty of room aboard," Captain Murphy replied, looking at Bev and then his officers.

"Are you sure you can't ask the aliens to reconsider?" Colonel Wolf said.

"They're done talking until we get to you know where," I replied.

"Any chance I could join your crew?" he said. "I'm a trained navigator, a quick study, and I don't get seasick."

This was getting weird. Some of our crew wanted to stay with *The USS Fields* and at least one of its crew wanted to come with us onboard *The Aquaholic*.

While having the colonel aboard might have been a good idea, especially if we were going to lose three very capable sailors, I vividly remembered that the aliens had said only those of us aboard *The Aquaholic* when it originally came through the portal could be returned.

"Sorry," I said. "They won't allow anyone to be returned who wasn't onboard when we first came through the portal."

Colonel Wolf stared at me for a second. Disappointment colored his face. He looked away, then down, and then shook his head.

Reid raised both hands. That got my attention, and everyone else's.

"Let's not make any hasty decisions," he said. His voice was calm.

"Captain Murphy," Reid said, looking at him. "Would you mind returning to your ship?"

Captain Murphy didn't reply,

Reid continued. "You can talk to your officers and I can talk to mine."

"That's a good idea," Captain Murphy said, motioning for Bev to let him out.

"Can we have a couple of hours?" Reid asked, offering his hand.

Captain Murphy shook his hand and then motioned his officers and Colonel Wolf to the stern. "Keep your radio on," Captain Murphy said as he beckoned for his dinghy to return.

CHAPTER 18

After Captain Murphy and all of his men left, Bev went inside the salon. She returned with a chart of South America and unrolled it on the cockpit table.

I moved, trying to get a better vantage point, but I could barely see. For a moment, I wished I was taller.

The chart showed the Pacific and Atlantic Oceans and a little of Central America but not Hawaii or the Caribbean. It did show the Galapagos Islands but not Easter Island, which I thought was in the same vicinity.

Bev pointed off the left side of the chart and said, "We are south-southeast of Hawaii, approximately here." She pointed off the other side of the chart and said, "The Bermuda Triangle is over in this area."

"Since the Panama Canal isn't an option"—she pointed to Panama—"we'll have to go the long way—around the tip of

South America."

I knew that was the only way. I didn't see a problem.

"Back the way we came and then around South America will be pretty slow," Reid said.

"How would you go back?" she asked. Her tone indicated sarcasm. Reid left the cockpit, not replying.

I took his spot and looked closely at the chart. I too didn't know of any other way back to the Bermuda Triangle without going around the bottom of South America.

A few minutes later, Reid rejoined us and unrolled another chart on top of Bev's South America chart.

It was a chart of the whole world. He pointed to the Hawaiian Islands. "Go due south," he said. "And turn left at the Southern Ocean. Take it past Cape Horn. Turn left again and we can work our way north to the Caribbean."

"That's a square turn and much farther than angling across," Bev argued, drawing a direct line with her finger.

"It may be further, but it will be much faster," Vee added. "Once we turn left, we'll have the currents of the Southern Ocean pushing us the whole way to Cape Horn."

"Taking this boat into the Southern Ocean is even more of a suicide sail than skirting the South American coastline," Bev retorted.

"Why do you keep saying it's a suicide sail?" I asked. I didn't like her saying that, and I didn't understand why we couldn't just go back the way we came.

"Assuming your boat doesn't break apart in a storm, you'll

exhaust your fuel long before reaching the Bermuda Triangle," Bev sneered.

"Aren't we able to sail without fuel?" I asked, trying to counter her negativity.

"Sail, yes. Recharge batteries and make water, no. No fuel, no engine, no power." Bev had raised her voice. She was obviously distraught.

"You have no backup and you have no spare sails," she said. "And you'll be shorthanded to face the Southern Ocean when at least three of us don't go with you." Then she added, "Not to mention you don't have the proper gear, clothing, and equipment for the conditions awaiting you."

I wondered why she was so negative. But what if she wasn't negative? What if she was frightened?

"Let's assume you do get approval to accompany Captain Murphy," Charles said.

Bev looked at him. I was glad her attention was on someone else.

"I'm sure we will," Bev replied.

I waited to hear Charles's point.

Charles quickly responded. "If he sets course to the West Coast, California, Oregon, or Washington, he'll use most of his fuel getting there."

"So?" Bev questioned.

"Once whatever provisions are aboard *The USS Fields* have been consumed, you'll be forced ashore," Charles answered. His voice was calm and smooth.

"So?" Bev questioned again. "There's safety in numbers."

"Imagine the logistical nightmare of feeding hundreds of sailors every day," Jane said quietly. "That's a lot of fishing or a lot of hunting. *The USS Fields* will have the same problem as *The Aquaholic* eventually. No fuel, no power." I was glad she wasn't taking Bev's side.

"Do you remember how malnourished Mo and Gert were?" Reid asked.

Bev nodded. So did Candy and Dreamgirl. Even though neither of them had spoken, it was obvious they were listening.

"That fate may well await you if you go with Captain Murphy," Reid said. He didn't sound threatening, just brutally honest.

"You should reconsider and come with us," Vee said, looking at Bev. "We'll make good time in the Southern Ocean, and I could use the help." Her voice was soft and comforting.

"I can't believe you'd take a risk like that in a boat like this," Bev answered, glaring at Vee.

Vee was quick to reply. "I can't believe you'd want to stay back here and not take every chance available to return to our time."

"I'd rather die ashore in the company of the United States' Navy that die frozen in a life raft in the Southern Ocean."

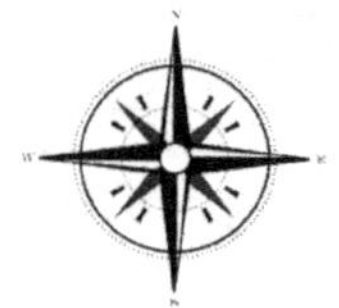

CHAPTER 19

"What about you two?" Vee asked, alternating glances between Candy and Dreamgirl.

They both took a moment to look at the world chart. Candy did some rough measuring with her fingers, muttering and adding approximate distances, but finally spoke. "Fifteen thousand plus miles in a catamaran with a half a tank of fuel, half empty propane tanks, no spare sails, no weather forecasts, no backup, and limited provisions is a risk that I'm not willing to take. I'll stay with Bev."

Bev took her hand and smiled a little but didn't say anything.

Vee looked at Dreamgirl. So did Reid. So did I.

"As much as I'd like to get back, I've read a few articles about boating and sailing in the Southern Ocean," Dreamgirl said. "Candy says you'll be in the Southern Ocean for over three thousand miles, which will take two to three weeks, maybe longer, and that's sailing nonstop."

I hadn't been listening all that closely to Candy's whispered calculations, but it was several inches across the bottom of the world chart, so three thousand miles was fair.

Dreamgirl paused and then continued. "This boat is likely to break apart in sustained gale force winds, and those are the norm in the roaring forties. Count me out."

"How about you?" Vee asked, turning to look directly at Charles.

"I want to get back, and the only way to do that is to stay with Tracy. Count me in."

"I lost my daughter once," Jane said. "I'm not going to lose her again for lack of trying." She paused a second and then smiled and said, "Let's make it a true daily double."

I thought her *Jeopardy* reference was appropriate. If the Southern Ocean was as bad as everyone was saying, it was literally all or nothing.

Marta pointed at Vee and then said, "You know who I'm staying with."

Bev didn't say anything except that she was going to use the radio and call Captain Murphy. Candy went with her.

Dreamgirl started to leave but then stopped and looked at Reid. She smiled at him. "You should reconsider and come with me." She leaned her head back slightly, which pushed her breasts up and out toward him.

Her body language was unmistakable. I didn't like that she was hitting on my man. I didn't like it at all. For a fleeting second, I wondered if this was how Pat had felt, overhearing what she had.

"You do know that Tracy and I are still an item," Reid answered, backing away slightly. "I'll go wherever she goes."

Dreamgirl didn't say anything, but she looked a little surprised at getting rejected. She left, heading into the salon.

I moved close to Reid. A terrible question was burning a hole in my brain. I didn't want to ask it, but I knew I needed to. I tuned out Vee, Charles, everything, focusing only on Reid. His eyes met mine.

"Can *The Aquaholic* make it back to the Bermuda Triangle?"

"I certainly hope so," he said, grinning. I wasn't expecting an almost humorous answer to a very serious question.

As if sensing my surprise, he took my hand. "I wish we were more prepared, but we're not. We'll have to be careful. If any one of a thousand possible things that can go wrong does, the Southern Ocean will magnify its effects tenfold."

"What are the 'roaring forties'?" I asked.

He took a breath and replied. "That's the area between forty and fifty degrees south latitude. It's characterized by rough seas and strong winds, because the Southern Ocean circles the globe, free of any land masses to obstruct it."

I blinked.

Reid continued. "With no continents to block the currents, they just proceed from west to east, unimpeded, all the way around. The winds build, the waves build, and the process repeats, feeding on itself. The Southern Ocean is not for a lone catamaran."

Images of massive waves, howling winds, and violent seas flashed through my mind. "Why the fuck are the aliens doing this to me?" I thought.

"Maybe we should stay in Hawaiian waters?, I thought. "Or we could follow *The USS Fields*? Or perhaps Bev is right; there is safety in numbers."

Those thoughts evaporated almost as fast as they appeared. I knew that I had to try to get returned to our time. I had to stop Pat. If I didn't at least try, I knew the aliens would stop her—their way. I owed it to Pat to take the chance.

Pat and I had sailed *The Lady Anne* through a gale once before. It was rough, but we made it. *The Aquaholic* was fast and seemed pretty stable. She had been repaired back in Bermuda. Reid had shown me the reinforcements to her hull. If the Southern Ocean was the fastest way back to Pat, then the Southern Ocean it would have to be.

CHAPTER 20

Reid motioned everyone to the cockpit table. He traced his proposed route with his finger. He repeated the likely conditions we would face once we reached the roaring forties.

I saw that to go around Cape Horn, we would be closer to sixty degrees south latitude. Hell, we would be going right past the Antarctic Peninsula.

If the area between forty and fifty degrees south was bad, it had to be worse closer to sixty degrees. I decided not to ask how bad. I really didn't want to know.

Sailing past a bunch of islands, including Tahiti, on the way to the roaring forties looked fun. Sailing close to Antarctica looked scary.

"I also need to mention the weather," Reid said.

The way he emphasized "weather," I knew something bad was coming. All I could do was wait for what was next.

"It will be winter in the Southern Ocean by the time we get there," he said.

Vee shook her head. Jane gasped. Charles didn't react, but I could see that he was thinking.

"The Drake Passage can be called 'The Drake Lake' or 'The Drake Shake,'" Reid added. "And that's in the summer."

To my questioning look, he clarified. "Sometimes the Drake Passage between Cape Horn and the Shetland Islands is as flat and smooth as a 'lake.' Sometimes it's so rough, the boats fear they will 'shake' apart."

I swallowed.

"I'm not sure what they call it in the winter," he added.

Nice, calm, always in control Reid looked worried. That gave me even more cause for alarm. Bev's words "suicide sail" echoed in my brain.

I had no more thought of Bev's dire comment when she appeared.

"I spoke with Captain Murphy and he's on his way over," she said. She looked pleased.

I didn't see Dreamgirl or Candy. I wondered if they had gone below to pack. I wondered if they were running scared. I wondered if maybe I should be following them. But then I thought about needing to try and talk Pat out of whatever bad choices she was making. Talk her out of them and hopefully save her life.

Fifteen minutes later, a dinghy approached. Captain

Murphy and the same lieutenant from before came aboard. The dinghy then motored away a short distance and waited.

Instead of wearing a pistol, Captain Murphy was carrying a book. He proceeded to the cockpit table and motioned for everybody to gather around. I got a clear look at the title: *Military Camouflage Explored and Explained.*

He opened it to the page he wanted and then held it up, turning slowly so we could see. There was a picture of a large warship with the same paint job as *The Aquaholic.*

Captain Murphy then asked how a sailboat from Eleuthera happened to have such a historic paint job.

Jane stepped forward and told him that her great-great-aunt Luverne was an artist and that razzle-dazzle paint scheme was her original design. She was smiling and obviously very proud.

Captain Murphy shook her hand vigorously. "I had a great-great-uncle that served on that ship during the war. Several vessels in the fleet were attacked by German U-boats, but his never was. The whole crew believed it was the effectiveness of their razzle-dazzle paint scheme that saved them."

Jane asked if she could look at the book. He handed it to her, asking if she'd mind autographing it for her great-great-aunt Luverne.

"I want you to know that the CIA and NSA agents I have aboard both insist *The Aquaholic* is a serious threat to national security and she be impounded at once," Captain Murphy said.

The good feeling I had from hearing about our paint job's

history was immediately replaced by a bad feeling. I wasn't sure what "impounded" might mean in our current circumstance, but I knew it would keep me from trying to sail back to the Bermuda Triangle.

"What are you going to do regarding their recommendation?" Vee asked.

Captain Murphy turned to face her. "Until five minutes ago, I was leaning toward towing *The Aquaholic* behind us."

If he hadn't prefaced his answer the way he did, I would have started shaking.

"And now?" Reid asked.

"Yes," Bev spoke up loudly. "What are you going to do now?"

I tensed and waited.

Captain Murphy removed his hat and scratched his head. He looked back toward his ship and then he looked at Jane. He replaced his hat and said, "Out of respect for my great-great-uncle and your great-great-aunt, I'm going to let you go on your way."

CHAPTER 21

I felt so relieved I nearly started applauding.

"Where will you go?" Vee asked. "Hawaii?"

Captain Murphy shook his head. "Hawaii is uninhabitable long-term. I'm going to set course for Astoria, Oregon."

"What's in Astoria?" Bev asked. I too was very curious. I had never even heard of Astoria.

"That's the mouth of the Columbia River," Jane announced.

"Fresh water?" Vee asked.

"Availability of game?" Charles asked.

Captain Murphy nodded to both of them.

"Will you take me and my two friends with you?" Bev asked.

He nodded again.

"Can you spare any diesel?" Reid asked. "Or propane?"

That was a really good question. If we could "fill up," our fifteen thousand mile sail would be a lot easier.

"We have F-76 and JP5," Captain Murphy replied. "I'll find out if either of those will work in your engine. I'm pretty sure we don't have any propane."

He gestured to the lieutenant, who removed a handheld radio from his pocket and went clear aft to use it.

Captain Murphy turned to face Bev. I knew what he was going to ask. "How soon can the three of you be ready?"

Bev didn't even hesitate. "We can be ready in thirty minutes, forty-five at the most."

I was sorry to be losing them, but I wasn't going to miss Bev's doom and gloom attitude.

Captain Murphy noticed the world chart. He looked at it briefly and then asked Vee, "What course will you take?"

"We haven't discussed it in detail, but we'll probably go due south to the roaring forties and then turn left."

"Taking this boat through the Southern Ocean in the winter is really risky. You do know that, right?" He seemed genuinely concerned.

"Apparently we have no other options," Vee replied, glancing at me.

I didn't say anything. Going on a "suicide sail," as Bev called it, wasn't my idea.

The lieutenant returned and reported their F-76 marine diesel fuel definitely would not work in our engines but JP5 might, short-term. They didn't have any propane but might be able to fill our empty propane tanks with acetylene they had for welding and cutting. He cautioned that while acetylene burned hotter than propane, it should work, theoretically.

Reid, Vee, and Captain Murphy agreed on a plan.

We would empty all of our diesel cans into *The Aquaholic's* fuel tanks. We would then send the empty cans over and Captain Murphy would fill them with JP5, which I finally figured out was jet propulsion fuel. The same for our empty propane tanks. They would fill them with acetylene, assuming the fittings would interchange.

During this period, Bev, Candy, and Dreamgirl would pack. Vee asked them to please leave any sailing related gear they wouldn't be needing. I figured Candy and Dreamgirl would honor her request. I wasn't so sure about Bev.

Jane asked if they could spare any food. She was told no.

Charles asked if they could spare any cold-weather gear. He was told maybe.

Captain Murphy returned to his ship, leaving the lieutenant behind with his radio.

One by one, tasks were completed. Our yellow diesel cans were refilled with JP5 and marked as such. Reid and Vee agreed not to test it and risk damaging our engines. They both felt it was prudent to use it as a last resort.

We also got two of our propane tanks refilled with acetylene and marked them accordingly. Again, they would be used only after our regular propane ran out.

With the refilled propane tanks was a large bag containing two sets of cold-weather gear, including boots and mittens. They looked really big, but they looked warm.

Marta carried all Bev's, Candy's, and Dreamgirl's bags topside, piling them on and around the cockpit table. She looked miserable. Vee looked heartbroken.

All of the bags were loaded into the dinghy and ferried over to *The USS Fields*.

As we said our goodbyes amid hugs and weeping, Reid went forward and returned with a trash bag. "Would you mind taking our trash with you?" he asked the lieutenant. "*The USS Fields* has more room than we do."

The lieutenant agreed, and while he look surprised at how many trash bags we kept producing, he helped load them on the dinghy and sent them over.

When the dinghy returned, Bev, Candy, Dreamgirl, and the lieutenant boarded her for the final trip.

"Good luck to you all," the lieutenant said, waving goodbye.

"And to you," Reid replied.

"Fair winds and following seas," Candy shouted through teary eyes.

Reid put his mouth close to my ear and whispered, "It's the following seas I'm afraid of."

<h1 style="text-align:center">CHAPTER 22</h1>

His remark confused me. "I thought following seas were a blessing," I said quietly.

"Not in the Southern Ocean," he replied.

Before I could question him, he waved goodbye to those in the dinghy. We all did.

We watched as the dinghy made its way back to *The USS Fields*. The dinghy was quickly secured. Some of the sailors were waving at us, some weren't.

We watched as Candy, Dreamgirl, and Bev followed the lieutenant out of sight. A few minutes later, *The USS Fields* motored away, sounding one long blast of her mighty horn.

I felt sadness creep over me. I wiped away a tear before anyone could see and went to look at the world chart.

Tracing the route with my finger, it occurred to me *The*

Aquaholic would be nothing more than an insignificant speck on the vast seas that awaited us.

I wiped away another tear.

One by one the others joined me and took a seat at the cockpit table. I wondered if they found *The Aquaholic* as suddenly lonely as I did.

Vee was the last to join us.

"Before we get underway," she said, "I have a few things to say."

I wondered if I should take notes, but I didn't see anything to write with so I just listened.

"I'm going to make a new watch schedule and I need to know who is comfortable taking the helm at night."

Reid's hand went up, followed by Charles's. I raised mine too. Jane and Marta didn't.

"Then Charles, Tracy, and I will split the night shifts," she stated.

Reid reminded her he was more than comfortable sailing at night, but she stopped him. "I've got other plans for you Mr. Adams," she said.

"What kind of plans?" he asked.

I didn't understand why she wouldn't want Reid taking a turn through the night. She knew he was a sailing instructor and immensely qualified.

She made eye contact. Reid didn't flinch, blink, or look away. He just waited, as we all did.

"You will have three tasks, and they won't leave you any time for night sailing."

Vee looked at each of us and then looked back at Reid.

"Number one: you are now responsible for navigation and ascertaining our position. I understand that Mo gave you and Pat celestial navigation lessons, and since neither of them are here, that duty is now yours. I expect you topside every day at noon to shoot the sun and determine our latitude."

"I don't have my notes," Reid answered.

Vee gave him a very stern look, as if she were Medusa, trying to turn him to stone.

He shook his head and in a lowered voice replied, "I'll do my best."

"Good. Second: you are also in charge of weather forecasts. I expect two a day. One for the morning, one for the night."

I knew that Mo had been doing that onboard *The Lady Anne*, not Reid. I watched and waited to see what Reid's response would be. He didn't say anything.

"Good. Third and perhaps the most pressing, you will use your remaining time to teach Jane and Marta how to sail. Start with the basics and get them up to night sailing solo as quickly as possible," she said. She paused a second, as if expecting an argument.

Hearing nothing, she added, "And don't tell me you don't have a textbook. Handwrite the curriculum if you must, but do it quickly. The quicker the crew is trained, the more prepared we will be for what's to come."

That certainly made sense to me. I watched to see if Reid would smile; after all, he should really enjoy that part. That's what he did—teach people how to sail. Hell, he taught Pat and me on a lake in Colorado and look at me now. I was ready to embark on a fifteen thousand mile "suicide sail."

I reminded myself to quit saying that. A fifteen thousand mile adventure, I told myself. It's a fifteen thousand mile adventure.

There were no comments. Marta and Jane looked at each other but remained silent. It was obvious they were surprised by their sudden enrollment in a "live-aboard" sailing class, but if they thought about it, they had to know that Vee was right.

"Until Reid can ascertain our current position, we're going to set course south," she said, sounding very much in command.

"Tracy, take the helm. Charles, assist her," she stated loudly but politely.

"What's our heading, Captain?" I asked, moving toward the helm.

"Until Reid can calculate compass variation between true south and magnetic south, just steer 180 degrees, magnetic."

CHAPTER 23

Charles got the sails up and I steered the compass needle to 180 degrees. He trimmed the sails a little and *The Aquaholic* quickly accelerated. I steered for course 180 degrees. I moved the wheel very gradually, trying to keep the needle within a few degrees of the course I needed.

Before long Marta appeared, handing us each a PFD with a tether attached. We put them on, got them adjusted, and hooked the free end of the tether to a solid handhold that was nearby.

My PFD smelled like perfume. I wondered if it had been Bev's, Candy's, or Dreamgirl's. But it didn't matter. I was glad to have one, having left mine aboard *The Lady Anne.*

Vee appeared, asked if I was doing okay, and when I replied that I was, she motioned for Charles to follow her. Once he left me, a feeling of aloneness took his place.

"You can do this," I told myself. "As Reid would say, 'relax and hold your course.'"

I sailed for over an hour, periodically flexing my hands and readjusting my grip on the wheel. I was uneasy at first but gradually felt more and more comfortable at the helm alone.

Vee had asked me to confirm our heading and speed shortly after Charles left. Besides that, I hadn't seen anybody, or anything, except I did watch as *The USS Fields* disappeared off the radar. Seeing their signal vanish only confirmed how alone we really were.

After another hour, I wondered if I had been forgotten. I knew that I'd have to pee eventually. I also wondered when I'd get a chance to eat.

I hadn't had anything since the cookie and that was a long time ago. But I tried to ignore my growling stomach and focused on keeping the compass needle as close to 180 degrees as I could.

Charles interrupted my focus when he came up to the helm. "My turn." He smiled. "Go below and get a bite to eat."

I didn't question him, quickly handing off the helm and then unclipping myself and going into the salon. I was thankful to have been relieved.

The salon was warm and inviting. It smelled like food. I made a quick pit stop below and then returned to the salon. Jane pointed me toward the table and placed a plate in front of me.

She had made nachos with tortilla chips, canned chicken, onions, and string cheese. It tasted really good.

While I was eating, Vee showed me the watch schedule and the cabin assignments. Vee and Marta would share a cabin, as would Reid and I. Charles got his own cabin, as did Jane.

I made a note of my watches. I had the seven to ten p.m. night watch, the four a.m. to seven a.m. early morning watch, and the eleven a.m. to one p.m. afternoon watch. Vee's watches followed mine; Charles's watches followed hers, except Reid had the three p.m. to five p.m. watch. Jane's and Marta's names were absent from the watch schedule for now.

I looked at the time and told Vee they didn't match and that she was supposed to follow me, not Charles.

"You're now officially off duty," she said. "Report to the helm at four a.m. This schedule takes effect then."

"My phone is onboard *The Lady Anne* and I don't have an alarm clock," I said, making sure it didn't sound like I was making light of my responsibilities or complaining.

"Marta and I have our phones and they're partially charged. Jane has hers and Angie's too. Borrow one, learn the access code, use the clock function, and try not to oversleep on your first day."

CHAPTER 24

I went below and found my new cabin. It came up short compared to what I had on *The Lady Anne*. The bed took up practically the entire cabin. There was a little space to stand up. There was a big drawer under the berth, a couple of dinky shelves, a couple of coat hooks, and that was it. No big closet, no television.

The head wasn't much better than the portable toilet back in Bermuda, except it didn't smell. The shower hose was connected to the sink's faucet. There was barely room to stand up or turn around. I really missed *The Lady Anne's* separate shower and double sinks.

The only thing I did like was the cabin's large overhead hatch and large window. They let in a lot of light. The port-hole in the head was pretty small.

I saw that my bag was already in there, laying on the berth

next to Reid's. He was seated on the cabin sole, thumbing through the owner's manual for the weather station. The sextant and the nautical almanac were on the floor next to him. So was a yellow spiral notebook.

He smiled but looked stressed.

"What are you working on?" I asked.

"Vee may not know this, but Mo wasn't overly successful in trying to duplicate *The Lady Anne's* professional weather faxes," he replied. He sounded distraught, in sharp contrast to his usual easygoing, always positive, joking attitude.

"Just do your best."

"What if I miss a storm?"

"Then you miss it." I smiled, hoping he would too.

When he didn't, I asked, "What's in the notebook?"

"I wrote a quick sailing lesson plan, and then I've been jotting down as much of Mo's celestial navigation lessons as I can remember. I wish I had my notes." Reid was obviously feeling the pressure of at least two of Vee's task assignments.

I sat down next to him and picked up the notebook.

The first page only had two paragraphs. The first mentioned safety, knots, rigging, point of sail, tacking, and jibing. That all seemed pretty basic.

The second mentioned more knots, reefing, anchoring, systems, maneuvering under power, sailing at night, bad weather, operating the dinghy, and man overboard drill. Those were intermediate to advanced topics. I was pretty confident that none of that material should be stressing Reid.

Hell, I knew enough to teach any of that stuff, with

the possible exception of retrieving a man overboard in a catamaran. Then I wondered why anyone would ever fall overboard anyway. I had a vision of *The Aquaholic* being tossed around by a storm. My vision got worse—it was at night.

I could visualize someone flailing about in stormy seas, their head completely disappearing under the pounding waves. I saw them gasping for air and screaming for help. That scenario flashing in my head was terrifying. I quickly stopped thinking about it. Maybe Reid had a reason to be stressed after all.

The next page was titled "Celestial Navigation." It contained many short sentences and bullet phrases. There were some sketches of overlapping circles and triangles. There were also some formulas. It looked vaguely familiar. I remembered trying to learn it from Mo.

Pat and Reid understood it, but I didn't, so I gave up. Now I was sorry I had. If anything were to happen to Reid, we might get hopelessly lost. I completely understood why he wished he had his notes. But he didn't. They were on *The Lady Anne*.

"If I'm off duty"—I smiled—"I can try and help you with your calculations."

"Thank you." He smiled back.

I debated asking him to clarify the comment he had made earlier about following seas being a problem in the Southern Ocean. Part of me didn't want to hear any scary stories, but part of me did. I decided to ask.

Very calmly, Reid explained that we were likely to encounter massive waves and ferocious winds.

"Define massive and ferocious," I said, anxiety starting to build.

He only took a second to answer. "The waves will be between thirty and sixty feet high, and we can expect sustained winds between thirty and fifty knots."

Sixty feet would be roughly the height of a six-story building. I tried to envision a wave that high. It was scary. I tensed up and felt my heart beating faster.

"Following seas of that magnitude, depending on how close together they are, will likely wreak havoc on the dinghy," he said.

"Why?"

"An overtaking wave that size can rip the dinghy right off of the davits." I saw another equally disturbing image of the dinghy being lost and the stern being damaged when the davits were ripped loose.

"Did I mention the Southern Ocean is full of icebergs?"

For a moment I was sorry that I hadn't gone with Bev and the others. "Fuck Pat," I thought. "Let the aliens deal with her."

Then Reid took my hand and smiled at me. Images of raging seas and a crippled vessel vanished.

"Do you want to tell me a joke, and then we can fool around?" I asked.

I was confident he would appreciate the break, and I needed to change the subject.

"I'm going topside to take a sight," he replied. "Maybe later." With that he kissed me on the cheek, picked up the sextant, the nautical almanac, and his notebook, and left.

It wasn't like Reid to reject me. I chalked it up to him being stressed from a long day. I refused to think about any of the scary things he had mentioned.

I went to find Jane. I wanted to borrow Angie's phone so I'd have an alarm clock, but it hadn't been recharged yet. Jane smiled and offered me an "old-school," wind-up alarm clock she had brought with her. I had never used one before, but it looked pretty simple.

I returned to my cabin, brushed my teeth, set out a jacket for the night watch, double-checked that the flashlight worked, double-checked that the alarm clock was set, and then climbed into bed. The bed was cold and lonely. I missed Reid.

CHAPTER 25

The alarm went off and immediately woke me. I managed to stop it on my first attempt. Reid was sleeping next to me. The bed was warm. I felt safe.

I got up, threw some clothes on, and headed topside to relieve Charles. I wanted a cup of coffee but didn't want to be late, so I settled for a bottle of water instead.

Charles was glad to see me. He had nothing to report other than *The Aquaholic* was on course and making good time. He left me at the helm, saying he'd make a quick log entry before getting a little rest. He was tired but not sleepy.

I connected my tether, double-checked our heading, and then concentrated on staying awake. It was really dark. I was on edge. I remembered to wind my watch.

Gradually the blackness was replaced by a magnificent sunrise. The sun looked like it came right out of the water to greet me. I remembered that I had forgotten my sunglasses below. I told myself to not do that again.

The brightness of daybreak quelled my anxiety. *The Aquaholic's* twin hulls sliced through the waves. Now that I could see, I made a minor trim adjustment to the sails and watched as our speed increased.

I congratulated myself on a successful night watch. I had held our course and kept our speed. I had done well.

Whatever nasty conditions may be awaiting us in the Southern Ocean, they were over five thousand miles away. I focused on enjoying this moment. I refused to worry about what was ahead.

Vee called out that she'd relieve me in twenty minutes. I looked at my watch. She was right on schedule.

As I relinquished the helm, she told me to be extra careful on my next watch so we didn't get flipped over or hit anything.

Both of those were obvious, so I didn't question her.

I knew that if a catamaran got flipped over by a large wave, she would float upside down. Then only another equally large or larger wave could flip it back over.

I also knew that *The Aquaholic* didn't have any escape hatches in the bottom of her hulls. If she flipped, anyone unlucky enough to be below when the cat flipped would drown.

If we hit anything like a log, a whale, or a big chunk of ice, we'd damage the hull and have a serious problem.

"Go get some breakfast," she said, grinning. "I'll take over."

I did as instructed. As I headed toward the salon, I heard the engines start. I glanced back at Vee. "Tell Reid he's got power for thirty minutes," she shouted. I gave her a thumbs-up and went inside.

Reid was showing Marta and Jane how to run the water maker. Jane was taking notes; Marta was just watching. I told him he had power for thirty minutes. He glanced at his watch and nodded.

Then he showed them how to set the battery selector switches. Charles was awake and plugged in some chargers.

Reid had made a nice breakfast using the last of our eggs. I had a piece of toast spread with peanut butter and the last serving of an egg and onion soufflé. His soufflé was really good. I was sorry we were out of eggs.

I finished eating and cleaned up my plate. Reid motioned Jane and Marta to follow him aft. He pulled a few pieces of line from his pocket. I guessed they were going to practice some knots.

Charles took out his small notebook and motioned me to sit down next to him. "Vee wanted me to inform you that she will run the engine every morning and the generator every evening," he said, reading from his notes.

"We will use that time to charge batteries, macerate our holding tanks, make hot water, run the water maker, and charge any handheld devices." Then he winked and added,

"And we can also use engine power to fish for the night's dinner."

"I like to fish," I replied, smiling.

He smiled back. "You can also troll when Reid is teaching reefing and we are sailing slow, or at least slower."

I nodded. Before I forgot, I'd have to go and see what kind of lures we had aboard. I wasn't sure what kind of fish were in these waters, but having fresh fish for dinner suddenly sounded really good.

I excused myself and looked through *The Aquaholic's* fishing gear. By the time I got a fishing pole ready, engine time was over.

I rejoined Charles at the salon table. He was looking at a chart. It was the same one we had been using on the way to Hawaii. Now our penciled course line went off the bottom of the chart.

I was a little down that we weren't going to see Hawaii. We had sailed so hard to get there, and then Pat did what she did and now we were sailing away from it. Damn her.

"Reid got a good fix last night," he said, pointing to a mark on the chart. "Reid believes we are within forty nautical miles of where we thought we were. He's also confident that compass variation is minuscule, so course one hundred eighty is fine."

"A forty-mile difference isn't that great." I sighed. "Given the radar's twenty-six-mile range, we could easily sail right past an island."

Charles reminded me we weren't trying to find an island, we were headed for the Southern Ocean.

Stopping at an island would give us a chance to get off of the boat, but it would also add time. Time wasn't on our side. If we used all of our fuel, there would be no way to run the water maker and no way to run the radar at night.

Sailing at night without radar was dangerous. Not having a supply of fresh water was disastrous.

I wished *The USS Fields* would have just happened to have a few drums of the right type of diesel fuel for *The Aquaholic's* engines, but they said they didn't. I hoped the JP5 jet fuel they had given us would work, at least long enough to reach the Bermuda Triangle.

"Reid's going to take noon sun shots every day," Charles said. "That will give us our exact latitude."

"This chart stops at the equator," I said. "Do we have another one once we sail off the edge, so to speak?" I managed a chuckle.

Charles smiled and retrieved the adjacent chart, lining it up below. The waters south were marked with numerous reefs, atolls, and islands. Lot of islands.

I was confident that when land came into sight, everybody would want to stop to take a break. Even an hour or two off the boat would be welcomed.

I found Easter Island on the chart. It wasn't even close to

being on the way. Charles saw me locate it and looked like he was going to say something, but he didn't. I guessed he was going to remind me those cool stone heads hadn't been carved yet. Like the Panama Canal, we were just too early.

I must have looked disappointed, because he touched my shoulder and said, "I'll bet the fishing will be really good as we sail closer to any of these islands."

"What kind of fish will I catch?"

"You might get a mahi-mahi tomorrow morning, or an ahi tuna, or a marlin, or maybe even an ono."

"What's an ono?" I asked. I had seen it on a Hawaiian menu but had never ordered it or tasted it.

"That's the local name for a wahoo, which is like a big, fast barracuda but very tasty."

Reid gave Jane and Marta some alone time to practice their knots. He took some readings from the weather station and noted them in his notebook. Then he took the Atlas of Pilot Charts and found the ocean and month he wanted.

I wasn't familiar with the Atlas of Pilot Charts, so he quickly explained that it showed average weather data, per ocean, per month.

After Charles relieved Vee at the helm, Vee looked at the pilot chart in more detail. Reid was teaching Jane and Marta again, so I sat with Vee.

There was a new symbol I didn't recognize—a wind rose. It showed the wind directions and wind speeds averaged over time. The pilot chart also listed the wave heights we were likely to encounter on our route to the Southern Ocean. She didn't want me to look at the pilot charts for the southern waters, not yet. I told myself I could sneak a peek later. Then I told myself not to. If I saw a strong historical probability of huge waves, strong winds, ice flows, and frequent cyclones, I knew I'd only be alarmed.

Vee included our average speed per watch into a formula to calculate distance, speed, and time. Her computations were then adjusted to match the exact time of Reid's celestial fix. Once she applied that correction to our projected course, Reid's fix was less than six miles different, not forty. I knew he'd be pleased when he found out.

The Aquaholic pressed on southward. We passed some distant whales, but they were too far away to positively identify.

My lunch shift was fun.

Reid and his students joined me at the helm. He let each of them steer for a while, and then they made several tacks. They also got some hands-on experience trimming the sails.

He had taught them the proper commands and responses and shown them exactly what to do, both together and solo. All three of them were smiling.

At the rate Jane and Marta were learning, I figured that Vee would be able to include them in the daytime watch rotation tomorrow or the day after. That would certainly make things easier.

My watch ended and I grabbed a snack and then took a quick nap, asking Reid to wake me in time for dinner. He smiled. I really missed him.

CHAPTER 27

After my early morning watch, Vee started the engines and motorsailed slow so I could fish. I let a green lure out, and five minutes later I had a fish.

The fish came in a little and then ran, so I let Marta take over. The fight didn't last very long, but Marta smiled the whole time she was cranking. Reid gaffed it. We had a yellowfin tuna.

Reid guessed it weighed about one hundred pounds. Marta lifted it a few times and said it was closer to eighty. Given all of the weights she had lifted, I figured her guess was closer.

Regardless, she and Reid cleaned it and wrapped several large pieces in plastic. Reid put them in the cooler, on ice. By then, engine time was over so we resumed our course, inching steadily toward the equator and a change of charts.

Charles had gone back to his cabin after his shift. When he came topside for his nine o'clock watch, he looked a little tired. Reid told him to go back to bed, saying that he and his students would handle helm duties for the rest of the day. He wanted us to get a break and needed his students to get hands-on experience under supervision.

I was glad to only have to sail two watches per day. It was neat that I had the time slots with both the sunset and the sunrise. I appreciated Reid, Jane, and Marta taking the day shift. I knew that Charles and Vee appreciated it too.

Four days later, we crossed the equator. Reid and Charles talked about having some sort of a ceremony for the rest of us who'd become "shellbacks"—one who has crossed the equator. They finally decided not to do anything special.

Charles did serve drinks and Jane made a loaf of bread. Reid told a joke. He asked where Bugs Bunny kept his boat. None of us knew. He said Bugs kept it at the "what's up dock." Nobody but Reid laughed. Except for the log entry and changing charts, that was pretty much it.

Reid was doing his best at forecasting the weather. He predicted wind every day and so far he hadn't missed. He also plotted our position when he felt confident with his sightings and calculations.

He was certain the Line Islands were west of us but not close enough to see or spot with the radar. I noticed the Line Islands angled south-southeast toward our projected course line.

Vee and Reid were optimistic we would spot either the

Filippo Reef or Caroline Island after we sailed much further south.

I noticed our projected course took us past the Marquesas Islands, but they were way east of us and we couldn't possibly see them. However, our projected course took us right through the Society Islands, the most well-known being Tahiti.

That was exciting. I was hopeful we could stop there and take a break. I planted a seed with Reid, telling him that he could use that area to teach anchoring. He smiled. I sensed he wanted a break too.

Getting closer to islands, however distant they might still be, had lifted my spirit and broken the monotony of nonstop sailing. Bird life was sporadic but at least we saw some. We passed lots of whales and were even surrounded by a large school of dolphins one morning.

Reid's lessons were progressing well, and he had Vee trade him my seven-to-ten night watch for his late afternoon watch. Jane and Marta would join him and get a safe exposure to night sailing.

Just before his first night lesson, I heard him tell Marta and Jane he was going to teach them the most important knot. I moved closer. I was very curious to hear which knot he thought was the most important.

"Do 'not' fall overboard," he said, making air quotes. He quickly added, "If you do, you'll be in the water until the next watch finds that you're missing."

That sounded bad.

"They will immediately sound the alarm and reverse course, but the odds of being recovered, much less alive, are one in a million." He certainly had Jane's and Marta's attention. Mine too. His tone was the most serious I had heard in quite some time.

CHAPTER 28

Notwithstanding Reid's dire warning about "not" falling overboard, the closer the islands got, the lighter the mood became. The change was obvious and most welcome.

Reid and I had sex for the first time since coming through the portal. As we snuggled after, I had something to ask him.

"Do you suppose Jane's got a vibrator?"

He started laughing. Finally, he shook his head and said, "That hum you're hearing emanating from her cabin is not a vibrator."

"How do you know that?" I asked.

"I heard the same humming noise, and when I couldn't figure out what it was, I followed the sound and then knocked on her cabin door. And guess what?"

"What?" I asked, very curious.

He smiled. "I caught her with her battery-powered, rechargeable toothbrush in her mouth."

The vision of Jane standing there with a mouth full of toothpaste and wondering what all the fuss was about was pretty funny. I laughed too.

The next morning Vee announced she wouldn't change the watch schedule until we made landfall. That was really great news. Not the part about changing the watch schedule, but the part about making landfall. I didn't mind sailing at night, but I really wanted to get off of *The Aquaholic*. Judging by everyone applauding Vee's comment, the others did too.

During his lessons, Reid started telling jokes.

"Where do sopranos go sailing?" he asked.

I wasn't sure, but Jane answered almost immediately, "The high C's."

She was correct.

Undaunted, Reid told another. "Where do zombies go sailing?"

Jane answered again. "The dead sea."

I figured Reid would stop since Jane was stealing his punchlines, but he didn't. "What kind of oranges do sailors eat?"

Once again, Jane had the answer: naval oranges.

Everybody was laughing, including Reid. He looked at Jane and asked, "What did the cyclops sailor say to his captain?"

She looked back at him and replied, "Eye, Captain." After she spelled "eye," I got it and laughed along with the others.

"Did you hear about the man who got lost sailing from Santa Cruz to Catalina?" Reid asked. He was really on a roll. I didn't know, but I waited for Jane to answer. She finally shook her head.

"He left his chart in San Francisco," Reid answered, smiling.

I groaned loudly and walked away. "That was really bad," I said. Vee walked away too; so did Charles.

But Jane and Marta couldn't walk away; it was time for more sailing lessons.

As we closed the distance to Caroline Island, Vee, Charles, and Reid had a quick meeting at the chart. Marta and Jane were at the helm, but I was free, so I listened.

Vee was afraid that if Reid's navigation calculations were off by much, we might sail right past Caroline Island and never see it.

She was also concerned about sailing into the Filippo Reef at night. It would be unmarked and not visible to the radar.

I hadn't thought about either of those possibilities, but thankfully Vee had.

I wondered what I would do had I been in charge. It was simple. I'd just "heave to" every night and wait until morning. But then I remembered that catamarans didn't "heave to" very well.

They discussed dropping sail at night and drifting until morning or trying to "heave to." Drifting along with the wind would waste time. Constantly adjusting a "heave to" at night would be tiring, and would also waste time.

The decision was finally made. We would assume that Reid's calculations were spot-on and we would slow down until our projected arrival time to either of those places would occur in the middle of the day. A few hours off either way would still give us lots of daylight to either avoid the Filippo Reef or assess landing conditions at Caroline Island.

Reid confided to me that he was uneasy about his celestial navigation calculations being so heavily relied upon. He was also concerned that the chart we were using wasn't accurate for this time period.

When I got him alone in our cabin, I jumped him. For a little while, he forgot all about navigating.

It was good for me too.

CHAPTER 29

The day we were supposed to pass the Filippo Reef arrived. Despite a vigilant lookout, we never saw it. Reid had gotten a good sighting the night before and was pretty confident of our position, but there was no reef.

One possibility was that the reef was likely there and we had just sailed right past it. It might have been totally submerged due to the water levels being different in the past.

The second likelihood was that the Filippo Reef hadn't been formed yet.

The third option was we weren't where we thought we were. While he didn't comment, I could see that third possibility made Reid a little anxious.

There was no way to verify any of those possibilities, so we pressed on.

Three days later, we began watching for Caroline Island, a

small, crescent-shaped atoll. A footnote on the chart yielded minimal information.

It had an area of less than one and one-half square miles. The highest point was less than twenty-five feet at low tide. There was a shallow central lagoon. A "no fishing" zone extended for twelve nautical miles around Caroline Island.

As daytime turned to evening, we resigned ourselves that we had somehow missed it. Reid was sure it was his fault, but Vee told him not to worry about it.

"What's our next possible landfall?" she asked cheerfully.

Reid looked at the chart, did a little measuring, and said, "We should spot the Society Islands in a couple of days."

"Tahiti?" I asked.

"Maybe Tahiti," he replied. "But if my calculations are anywhere near close, which is becoming more and more questionable, I predict we'll spot Huahine first."

I looked over his shoulder. Huahine was between Bora Bora and Tahiti. There were several other islands nearby as well.

"I have confidence in you," Charles said, patting Reid on the back.

"Me too," Jane added.

Reid looked at me. I smiled. I was glad he was along. I was sure we'd spot something eventually. I hoped his prediction of spotting land in a couple of days was right, or at least close.

He needed a confidence boost and I needed to get off the boat. As nice as everybody was trying to be, we didn't have much personal space. *The Aquaholic* seemed to be getting smaller with every passing hundred miles. I hoped that we wouldn't all hate each other when we finally reached the Bermuda Triangle.

Reid took his evening weather readings and announced that we might be getting some unsettled weather. We sailed through a moderately heavy rain for the better part of the next day. He smiled, glad he had called it.

If we hadn't had a water maker, we could have caught the rain and replenished our drinking water supply.

Vee and Marta used the rain to shower on the stern in the nude. Vee was cute. Marta had more muscles than most men. She had six-pack abs and nice pectorals. I saw zero body fat.

I remembered back to when I taught fitness classes part-time at a health club. Ironically, that's where I met Pat. Working there, I saw a lot of people and a lot of great bodies. But I didn't remember many that would have compared to Marta's.

I wondered if Reid would linger about, pretending not to look. If he did sneak a peek, would it be of Vee or Marta? Would he be intrigued by Marta's body and wonder how she'd be in bed? If Dreamgirl had been there, would he have been able to control himself?

I looked for the only two men aboard. Reid was close but wasn't watching. Charles was at the helm and facing the other direction. I smiled, thinking that they were missing an erotic shower scene.

I hustled below and got my towel. Then I stripped and joined them in the rain. Vee pointed to their shampoo and body wash and told me to help myself. She and Marta finished rinsing off and went inside to dry.

The rain was surprisingly warm, and it felt really good to just stand there and let the water stream off of my body. I enjoyed being able to move about. This was way better than fussing with a handheld showerhead in the small heads below.

I took my time washing my hair, enjoying every minute of the unlimited, free, natural shower. The rain's smell added to the experience. To quote the old credit card commercials, this shower was priceless.

Finally, I finished and went inside to get my towel. I was pretty sure Jane wouldn't shower after me, but I was wrong. She did, although she wasn't naked like we had been; she had put on her ugly, brown swimsuit.

After Jane was done showering, Reid took a shower in the raw. Jane raced below, never looking back, but I noticed that Marta and Vee took their time in the galley, towel-drying their hair.

When Reid had finished, Charles called me to the helm. I spelled him while he took his shower. Unlike Jane, he didn't wear a swimsuit. I noticed he was partially aroused. I couldn't see if Vee and Marta were checking him out like they had Reid.

I thought back to the crazy poker game when Pat won *The Lady Anne*. Had any other card come up, I would have spent the weekend indulging Charles's sexual fantasies. I wondered if he ever thought about what almost happened. I wondered if he had been watching me shower and fantasizing.

I knew I'd get lucky with Reid later. I was sure he had managed more than a few looks at the three naked women showering on the stern. What man wouldn't have looked?

Reid had borrowed Charles's electric razor and was now clean-shaven. I wasn't going to miss his scratchy beard growth when he kissed me.

When Charles returned to the helm, I went below to find Reid. He was waiting for me in our cabin. We didn't even try to be quiet.

CHAPTER 30

Land showed up on the radar early the next afternoon. Vee saw the signal and made the announcement. My shift had just ended, and I was disappointed that I didn't get to announce the radar contact.

Nonetheless, I was really excited to finally be approaching land. The last time any of us were on land was in Panama City, and that was weeks ago.

Our chart showed that Huahine was composed of two large, mountainous islands separated by a bay. Reefs encircled much of the island, but there appeared to be good access to the bay.

If the island ahead looked anything like the island on the chart, Reid would gain a lot of confidence in his celestial navigation calculations.

An hour later, Charles gave the "land ho" shout.

An hour after that, we changed course to follow the eastern shore of the island.

We stayed well clear of the lighter water, which indicated reefs. Dolphins swam along with us. Birds flew overhead. The island was green with vegetation. Past the shoreline, there were lots of ridges and cliffs. The top of a mountain was clearly visible.

Vee thought it prudent to launch our dinghy and use it to explore the entrance to the bay's protected waters. After the dinghy found a safe way through the reef, *The Aquaholic* could follow.

I wanted to join Reid in the dinghy, but he insisted that Jane and Marta accompany him. Dinghy operation was on his curriculum but hadn't been covered yet. I was disappointed but knew he was right.

As we passed the first mountain peak, the land got lower, and then began to rise again toward the second peak. According to the chart, the Maroe Bay would be between them.

When the bay came into view, we launched the dinghy.

Reid took Jane and Marta and a radio. He also took a weighted line to check the depth through the reef and inside the bay.

Marta started the outboard's engine on the third pull. She drove with Reid in the middle and Jane at the bow. We reduced sail and made lazy tacks while we waited.

The dinghy held a fairly straight course right into the bay. Reid radioed there was a minimum of ten feet of depth, which was more than *The Aquaholic* needed. He reported the reef was clearly visible and the channel was plenty wide for us.

A minute later, he radioed the bay's depth was good for anchoring and we should come on in.

Vee relieved Charles at the helm and started the engine. He and I quickly furled the sails. We then went forward for lookout duty. When we were in position, she motored toward the reef.

The dinghy came back toward us, then turned and putted back in, waving for us to follow. We did, slowly. Once we were in the bay, Reid radioed that they were all coming back aboard. Jane and Marta were going to learn how to anchor *The Aquaholic*. I smiled, knowing that was also on his curriculum.

Charles manned the helm while Jane and Marta deployed the anchor with Reid's coaching. Maroe Bay was a beautiful shade of light blue. The bottom was clearly visible. There were rocky cliffs on three sides. Seeing all of the birds flying around made me repeat the story about what happened to Reid, Pat, and me one time when we got attacked by birds.

I wanted the story to be informational, but it might have unnerved Jane. That wasn't my intention. However, I was positive that none of us would drop any food, intentionally or accidentally.

While we waited to make sure the anchor was holding, Reid, Jane, and Marta took the dinghy and deployed a second anchor. Once both anchors were set, Charles and I launched the sea kayaks and tied them to the stern. With them out of the way, we then swabbed the salt off the deck.

Vee let the engine run long enough to completely recharge the batteries.

I was anxious to take the dinghy ashore with the others. Vee said that half of us could go, then the other half. I questioned why we couldn't all go together, since it was obvious the anchors were holding and the bay was deserted.

"Are you sure we're the only ones in here?" she asked. I thought that was a stupid question, and I didn't like her tone. I hoped that Reid would come to my rescue and say something.

I looked at him. His facial expression said that he was waiting for me to reply.

"We're tens of thousands of years ahead of the Polynesians," I said, remembering Reid's conversation with Jane. "There is nobody else here."

Vee looked right at me and said softly, "We're here."

"Only because of alien technology," I replied, slightly raising my voice.

"Are you one hundred percent certain that alien technology hasn't put anyone else here?" she asked, keeping her voice low.

I released a breath. She was right.

CHAPTER 31

Before I could admit it, Reid said, "She's right. If anything happens to *The Aquaholic*, we'll be stuck here on Huahine, alone, forever."

I suddenly felt foolish. I should have remembered the close calls we had experienced aboard *The Lady Anne* on our first trip through the portal.

"Should I stay behind to keep a lookout?" I asked.

"I'll stay behind to watch the boat," Charles said. "In fact, I'm going to get the shotgun."

"I agree," Marta said. "We've had to repel boarders before. It doesn't cost anything to be vigilant and prepared. You go ashore; I'll stay with Charles."

Reid, Jane, and I took the dinghy ashore. Jane drove, I sat in the bow. We brought two radios, a flashlight, and a can of bug spray, just to be prepared.

Reid had Jane gun the engine and then stop it and tilt it up, out of the water. The dinghy glided to a stop on the beach. The sand was very coarse and crunched as I walked across it to tie the dinghy's bow line to a rock. Reid radioed we had arrived. Charles acknowledged.

After weeks at sea and thousands of miles on a boat, it felt weird to be walking on land.

There was maybe fifty yards of sandy beach, followed by another fifty more yards of smooth, black rocks. Those gave way to some larger, more jagged rocks. Beyond that, the island had patches of green.

Jane pointed at some animal tracks in the sand. "These are birds and those are some kind of lizard," she stated. Reid looked at the tracks and agreed.

As long as there weren't any poisonous snakes or something else that could eat or hurt us, I didn't care all that much. I was a little disappointed that solid ground was "moving" under my feet. It felt like I was still at sea.

"It will pass," Reid said, taking my hand.

"Do you feel it too?" I asked.

He nodded. So did Jane. The three of headed toward the green area. Jane wanted to see what kind of flora and fauna lived here. Reid wondered if there would be anything to eat. I was glad to be off of *The Aquaholic*.

We saw scads of small lizards. Jane apologized for not being able to identify the exact species. A lot of birds flew around us, but we didn't see any nests. The jagged rocks weren't all that jagged, and we easily crossed through them.

The green patch was indeed plants, but they were low growing. I didn't see any fruits or berries.

Charles radioed, asking if everything was okay. We acknowledged and returned to *The Aquaholic*. Then he, Marta, and Vee took the dinghy but went across the bay to explore the other side. When they returned, their report matched ours.

"So what's the plan?" I asked, finishing a bottle of water.

"We take a day or two to rest here," Vee replied. "We can do our laundry, burn our trash, do some snorkeling, and basically take a break from sailing before we continue."

I hadn't thought about burning our trash, but that made sense. Reid and I desperately needed to do laundry. My pants were practically standing up by themselves. Snorkeling also sounded like a nice diversion.

"We've got one frozen roast left," Jane exclaimed. "How does that sound?"

That sounded really good. I was glad our tuna was almost gone. Baked, broiled, fried, or sautéed, it was beginning to all taste the same.

Jane looked at Vee and added, "I'll be efficient when the oven is on." Vee smiled but didn't comment.

One or two days turned into four. We got a lot of use from the kayaks, trying to avoid using the dinghy as much as possible.

Reid and I kayaked every day. The slow pace was relaxing. I enjoyed the alone time with him. Several turtles swam along with us. I thought back to when I tried to rescue baby turtles from getting eaten by swarms of hungry gulls. I wondered if there were any barracudas around.

The snorkeling inside the bay was really good. There were tons of colorful fish. When I asked Reid if he knew what kinds they all were, he just smiled.

When we got back to *The Aquaholic*, he showed me a waterproof card he had found. It showed color pictures of reef fishes of the Bahamas. It was interesting that several of the fish found in the Bahamas were also found in Huahine's Maroe Bay.

I wondered why there were hardly any starfish, unlike the San Blas Islands. Reid didn't know. Neither did Jane.

One time I spotted some long, slender, snake-like looking fish. What caught my attention was these fish had blue eyes. Later Reid told me they weren't fish, they were eels.

My mind raced back to where I found Buster. He was the only survivor of *The Obsession*, a forty-foot sailboat out of Nova Scotia. His owners had put all of their supplies in their dinghy in a pond for safekeeping. That pond turned out to be filled with poisonous eels. Those eels killed both owners.

I wondered if these blue-eyed eels were poisonous. Reid wasn't sure, which wasn't a very comforting answer. The eels weren't aggressive; in fact they completely ignored us.

But there was no way to get the memory of Cookie Cook's last log entry about dying from a poisonous eel bite out of my mind.

It also made me miss Buster even more; his companionship had become a welcome part of my life. I hoped they were being good to him.

As good as the snorkeling was in the bay's protected waters, I insisted on a change of venue. Kayaking in the bay was still fine; snorkeling wasn't. Nobody argued.

We decided to check out the snorkeling outside of the bay. The first time out, we stayed inside the reef.

The water was a little deeper but still quite warm. There were bigger fish but, thankfully, no blue-eyed eels. There were more turtles. There were also sharks.

Jane identified them as blacktip reef sharks and said they would leave us alone. There were a few dozen of them, and while they followed us around, they didn't get close enough to be a problem.

After I got over the presence of sharks, I enjoyed the new undersea wonders to behold. I liked it when a cute turtle swam right alongside me. I suppose one of them could have bitten me but, thankfully, none of us had a problem. I figured the turtles were checking us out, just like we were them.

Besides snorkeling inside the reef, we explored the waters outside the reef when the wind was calm. The water was noticeably cooler and deeper, and there were fewer fish, but they were bigger.

Much bigger.

I saw some big blue/green fish that had a strange dent in their heads. Reid told me they were wrasse. Jane confirmed later they were Napoleon wrasse.

There were also lots of groupers. Most were dark brown

with white spots. They seemed to stay clustered together. Reid pointed out a moray eel that was hiding in the rocks, near the bottom. I tensed up.

When we surfaced, he promised that both the wrasse and the groupers, while large, were harmless. He also swore that moray eels wouldn't attack a human unless we encroached on their space and they felt threatened.

Beside blacktip reef sharks, we saw other sharks too. There were several whitetip sharks. They were about the same size as the blacktip sharks, about five and a half feet long, but the tip of their fins was white, not black. It was easy to tell those two kinds apart. I thought their names simple and accurate.

The lemon sharks were about twelve feet long, but Reid assured me they weren't aggressive unless feeding. They weren't very numerous and kept their distance.

When a giant shark swam by, I started to panic. Reid directed us back to the kayak. We climbed into the kayak and immediately returned to *The Aquaholic*.

"What the hell kind of a shark was that?" I asked, paddling quickly but steadily. Seeing that monster was super frightening. It didn't get close and it didn't even really look at us, but it was way too big for my comfort.

"Tiger shark," Reid calmly replied, not missing a stroke.

"Are they dangerous?" I asked.

"Not usually," he answered. "Keep paddling."

We got back to *The Aquaholic*. Vee noticed I was shaking. "What's wrong with her?" she asked Reid.

"A big tiger shark swam by."

Charles came right over. "How big?" he asked.

"Eighteen feet, maybe twenty," Reid answered. His voice was calm. It was like nothing scary had happened at all.

"If you saw a twenty-foot tiger shark, we should not snorkel outside the reef anymore," Vee said.

Reid nodded.

So did I.

CHAPTER 32

Vee called a meeting for later that afternoon.

"We've been here long enough," she announced. "It's time to get going."

I looked at the chart. There was way more ocean ahead of us than behind us. Even after we passed Cape Horn, we had to sail all the way up South America to even get close to the chart of the Bermuda Triangle.

"Make sure you've got your fill of dry land," she said, smiling. "I'm not sure if we'll stop at another island."

"We won't stop again until we reach the east coast of South America," Reid added.

That was a long way off, but he was most likely right.

"There are going to be some changes," Vee said. The way she said it made me worry. Her emphasis on "changes" sounded ominous.

"What sort of changes?" Charles inquired.

"I've got good news and bad news," she replied.

I thought back to the joke she told about the wife telling her husband that of all of his friends, he had the biggest penis. The joke had made me smile. But judging by her demeanor, she wasn't going to tell another joke.

"The good news is that thanks to Reid, we now have two more qualified sailors that will be added to daylight watches beginning tomorrow." She looked at Jane, then Marta, and then Reid. She applauded in Reid's direction. Charles and I joined her.

Reid blushed. Jane and Marta fidgeted but smiled.

"The bad news is we're burning through our fuel way too quickly."

Her words hit me like a ton of bricks. Out of fuel would mean no water maker. No water maker would be really bad.

Reid spoke, stopping my thoughts from running further down the proverbial rabbit hole. "What do you propose?" he asked. That was a simple question. I hoped that Vee had a good answer.

She looked at each of us and then answered. "We will now run the engine every third day, and then only briefly."

Charles put my thoughts into words. "So when the house batteries are dead, we'll be without lights or instruments, right?"

"Right," she answered.

Reid replied. "So we'll just conserve battery power and keep the survival flashlight that doesn't use a battery at the helm. Compasses aren't electric, so they will still be working."

He didn't sound fazed by Vee's edict about conserving fuel. I sensed he would be happy to sail without using the engine at all.

If Reid wasn't concerned, then why should I be? "Okay," I replied, giving Vee a thumbs-up.

Charles spoke. "Then I'm buying dinner."

Everybody looked at him. There was obviously nowhere to eat ashore and the last of the roast was gone. We were also out of tuna.

"We've got one bottle of a hearty red wine left." He smiled. "And I believe there is pasta and spaghetti sauce onboard, so tonight we'll be eating Italian."

Reid and I washed our laundry in a bucket and hung it on a makeshift clothesline to dry. So did the others. Jane provided music while Charles and Reid worked in the galley.

I savored my glass of wine, knowing it was the last one. Reid said he had a joke. I hoped he wouldn't ruin our nice dinner with another of his lame jokes, but there was no way to stop him without hurting his feelings, so I just waited.

"Why do pirates avoid sailing in shallow water?" he asked, grinning. I waited to see if Jane would steal his punchline, but she didn't say anything.

I was trying to think of a reason when he answered. "Because with only one eye, they have terrible depth perception."

I shook my head. He told another.

"What does Captain Jack Sparrow use to cook?"

There were a lot of blank stares, followed by silence.

He waited and then told the punchline. "Pyrex of the Caribbean."

Everybody laughed but me. I looked down and shook my head. I wondered how he managed to tell so many jokes without repeating any. I wondered why he only knew lame jokes. I wondered if he'd ever run out.

Of course, he told another. "Why can't you tickle a sailor?"

I rolled my eyes and waited.

"Because they're nautical-ish."

I laughed. I didn't want to encourage him, but that one was very clever. Jane went to get some paper. She began writing them down. I wondered why anybody with a memory as good as hers would need to write anything down. "Maybe she isn't good at remembering jokes," I told myself.

When she was caught up, Reid told another. "What do sailors eat for breakfast?" He grinned and finished it. "Boat-meal." Everybody chuckled. Jane kept writing.

Charles said he had a joke. "In the Canary Islands there are no canaries." He paused a moment before continuing. "Same thing in the Virgin Islands . . . No canaries." I laughed some more. Charles didn't tell very many jokes, but his were pretty good.

"Speaking of jokes," Reid said, looking at Vee. "You never finished your three martini joke."

Vee suddenly looked very serious. "Candy, Bev, and Dreamgirl have forbidden me to tell that one," she said.

"Candy, Bev, and Dreamgirl aren't here right now, are they?" Reid replied.

He had a point.

Vee stiffened. "Sorry," she said, managing a faint smile.

Reid shrugged but didn't say anything.

Vee walked away.

CHAPTER 33

The *Aquaholic* motored out of Maroe Bay the next morning, following the dinghy through the reef. When we had cleared Huahine, we stowed the dinghy and resumed course south.

Vee reefed the sails so I could fish. I caught a marlin right away. When it jumped, it was really big. Vee ordered the sails furled. Charles got us stopped while Reid got Marta the fighting belt.

She reeled it in all by herself, battling it for nearly an hour. She was tired but happy. Jane took some pictures. Reid thought it weighed close to a thousand pounds. He released it without incident. I got Marta a chocolate milk. She smiled. I did too. Real chocolate milk was so much better than a Snickers bar and some half and half.

We got the sails up and resumed course. Reid told Vee he'd

like to fish for something smaller, something we could eat. She agreed. He put the lure back out, and less than ten minutes later, he caught another marlin.

He, Charles, and I took turns reeling this one it. Jane even took a turn. It was smaller but still too big to keep, so after a few more pictures, we let it go.

Since we were in a good spot, we changed lures and tried again. This time we caught a shark.

It put on a more acrobatic show than either marlin had, jumping completely out of the water several times. Marta got it in close enough to identify. It was a mako, around twelve feet long. Rather than risk getting bitten, Reid cut the line.

I was sorry to lose the lure but completely understood. Vee wanted to reel one in, so I switched places with her. Charles got another lure and we started trolling again. Twenty minutes later, Vee had one.

"Fish on," she yelled.

I turned *The Aquaholic* into the wind. Jane helped with furling the sails.

She had caught a dorado, or mahi-mahi as Charles said we should call it in this area. It was only about fifty pounds, so we kept it. She admitted she didn't fish much but really enjoyed it.

While Reid was cleaning the fish, I resumed course. Our fish icebox still had room, but we all agreed we had done enough fishing for the day. I smiled when Reid cleaned the fish wearing only his swimsuit. He didn't want to get his newly washed clothes all fishy.

After he cleaned up and got dressed, he discharged a CO2 fire extinguisher into a pillowcase and, wearing heavy gloves, pulled out several small chunks of dry ice. Then he froze some big baggies of water, refilling the ice cooler.

Later that day we spotted another island. Based on Reid's estimated position, it had to be Maiao. It was much smaller than Huahine and much lower. We steered closer and discussed if we should stop or not.

The chart showed the Austral Islands were the next island group we would pass. The island of Tubuai was pretty close to our projected course line. Since we would reach Tubuai in a couple of days, and since we had stayed longer than planned in Huahine, Vee wanted to keep going. We all agreed and pressed on, still on course 180 degrees, magnetic.

Just south of Maiao, we passed through a big school of turtles. Following that sighting, we went through a school of dolphins. They stayed with us until dark.

Reid was true to his word and had gotten the survival flashlight. It was pretty cool that it worked by just shaking it. It was easily bright enough to read the compass.

After dinner, Vee ordered all of the circuit breakers turned off except for the bilge pump, which she left set to automatic. She didn't want to drain the house battery any further, hoping the solar panel could keep it charged during daylight hours.

With the circuit breakers switched off, we had no lights, no running water, and no power to the inverter to charge anything. We also had no instruments. Vee would no longer have average speed per watch to adjust her calculations.

Reid reminded Vee that without power for the weather station, he could no longer make his weather forecasts. She looked surprised for a second but quickly added that he could certainly use the house battery for that.

Jane found a citronella candle aboard. I surmised that Angie must have had it to repel mosquitos when dining at the cockpit table. Whatever she used it for, it was a welcome addition to the main salon. Its single flame was surprisingly comforting. Vee cautioned us against having it burn unattended. That certainly made sense. A fire was the last thing we needed.

Jane could play her violin without much light, and she played one or two songs every evening. We had been playing a CD with a steel drum, island version of "Call Me the Breeze." Jane now played that, and whoever was close by joined in singing the chorus: "I keep blowing down the road."

I could see Reid missed having his trumpet.

CHAPTER 34

The night shift was eerily dark. While the stars above twinkled and sparkled, the ocean was encased in blackness. Unless I pointed the flashlight's limited beam at the nearby waves, it felt like I was sailing with my eyes closed.

With the flashlight's help, I could easily see the compass needle. But I didn't want to keep shaking the flashlight to get light, so I found another way.

When I knew I was on course, I picked a bright star that was just above the horizon. I pointed at it and then tried to steer in the direction I was pointing.

I'd sail for about fifteen minutes, holding the wheel steady, before I checked my course against the compass. My makeshift target turned out to be pretty accurate, and I didn't stray much from course 180 degrees.

Later that evening, I heard a whole bunch of clicking

sounds. It sounded like the telegraph office in an old Western movie. The clicks varied in speed and were pretty loud. A few times I heard something breaking the water nearby.

I guessed that we were sailing by some whales, but I couldn't see anything. With the radar off, I was completely blind. There were occasional patches of bioluminescence, but the ocean was blacker than ever.

I was stressed during my entire watch, concerned I'd get off course. Worried I'd hit something. Terrified that something would hit us. The louder the clicking noises got, the worse my nerves became.

Remembering what Reid had told Marta and Jane about "not" falling overboard took on a profound importance. I kept double-checking my safety tether, knowing that my life totally depended on six feet of webbing and two snap hooks. By the time Vee relieved me, I was worn out from worrying about not messing anything up.

We kept heading south. None of us pushed the boat very hard. We all knew that if anything critical broke, we'd have a major problem. The next landfall past the Austral Islands was Antarctica.

We used the reduced speed to fish more. Since the galley's refrigerator was basically empty, Reid moved the dry ice to it and used both of our coolers for fish storage.

Besides keeping two more mahi-mahi, we now had swordfish, another yellowfin tuna, and a nice wahoo.

The blood trail from cleaning fish drew sharks. Sometimes

they'd follow us all day. When several fins were visible, it was a little nerve-racking.

When a single fin was announced, it wasn't paid much attention to. Several fins close behind us ended the fishing. We didn't want to have to cut off any more lures if a shark hit.

One shark that followed us had a really tall tail. Jane said it was a thresher shark. She said they weren't dangerous, and then added, "Unless you grab their tail." I wondered why in the hell anybody would ever do that, but I didn't say anything. Then it hit me. She had made a joke.

Reid donated one of the last beers to the galley. He used it to make a beer batter. Beer batter mahi-mahi fillets were excellent and my new favorite.

Jane surprised us one day with a spicy tomato fish soup. When asked where she found the tomato soup, she laughed and replied, "It's not tomato soup; it's Bloody Mary mix."

Having Spam for breakfast was no longer questioned or joked about. We were all glad to have it, regardless of how it was cooked. Jane was sorry that her daughter hadn't bought more of it at the PriceSmart in Panama. We were too.

We were no longer smashing our empty plastic water bottles. We were saving them to refill when the water maker was running. Bottled water tasted better than desalinated water, but we didn't have many choices. A little powdered drink mix helped. I liked the orange flavor but not the grape.

Three days after sighting, but not stopping at, Maiao, Tubuai came into view. With the radar off, we had been using binoculars when Reid thought we were close.

Jane and Charles were at the helm together. Charles spotted it first and gave the "land ho" shout. Those two words sounded really good. Much more pleasant than "fin."

The island was a little east of where Reid expected it to be, so we changed course and headed straight for it.

Vee sent Marta and me forward with binoculars to watch for any reefs. She then switched on the battery so the depth meter and radar would work.

Her plan was to get close and look for a suitable anchorage. According to our chart, there were no lagoons or bays, but she was hopeful we could find some protected waters to anchor in for the evening.

We had nearly circumnavigated the entire island when a likely looking spot came into view. We stopped and launched the dinghy. Jane and Marta expected Reid to accompany them, but Charles wanted to go this time.

They quickly reached sheltered water, radioing back that the reef was deep and wouldn't be a problem, clearance wise. *The Aquaholic* motored in, making water and charging her batteries on the way.

The anchorage was the right depth but would be completely unprotected if the winds changed during the night. Vee's solution was to maintain the watch schedule through the night. But instead of sailing at night, the night watch would keep an eye on the winds.

We deployed the main anchor and then sent our second anchor with Charles in the dinghy. Once it was dropped, the dinghy returned.

Reid motioned Jane and Marta to the anchor line, saying he had a trick to show them. Vee, Charles, and I went to see too.

Reid got two fenders, placing one near each anchor line. The anchor lines were cleated, but Reid loosened them long enough to tie a simple loop on the water side of the cleat. Each fender had a short piece of line tied to it, and Reid tied that off to his loop. He then secured a galley knife near each anchor line.

Vee and Charles smiled and nodded, obviously pleased, and obviously knowing why he had done that. I wasn't sure. Neither were Jane or Marta.

Reid explained that if the winds suddenly shifted and the anchors failed, rather than run aground while trying to retrieve both anchors, the night watch could start the engines and then quickly cut the anchor lines and motor out of danger.

He assured us the fenders would float and keep the anchor lines from sinking. We could retrieve them later with the dinghy after *The Aquaholic* was safely out of danger.

I thought back to all of my sailing lessons. I couldn't remember him ever mentioning having to ditch the anchor to avoid being shipwrecked.

Needless to say, his little demo with the fenders kept me stressed throughout my entire anchor watch. Although I couldn't see very well, I was positive the shoreline kept inching closer and closer.

CHAPTER 35

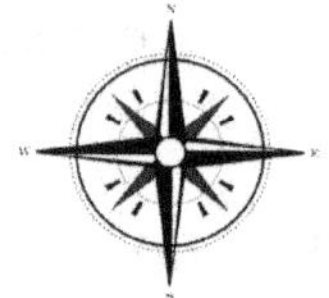

The unprotected anchorage wasn't very restful. Since Tubuai Island didn't appear to offer anything except for thousands of squawking birds, we discussed our options during breakfast.

By Reid's calculations, we had over 1,500 miles to go to reach the "roaring forties." Once there, we would turn left and have strong winds behind us all the way to the bottom part of South America.

When we got closer to that continent, we would angle south to round Cape Horn.

The Southern Ocean technically didn't begin until sixty degrees south latitude. According to Reid's fix yesterday, we were currently at twenty-three degrees, twenty-two minutes south.

He and Vee agreed that staying out of the Southern Ocean for as long as possible was our best course of action. We might have to dip into it to round Cape Horn, otherwise tackling it in the winter, with no backup, could either break the boat or break the crew.

The whole discussion made me apprehensive. Reid and Vee weren't very good salesmen. I thought back to Bev calling it a "suicide sail." That didn't help calm my fears.

Our chart showed other Austral Islands south and east of us. We could alter course to pass by those, or we could keep heading due south.

Having a few more stops before the roaring forties would have been a good idea if we hadn't been running so low on fuel and food.

With no guarantee the JP5 we got from the Navy would actually work in our engines, we decided that the Austral Islands route was out of the question.

We left Tubuai without going ashore and resumed course 180 degrees. We had a long way to go before we turned left, but I felt pretty good about our chances.

Vee was conserving our fuel by not running the engine every day. We were using our batteries sparingly and the solar panel was keeping them pretty well charged; we were being efficient with the water maker by filling our tanks and extra water bottles together; we had two more qualified crew; we had plenty of fish and they were easy to catch; *The Aquaholic* had handled all sea conditions so far without any problems;

Vee was proving herself a very qualified captain; and Reid was doing a great job with navigation and weather forecasting.

As we clicked off the miles south, the bird life gradually diminished. But we encountered vast schools of dolphins, a few whales, and of course, the ever-present sharks.

The dolphins would jump out of a wave right across the front of our hull. Some of them got really close, and I kept expecting to hear a thud.

We also spotted lots of turtles. Jane had been keeping an unofficial log of the turtle species she had positively identified. Her list included leatherback, hawksbills, green, black, and loggerhead.

I thought all turtles had a shell, but not the leatherback. Jane proved the scope of her knowledge bank once again by telling us that leatherbacks were not only the largest turtles on Earth, but instead of a shell, had a somewhat flexible and almost rubbery carapace.

She was in her element as she continued. "They can grow to over five feet in length and weigh up to fifteen hundred pounds—the fourth heaviest modern reptile behind three species of crocodile. They are among the deepest diving marine animals, having the most hydrodynamic body design of any sea turtle. They can dive to forty-two hundred feet and stay down for up to eighty-five minutes." She sighed. "Their population is rapidly declining in the modern world. We are very lucky to be seeing a specie that might soon be extinct."

She paused and looked at us. "Did I do it again? I guess once a *Jeopardy* contestant, always a *Jeopardy* contestant."

We laughed. I admired her ability to retain so much diverse information when I could barely remember what I had for breakfast from one day to another. On the other hand, I hoped her good memory would help when we got back to our own time since our logbooks, like any other record, would no doubt have to go before we made the transition.

While leatherbacks were the biggest turtle we had seen, the hawksbills were consistently the smallest. The loggerheads were the second biggest.

We only saw a few whales. Jane said they were sperm whales. They were making the same clicking noises I had heard before. Their name made me chuckle. I wondered how they got it and finally asked.

Jane said the sperm whale's large head contained spermaceti, a waxy material used in candles, oil lamps, and ointments.

As usual, I was impressed by her knowledge.

We also saw sharks, so many that we quit announcing "fin." Lots of the bigger sharks would swim right alongside us, pacing us, less than five feet away. Often they would stay there for twenty or thirty minutes. Sometimes they would roll their head slightly. I could swear that several times one of those big sharks was looking right at me.

I saw in the log that Reid had noted a great white shark had followed us for almost an hour. I was glad he hadn't told me.

I wondered if there were great white sharks in the roaring

forties. I knew that Reid and Jane would know, but I didn't inquire because I didn't want to know.

I also found a log entry where Charles had noted a shooting star. I wished I could see one of those too. Given the absence of "light pollution," as Jane called it, I was sure I would eventually.

The day Reid announced we had just hit forty degrees south latitude arrived. I expected strong winds for the foreseeable future, but the weather wasn't any different.

In the absence of the expected westerly winds, we held our course south. The following days and nights merged with one another, but the weather remained basically the same. Part of me thought it was a letdown, given all the stories I had heard about strong winds and following seas. Part of me was glad to just see occasional downpours, not ferocious storms.

The helm had been mine since my watch began at four a.m. Even in the blackness, I could feel the winds increasing.

I vividly remembered Reid's lessons about reefing the sails. He had emphasized that the time to reef was ten minutes before you needed to.

Working alone, by flashlight, I got both sails reefed. There was no power to the instruments, but I could feel that our speed had increased.

It was also evident the winds were shifting, so I trimmed the sails, again by flashlight, trying to maintain course 180 degrees.

I was proud for doing what needed to be done without

calling for assistance and waking everybody. I kept telling myself that it was okay to be jittery but not to get scared.

Watching the sunrise always told me two things: One— my shift was nearly over. Two—we were one day closer to reaching the Bermuda Triangle.

Today the sunrise gave me different information. There was trouble ahead.

CHAPTER 36

Vee came topside early. She took one look at the reefed and trimmed sails and immediately switched on the radar. There were surface contacts ahead of us.

I asked her if the blips were scattered islands. She replied the contacts weren't islands. They were storm pockets. She smiled and told me that we had reached a waypoint and it was time to change course.

Vee took over, which was fine with me. Within ten minutes, the waves were higher than usual and the winds were stronger. She gradually steered *The Aquaholic* until we were angling east. I trimmed the sails as directed.

Even with the sails reefed, our speed increased dramatically. We were no longer taking it easy. *The Aquaholic* was flying. Vee was smiling. I was on edge.

Ten minutes later, all hands were awake. Our normally

smooth ride had changed. It felt like we had a flat tire on a gravel road. Maybe two flat tires.

The Aquaholic was now pounding through the waves, vibrating way more than before. Waves splashed over the hulls, coating everything with salt spray.

Reid appraised the situation, telling me I had found the roaring forties. He looked at his watch and said he'd guesstimate our position and give Vee a new course heading.

Charles saw how fast we were going and told me he'd slow us down. When he disappeared inside without further reefing the sails, I was curious how.

A few minutes later he returned, carrying some line. He tethered himself to the stern. He cleated one end and then let the line out, dragging it behind us. We slowed a little. He repeated the procedure on the other hull. Our speed significantly decreased.

Vee explained that dragging those lines would not only slow us down, they would also give anyone who fell overboard a second chance at being rescued.

She looked at me and said, "If you find yourself in the water, get behind the boat and grab hold as the line passes." That seemed like a terrifying situation, but I knew I'd remember her advice.

Based on Reid's rough calculations, he believed we were close to forty-three degrees, forty minutes south latitude. He said he'd know better the next time he got a fix. He gave Vee the new course to steer.

Then he replaced me at the helm. I watched as he reefed

the jib some more and fine-tuned the mainsail. He applauded me for having already reefed the sails. I told him I had tried to do it ten minutes before I needed to. He smiled, knowing that was what he always told his students during their reefing lessons.

He stayed with Vee at the helm, saying I could go. The decks were wet and slippery. I carefully made my way inside, staying tethered the whole way.

Jane was frying some Spam. She looked nervous. So did Marta. Charles was looking at the chart. He didn't look the least bit uptight. I went below to use the head.

The first thing I noticed was that waves were covering the porthole. I felt like I was looking into a fish tank. The second thing was the noise. The hulls were literally humming from the force of the water passing by. It soon occurred to me why these latitudes were called the roaring forties.

I made sure there were no loose items in our cabin. For the first time, it felt claustrophobic. The waves pounding the over-head hatch startled me. I made sure it was tightly closed and latched. I hoped it wouldn't leak. A wet bed would suck.

I realized I was shaking. I sat down and told myself I was okay. I congratulated myself on reefing the sails alone, in the dark, without being told.

Jane called out that breakfast was ready. She had made "boatmeal," (my new name for oatmeal), fried Spam, and hot coffee. We all agreed that a hot breakfast really hit the spot.

Charles took some food topside to the helm. I carried the

coffee in half-full cups. Both of us clipped in the second we left the salon. Being outside was now dangerous.

Reid asked Charles if there were loops in the lines we were dragging. Charles shook his head but offered to fix it. He pulled in the lines, and I tied a large bowline in the end. He made sure it was tight and then let the lines back out.

I thought back to transiting the Panama Canal. Our line handlers had done the exact same thing, except for a different reason. These lines weren't to get us through the locks; their purpose now was to save someone's life.

"How far is it to South America?" I asked Charles after we completed our tasks and were returning to the safety of the salon.

"Probably close to four thousand nautical miles," he replied. "More or less."

"And it will be like this the whole time?" I asked, trying not to sound intimidated.

"Yup."

I felt weak in the knees. Another month in these conditions suddenly sounded impossible.

CHAPTER 37

The watch schedule had to be adjusted for Charles. He was the oldest one aboard, and the early morning watch was taking its toll on his health. He didn't complain, but he was moving a little slower. He was also wearing more clothes and looked cold sometimes.

Marta now followed Vee's ten p.m. to one a.m. watch. Jane took his nine a.m. to eleven a.m. watch. Charles insisted he was able to do more than the five p.m to seven p.m. watch, but Vee was unmoved.

Now that Reid was nearly done with his sailing lessons, he wanted more than his late afternoon shift. His request, like Charles's, fell on deaf ears.

Vee reminded him not to minimize or devalue his weather forecasting duties or his celestial navigation. The further south we went, the more important those two duties became.

Vee and I still had three watches each. I took it as a compliment that Vee trusted me at the helm so often.

Jane was assigned to shadow Reid when he made his weather forecasts. Vee wanted backup in case something happened to Reid.

Likewise for the navigation. Vee wanted Jane and me to learn the basics of celestial navigation. Reid made detailed notes and walked us through the process. Jane caught on right away. I struggled.

The dolphins and whales were abundant. We spotted more sperm whales. Jane told us they could stay underwater for over ninety minutes. She also said they didn't sleep but took vertical naps instead.

When asked what they ate, she replied, "Giant squid."

I had a nightmare about a monster octopus attacking *The Aquaholic*. It had all of us wrapped in its tentacles. As one of its tentacles started pulling our mast down, I woke up, yelling and quivering.

When I told Reid about my nightmare, he laughed. "Jane said squid, not octopus. Go back to sleep."

The fishing was good. When conditions allowed, Marta and I kept the fish cooler full. Marta even caught a swordfish. It was really fast and nearly took all of her line, but she managed to land it.

Reid kept as many steaks as we could and threw the rest of the fish overboard. It wasn't long before the sharks showed up. I thought we were too far south for sharks, but apparently not.

I had never eaten swordfish before, but with a generous

blend of spices, it was quite tasty.

Our course angled us across the roaring forties, toward Cape Horn. The further south we sailed, the harsher the conditions became.

Even with her sails furled and dragging two lines, *The Aquaholic* was averaging fifteen knots during the day and almost twelve at night. The wind in the rigging made a sinister sound.

We would fly down a wave only to run into the next wave's trough. When our hulls hit, there was a loud smack, and foamy water sprayed everywhere. As high as the helm was, whoever was steering frequently got soaked.

Our rain gear kept us dry for a few days but then just seemed to get clammy. I wore as many layers as I could, but fifteen minutes into any of my watches, I'd be cold and fighting the shivers.

The Aquaholic did not have very many blankets on board, but Vee had an ingenuous solution. She got all of the beach towels from the forepeak cabin and passed them out to eager hands.

I had never slept with a towel before, but between two towels and Reid's body heat, my berth was warm and inviting.

I was usually too tired for sex, preferring just to snuggle and steal Reid's body heat. He never complained about my cold hands on his back, or anywhere else.

I saw Easter Island on the chart, but it was way out of our way so I didn't say anything. I knew those big stone heads hadn't been carved yet.

I sorely missed the Panama Canal. I never fully appreciated how wonderful that transit had been until now.

One morning, as my four a.m. to seven a.m. watch was ending, I saw a giant bird fly alongside of us. It looked a little like a seagull, except its wingspan had to be at least twelve feet across, minimum.

It stayed even with me for a few minutes, as if it were watching me watch it. Then it flapped its massive wings and veered away.

When I told the others, Jane was positive I had seen an albatross. Everyone was excited at the prospect of seeing more except Marta. She said they were a bad omen.

As the days went on, we saw more and more albatrosses. They were quite magnificent, with their white bodies and contrasting massive, dark-colored wings.

The seas had been running between twenty and twenty-five feet, with sustained winds in excess of twenty knots, gusting to forty. Waves regularly washed over every inch of the deck.

The skies were cloudy nearly all of the time, rendering the solar showers useless. I tried to take a shower below once, with Vee's permission, but swaying and bouncing in the enclosed head made me nauseous. I was cold, tired, damp, and smelly. I also had headaches from the noise of the wind and the crashing of the waves.

And we hadn't even reached fifty degrees south latitude yet.

CHAPTER 38

One morning I spotted huge streaks of red right below the surface of the water. Even with the large waves, the color was obvious. I was pretty sure it wasn't one of the biblical plagues, but I honestly had no idea what all of those red blotches were.

A big red whale? If Moby Dick was white, why not a red one? The blood from a school of giant squids that a pod of sperm whales had just devoured? A mirage? An alien sphere, desiring to make contact?

Jane took one look and smiled at me. "Krill," she said. "It's only krill."

Having a *Jeopardy* champion aboard proved to be a huge asset again.

I had been thinking that Jane was perhaps the smartest

woman I had ever met. I grinned. Jane *was* the smartest *person* I had ever met.

I had heard of krill but had never seen any. Jane announced that with all the krill, there should be baleen whales around. "What kind of whales?" I asked, never having heard of a baleen whale.

"Baleen whales eat krill," she answered. "Toothed whales, like the big sperm whale, eat seals, fish, and squid." Her answer impressed me; it was straightforward, not conceited or arrogant.

"It's one thing to be the smartest person in the room, or on the boat in this case," I said to myself. "It's another to be humble, like Jane is."

"With all of the krill in the area, keep your eyes open for blue whales, fin whales, and humpbacks," Reid said, looking around.

"Aren't blue whales really big?" I asked, starting to get worried.

"Largest animal on the planet," Vee answered, looking around as well.

"Over one hundred feet long and weighing in excess of one hundred thousand pounds," Jane added.

"Will we hear them, like the sperm whale's clicking noises?" I asked.

Jane shook her head. "They make sort of a 'woo, woo, woo' calling sound."

Later that afternoon, I heard the sound Jane had

described. It was fairly loud and sounded pretty close. I grabbed my PFD and headed outside.

Reid was at the helm, pointing and grinning.

I looked just in time to see a giant tail disappear in the large waves.

I was sorry I had missed it until I heard a loud blowing sound, followed by another. That had to be blue whales on the surface, close by.

I joined Reid at the helm and clipped in. We were passing right through a whole bunch of blue whales. They were making Jane's "woo, woo, woo" noises as they leisurely swam around us.

As massive as some of them were, their calls were strangely calming. I should have been freaking out, between the strong winds, big waves, and being literally surrounded by the "largest animals on the planet," as Vee had called them, yet for some odd reason, I wasn't at all.

It was too rough to go forward, so Vee, Marta, and Jane were content to watch the magnificent spectacle from the area near the cockpit table.

Charles had been resting, complaining of being cold. In fact, Vee was concerned he was getting pneumonia, so Jane got him some of her daughter's extra heavier clothes to wear. I smiled when Charles joined us outside wearing a women's fleece top and a pink stocking hat.

The whale's strange calls had woken him. His tired look was replaced by one of happiness. He admitted he had never seen a blue whale in the wild before and seeing one was on his bucket list.

I believe we all felt glad he was able to get out of bed long enough to realize one of his dreams. I know I did.

CHAPTER 39

The winds, waves, and currents continued pushing us southeast. The ride stayed rough and bumpy, but *The Aquaholic* continued to make excellent time.

Reid figured our coordinates as often as he could get a decent sighting. Jane double-checked his work and then started the log entry.

My job was to plot his coordinates on the chart, ascertain if we were on course, and give the distance made since the last fix to Jane for her log entry.

It was easier to see during the day, but at night I'd need a little battery power for the salon lights.

Using a straight edge and the latitude and longitude markings on the edge of the chart, I'd mark his coordinates and the day and time.

If we were close to our projected course line, nothing had

to be done. If we weren't, I'd tell the helm to adjust as necessary.

The last thing was to draw a line from Reid's most recent fix to the previous one. I'd use a divider to find the distance between them. I'd use the calculator in Jane's phone to provide the average speed between fixes. Jane would note that in the log. South America kept inching closer.

I knew Reid had raided our emergency supply of freeze-dried rations, because that's where the orange and grape flavored drink mixes came from. With our food supply rapidly diminishing, Vee called a meeting. We had plenty of fish, but all of us were getting tired of eating straight fish. It was unanimously agreed that we begin using our emergency rations. The cold was sapping our strength, and in these challenging sailing conditions, we couldn't afford any fatigue-related mistakes.

Our traditional morning breakfast of "boatmeal" was augmented with cinnamon apple cereal, brown sugar and maple granola, biscuits and gravy, and scrambled eggs with bacon pieces.

While most of the meals were theoretically edible just by rehydrating with water, they all tasted much better when cooked with hot water.

"Tasted much better" was relative. So far, with the exception of the orange drink powder, freeze-dried food sacrificed taste and texture for weight and shelf life. But, it had nutrients and calories and did keep my stomach from growling.

I had missed Jane's Bloody Mary mix soup, but now we had four different flavors of freeze-dried soup mixes. We also had assorted lunches, dinners, and one dessert—vanilla pudding, which was a little runny but not bad.

One day Reid brought lunch to me at the helm. I was expecting macaroni and cheese, but judging by his mischievous grin, there was obviously something else happening.

He handed me a bag of corn chips and a spoon. I looked inside. The corn chips were covered in chili. Thinking he had found ingredients to make his chili, I didn't hesitate to dive in.

After one bite I knew it wasn't Reid's chili. It tasted flat and processed, but I was hungry and kept eating. He held the wheel, allowing me the use of both hands.

While I ate, he explained that he had rehydrated and heated southwest chili and then scooped some over the chips.

His concoction was pretty smart. It tasted like freeze-dried chili, but with all the chips, it was surprisingly filling. It was easy to eat, and the foil bag was radiating heat, which helped warm my hands. He got a kiss for his efforts.

As the days passed, I noticed something I had not expected. The days were getting shorter.

I knew this because my four to seven a.m. watch had always included the sunrise. Likewise, my seven to ten p.m. watch had always included the sunset. Until recently.

The further south we sailed, the later the sun was rising and the earlier it was setting. The worst part was now two of my three watches were in the dark.

It wasn't so bad when the moonlight illuminated the frothy seas or when I had a bright star to steer toward. But when the clouds assisted the blackness in engulfing us, it was scary.

I couldn't figure out why I couldn't get comfortable with being alone at the helm in the dark.

Since leaving Panama, I certainly had gotten a lot of practice. And I hadn't had any major problems and was making almost as many miles during my night watch as Vee was. But scare me it did.

When Reid calculated our position as reaching fifty degrees south latitude, we made a course change. We were still a long way from South America and didn't want to go any further south until we were ready to round Cape Horn.

We steered a new course, due east.

I noticed Charles seemed to be feeling better. He was no longer shivering and his appetite had increased. When I asked him about it he smiled and replied that Jane was a good nurse.

There was something about the way he said "good nurse" that made me inquire further. After a little prodding, he confided that they were now sharing a cabin.

I grinned, but he quickly explained that they were sharing a bed but strictly for warmth.

"Do you expect me to believe that?" I asked.

"I don't care what you believe, but two can sleep much warmer than one and that's all that's going on," he replied.

He had a point. He also offered their extra cabin to be used as a permanent clotheslines for drying our nearly constant supply of laundry.

I really looked forward to climbing into bed with Reid

when my one a.m. watch ended. No matter how cold I had gotten at the helm, the bed was always hot on his side.

Of course I kept Charles's secret.

One morning, Jane surprised us with fresh bread for breakfast, spread with peanut butter.

"How did you get the yeast to rise?" Reid asked when he took his second piece.

Jane looked uncomfortable for a second but answered. "I put the bowl of dough in bed with me and my body heat did the trick."

I knew the whole story but kept quiet and joined Reid in seconds. Jane's loaf wasn't as attractive as her daughter's, but it tasted wonderful.

I was tired of "fiberglass camping," as Reid often called it, and taking a sponge bath with a few cups of tepid water.

As usual, Reid came to my rescue.

He heated water on the stove and added that to a solar shower that was mostly full of cold water. The sun didn't shine long enough to get the solar showers hot, but a small quantity of almost boiling water got the whole container to a usable temperature.

When the seas calmed enough so I could stand up without crashing into the bulkhead, he'd prepare a solar shower and hang it in our head. Maintaining my balance was challenging, but I was able to take a super-fast shower with warm, almost hot, water.

I bragged about his resourcefulness, and the others copied

what he had done. Being cleaner visibly improved everyone's attitude.

I stared longingly at the chart, wishing we would reach the South American coastline faster.

I was cold, tired, and had a headache from the constant noise of the pounding ocean. I also had an upset stomach and gas from eating so much freeze-dried food.

It was slightly funny that everyone seemed to have a flatulence problem, so I didn't feel too embarrassed whenever a fart sneaked out.

There was no scale aboard, but judging from the way my clothes were now fitting, I was losing weight. With the possible exception of Marta, we all were.

I thought back to how thin Mo and Gert had been after we found them. I forced myself not to think about getting sickly thin.

I remembered hearing somewhere that the old-time sailors got scurvy and ate limes for a remedy. I wasn't sure what scurvy was exactly and didn't want to ask Jane.

We didn't have any limes, and the bottle of lemon juice had been used up cooking fish. I wondered if weight loss was a side effect of a diet lacking in fruits and produce.

I wondered how much weight we could afford to lose before getting too weak to sail in these increasingly challenging conditions.

CHAPTER 40

Before we were within in sight of the Chilean coast, we altered course south-southeast.

We had been sailing east, keeping very close to fifty degrees south latitude. We would need to reach fifty-seven degrees south to round Cape Horn.

Using the chart, Reid presented his rationale for the course change. Vee double-checked his calculations. Everyone agreed now was the time to angle toward the Cape.

The course change was both welcomed and problematic.

It was very comforting to see how far we had come.

The problem was we were no longer running with the wind behind us. The winds were now blowing from the side.

It was easy enough to trim the sails for a broad reach. Our biggest worry was the waves. Instead of running along with them, we were now angling through them. If we got each of our hulls in a separate wave, *The Aquaholic* would be ripped in half.

Steering was now critical. Any miscalculation at the helm could spell instant disaster.

Vee adjusted the watch schedule again to reflect sixty minutes at the helm, maximum.

Charles had been wearing one of the two sets of cold-weather gear *The USS Fields* had given us. He wore it all the time, saying it kept him warm. Nobody disagreed, but now we had another problem.

The night watch now needed cold-weather gear. With only one set, it had to be shared.

The best way we found to do this was for the new watch person to report wearing their heavy clothes. Whoever they replaced would go into the salon and change from the cold-weather gear into their heavy clothes. They would then return to the helm so their replacement could change into the cold-weather gear for their watch.

This process wasn't overly efficient and added time, but until Charles was willing to part with the gear he was home-steading, there wasn't any other way.

One benefit of sharing one set of cold-weather gear was it was already warm when you put it on. The negative was the previous wearer's body odor. Vee donated a bottle of perfume and that helped.

We continued to see albatross and whales. Jane positively identified the massive blue whales, the almost-as-massive fin whales, a few solitary humpback whales, much smaller minke whales, the slow swimming right whales, the speedy sei whales, and of course, more sperm whales. She also noted some small dolphins she thought might be hourglass dolphins.

The only whale she expected to spot but didn't was the killer whale. I asked her to please call them orcas instead. She smiled and said she would try. She might have thought I was a scaredy cat but too bad.

Each wave risked being a "killer wave" if we got the hulls out of step. I didn't need the local wildlife sharing the same name. I didn't even like it when she served a loaf of "killer French bread" as she called it.

The Aquaholic continued toward Cape Horn. The winds were still ferocious, and we sacrificed speed for safety. We kept the sails reefed and sailed very conservatively.

A few times a large wave washed right over the dinghy. I expected it to get ripped away and lost, but it stayed put.

We had long since removed the outboard motor and were storing it below. Reid did tie a long line to the dinghy, reasoning that if it did get torn away, we might have a chance to retrieve it.

Watching the huge waves surrounding us, I doubted we be able to pull the dinghy back in.

The waves crashed over the bow, drenching the decks. They also played havoc with the sea kayaks that were tied to the lifelines. When a wave completely covered them, I was sure the kayaks would be torn away, damaging the boat in the process.

Reid and Marta tried stowing one of the kayaks in the

salon, but it was really in the way. They discussed tying it to the dinghy but agreed it would be even more vulnerable to a following sea than the dinghy was. Eventually they returned it to its place, lashing it as securely as they could on the heaving, pitching deck. Reid managed to tie a safety line to both kayaks, just in case.

We could have used some more fish, but it was too rough to try fishing until we got around Cape Horn and presumably reached calmer seas.

We continued to conserve battery power, propane, and fuel. The only circuit we left on full time was the automatic bilge pump.

When it ran intermittently one morning, Reid knew we had a leak.

A quick search revealed water in the bilge of the starboard hull.

After a little more investigating, Reid and Vee determined the leak was coming from the forepeak head.

Knowing that heads contained thru-hull fittings to allow the plumbing fixtures to bring in seawater or let out wastewater, I asked if one of those fittings had possibly failed.

They didn't think so because there wasn't that much water in the bilge.

"One of us is going to have to go forward and see what's leaking," Reid said. "I volunteer."

Nearly every wave we hit caused water to wash over the hulls. Beside getting soaked, anybody going clear forward would be in constant danger of getting washed overboard. In these rolling, churning seas, going forward was inviting disaster.

Reid repeated his statement. As if confirming his observation, the bilge pump hummed, cycling on and then off.

He looked at Vee for her approval.

She nodded and said, "I'll take over the helm. Be careful." Then she added, "And remember, we are dragging lines with loops."

Reid put on his offshore rain gear. He then got some lines but no tools.

Jane had been relieved of her helm duties and joined me, Marta, and Charles clear forward in the salon.

The view over the foredeck was spectacular and frightening. The rolling waves were very powerful, yet strangely simple.

Hundreds or maybe thousands of gallons of water were washing over our hulls with every splash, but the water didn't care that we were in its way. The salt spray just rejoined the next wave and continued on its way.

The thought of Reid being forward and alone to face those waves made me shiver.

"I'll go forward and see what's happening," he said.

If he was afraid, his voice didn't reflect it.

He held up one piece of line. "I'll attach this for a jackline," he said.

I knew that once that line was securely fastened, he'd be able to attach his safety tether to it and move about freely.

I nodded my approval.

"I'll attach this to my harness," he said, holding a long length of yellow, floating line.

He then handed it to Marta. "If I fall in before I get the jackline secured, you'll have to help me back to the boat."

She took the yellow line and nodded.

I swallowed. Now I was alarmed. I looked at the massive, churning seas. There was no way that anyone who fell overboard in these conditions would live to tell about it, yellow safety line and dragging loop lines or not.

Reid looked at Charles and Jane next. "I'll let you know what tools I need."

They both nodded.

Then he looked at me. "I'll be right back."

I was speechless. I needed to tell him I loved him, but would that imply that he wasn't going to make it? Was I seeing the last of Reid Adams, sailing instructor, fiancée, friend, and lover? Would he die doing what Cookie Cook might have referred to as "a sailor's death at sea?"

He gave me a hug and then went outside. We followed.

The air was cold. The foredeck area was wet and slippery.

Reid carefully made his way forward on the starboard hull, immediately clipping his tether to the lifeline.

Marta moved to where she could let out her yellow line without it getting tangled. Charles held onto Marta. Jane began paying out the jackline. I held Jane with one hand and the boat with the other. This suddenly seemed crazy.

Reid reached the bow and tied off his end of the jackline. Then he hunkered down and waited for the next wave to pass.

He was momentarily covered by water but never moved. He raised up, tugged on the jackline, and then signaled a thumbs-up. I could see he was smiling.

Jane tied her end off while I watched. She pulled the line tight and I kept it tight while she tied her knot. I watched carefully. It looked like it would hold.

I waited for the next wave to soak him and then signaled with another thumbs-up. He moved his tether from the life-line to the jackline.

Marta was holding her yellow line. Charles was still holding onto her. We all waited for Reid to make his way below into the forepeak crew head to assess the leak.

I wondered how he'd close the hatch behind him, since he was tethered to the jackline. I wondered if the bilge pump could keep up with the amount of water that would pour into that compartment if the hatch was open when another wave hit. When Reid didn't go below but turned and made his way back, I wondered what was wrong.

CHAPTER 42

"**G**o tell Vee the hatch is cracked but we'll fix it."

That's all Reid said when he returned, motioning us to follow him into the salon.

"The hatch cover is cracked, that's all," he said. "Easy fix."

I relaxed. That didn't sound so bad. Probably nothing that duct tape couldn't handle. Of course he'd have to go back up there, but the jackline was already in place and he didn't seem all that concerned.

"I'll need duct tape, a towel, one of the blue tarps, bungee cords, and the galley scissors," he said, wiping the water from his face.

"How was it up there?" Charles asked.

"All you have to do is hold on and time the waves," he replied. His voice was calm. He didn't seem at all worried.

When he grinned at me, I grinned back.

When he told me to get into my rain gear, I started shaking.

"You're kidding, right?" I asked. There was no way I was leaving the safety of the foredeck. Being on the foredeck had been scary enough.

"I can't do it alone," he replied. "I need another set of hands."

I gulped. He was serious.

I put on my rain gear but felt numb the whole time. Even though it wasn't cold inside, I was shivering.

He gathered what he needed, giving me the bungee cords and the towel.

"This will keep the towel dry," Jane said, handing me a plastic bag.

I took the bag. It felt surreal, like everything was happening in slow motion. I could feel my heart pounding.

I watched as Reid tied another safety line to my harness. I didn't know what to say. It was obvious I would have to go forward with him.

He took my hand and looked into my eyes.

"Relax," he said. "Relax and follow me."

We went outside. Marta and Jane let out our safety lines. Charles held both of them.

"Clip to the jackline," Reid said. The wind was whipping past us and it was hard to hear. I did as instructed.

"Follow me after the next wave, and be careful," he said, raising his voice to be heard above the wind.

A big wave washed over the bow. That was our signal.

The hull was as slippery as an ice rink. I went slowly. My tether to the jackline slid effortlessly with me as I moved forward. I could feel the safety line's slight drag as it was played out. I hoped that Jane wouldn't let go. I remembered that we were dragging long loop lines behind us, one on each side.

I fought hard to keep going and not turn back.

We reached the hatch.

"Brace yourself," Reid hollered, kneeling down.

I knelt as he did, holding on with both hands.

The boat slammed into a wave. Frigid water hit me with such force that I screamed.

That was a mistake because I suddenly had a mouthful of salt water. I started gagging. As the water rushed past me, I felt it pulling, like receding waves do when you're at a beach.

But I didn't let go.

"You okay?" Reid asked.

No, I was definitely not okay. This sucked. But for whatever reason, I spit out some seawater and nodded.

"See the cracks?" he said, pointing with one hand while holding on with the other.

I quit gagging and tried to focus. My eyes stung from the salt water. I tried wiping them, but my hand was also wet, so that didn't help.

Finally I saw there were three cracks in the hatch. There was a line of bubbles where water from the last dunking had made its way below.

"Got it," I replied, trying not to cough.

"After the next wave passes, I tell you what we're going to do. Get ready for another bath."

Bath was not the word I would have used to describe getting pummeled by giant waves in the middle of fucking nowhere in the South Pacific. But this time, I closed my eyes and my mouth and held on tightly until the last tug of the receding wave had ended.

"After the next wave, get your towel and dry off the biggest crack." Reid's voice made me open my eyes. They still burned but not as bad as before.

"I'll tape it right behind you, so don't make a career out of this. The hatch doesn't have to be totally dry, just dry enough for the tape to stick. Got it?"

I understood and nodded, feeling for the plastic bag and then bracing myself for the next wave. "Now I know what a car wash feels like," I said, but he didn't hear me.

After three waves, we had successfully taped the three cracks. I wiped, he taped, and we didn't waste any motions or time.

"Are we done?" I asked. I was cold and soaked but not as spooked as I had been.

"Not quite," he answered. "Now we have to bungee the tarp in place."

I held on as Reid worked in between soakings. Once the tarp was cut bigger than needed to cover the hatch, he held it in place while I stretched the bungee cords all the way around the hatch's frame, finally hooking the last hook to the first one.

He had been right; it was a two-person job. But once you

figured out the interval between the splashings, there was about fifteen seconds to get work done before having to brace for the next wave.

I really felt proud when we finally returned to the foredeck. Jane, Marta, and Charles were all smiling. I looked back to the hatch we had just fixed. The blue tarp was still in place. I hoped the bungee cords would hold, because they were as tight as we could make them.

"Ready to do it again?" Reid asked, squeezing my nearly frozen hand.

"What?"

He pointed toward the port side hull. I shook my head.

"That hatch is stressed as well," he said. "We should fix it while we're out here."

I didn't argue. I knew he was right.

Despite my shivering, I stayed outside and watched while Reid rigged another jackline. Once it was in place, we went forward and repeated the repair.

The port hatch had one crack, not three, and didn't appear to be leaking, but we taped and covered it anyway.

We all got back inside without incident. Reid left the jacklines in place, just in case. Jane heated some soup while Reid and I got out of our dripping rain gear and dried off.

Marta went to relieve Vee at the helm.

I went to the stove and rubbed my hands near the burner, trying to warm them.

When Vee joined us in the salon, she looked at Reid and me and said, "I'm glad neither of you fell overboard."

She was glad. That seemed an odd thing to say.

Reid and I exchanged glances.

Vee got out of her cold-weather gear and swapped it with Marta. Once the exchange of gear had taken place, Vee joined us at the galley table.

"I don't know if you noticed," she said, "but there were killer whales following us the whole time you two were forward."

Reid had a bite of soup and said, "I saw them."

"You saw killer whales and didn't tell me?" I squeaked, glaring at him.

"What good would it have done?" he replied. He was very calm. "You were already pretty scared. I didn't see any reason to make it worse."

I wanted to argue that I should have known if for no other reason than I needed to be prepared if anything happened, but something held me back. I took a moment to digest what he had said.

The whales were apparently all around us. Knowing they were there wouldn't have made a difference except to frighten me even more than I already was.

The more I thought about it, the more I knew Reid was right not to have said anything.

And even as frightened as I was, I was able to overcome my fear and help keep the boat safe, something I was proud of. Hopefully the tarps would stay in place long enough for us to get out of these terrible conditions.

But when we saw our first iceberg, I knew that things might get worse before they got better.

CHAPTER 43

Vee was at the helm and shouted, "Iceberg ho."

The salon emptied. Breakfast would have to wait.

Reid joined Vee at the helm. Marta and I just held on and watched the iceberg come in and out of view. Charles and Jane were below, but if they heard Vee's cry, they would be joining us shortly.

I was mesmerized by the size of the iceberg ahead. When we were atop a wave, I'd get a really good look at it. It had to be over one hundred feet high. It was ten times longer than a cargo ship, and its top was flat.

Reid trimmed the sails and we steered away from it.

Two days ago we had reached fifty-four degrees south latitude and had changed course due east. We would hold that heading until the Chilean coast came into view. Then we would angle southeast toward the northern boundary of the Drake Passage, Tierra del Fuego.

After that course change, Vee had warned us all to keep alert for icebergs. She said that ninety percent of an iceberg was underwater, and the part you didn't see was the problem. Its submerged jagged edges could severely damage even the largest vessels.

I got another good look at our first iceberg. It was hard to imagine that thing being ninety percent underwater.

Marta left me aft, going back inside. I stayed put, wanting to see it again. When I got soaked by a wave, I quickly retreated to the dryness of the salon.

Charles and Jane had come topside. They were forward with Marta, catching glimpses of the iceberg as the roller coaster waves hurtled us up and down. Still dripping water, I joined them. Wet or not, I wanted another look.

Reid touched my shoulder. I jumped.

"Pretty cool, huh?" he said. His smile was gigantic.

Jane made breakfast. Reid and Charles looked over the chart. Marta kept an eye on the iceberg. I got dried off-again- and changed into drier clothes.

Jane fried our last can of Spam. She had been saving it for a special occasion. Our first tabular berg sighting certainly qualified.

In response to our questioning looks, she explained that icebergs carried different names based on their general shapes. The flat-topped ones were referred to as tabular bergs.

"If an iceberg is ninety percent underwater, then why doesn't it sink from its own weight?" I asked.

Jane replied almost immediately. "I know three reasons, but there might be more."

I waited for her answer. Three reasons? I couldn't even think of one. Again, I was impressed.

"One: liquid water is slightly denser than solid water. That's why ice cubes float in your glass."

She looked at me as if waiting for me to acknowledge that I understood. I did and nodded.

"Two: icebergs aren't solid but are riddled with millions of tiny air bubbles. The trapped air adds to its buoyancy and is what gives icebergs their white appearance."

I nodded again.

"Three: there are dissolved solids in seawater, making it denser than freshwater. Icebergs are composed of freshwater, hence they are more buoyant."

"So why doesn't the seawater melt the iceberg?" Marta asked.

I wondered that too, but Jane didn't even blink before she answered. "Saltwater has a lower freezing point than freshwater. As long as the temperature of the saltwater remains below that of the freshwater iceberg, the iceberg may melt a little from the sun, but not from the ocean water it's floating in."

"Do you know about Bluetooth icebergs?" Reid asked.

As we shifted our attention to him, he answered. "Any vessel that goes near one will sync." He then spelled out sync and started laughing.

Jane laughed. So did Charles. I just shook my head at another of Reid's seemingly endless supply of lame sailor jokes.

Marta delivered a cracker and Spam sandwich to Vee and then rejoined us.

Reid hadn't been able to get a fix for two days as the stormy weather obscured everything. But based on our course and speed, he estimated we'd spot land today or tomorrow, or perhaps the day after.

I took another look at the chart. Tierra del Fuego, at the tip of South America, was full of islands. The islands dotted the waters between fifty-five and fifty-six degrees south latitude.

Since we had spotted an iceberg at our present latitude of fifty-four degrees, I figured there would be more icebergs in the waters to the south.

Reid predicted the weather might be improving. That was really good news. I was half-scared of what I had overheard about the Drake Passage—that it could be mostly calm or treacherous. Adding bad weather into the mix would only make things worse. I tried thinking of a word for worse than treacherous. I finally came up with two: fucking treacherous.

Just before dark, we spotted two more giant icebergs. They weren't in our path, but they could have been. It was now time to leave the radar turned on.

The radar required more power from the batteries than the solar panel was capable of keeping up with. *The Aquaholic* had two choices: run its engines or run its generator.

Since we had wind, Vee opted to use the gasoline powered generator and save our precious diesel for when we needed the engines.

CHAPTER 44

Vee modified the watch schedule to add one lookout in addition to the helmsman.

I couldn't stop thinking about the *Titanic* and even got the song from the movie stuck in my head. I had a dream of being in a lifeboat and finding Reid floating in the water, frozen. It was horrible.

We continued on course. Before we sighted land, we spotted lots of large birds. There were hundreds of them, filling the sky.

They had dark bodies and a white head. I thought they might be bald eagles, but Jane announced they were Andean condors taking advantage of the air currents.

A little while later, the radar signaled land. An hour after that, Charles gave the "land ho" shout.

Reid was next to me and whispered, "Who's he calling a ho?"

I almost chuckled but didn't want to encourage him and get him started with more jokes. I was getting joked out.

We changed course again, following the coast more than the compass.

Once we had gotten into krill waters, we saw numerous whales but only occasional seals. These coastal waters were teaming with seals. Jane identified most of them as crabeater seals. They were lightly colored and ate mostly krill, not crabs.

She was surprised there were so many this far north. She also said the crabeater seal's chief predators were orcas and leopard seals. Fortunately for the seals, we hadn't seen any orcas lately.

We sailed past many icebergs. What bothered Reid and Vee more than the giant icebergs were the smaller ones.

We passed one the size of a minivan. Reid told me it was a growler. Before I could question its name, he said, "That's from the noise the smaller icebergs make as the trapped air escapes."

I listened but couldn't hear anything over the rushing, noisy waves.

We sailed past more growlers. They ranged from car sized to school bus sized. Most of them stuck about three feet out of the water, but some were twice that high.

Vee told us they were more dangerous than the big ones because they were too low to be visible to the radar. If we hit one, we'd get a hole in the hull.

I looked at the growlers floating all around us and thought, "This really is a suicide sail."

Vee talked to Reid. I couldn't hear what she was saying, but he kept nodding. Finally, she directed him to the helm, assigned Marta lookout duties, and motioned for me, Charles, and Jane to join her in the salon.

I had a bad feeling.

"There's too much floating ice to try and sail through the night," she said. She sounded concerned but not alarmed.

I glanced at Charles. He was listening and looked cold but not worried.

"Are we going to anchor every evening and restrict our sailing to daylight hours?" Charles asked.

Vee nodded. "We had planned to clear all of Tierra del Fuego's island coast by sailing south to fifty-seven degrees before changing course due east."

I remembered that was the plan.

"That's clearly impossible now given the crap in the water. We'll do exactly as Charles suggested. Anchor in protected waters at night and only sail during daylight hours."

"All that stopping will add time," Charles stated. "Do we have enough food?"

"Maybe Tracy and Marta can catch us some Chilean sea bass," Vee answered, smiling.

"Chilean sea bass is really Patagonian toothfish," Jane said.

I looked at her. I had never heard of a Patagonian toothfish, but I knew that whatever she was going to say would be accurate.

"The Patagonian toothfish is delicious, but its name doesn't sell well. In nineteen seventy-seven, a fish wholesaler named Lantz rebranded Patagonian toothfish as Chilean sea bass and demand for the fish soared."

"Ever catch one?" Charles looked at me and grinned.

"Not yet," I answered. I had heard of Chilean sea bass but had never seen one. But if they were in these waters, and if we needed more fish, then I would give it my best shot.

CHAPTER 45

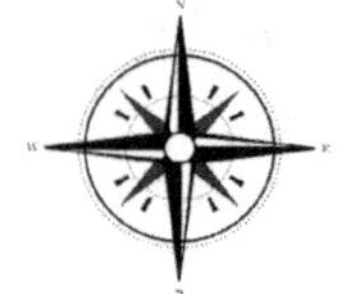

I t was Marta who got the first strike.

We had made our way across the southern end of Tierra del Fuego, basically island hopping without accurate charts.

Marta was fishing, trolling deeper and deeper until she caught one. Reid gaffed it, carefully controlling its mouth, which was full of short teeth. Its body was dark green with wide, vertical black stripes. She proudly announced that her fish weighed thirty pounds. Jane identified it as our first Patagonian toothfish.

Later that day, I caught one too. Mine looked the same except it was longer and fatter, with a bigger mouth. Reid judged it to be close to seventy pounds.

"More like eighty," Marta corrected him after lifting it.

Between our two fish, the cooler was full of nice fillets, stacked under a blanket of frozen water bottles.

Jane cooked a pan full for dinner. The fact that there were no leftovers confirmed the fish was delicious.

Reid had been right in his prediction of improving weather, but that was relative.

The winds had weakened some but were still strong. The waves were smaller but still large. The skies were still threatening but less so. Icebergs, small and humongous, were pretty much everywhere.

Without a steel hulled, specially designed vessel, our only chance to survive the Drake Passage was to avoid its iceberg sentinels.

The only way to do that was sail in behind the islands to where they provided some protection from the waves, but not so far behind them as to lose the wind.

We noticed flatter areas where the waves were reasonable and the wind sufficient for relatively safe travel. We still kept one lookout per watch.

Most of the islands were rocky and desolate. Seal colonies were plentiful. I got a good look at some condors on shore. I had never known that condors were a specie of vulture. They had a mean looking, ugly head. They were much prettier gliding over us.

A few of the islands had some vegetation. Jane pointed out "flag trees" and explained they grew almost sideways because of the strong winds.

As it got darker, we'd find a relatively sheltered spot and

drop anchor for the night. We kept a night watch in case the winds shifted or an iceberg invaded our anchorage.

We also checked the forepeak cabin hatches. The cabins were dry thanks to our improvised tarp covers. Reid used some more duct tape and then resealed both hatches as before.

Besides the winds, it began to rain, which usually turned to snow. Nearly every morning, the rigging would be covered with icicles. It was pretty, but obviously humid and cold.

As if the decks weren't slippery enough from the constant waves, the freezing temperatures made everything worse.

Reid commented that it was cold enough to freeze the balls off a brass monkey. To the questioning looks, he explained that the old ships kept their cannonballs stacked near the cannons.

They were stacked on a dimpled piece of brass that was called the monkey. When it got cold, the brass would contract, the dimples would recede, and the cannonball stack would fall.

Jane thanked him, saying she'd remember that. So did Charles. I had heard the expression before but didn't know where it had originated.

Reid hadn't been able to get a decent fix for nearly two weeks, but he was fairly confident we were getting close to changing course out of the Drake Passage.

Jane served fish and then used the last packaged cake mix and made dessert. For a cake made without eggs, filling, or frosting, it was really yummy. After the galley was cleaned up, she played a few songs about snow on her violin—most were

Christmas songs but appropriate. Everyone was in good spirits.

Reid said he had a long joke but it was worth it. He looked at me as if silently seeking approval. As much as I feared he'd tell another clunker, a joke sounded like a good idea. I smiled and nodded.

"A magician got a job on a cruise ship. After a few weeks performing, the magician figured out that since his audience changed every seven days, he could just repeat his act. So he did, week after week, cruise after cruise, audience after audience. It was a very easy gig, except for one thing.

"The captain owned a beautiful parrot and kept it on the stage. The parrot watched this magician's act show after show and after a few months started talking. 'That's not the same hat. Look at his other hand. All the cards are the queen of hearts.'

"The magician quickly began to hate that parrot, but what could he do since, after all, it was the captain's parrot?

"One day at sea there was a terrible accident. The ship sank, and all hands were lost except for the parrot and the magician, who were both clinging to a piece of the wreckage.

"The day passed and neither of them said a word. The night passed and once again, complete silence.

"Finally on the second day, the parrot looked at the magician and said, 'Okay, I give up. What did you do with the ship?'"

Reid didn't break into his customary punchline laughter and instead waited, watching for our reaction.

I started laughing. It was one of his better jokes. The more I thought about the bird saying that, the harder I laughed.

The others laughed too, except Marta.

"It's bad luck to tell a joke about a ship sinking," she said.

Her comment ended Reid's joke telling for the evening.

CHAPTER 46

T*he Aquaholic* and its nearly exhausted crew finally rounded Cape Horn and changed course north into the vastness of the South Atlantic.

Getting behind South America lessened the waves and the winds, but not the icebergs. There were still giant icebergs everywhere, but at least they were big enough to show up on radar.

There were fewer growlers but plenty of orcas and sperm whales. Those didn't show up on the radar.

We continued with two-person watches: one at the helm and one on lookout duty.

Jane fished and caught a huge Patagonian toothfish. Charles helped her reel it in, and Reid landed it. It easily weighed over one hundred fifty pounds. That refilled the fish cooler.

Rather than sail due north, we set course north-northeast toward the Falkland Islands.

In order to clear the easterly bulge of Brazil, we needed to get a lot further east. Vee decided that we could make a quick stop in the Falklands and then angle north-northeast toward Brazil.

I looked at the chart and shook my head. According to Reid's course line, it was over thirty-four hundred nautical miles to round Brazil's far eastern shore. There we would change course for our push toward the Caribbean. Then we still had to get to the Bermuda Triangle.

I silently cursed Pat for what she had done. I wondered if *The Aquaholic* and its crew would make it.

I debated trying to contact the aliens to ask if they would change their mind about making us sail all the way to the Bermuda Triangle.

I finally decided against it, not wanting to risk antagonizing them and being stuck here, in the past, with no hope of ever being returned.

We were still dealing with freezing rains that felt like bee stings if you got caught outside without your rain gear, but thankfully it had quit snowing.

Rounding Cape Horn had been rough, so rough in fact that everyone but Reid had been fighting sea sickness. I was glad that I hadn't thrown up like most of the others, including Vee.

I looked forward to taking a break in the Falkland Islands. The chart showed lots of promising anchorages. We might even get a chance to explore the channel separating the two islands, the Falkland Sound, by kayak if the weather permitted.

Our condor sightings had stopped but the albatross returned. So did the dolphins. One day there were thousands of them.

I was tired of eating fish and kept thinking about food.

I imagined myself at a marina in the Bahamas, ordering from a friendly waiter. I sorely missed fresh vegetables and fruit, like a crisp apple that crunched loudly when I chewed it.

I also missed water that hadn't been desalinated first. A tall glass of nothing but pure ice water sounded fantastic.

I wondered how long after returning to civilization it would take me to find a buffet that had one whole section devoted to hot soup and another section that housed a twenty—foot-long salad bar.

I also looked forward to getting warm in either a hot tub by the hotel pool or at a couple's spa with Reid. He and I could alternate between the steam room and a private Jacuzzi tub, where we could fool around.

"Yes, sir, the first thing I'm going to order are two salads and a pitcher of ice water, served while I soak in a hot tub," I said to myself.

I wasn't going to order any fish for the foreseeable future or go camping. I had had enough fish, freeze-dried food, and solar showers to last me for the rest of my life.

But I never mentioned my food fantasies. There was

nothing to eat but what we had left or what we could catch. Why start salivating with so far to go?

Reid and I had finished a late watch, replaced by Vee and Marta. Charles and Jane would replace them, and then it would be our turn again.

The watches were now ninety minutes, having been lengthened to allow for clothing changes.

The person at the helm wore the cold-weather gear and, except for Jane, the person on lookout duty wore damp rain gear. That choice was simple because the helmsman was stationary while the lookout could move around, within the limits of their tether.

I envied Jane having her own cold-weather gear when she was on lookout duty, but she deserved it.

Reid and I were snuggling in our cabin, trying to get warm and debriefing about all of the cool dolphins we had seen.

We both heard a strange noise, a pounding sound. It was coming from above.

"Did we hit a growler?" I asked, afraid that we had punctured a hull and were sinking.

"I don't think so," Reid said, shaking his head. "But something's wrong."

I listened hard. The pounding was fast and steady, like a drum roll. I could feel the vibrations. It was definitely not normal wave rhythms.

He opened our cabin door.

We both heard screaming. It sounded like Marta.

I grabbed my jacket and followed Reid topside.

CHAPTER 47

Charles and Jane arrived in the salon at the same time we did, obviously hearing what we heard.

"Vee, Vee, Vee," Marta kept hollering. Her voice was piercing and frantic.

Reid raced toward the helm without his PFD or safety tether. The rest of us followed. My heart was pounding.

"What's wrong?" Reid asked, holding on as *The Aquaholic* bounced through a wave.

Marta quit stomping her feet, which was the pounding sound we had all been hearing.

"Vee's in trouble," Marta shrieked. "She's not answering and I can't see her."

"Where?" Reid asked.

"Forward, port side," she yelled. "Take the helm. Now!"

"I'll get it," Charles said, raising his voice. "Go see what's wrong."

Reid whirled around and headed forward. I waited until Marta had handed off the helm to Charles and then followed her. Jane followed me, grabbing a flashlight as she passed through the salon.

Reid had gone forward to the deck area. Marta passed me, pushing me out of her way.

I exited the salon right behind Marta just as a large wave splashed over the hulls, soaking both of us.

"Vee," Marta screamed. "Where are you?"

"She's over here," Reid answered. "I need help."

I could see him by the kayak, but I didn't see Vee.

The deck was heaving and rolling. Marta scrambled toward him, practically leaping in time to the rolling waves.

I went slower. I wasn't tethered in. Getting washed overboard, with no PFD, in these waves, at night, would be the end.

Jane grabbed my hand and we made our way to Reid.

"No, no, no," Marta screamed, her wail like something in a horror movie.

I reached the kayak and held onto the lifeline. So did Jane. Reid and Marta were pulling something out of the water. Before I could see what it was, another wave soaked me.

I shook my head. My eyes stung, and I was starting to shiver. But I focused on Reid. Jane aimed her flashlight's beam at him.

He had a hold of Vee's tether. Marta had one of her arms. She had somehow fallen overboard.

"Help us," Reid said. His voice was loud but not frantic. Compared to Marta's near hysteria, he was surprisingly in control.

I moved close and wrapped one leg over the lifeline, hooking my other foot behind it. I felt stable enough to use both hands to help.

I leaned over the side and grabbed Vee under her armpits. I straightened up, pulling her body out of the water. She was limp. I feared the worse.

Another wave coated all of us. Its drag tried to pull Vee from my grasp, but I held on.

Marta repositioned herself and got a hold of Vee's leg. Reid held onto the tether with one hand and grabbed her other leg.

"On three," Reid said. I had stopped shivering and felt strangely strong.

As the wave passed, he counted, and on three we pulled together, dragging Vee out of the water. She wasn't moving.

Reid grabbed the back of her PFD's collar and drug her to the salon. I unclipped her tether and extricated myself from my precarious position on the lifeline.

Marta helped Reid. Jane helped me. Together we all made it back to the salon.

Reid felt for a pulse. He shook his head. He quickly removed her PFD and the top of her rain gear. I noticed that Vee was pale. There was no color in her face. Her limbs were completely limp.

My heart pounded harder. This was bad. Vee dead? She couldn't be. Our only hope was to revive her.

Marta kept screaming Vee's name. Jane held her back, moving her out of our way. I assisted Reid. I knew CPR, courtesy of the health club where I used to teach fitness.

Reid unzipped her fleece top and started the chest compression cycle. After a couple dozen chest compressions, I opened her airway and gave her one rescue breath. Her chest didn't rise. I gave her another breath. No response.

Reid continued the chest compressions. We worked together, repeating the process. When Reid tired, we switched positions. When I tired, we switched back.

Vee was unresponsive, but we didn't stop. Marta was sobbing. Jane left long enough to tell Charles what was happening. When she returned, all she could do was watch and hold Marta.

Reid finally stopped administering chest compressions and looked at his watch. Tears streamed down my face. Marta began shrieking. We had lost her friend.

Marta broke free of Jane's hug and pushed Reid out of the way. She began chest compressions. Reid moved alongside and placed her hands where they went. He helped her get the rhythm and then let her continue. He administered the rescue breaths at the proper interval.

I knew that Vee was gone and their efforts were pointless, but I moved out of their way in silence.

Reid and I had tried to resuscitate Vee for nearly an hour.

Marta and Reid continued for another hour. Finally Marta stopped.

"Do you want me to take over?" Jane asked softly.

Marta shook her head and wiped her eyes.

CHAPTER 48

I went below and got a beach towel from our cabin. I returned, quietly placing it over Vee's body. I didn't want to look at her corpse and didn't know what else to do.

"What do you suppose happened?" Jane asked.

"That kayak is coming loose," Reid answered. "She must have noticed it, but when she tried to fix it, she must have lost her balance and fallen overboard."

"She was tethered to the lifeline," Marta said. "We all saw that she was. Why wouldn't that have saved her?"

Reid didn't reply right away. He was obviously carefully considering his answer. "The near freezing water must have disoriented her. All of her heavy clothing suddenly became a liability. Sort of like how medieval knights feared getting into water that was deeper than they could stand up in. Being so heavily weighted, it wouldn't have taken long before she succumbed to exhaustion, followed by hypothermia and eventual drowning."

That seemed a terrible way to die. Being dragged through frigid water until your death, with the safety of the boat less than six feet away. I shivered at the very thought.

Marta didn't ask any more questions. Reid put on some heavier clothes and went to spell Charles at the helm. As he headed to the helm, I followed and whispered, "You'll be the captain now, right?"

He nodded. "I suppose so."

I returned to the salon. Jane had gotten dressed and was going forward for lookout duties.

"Be extra careful," I warned her. She nodded.

I explained our failed CPR attempt to Charles. He looked mortified that Vee had died such a tragic death. He told Marta he would cover her watches for the next few days. She thanked him but declined, saying we needed to keep sailing twenty-four sevens and didn't have the luxury of sparing any crew.

Knowing she'd have to return to helm duties in a few hours made me feel worse. I didn't know if Marta and Vee were lovers or just really close friends, but it didn't seem fair to have to suck it up and go back to work before Vee's corpse had been given a proper burial.

I looked at the chart. Based on our last noted position, we were about halfway between southern Argentina and the Falkland Islands. Reaching either place would take a couple of hard sailing days.

Tierra del Fuego had been really rocky. Southern

Argentina would likely be more of the same. I wasn't sure what the Falkland Islands would be like in this time period.

Trying to dig a grave in rocky ground would be hard. If we buried Vee on nearby land, we'd have to just pile rocks over and around her body. That didn't seem right.

My other thought was a burial at sea. That wouldn't take much time and would be appropriate for a sea captain. The part of that option which bothered me was the sharks.

We hadn't seen any fins for quite some time, but given all of the whales and dolphins in the area, the sharks had to be close by. Giving Vee's body to the sharks didn't seem right either.

Both choices sucked. I decided that Reid, as captain, or Marta, as the closest there was to next of kin, could make the decision.

I was sorry that Reid wouldn't be able to play "Taps," but his trumpet wasn't onboard.

Charles and I took the next watch. He took the helm and I went forward to watch for growlers. Before Reid went below, he helped me with the kayak.

It had indeed come loose, but we quickly retied it and checked the other one too. Securing those kayaks made me sad. I remembered Reid saying that kayaks on board would be in the way. How right he had been.

I tried to remember who had last tied them. I started shaking. What if it had been me? That would have made me responsible for Vee's senseless death. At least indirectly.

I concentrated on thinking about retying those kayaks.

Then I remembered. Marta and Reid had retied them after we spotted the blue whales but before we rounded Cape Horn.

They tried moving one to the salon, but it wouldn't fit so they had to put it back. I wasn't sure which one of them had tied that kayak, but selfishly, I was glad it wasn't me.

I wondered if Marta remembered. If she did, and it was her knots that had come loose, did that add to her sorrow?

What if Reid's knots were the ones that failed? He tied knots for a living. How would he feel knowing he was indirectly responsible for Vee's tragic demise?

I shook my head, trying to make those thoughts go away.

I focused on a new thought. Knowing the pounding waves were trying to wash the kayaks away, we all had a responsibility to check their lashings. Maybe not during every watch, but certainly checking them every day would have been prudent.

I made a mental note to do that from now on. It couldn't bring Vee back, but it might save someone else from a similar fate.

Jane and Reid relieved us two hours later. It was freezing, and the blowing froth from the waves stung my exposed face like hornets.

I was glad to return to the salon and get out of the wind and constant splashing.

Vee's body was still in the same place, covered by our towel. I didn't see Marta but hoped she was trying to get some sleep.

Until today, my divorce had been the worst day of my life.

I remembered lying in the fetal position and crying so hard I'd started shaking.

This was worse. Much worse. Vee was dead. Her death was completely senseless. It could have been prevented if we'd had only been more vigilant in checking the condition of the kayaks.

"People aren't supposed to die from a failed knot," I told myself. "I need to be extra careful. I don't want to join her."

CHAPTER 49

I managed an hour's nap before being awakened for the next watch. Charles took the helm and Jane stayed forward as lookout until I could take her place.

Reid had made coffee, and the salon was warm. I noticed that Vee had been dressed in Bacardi clothing. She looked peaceful.

Reid told me there would be a funeral later. Marta had agreed that Vee could be buried at sea. The Bacardi outfit was Marta's idea. She told Reid she wanted to keep Vee's uniforms but that Vee liked her Bacardi outfit. I tried not to think about sharks.

Later that morning, we had a service. Charles took over the helm without a forward lookout. Reid and I carried Vee aft and placed her body on the cockpit table. Reid then draped

The Aquaholic's Bahama's flag over Vee's body, tucking it underneath to hold it in place.

Jane comforted Marta. They were both sobbing. So was I. Reid's eyes were moist. I couldn't tell if Charles was crying or not.

We all said a few words. Reid praised her prowess as a captain. Jane echoed that, saying she was proud to have crewed for her. Charles shouted from the helm that he was glad to have known her.

I said that Vee was a great captain and a good friend. My remarks were intentionally brief. I deliberately avoided any mention of her accident. I already felt guilt about not checking the kayak's storage. I wondered if Marta or Reid did too.

When she spoke, Marta was sobbing so hard we could barely understand her. She said she missed her friend. She recounted how they met and their first job, stealing diamonds from bad men: a perfect crime.

She talked about Bev, Candy, and Dreamgirl and the bond they forged together. She shook her head. "Maybe we should have listened to them, Vee," she said. "What did they call it? A suicide sail? After everything we survived in our former life, how could it have come to this? Dying in an accident at sea. Not how any of us would have expected you to meet your end."

Her voice dropped.

I cried even harder. I wasn't sure if I was shaking from

grief, the cold, or my knowledge of who had last tied the kayak that came loose and caused Vee's death.

Reid removed the flag and folded it into a triangle with military precision. He then retrieved the shotgun and fired three shots, saving the spent shells. He placed the used shells into a small baggie. He then handed the flag and the baggie to Marta. She held them tight. Reid gave her a salute and then pivoted and marched away a few steps.

I wasn't sure of the significance of the fired shells, but was sure it followed some military tradition. Regardless, he had done a nice job presenting Marta with the flag.

Reid motioned for me to help him. We carried Vee's body to the stern and held it while Marta said her last goodbyes. We then lowered Captain Veronica Kline into the water and let her go.

She slowly sank behind us. Marta watched silently, holding my hand as we watched Vee drift away.

Jane used that moment to get her violin. She played "Taps." It was even more haunting when played on a violin. I looked back, but Vee was gone. Her body had disappeared. The ocean had claimed her.

We were still dragging the long lines behind us, but they would not do Vee any good. She would pass by one of them as she sank. She was dead and wouldn't see it. Marta's words about our journey being a "suicide sail" flashed in my head once more. Maybe Bev and the others had been smart to not attempt it. They were safe with hundreds of good-looking sailors thousands of miles from here, where it was warm.

We were onboard a tiny sailboat that was trying to defy the odds and make the passage from close to Hawaii to the Bermuda Triangle. We didn't have the expediency of the Panama Canal. We were relying on fish to eat and were close to using untested fuel.

Were we all awaiting a fate similar to Vee's? Instead of a line failing, would we hit a stray growler? Or would a gigantic whale ram us for getting too close to its calf?

What if we ran into really bad weather, like a hurricane? What if we ran out of food and the fish quit biting? Would we resort to cannibalism, like the aliens said the crew that Reid and Mo rescued Marta and Elouise from had?

I blinked and forced those thoughts out of my head. I didn't need any pointless what if scenarios adding to our already scary situation.

I wasn't ready to die. Especially not like Vee had. She was gone, and I had to let her go.

Jane then played the theme from the *Titanic* movie, "My Heart Will Go On." I wondered if she had heard me humming it before when it was stuck in my head. The music made us all cry; even Charles was wiping his eyes.

And then the service was over. Reid, Jane, and I gave Marta a hug and told her we were so sorry. Charles bowed his head. Jane dried off her violin and put it away. And then we got back to the business of sailing.

Reid assumed the duties of captain without any fanfare or objections. Everyone knew that he was the logical choice.

The five of us rotated, two at a time, one at the helm and

one on lookout duty. The three that weren't on duty could rest.

When I was forward, I made sure to check the lines holding the kayaks. I didn't say anything, I just did it, quietly.

Both Reid and Jane did the weather forecasting and took fixes. The Falkland Islands kept inching closer.

The boat was different with Vee gone. The mood aboard was very somber. Everyone felt the loss.

When Reid and I were alone, he told me he had written down the music for "Taps" for Jane. I said she had played it beautifully. He nodded his agreement.

I asked what the three shells symbolized. He said they signified the dead had been gathered from the battlefield. I wondered if Jane knew that.

I thought about mentioning that he and Marta had last tied the kayaks. But that discussion would only bring guilt. I didn't say anything but snuggled in his arms instead.

WE REACHED THE BERMUDA TRIANGLE, AND THE ALIENS returned us to our time. Charles called for his plane. Pat met us at the dock.

I wasn't expecting to see her. She slowly approached and said she was sorry. Then she gave me a hug. I hugged her back. I wasn't sure that I could forgive her that quickly, but it was nice that she had apologized.

She looked at me. Her eyes got big. I felt her go limp and she began sliding down, nearly pulling me down with her.

"What's wrong?" I asked.

Pat's head fell forward and I staggered, trying to control her weight.

Marta was standing behind Pat. She pulled a big knife out of Pat's back. "That's for Vee," she hissed.

I tried to keep my balance and keep Pat from falling. Marta stabbed her again. "This one's for Bev."

Pat didn't move. Marta wasn't finished.

"This is for Candy," she menaced, jabbing the knife back in.

I didn't know what to do. My knees buckled, and Pat's weight forced me to the dock. Pat's blood spilled over me and pooled on the dock.

"This one is for Dreamgirl."

As Marta stabbed Pat again, I began screaming.

"And this one's for me," Marta announced, raising the knife high overhead.

Would she ever stop? I screamed again and felt arms around me, pulling me away . . .

"Wake up," Reid said, holding me tightly to his chest. "You're having a nightmare."

CHAPTER 50

It was pretty quiet all the way to the Falkland Islands. Nobody had much to say. The memory of Vee's unfortunate accident and dreadful death was fresh in my mind and everyone else's too.

The sailing conditions were still harsh, but we pressed on. There wasn't anything else we could do.

Two days later we sighted the Falklands. When we got close, Marta pulled in our long lines. She used to do it with the high energy of a gym workout. This time was different.

She pulled them in without complaining, but I could see that her heart wasn't in it. She had no spark for exercise. I felt bad.

As soon as the long lines were secured, Charles and Jane took the helm and motored us into the Falkland Sound. It was over one hundred feet deep, way too deep to anchor.

Reid pointed toward the shore and Charles changed course, with Jane calling out the depth. While the water got shallower, the smell of bird shit was overpowering. We finally found a suitable depth that was far enough from land to be relatively free of the smell. We anchored.

What a disappointment.

There was hardly any vegetation and no trees ashore. There were thousands of squawking gulls, making a quiet night's sleep out of the question.

But there were also lots of penguins about. Until now, the only penguins I had ever seen were at the zoo. As ungainly as their waddling gait was on land, they were graceful swimmers, as nimble as any dolphin.

I especially enjoyed watching as they shot out of the water when returning to the snowy shoreline. Jane identified four different species, but the most common were the gentoo penguins. They were bigger and had a white stripe across the top of their head.

It snowed all the time, and the wind blew fiercely. The temperature never got above twenty-eight degrees.

We took advantage of the cold temperatures to freeze fresh water in two of our steel mixing bowls, thus prolonging our dry ice.

Even in the cold, the smell from thousands of birds pooping was unmistakable. I didn't want to even imagine what it would smell like when it got warmer.

Whatever thoughts I had entertained about kayaking,

snorkeling, and exploring ashore had been a waste of my time. There was absolutely nothing to do here except leave.

As soon as we got a lull between storms, leaving was the plan. There were no objections.

On two separate occasions, a massive school of penguins circled the boat in a tight formation. It looked like the swirl of a giant bathtub draining. But, outside of the penguin's maelstrom, there were lots of big fins.

The sharks had returned. The penguins were encircling us. The sharks were patrolling the perimeter. I had figured the waters were too cold for sharks. I was wrong.

I also wondered if we would see penguins getting eaten but fortunately, we never saw any bloodstained waters.

Our diesel fuel was nearly exhausted, and we were on our last propane tank. Reid used the relative shelter of the Falkland Sound to use the JP5 jet fuel we had gotten from *The USS Fields*.

He carefully siphoned it into *The Aquaholic's* tanks. He did so after her engines had been running. He didn't want to try and start cold engines with untested fuel.

When all of the JP5 had been transferred, he turned off the engines. It was time to see if the engines would restart. I held my breath. If they wouldn't run on the jet fuel, we'd have some serious problems.

Reid turned the key. The piercing alarm tone scattered the penguins that had been swimming close by. It also got the attention of all of the birds ashore.

It was weird how silent they got when that tone sounded.

It was as if they had all gotten the memo. When the engines roared to life, Charles and Jane applauded. I silently exhaled. The bird squawking resumed.

Reid let the engines run for fifteen minutes while he changed from propane to acetylene. He had Jane try the stove. She reported it was working.

Reid shut down the engines, waited a bit, and then tried starting them. They started right up, no problems. The alarm tone didn't scare the birds this time.

I joined Marta at the chart. She was tracing our route line from Cape Horn. Reid had marked an *X* where Vee had died. Her fingers lingered at that spot. I gave her a hug. She tensed up.

I was going to ask if she was okay but knew that was a stupid question. I wondered if she blamed Reid for the kayak coming loose. I wondered if she blamed Pat for sending her and her friends back in time. I hoped I wouldn't have another stabbing nightmare. I left her alone with the chart.

We got a break in the weather and left the Falkland Islands. We motorsailed until we cleared the sound. The engines seemed to be working fine.

I resigned myself that there wouldn't be another landfall until we rounded the "Brazilian hump," as Reid called it. That hump was over two thousand eight hundred nautical miles away.

In these menacing sailing conditions, it might take a month to go that far. And reaching the easternmost part of

Brazil only signified a course change. Reid didn't plan to stop unless we needed to.

However, I had noticed that once we reached twenty-three and a half degrees south latitude, the Tropic of Capricorn, we'd be sailing parallel to the coast.

We'd sail right by Rio de Janeiro. It was too bad it hadn't been discovered yet. I had never been there but heard they had great parties.

After Rio, the next major point of interest on the chart was the Amazon. Even in this time period, that big river would be there and it might be worth stopping and checking out. I wondered if a piranha would hit a lure. I had always wanted to see one—from a safe distance.

We got *The Aquaholic* under sail and on course. I let the long lines out, sparing Marta the job. I could still smell bird shit.

CHAPTER 51

We sailed through the night. Reid and Jane predicted the weather would improve.

They were right. Too right. The waves gradually diminished, but the wind stopped.

The Aquaholic had entered a high-pressure system, devoid of wind. Since drifting wasn't an option, we had no choice but to motor-sail. I helped Reid pull in our long lines. We no longer needed their drag to slow us down.

We motorsailed nonstop, burning our precious fuel hour after hour.

The ocean and the skies were blue. There wasn't a wave or a hint of a cloud in any direction. It was hard to tell where the water stopped and the skies began. It was as if an artist had painted the seascape and the sky with one color and a paint roller.

The night skies were completely clear, allowing the thousands of stars to shine, blink, and twinkle without any clouds to obstruct their view. The Milky Way looked even more spectacular than usual.

Its band of stars angled across the sky. There was a circular shape in the center that was half brown and half red. A wide swath of white stretched to the left. A slightly smaller grouping of blue-white stars was toward the right. The entire band was framed in gray, which gradually turned to black.

"What causes the red and brown colors?" I asked, awestruck by the clarity I had never seen in our own time.

"Interstellar dust and gas," Jane responded.

I figured she would know.

"No one knows what ionized the hydrogen gas to produce such color," she continued. "In fact, it's only recently been observed through powerful telescopes. It's remarkable that we can see it with the naked eye."

I think her hushed tone reflected what we were all feeling.

She and Reid were able to get good navigational sightings and were confident of our position.

Since leaving the Falkland Islands, we had the Malvinas Current with us. Until we reached forty-five degrees south latitude, that current would continue to help us. North of that point, we'd be fighting the Brazilian Current.

I spent the time before my night watch relaxing by looking at the stars. I couldn't tell one constellation from another, but they were incredibly beautiful.

I got used to the noise and throbbing of the engines as *The*

Aquaholic chewed up the miles. Helm duty was borderline boring, thanks to the autopilot working perfectly in the flat conditions. It was nice to have hot water and power, but I feared we would run out of fuel before the wind returned.

At forty-five degrees south latitude, we passed an iceberg. It was too big to be a growler but much smaller than the ones we were accustomed to seeing. This one had a jagged peak and two big archways, one toward each end. The one on the left looked like it went all the way through.

Reid didn't believe we'd see very many more as the water was getting warmer. Later that day, we passed through a stretch of water that was filled with swirls and eddies.

I asked if whales or something equally large were feeding below the surface. He said we were crossing the area where the Malvinas and Brazilian currents intersected. It was really easy to see the swirling motions on the flat water.

I thought about the ancient mariners. I wondered what they thought when they encountered this phenomena. Perhaps they thought they might be nearing the edge of the "flat Earth" and would soon be sailing over its edge to their death.

The next day, Captain Reid announced that an extra lookout was no longer necessary during daylight hours. He also announced that based on our speed and actual distance traveled, we were now definitely fighting the Brazilian Current. We would fight that current until we rounded the Brazilian hump. Then it would be helping us all the way to the Caribbean Sea.

The following day, having not seen any more icebergs, and

based on the temperature of the water, the additional evening lookout was eliminated.

Charles gave an unusual shout the following morning. "Cloud ho."

That was as welcome as "land ho" had ever been. I charged out on deck, tilting my head skyward.

I panned the horizon and then I saw it. Far, far away and high up were some clouds—long, thin, swirly streaks of white in a loose formation. They looked like the tails of falling meteors. Finally an artist was using a color besides blue. I got excited, hoping those clouds signified wind. Jane said they were cirrus clouds and was anxious to check our barometer. It indicated the pressure was falling. She and Reid gave each other a hug. They were very excited.

The winds returned that evening. *The Aquaholic* shut down her engines and resumed sailing. The absence of the engine's noise was welcomed by all.

We had used up a lot of our fuel. After continuous use, the engines sounded a little different but weren't smoking. Reid wished he had some diesel conditioner or lubricant to add to the JP5 fuel, but there wasn't any onboard.

He hoped we wouldn't have to motor for another long stretch. I agreed. The Navy's substitute fuel worked, but I didn't want to press our luck.

The winds gradually increased during the night. By morning, the conditions were perfect for sailing. Jane got her violin and played "Call Me the Breeze." It was time to resume "blowin' down the road," just like the lyrics said.

As if to celebrate the conditions, we were treated to a show of humpback whales breaching. They would launch out of the water and then smack upon re-entry. A few of them would even rotate, like they were competing in a gymnastics event and performing with a higher degree of difficulty.

The temperature was still cool, but with the sun shining for the first time in several weeks, I no longer felt cold all the time. This was much better than Cape Horn or the Falkland Islands.

Marta had begun asking me questions about Pat. They were general questions about her work, her family, and her hobbies. The questions seemed innocent enough, and I didn't mind answering them.

The problem was that Marta kept asking them, two or three times a day. After I would answer, she'd go away for a few minutes, somewhere I couldn't see her.

It occurred to me that Marta might be making a file on Pat. I mean, according to Agent Washington of the CIA, Marta used to be an Interpol agent, a spy.

Why would Marta suddenly want to know all of these little things about Pat Taylor? That was a question I couldn't answer.

The Aquaholic pressed on. Since there weren't any more icebergs, Reid reverted to Vee's original plan to only run the generator every three days and not run the engines unless absolutely necessary.

One morning, Charles wanted to fish. Reid and I watched from the helm as he and Jane got a heavy rod, the gaff, and the fighting belt. They were obviously optimistic.

Charles selected a big, blue-and-green striped lure with red eyes. It was a foot long and had two shiny hooks that were nearly the size of the hook on a coat hanger. When he let it out, it immediately submerged out of sight.

In less than fifteen minutes, Charles yelled, "Fish on!"

Line began screaming out. He had a nice one.

"What are we going to do?" I asked Reid.

"We can't heave to in a cat, so I'll turn into the wind and you furl the sails," he replied.

I worked as fast as I could. I didn't want the fish to take all of the line before we could stop. Five minutes later, the sails were down and *The Aquaholic* began to drift.

Charles tried "pumping" the fish to the surface, but it stayed deep. He couldn't even reel in a foot of line. Jane fastened the fighting belt around his waist. Marta guided the gimbaled end of the rod into the fighting belt. Charles smiled and held on with both hands.

As time wore on, we all offered to take over the rod so he could get a break. He politely declined, saying he wanted to land it himself.

The fish circled the boat a few times. Charles scrambled over the deck, keeping the rod pointed out so the line wouldn't catch on anything metal and get cut.

Going around the dinghy davits was challenging, but he still didn't want any help.

It was nearly three hours before we even got a glimpse of his catch. It looked like a whitish torpedo.

It was another fifty minutes before the fish tired enough for him to get it close enough for a positive identification.

Charles had hooked a giant Atlantic bluefin tuna. It had to be at least fifteen feet long. Reid guessed it weighed over a ton. How that colossal fish didn't break the rod or the fishing line, I'll never know.

Of course there was no way to keep it. We might have been able to slip a line over the narrow part of its tail and all of us and a winch might have been able to drag it up on the stern, but there was no way we could eat even a small fraction of that behemoth.

Reid twisted the lure free and the fish swam away, splashing the boat in the process.

Marta gave Charles her last chocolate milk. He chugged it and then took a seat at the cockpit table. He was exhausted but managed a big smile. Jane got pictures and video. Again, I didn't have the heart to tell her the aliens would insist on her phone being destroyed as a condition of our return.

Jane said a fish like that would have easily fetched twenty thousand dollars in the Japanese fish market. I understood that most fisherman would have sold it for big money. A fish like that represented a lucrative payday. But I was glad we had released it.

Charles excused himself to lie down. He looked beat. Jane went with him. Marta, Reid, and I got the sails back up and resumed course.

Charles missed his next watch, but it wasn't a problem to cover for him. When he missed dinner and Jane asked if there was any soup left, I got concerned.

"Is Charles alright?" I asked.

"His breathing is shallow, he's tired, he has the chills, and he's running a fever," Jane answered.

None of that sounded good. Unfortunately, she wasn't finished.

"He's also coughing up blood and says his chest hurts when he coughs."

That was worse.

"We shouldn't have let him fight that big tuna all by himself," I said.

"I offered to help," Marta said. "But he was determined to land it alone."

She didn't sound overly sympathetic.

I went to the helm and informed Reid of Charles's condition. He wanted to see for himself, so I took over.

Nobody came back to report, so I just stayed at the helm, holding our course and watching the occasional sea birds fly by.

Finally Reid returned. He looked worried.

CHAPTER 53

"I believe that Charles might have pneumonia," Reid said.

"Why do you think that?" I asked.

"Vee and Dreamgirl brought a decent medical kit along with them," Reid explained. "When Dreamgirl left for *The USS Fields*, she left the kit with Vee. She thought we would need it more than she would since *The USS Fields* would have substantial medical facilities onboard and we don't."

"That was nice of her," I replied. I remembered that Vee and Dreamgirl had been taking care of Charles's gunshot wound. I didn't remember any medical kit. "But you still haven't answered my question."

"Marta got the stethoscope from that kit and we listened to Charles's lungs."

"And?"

"And his lungs sound different than mine, Jane's, or

Marta's."

"So you think it's pneumonia?"

"We all agree we hear a lot of wheezing in Charles's chest, and Jane says that wheezing is a symptom of pneumonia."

"But it might not be pneumonia," I said. "None of you are doctors."

"Jane is hopeful that it will go away, whatever it is," Reid said softly. He looked concerned. "I sure hope she's right."

I knew people who had caught pneumonia. Some of them required hospitalization, but all of them had recovered.

"Is there anything I can do to help?" I asked. With our limited resources, I was sure there wasn't much that could be done except give him liquids and let him rest, but I thought I'd ask anyway.

"All we can do is cover his watches and see that he gets plenty of rest," Reid answered.

"What about soup?" I asked, changing the subject. "Do we have any left? Has Jane looked?"

"As a matter of fact, she has. We're out of canned soup, but Angie had a box of onion soup mix aboard. Angie used it to make sour cream dip. Now Jane will use it to make Charles some onion flavored broth." Reid shrugged. "Better than nothing."

Allowing Charles to stay in his cabin and rest meant that the four of us sailed nonstop. After a day or two, Jane reported his labored breathing still sounded bad but at least it wasn't getting worse. I took that as a good omen.

Charles insisted that he had recovered enough to resume

his turn on the watch schedule.

But he wheezed as he spoke, and his eyes looked tired. I was skeptical. Reid was too, and denied his request, telling him to keep resting.

One afternoon, Reid trolled a line and caught a twenty-pound wahoo. It didn't fight much and was quickly gaffed. He was surprised to catch a wahoo this far from land. He filleted it, commenting that it would be a nice addition to our Patagonian toothfish stores.

Jane used some of the smaller pieces to make a weak fish soup with spices. I didn't care for it and barely ate any, but Charles and the others liked it, especially Reid, who made sure there were no leftovers.

Later that evening, Reid told me his stomach hurt. I checked with Jane, Marta, and Charles to see how they were feeling. They all felt sick and blamed Jane's wahoo fish soup. Since Jane was sick too, and that was the only thing everyone on board ate, she didn't argue.

The good news was that I hadn't eaten much and felt fine. The bad news was that I was the only one left able to sail.

I sailed through the night, alone and without using the radar. We went through some whales. I could hear whale song but couldn't see them. Thankfully, none of them hit us.

Daylight came and I hoped that somebody, anybody, would be feeling well enough to relieve me. Reid came topside long enough to inform me the whole crew was sick and that I could either keep going or drop the sails and take a nap while we drifted.

Reid took the helm long enough for me to use the head and get my sunglasses and a bottle of water. He looked terrible. He told me that everyone had stomach cramps, nausea, diarrhea, and vomiting that gave way to dry heaves.

I resumed helm duties. Sleep would have to wait. I was yawning a lot but forced myself to stay alert and keep my eyes open.

During one of my yawns, I noticed several dark clouds ahead. Our current heading took us right into them.

I furled the jib and reefed the mainsail. Scarcely twenty minutes later, the winds picked up and the waves got bigger. I reefed the mainsail some more.

We ran smack into a storm. *The Aquaholic's* hulls pounded through the waves. The foam was blowing right off the tops of the waves, coating the deck.

I couldn't leave the helm unattended to go below for my rain gear, so I stayed put. Two minutes later, I was thoroughly soaked. I called out for a little help, but no one answered. I realized nobody sick in their cabin could hear me over the howling of the wind.

Thunder roared. A second later, lightning struck the water. I could smell ozone. It reminded me of going through the alien's time portal. But there were no aliens around, just nasty weather.

I was suddenly wide awake, focusing on keeping our twin hulls in the same wave. If they got out of step, the catamaran would be ripped in half. That would be worse than tragic.

A lightning bolt flashed again, hitting the water. It was

even closer than the last one. I could feel the tingle of electricity and smelled more ozone.

I wondered what would happen if the lightning hit our mast. I wasn't sure but figured it would fry our electronics, switched off or not. I hoped it wouldn't start a fire or burn a hole in the hull.

A massive wave crashed over the hull, slamming directly into one of the kayaks. The kayak didn't move, but I wasn't sure how many more of those it could take before it broke free and damaged something.

My hands were cold and my teeth were chattering. I cursed myself for not getting my rain gear when Reid had taken the helm earlier. A big wave overtook us, threatening to rip the dinghy right off of its davits. Luckily, the dinghy stayed put.

I would have liked to have started the engines and motored out of this mess, but the starting battery had been switched off, preventing it from being accidentally discharged.

There was nothing to do but wipe the salt water from my eyes and keep sailing.

The *Titanic* song played in my head. I refused to think about sinking. I started singing "Call Me the Breeze." I sang softly at first, and then as I fought the wheel to keep from getting blown sideways, I sang louder.

Before long I was shouting song lyrics, lowering my head to keep from getting salt water in my mouth when the waves crashed and splashed over the hulls. I was determined to get through this. Shivering or not. Tired or not. Soaking wet or not. Failure and panic were not options.

Losing control of *The Aquaholic* would be the end for Reid, Marta, Jane, and Charles. They were below, sick in their cabins. I knew they could feel the boat slamming into the waves, but I wasn't sure they knew how bad it actually was. Their lives were literally in my hands.

None of my sailing experience prepared me for this freakish storm. I wanted Reid or Vee to be with me at the helm.

But Reid was sick and Vee was dead. I was alone, facing the ocean's fury.

A thought flashed through my mind. I remembered the party we had on our way to Hawaii. We had just made a major course change and were celebrating. Reid had made nachos and margaritas. Angie had baked chocolate chunk cookies with Toblerone candy bars. Pat had made a toast: "The meek will inherit the earth. The brave will get the oceans."

That thought was replaced by another—Bev leaving us to join the others on the Navy ship because we were embarking on a "suicide sail." Those two words were so ominous, I swore I heard the wind repeating them. But it was just the wind's locomotive noise screeching in the rigging. I clenched my teeth and forced that thought out of my head.

I ignored the cold and concentrated on doing my job. I was scared as fuck, but I had to be brave. Failure was not an option.

Neither were mistakes.

CHAPTER 54

The storm finally abated and the skies cleared. We had made it through a serious blow. I felt weak but extremely proud.

Thankfully, Marta and Jane came topside and told me they were feeling well enough to take over.

"How are Reid and Charles doing?" I asked.

"Charles still has noisy lungs," Jane reported. "Pneumonia coupled with cramps and diarrhea is really taking its toll. Now Reid is pretty sick."

"We need to throw that wahoo away," I told her. "It's bad fish."

Marta left to get it out of the cooler. I hoped it hadn't contaminated our Patagonian toothfish or Chilean sea bass or whatever the hell it was called.

Luckily Reid had put the wahoo in its own plastic bags.

Marta dumped it over the stern. I was sure the sharks would eat it but didn't see any fins.

I handed off the helm to Jane and went below. My knees were weak and I felt on the verge of exhaustion. I hadn't eaten in a whole day and should have been starving, but at this moment, all I felt was bone weary.

I found Reid in our cabin. He apologized for being sick. I told him not to worry about it.

"Don't tell me you handled the helm alone through that entire storm?" he asked.

"Okay," I replied with a grin. "I won't tell you."

With that, I stripped and crawled into bed. It was warm. I snuggled against Reid. He didn't complain about my cold hands and feet. I don't remember falling asleep.

When I woke up, my watch said four fifteen. It was dark outside, so it had to be a.m. Reid was gone. I was covered with both of our beach towels and the blanket. It was warm.

I could feel the boat moving and didn't hear the engines, so we had to be under sail. I used the head, got dressed, put on my PFD, and headed topside.

Reid was at the galley table and motioned for me to join him. He told me Jane and Charles were sleeping and Marta was at the helm. He said he was feeling fine and would be taking over for Marta shortly.

"How is Charles doing?" I asked.

"Weak but hanging in there," Reid answered. "You must be starving."

I nodded.

Reid made me a bowl of boatmeal, which I quickly devoured. I was surprised to hear that I had been asleep for a whole day.

Reid thanked me for bringing us all through the storm safely. He then showed me the chart.

We were headed northeast, along the Brazilian coast. Our next course change would be after we rounded the hump. We would then swing northwest and follow the coast all the way to Trinidad. There we would change course to angle across the Caribbean Sea.

Reid knew the aliens had agreed to return us to our time when we reached the area we called the Bermuda Triangle. Puerto Rico was generally accepted as being one of the corners of that triangle, with Florida and Bermuda being the other two.

Reid said he'd get me to Puerto Rico, or at least the latitude and longitude of where it should be. Then it would be up to me to establish contact with the aliens and get us returned.

I traced our projected course line with my finger. The route to Puerto Rico took us along the coast of Brazil. We would pass the Amazon, French Guiana, Suriname, Guyana, Venezuela, and then at least three Caribbean islands— Trinidad, Tobago, and Grenada. We still had a long way to go.

I noticed Devil's Island off the coast of French Guiana. I remembered something about a penal colony being built there. "Devil's Island" sounded really spooky. I was sure that Jane could tell me all about it. Maybe we could stop there and check it out.

I also wanted to see the Amazon if we got a chance. Perhaps we could take the dingy and go exploring. That might be a nice diversion.

I hoped that Reid wasn't planning to sail nonstop all the way to Puerto Rico. I wanted to anchor and get off the boat at least a few times.

The Falkland Islands had been very disappointing. I was sure that Trinidad, Tobago, or Grenada would have pleasant anchorages with an opportunity to rest and go ashore. The chart showed lots of small islands scattered along the Brazilian coast. Maybe some of them would be potential stops as well. I figured it would all come down to how our food was holding out and even more importantly, how Charles was feeling.

His cramps and diarrhea had stopped, and Jane was keeping him well hydrated. But when it was quiet, you didn't need the stethoscope to hear his wheezing. I feared that if his pneumonia didn't improve, we might be facing another burial at sea. Thinking about him actually dying on us was more than depressing.

When I got a chance to be alone, I tried communicating with the aliens. I asked them to return us from here and not make Charles wait to get medical attention. There was no response.

We continued sailing. Charles stayed in his cabin. When Jane wasn't sailing, she was with him. While she never said anything, it was pretty obvious that she cared deeply for him.

Marta reported that his lungs were sounding worse. That

only added to my fears of another funeral. When I told Reid I was worried about Charles dying, he squeezed my hand.

"Charles won't die onboard," Reid said softly.

"How can you know that?" I asked, fighting back a single tear.

Reid paused a second. He grinned and said, "Because we don't have another flag big enough to cover his body."

I rolled my eyes.

"I have a funeral joke," he said.

I shook my head.

He waited for me to say something.

I shook my ahead some more.

He kept waiting.

Finally I said, "You can't possibly know a joke about a funeral that will actually be funny."

"Request permission to tell my funeral joke?" His expression reminded me of a little kid who wanted to open his birthday presents a day early.

I can't believe that I agreed, but I said, "Go ahead. Tell me a funeral joke."

Reid smiled and began immediately, before I could change my mind.

"This guy got an invitation to a party that his friends threw to celebrate opening a second location for their business. He wasn't able to attend, so he sent flowers instead.

"Then his schedule changed and at the last minute, he was able to go. He arrived, saw the lone floral arrangement, and looked at the card. It read, 'Our deepest condolences for your loss.'

"Well, that wasn't what he had ordered, but he enjoyed the party and didn't say anything. The next day he called the florist and explained what had happened.

"The florist started laughing. 'I don't think that's funny,' the man said. The florist said, 'I'm thinking about the people who got your card. *Good luck in your new location.*'"

Okay. That *was* sort of funny. I chuckled more than laughed.

Reid smiled and nodded. I could see he was relieved to have gotten a chuckle and not a boo or a hiss.

Later, I saw Jane looking at the chart. I joined her and mentioned that perhaps we'd be able to stop at some of Brazil's coastal islands, the Amazon, Devil's Island, or perhaps a few of the other islands that lay along our projected course.

She told me she was fine with any stops except for the Amazon. When questioned about why not the Amazon, she said that even in this time period, it would be filled with insects carrying dangerous or even fatal diseases.

I stopped her before she elaborated. I didn't want to get creeped out by stories of deadly bugs. Going through the time portal had killed all of the bugs onboard, and I was fine with that.

The days blurred. *The Aquaholic* sailed on.

I visited Charles twice a day. He was always glad to see me but didn't seem to be getting better. The bout with food poisoning set him back. His cabin smelled like death, so I didn't linger.

On one of my quick visits, he told me to ask the aliens if they would return him to a time before his wife died. I told him I would.

During another visit he asked me to please close the door. The way he asked spooked me a little, but I did as instructed.

"I'm realistic enough to know that I might not live to be returned to our time," he said.

I shook my head. "Don't talk like that. Of course you're going to make it."

"Maybe to the Bermuda Triangle," he said. "That's one thing." He wheezed, gasping for breath before continuing. "Surviving the passage through the time portal is another."

I listened but didn't respond.

"I remember the condition the boats were in after going through the time portal—blackened metal, charred sails, etcetera."

I remembered all of that too. The electromagnetic fields generated by the alien's time portal left their mark on anything metal or even touching metal.

"The last time through, it felt like I had been involved in a serious car crash, not to mention having the headache from hell."

He started to cough again. It sounded like his ribs were breaking. When he recovered, he motioned me closer.

I took a hesitant step, not sure what was next.

He reached for my hand. I let him have it. He squeezed it lightly. I squeezed back and waited.

"One of the captains I hired, Beverly Thompson, called what we are attempting a 'suicide sail.' She may have been right."

I thought back to the night of the storm and how that had been on my mind too. Still, I remained quiet.

"Our own captain, Veronica Kline, didn't make it. If I continue to get worse, I fear I might be joining her."

Charles let go of my hand and retrieved some folded sheets of notebook paper from underneath his blanket. He held them out to me.

To my questioning look, he said, "I've made a change to my will. Put these in a safe place. In the event I don't make it, read them and follow the instructions."

I took the papers in both hands and nodded. "I'll take these," I said. "But you're going to make it. And then I'll give them back to you."

He smiled. "I appreciate your optimism. Now go put them somewhere safe."

He was overcome with another fit of coughing. I cringed. It was as if the mere act of smiling brought it on.

"Don't tell Reid or Jane," he said after recovering himself again. "This is just between us."

He looked so tired that I motioned him to lay back down. "Can I get you anything?"

He shook his head. "There's something else," he said. "I know why Mo fell in love with Gert and why Reid proposed to two women. Being back in time changes your point of view about being alone."

"Are you falling for Jane?" I asked softly.

"That would be highly improper given the relatively short amount of time I've been a widower." He turned and looked away, but not before I read the truth in his eyes.

"You're right. What we've experienced changes your perspective about a lot of things," I said. "And one of the most important is rethinking what's 'highly improper.' You don't have to be alone, Charles, if you don't want to be."

I left Charles with that thought, hurrying to my cabin to stash the papers under my side of the berth.

I resisted the temptation to look at them.

CHAPTER 55

The *Aquaholic* pressed on. Reid and I managed most of the night sailing. Marta and Jane took most of the daytime watches. We caught another wahoo but let it go. There was no way any of us wanted food poisoning again.

I caught a strange looking fish. It had dark black scales that were diamond shaped. White flecks covered its body and head. The edges of its fins were blue green, and its mouth was full of teeth. The tail was one piece and shaped like the fish's head. Its dorsal fin was triangular and ribbed, while its other fins were tulip shaped. It was about three feet long.

I had no idea what it was. Neither did Reid. Surprisingly, even Jane was baffled. She took several pictures and showed them to Charles. He didn't know what it was either. I told Reid to let it go.

I caught several dorado. Reid kept and cleaned enough of the smaller ones to refill the fish cooler.

Our freeze-dried food was gone, even the drink mix. So was the bread flour, the boatmeal, and the granola. We did have sugar, salt, yeast, olive oil, vinegar, assorted spices, and fish. That was it.

One day Jane announced that some of our spices had spoiled. She retrieved jars of rosemary, oregano, and basil. She slowly removed the lids.

Sure enough, there was gray-yellow-green mold growing on the dried spices. I didn't know that spices could spoil. I wondered if eating bad wahoo had made the others sick, or if it was the moldy spices?

If it was the moldy spices, I felt bad for throwing away perfectly good wahoo. Jane threw the jars in the trash.

After one of Reid's watches, he pulled me aside and confided that Marta had been asking him questions about Pat. I told him she was doing the same with me. We decided she obviously blamed Pat for our situation and for Vee's death.

Reid told me about the day that Pat, Mo, and he had gone back in time and rescued Marta and Elouise from the bad men aboard the Chinese spy vessel.

I had never known the whole story about how Marta had found a knife and wanted to take revenge on her captors. I wondered if she was gathering intelligence about Pat to avenge Vee, Candy, Bev, and Dreamgirl.

My clothes were looser than ever. I felt tired a lot, but at least I was no longer freezing all the time. The further north we sailed, the warmer it got.

The sunshine was very welcome. It made the solar showers work. It also enabled us to completely dry our laundry.

Jane served Charles his meals in their cabin. She worked tirelessly to keep him warm, fed, and hydrated. Jane hoped there wouldn't be any permanent damage to his lungs. We all did.

We were all sick and tired of eating fish, but besides making faces, no one complained.

There was no fanfare when we crossed the equator. We never stopped at any islands, not even Devil's Island. I watched it go by on the chart, but we never got close enough to even see it.

Off the coast of Guyana we got hit by another storm. It wasn't as bad as the big one I had taken us through, nor did it last as long.

Reid rigged a tarp to catch the rainwater. Standing in the rain, I refilled a bunch of our water bottles. The rainwater was a nice change from drinking desalinated water from the water maker.

We arrived at the coordinates where Trinidad should have been. Forty-five minutes later, we spotted land. The island was fair sized. Even though its coordinates didn't exactly match the chart, it had three distinct mountain peaks, so it had to be Trinidad.

I congratulated Reid for his navigation skills that had

brought us this far. He winked and said I could thank him the next time we were alone. I winked back.

We anchored in a nice cove. It was sheltered from the wind and offered a safe anchorage. There wasn't much vegetation ashore, just a lot of rocks and noisy birds.

Regardless, it felt good to be anchored. Charles made his way topside, looked around, and then took a seat at the cockpit table.

I'm sure he was happy to get out of his cabin.

His body odor was obvious. Thankfully Jane was aware of it without us having to say anything. She had him strip and then used one whole solar shower on him, soaping and washing him pretty much everywhere.

While we were waiting to be certain the anchor was holding, I helped Reid swab the salt accumulation from the decks. Marta unloaded both kayaks by herself. She tied them to the stern and got the double-ended paddles assembled and ready for use.

Charles finished cleaning up. Jane helped him get into some clean clothes. He managed a smile, but he still looked sick and his cough sounded terrible. It still sounded like his ribs were breaking. I was certain he felt pain with each cough. I hoped I was right about being able to give those changes to his will back to him soon.

I looked at all the seagulls flying around and asked if they were edible. Anything besides fish sounded appealing.

"They're going to be tough and taste fishy," Reid answered.

"We might be able to eat a gull or a pelican and not get sick, but I'm not that desperate."

Jane added that since that since gulls were scavengers, they might contain worms that we wouldn't want to ingest.

Marta said she didn't want to eat a cute seagull.

Charles just shook his head.

I resigned myself to another meal of fish.

CHAPTER 56

We spent a whole day at anchor, resting and getting our laundry caught up. To save gasoline, we didn't even unload the dinghy. Charles stayed aboard, but the rest of us did take the kayaks ashore.

The birds had no fear of us. I figured we were the first people they had ever seen. It would have been pretty easy to hit a seagull in the head with a rock, but I didn't want to eat anything that might have worms.

We wandered around. The ground was solid but uneven. Like the last time we were on land after weeks of sailing, it felt funny to walk, as if the ground was unstable. It made me a little nauseous. There were lots of little lizards scampering about. It reminded me again of where I found Buster. I hoped Pat was taking care of him and wondered if he missed me as much as I missed him.

Jane identified three species of geckos and pointed out two more species that she couldn't identify. I thought about the insurance commercial with the talking gecko. I suddenly missed television too.

Back aboard, I helped Jane wash Charles's bedding and linens. They sorely needed it. Jane then got some orange cleaner and wiped down his cabin.

Reid and Marta took the kayak to do some snorkeling. They soon returned, handing me two large lobsters. They said there were hundreds of them, all shallow and easy to catch.

At my urging, they went back and got four more. Reid agreed that since he'd have a pot of boiling water, cooking six was no more work than cooking two. He'd cook them all and we could eat them at our leisure.

Halfway through boiling lobsters, the stove quit. Reid checked. The acetylene tank was empty. He was a little surprised that it hadn't lasted longer than it did. He said the Navy must not have been able to fill the tanks as full as a regular propane distributor could. He switched the hose over to our last tank and finished boiling our dinner.

Even without butter and lemon, I enjoyed their catch immensely. After dinner, Jane got her violin and played a sonata and a concerto. I didn't know either of them, but they were easy to listen to.

It had been a good day. Maybe it was the change from fish to shellfish, or perhaps it was being anchored in a nice spot. And to make the day totally perfect, Reid and I had Olympic-caliber sex later that night.

Early the next morning, we raised anchor and set course for Tobago. The winds were favorable and it didn't take us long to get there. A small pod of maybe twenty dolphins swam just ahead of us most of the way.

Tobago was rocky with sparse vegetation. It did have one fairly big mountain range. As usual, there were large numbers of birds flying all around. It was too early to anchor, and Grenada was less than ninety nautical miles away, so we sailed on without stopping.

We were on our last acetylene tank. I was worried that it wasn't full. I didn't know what we'd do when we were no longer able to cook our fish. "Eat sushi I guess," I said to myself.

Reid went forward to recheck the kayaks, and I followed.

"Can I ask you a question?" I asked, keeping my voice low.

"Is something wrong?" Reid turned and looked at me.

"Assuming the aliens do return us to our time, what are we going to do when we find Pat?"

"What do you mean?" he whispered, moving closer.

"When I first made contact, the aliens told me Pat was headed down a path of bad choices. They said we'd have to stop her from using what she had learned from them for personal gain."

Reid nodded. "I remember you telling me we'd use the time from Hawaii to the Bermuda Triangle to reflect on the consequences of her bad choices."

"I'm worried that Marta may kill Pat on sight before you

and I get a chance to find out what's she's doing that has angered the aliens."

"Do you believe Marta blames Pat for everything that has happened?"

"Wouldn't she'd be right to do so?" I whispered. "If Pat hadn't sent us back in time, we'd have reached Hawaii, Charles would have paid them for their services, and Marta and her friends would be on their way."

"You're forgetting about the Navy and the CIA," Reid said. "We might not have ever reached Hawaii, at least not without being in handcuffs or in the brig. We likely would have been detained indefinitely and questioned repeatedly. That's why Pat did what she did."

Oh shit. I had forgotten about that. Reid had a good point. Hearing we were "totally fucked," as Vee had said, and then hearing me tell Reid we should join Vee and her crew and get lost on a Clarriage ninety-five had been the reason Pat initiated the alien's time portal device and sent us back to this time.

"I'm still worried about Marta. She's a former spy. She's trained in espionage. She's not afraid to take revenge with a knife. And lately, she's asking too many questions about Pat," I exclaimed, my frustration growing.

Reid didn't respond. He glanced about. I sensed he was processing what I had just said.

Reid finished inspecting the kayak's lashings. I waited to see if he was going to talk more about Marta.

He didn't. He just made his way across to the other hull to inspect that kayak. I shrugged and went back into the salon. I figured we'd talk later.

Just before the sun went down, Jane shouted, "Land ho."

Grenada was barely visible. Reid wanted to see it with the radar.

The engines started but didn't sound happy. Using the JP5 jet fuel was taking its toll. I wondered how many more times they would start.

He made a decision to bypass Grenada and used the radar to determine a safe heading to do so. Once we were clear, we would change course for Puerto Rico.

I joined him at the chart. Puerto Rico was almost five hundred nautical miles away. There was nothing between us and there but open water.

The winds today had been steady, enabling us to average thirteen knots. If we could maintain that, we were less than two days away.

Reid sent me to the helm so he and Jane could get a fix and do the nightly weather forecast. Marta accompanied me. I hoped she wouldn't ask any more questions about Pat.

Later, Reid announced he'd let the engines run long enough to use the water maker and fully charge the batteries.

When we were alone, he confided that Jane expressed concerns about how the engines were sounding and about being on our last acetylene tank.

"What did you tell her?" I asked.

He smiled and said, "I told her to refill the water bottles, refill the solar showers, and . . ."

"And what?"

"And pray the winds hold."

CHAPTER 57

When Reid calculated we were about one hundred nautical miles from Puerto Rico, I went into my cabin and tried contacting the aliens. There was no response. I was disappointed but decided to try every hour when I wasn't napping or on duty.

The second time I tried to establish contact, I got so relaxed that I fell asleep and woke up two hours later.

The next time I wasn't on watch I tried again. I relaxed, counting backward from ten. I cleared my mind of all thoughts and focused on one thing—making contact with the aliens.

I mentally projected two thoughts: "This is Tracy calling the aliens. Can you hear me?" I kept repeating those words, slowing my breathing after each attempt.

We hear you.

Their answer resonated in my head. Finally. I had made contact.

"We have done what you asked," I said. "Will you return us to our time?"

Yes, the answer came through clearly. *But be aware that one of you is very weak and might not survive the transport.*

I knew they were referring to Charles. It was a concern we all had. He was still very sick. My next question then was "What are that person's options?"

Their response was quick and clear.

He can be left behind while the rest of you are returned or he can be returned with you and take his chances on survival.

The first option was unacceptable. I tried "asking" something else.

"Can you return him to a time before his wife died?"

We can.

Too quick. I sensed that something wasn't right, so I rephrased the question. "*Will* you return him to a time before his wife died?"

No.

"Why not?"

The past is set. We cannot change what has happened. Just as we cannot allow you to do anything in this time that may affect the future.

That answer wasn't going to be popular, but at least now Charles would know for certain. I also had to ask him if he wanted to go back with us or not. After all, it had to be his decision, even if it meant picking between two unfortunate choices. I couldn't imagine Charles would choose to stay, even at the risk of his life.

It occurred to me to try something else.

"Will you return us then to a time prior to Vee's unfortunate accident and then return all of us together?"

No.

"But it happened here in this time. Bringing us back just a few weeks earlier could hardly make a difference. Her death changed nothing."

You cannot know that. The number of one's days are preordained. Whether here or back in your time.

I drew in a breath. "You mean if we had been back in our time, Vee would have died anyway?"

It is assumed from our experience.

I wasn't prepared for that, or sure I could accept it. It was a cinch Marta wouldn't. "What's next?" I asked after a pause.

Continue on your present course. If the decision is made to leave your failing person ashore, do so. Be fifteen of your nautical miles away from land on this heading and simply stop. At that location, this vessel and all aboard will be returned.

That seemed clear enough, and Reid's navigation skills were certainly good enough to put us fifteen nautical miles offshore on this heading. But there was a burning question that I had to ask.

I focused and thought, "What about Pat?"

Patricia Taylor must be stopped, permanently. Do so as quickly as you can.

That message hit me like a brick. "Stopped permanently? What does that mean?"

We made a mistake granting her the powers that we did. We ourselves cannot correct the mistake, but you can. You must. It is the condition of your return.

Condition of our return? Before I could ask why or how, the connection was terminated.

I opened my eyes. My thoughts were my own. My head was clear. The communication was over. I needed to tell the others what was coming, even though I still reeled from the implications.

I charged topside so fast I tripped on the steps and nearly fell.

Reid was at the salon table, picking at a cold piece of fish. "What happened?" he asked.

I glanced around. Nobody else was near. I sat down next to him and said, "I know what we have to do."

Reid quit eating and listened as I told him. He didn't interrupt or ask any questions or take any notes; he just listened.

When I finished, he thanked me for making contact. Then he said, "Go talk to Charles. See what he wants to do given his two options. Then report back."

"But what about Pat? Stop her permanently? What else could that mean but kill her?"

Reid shook his head. "When we're back, we can figure out what to do. First, we need to get back. Go see Charles."

I nodded, took a few bites of fish, and then headed below.

I hoped that Charles would be awake and alone. He was. I closed the door behind me and leaned against it.

He looked at me and coughed. I told him everything. Like Reid, he listened intently.

When I had finished, I waited. He only took a second to say, "Of course I'm going back with the rest of you."

I nodded and left. I was glad he had decided to return with us. That would have been my decision. Remaining ashore, in his condition and alone, would have been suicide. At least this way he had a chance. I purposely left out that the aliens refused his request to be sent back before his wife died, or before Vee's death. I didn't think it would help anyone to repeat their conviction that one's days were numbered and, regardless of the circumstances, death would come when those numbers were up.

CHAPTER 58

I went back to Reid. Jane was with him.

"Did you tell her what the aliens said?" I asked.

"I did," he replied.

"Please say that Charles is going to come with us," Jane begged. Her voice was shaky, her eyes intense with concern.

I smiled and nodded. "Of course he is."

She smiled, looking immensely relieved. "I'm glad. But I want you to know I would have stayed with him."

She said it defensively, as if thinking we were going to argue with her. Neither of us did.

"Go tell Marta what's happening," Reid said. "I need to look at the chart."

I joined Marta at the helm and told her what would happen next. I left out the main reason we were being returned was to stop Pat "permanently and quickly." It might sound like I was giving her permission to go after Pat herself. Pat was my problem, and Reid's. Not hers.

"What did Charles decide?" she asked.

"Charles is coming with us."

She nodded. "What do you want me to do?"

"Hold your course," I replied.

She nodded again. I left the helm and returned to the salon.

Reid and Jane were at the chart. He showed me where he had marked an *X*. It was on our present course line, fifteen nautical miles this side of Puerto Rico.

I heard Charles coughing. He joined us. Jane helped him take a seat.

"How much time have we got?" he wheezed, gasping for air.

Reid answered. "At our present speed, we'll reach the required position around one o'clock in the morning. Or . . ." His voice trailed off. I could tell he was thinking.

"Or what?" Jane asked.

"Or we slow down a little and try and time it so we're in position after the sun comes up."

"That sounds better," I said.

Jane and Charles both agreed.

Reid went topside, presumably to adjust the sails to slow us down.

Jane got Charles a bottle of water and then sat next to him. He smiled and thanked her. They looked happy together.

I looked at him now in a new light. If he died during the transit back, it was meant to be, wasn't it?

As the last rays of the sun battled the encroaching darkness, Reid joined me at the helm.

"I've got this," I said. "Go get some rest."

He gave me an odd look and said, "I know I won't sleep."

I understood. Had his watch been first, I couldn't have slept either. I snuggled. "Do you think Charles will make it?" I finally asked.

"Hope so. He's more than just a rich eccentric. I feel that he's become one of the family."

We sailed on. Our speed was now six knots. It felt like *The Aquaholic* was crawling more than sailing. But six knots would get us fifteen nautical miles offshore in daylight, which was the plan.

"How much stuff do you suppose the aliens will make us get rid of?" I asked.

"Probably everything that could be tied to this time period."

"Do you suppose we'll see a little green man again?" I asked with a chuckle.

"Maybe."

We sailed on through the night. Going this slow made me antsy, but I knew it was the right decision. I figured Reid would start telling jokes to pass the time.

Thankfully he didn't. He put his arm around my shoulder and we held the wheel, together.

I wanted to talk about Pat but decided against it. I tried

not to think about her or Charles. Both of them had a bleak future.

If Charles didn't make it, there would be a funeral. Perhaps another burial at sea. Possibly a service ashore.

If we made it, I'd have to find and likely kill Pat. She must have really gone on tilt to face that consequence. What she had done, I couldn't even imagine.

And what about Marta? Would she kill Pat on sight? I figured she would. I wondered how I'd stop her. Or if I should.

There were so many scenarios flashing though my head that I started to get a headache.

I tried to relax by keeping the compass needle on course and waiting for the miles to pass.

Reid left to take readings and confirm our position. He wasn't gone very long. When he came back, he told me we were right on course and on schedule. He also said the others were in their cabins.

When Reid calculated we were twenty nautical miles from Puerto Rico, he said he would see if land was visible to the radar. That seemed logical.

He tried to start the engines, but they wouldn't start. Their pesky alarm tone woke everybody. Marta joined me topside, telling me that Jane and Charles were awake and in the salon.

Reid ran the radar with battery power. It showed a large land mass seventeen nautical miles away. We were nearly in position.

Twenty minutes later, Reid had me turn into the wind

while he furled the sails. *The Aquaholic* slowed and then stopped. Reid disconnected the main and starting batteries. Jane took the batteries out of the flashlights, portable radios, and GPS units.

The rest of us waited restlessly.

Thirty minutes later, Reid pointed at a disturbance on the surface, about one hundred yards away.

"There's something there," he shouted. "It doesn't look like currents fighting each other."

CHAPTER 59

I moved to where I could see. Sure enough, a vivid, greenish-yellow glowing light was heading right toward us.

As the light got closer, the wind stopped blowing. Almost immediately, the ocean became completely flat. There wasn't so much as a ripple nearby. *The Aquaholic* came to a complete stop and just sat there, motionless, not even rocking.

An intense, dazzlingly bright light nearly blinded me. I closed my eyes and covered them with my hands, but I could still see it. A second later, the bright light subsided.

As things came into focus, the alien's sphere surfaced nearby. It levitated about two or three feet above the flat surface and then stayed there, suspended and glowing yellow.

As I vaguely remembered from the first time I saw it, the

sphere displayed various colors and then several sounds ranging from low to high and then soft to loud.

Not being drunk this time, I enjoyed the aliens calibrating their sphere so we could see and hear them. An actual conversation was preferable to only hearing them in my head. I also wanted Charles, Jane, and Marta to hear them so any thoughts they may have entertained that I was crazy for hearing alien voices would be dismissed.

Before long, an alien image of the proverbial little green man appeared on the sphere.

Congratulations on making it this far, Tracy.

I didn't think that congratulations were in order, and I was ready to tell him so.

Marta beat me to it. "Had you simply returned us from Hawaiian waters when we were almost there," she said bitterly, "one of my friends wouldn't be dead, three more wouldn't have been left behind, and my friend Charles wouldn't be deathly sick."

There was silence for a moment, and I had a quick, panicky thought that maybe Marta made them so angry, they would refuse to return us now.

We made an error in showing some of you advanced problem-solving techniques. You will be returned to correct that error.

They were obviously referring to Pat abusing the gift of alien technology.

"*Your* error," Marta continued. "Why couldn't you have corrected your own damned error?"

I put a hand on Marta's arm. "Not now," I whispered. "Let them get on with this."

But the alien obviously heard because he continued speaking.

Those of you on your vessel demonstrated a strong will to be returned to your time. We will honor our promise to return you from this area. We apologize that not all of you will make it back.

I wondered if they were referring to Charles or Bev, Candy, and Dreamgirl. I didn't ask. We had made it from Hawaii to Puerto Rico, and the aliens were going to send us back to our time. I was glad to be returning. I certainly didn't want to argue. Marta, too, remained quiet.

"What's next?" I asked finally, though I could have guessed.

As before, all records must be destroyed.

"Wait a second." It was Jane interrupting this time. "I have lots of questions."

I looked at her. Her outburst didn't surprise me all that much. Actually, I wondered why none of the others hadn't spoken up.

Future communication is only with the human female known as Tracy Palmer.

I waited to see if Jane would accept that or start asking questions. She looked perplexed but stayed silent. I figured Charles would ask to get returned to a time before his late wife died. I didn't think that Reid would ask anything. I wasn't sure about Marta.

Thankfully, nobody had anything further to say.

Suddenly, *The Aquaholic* was bathed in light. I had forgotten about being scanned. The aliens were determining which things on board would have to be incinerated before they'd send us back through their time portal.

The light only engulfed us for a few minutes. When it finally stopped, the alien image spoke again.

Destroy all documentation of your participation in this time period.

Participation wasn't exactly how I would have put it, but their message was unmistakable. I waited for the aliens to create a fiery hole in the water. I also waited for pictures of everything that could tie us to this time period to appear on the sphere.

An image of Bev, Candy, Dreamgirl, and *The USS Fields* flashed in my head. I had one more question, and I figured it was now or never.

"How are the others who were sent back to this time period fairing?"

The warship has disbursed its personnel over a large geographic area. The three females from this vessel have stayed together. That group has no casualties. That group is minimizing its impact on the local flora and fauna.

Now I knew the fate of Beverly Thompson, Candice Glover, and Penelope "Dreamgirl" Porter. Marta knew it too. They were still alive and together, somewhere.

Of the other two groups to transit the portal, only one survivor remains.

I wasn't expecting a status report on the others and I

jumped. I wondered which of them was still alive, but deep down, I really didn't want to know. I didn't ask for specifics. I silently hoped that Captain Daniel Pincus hadn't made it. He was an evil man.

The alien voice resumed. *All records must be destroyed.*

That message had barely stopped when pictures of items to be destroyed appeared on the sphere. As I was looking at the pictures, I felt an intense heat behind me. I whirled and saw a ring of fire and rising steam in the water.

I looked back at the pictures. The ship's logbook was there, along with several charts and some spiral notebooks— all of the notes Jane had taken along the way of the sea life we'd encountered. Pictures of all our cell phones—further documentation of what we'd seen—and anything that might give credence to the story of what we'd survived. All had to go.

Reid and I had known this was coming, but the others hadn't. I watched Jane's reaction, expecting disbelief or outrage. Instead, I saw simple acceptance. Maybe she was thinking of Charles and how arguing would delay him getting the medical attention he needed. Or maybe she was thinking that a brain that could memorize a million *Jeopardy* answers could recall any detail of our twenty-five-thousand-year journey without the aid of notes.

Our two propane tanks marked for acetylene were there. So were the yellow diesel cans that had been marked for JP5.

There was even a picture of the arctic gear the Navy had given us.

The propellant in your fuel tanks must be destroyed.

I knew they were referring to the JP5 jet fuel that Reid had siphoned into our fuel tanks. I wasn't sure how we could get it out of the tanks, but I noticed that Reid was nodding.

Then some pictures of all the fish we had caught appeared. I didn't know why dead fish fillets would be a problem, but obviously they were.

"Before we discard all of our fish, we might take a few bites," Jane said. "Who knows when we'll have a chance to eat again."

I nodded. That was a good idea.

Reid got an empty yellow diesel can and went below.

Charles remained seated, but the rest of us began gathering items. I took *The Aquaholic's* logbook to the stern. Marta joined me with her cell phone.

She hesitated until I tossed the logbook into the fiery hole. It vanished in a puff of smoke. Marta's phone met the same fate.

Jane set out the cooked fish in the galley. Every time I went by, I took a piece. I wasn't hungry but ate anyway, not knowing when I'd get another opportunity.

Reid came topside, carrying the yellow diesel can marked JP5. He smelled like jet fuel. He went aft and poured the fuel into the fire. Thankfully nothing exploded. He repeated the procedure before finally disposing of the cans themselves.

When Reid had finished disposing of our fuel, pictures of his clothes appeared. He stripped in front of all of us and threw his clothes into the fire. Then he got the orange cleaner and a solar shower and washed himself off. His skin was red, but he didn't smell like JP5. He was naked in front of three women but didn't seem concerned.

Our shoes were next—Reid's and mine. They did have a foul odor from being constantly wet. Reid liberally doused them with orange cleaner when we weren't wearing them but that evidently wasn't enough. The aliens wanted them destroyed. They must have contained some bacterial organism or something. We discarded them.

Item after item was thrown into the inferno circle. Picture after picture was removed from the sphere. When the last of Jane's cooked fish was incinerated, the sphere went blank.

A moment later, the alien's image returned.

Public discussion of this encounter or related events will cause swift authoritative intervention.

"Will you return my friends Bev, Candy, and Dreamgirl?" Marta asked suddenly. Her tone was unmistakable. She was not so much asking as demanding.

There was no response. Marta glanced at me, a look of desperation in her eyes. Remembering the aliens were only going to talk to me, I repeated her question.

Not possible.

"Why not?" Marta's response was loud and swift. She was furious. I sympathized with her position but hoped she wouldn't blow it for the rest of us.

I calmly repeated her question.

Desire to be returned required compliance with our directive. Your three friends chose not to comply. They now face the consequences of their choice.

Jane put her arm around Marta's waist and whispered she was sorry but it was time to let them go. Marta pulled away.

I looked at the alien and said, "Thank you for sending us back."

The alien image went away and the sphere receded beneath the surface.

I grabbed the pieces of a disassembled flashlight and put them and the battery in my pocket. Jane let go of Marta and pointed. "Fog ho."

We made our way to our cabins and prepared for the journey through the time portal. While I waited for Reid to get dressed, I took two Tylenol and then stuffed some tissue in my ears. I hoped Charles would make it.

CHAPTER 60

I woke up. My head hurt. Every bone and muscle ached. I looked at the porthole. It was dark outside. So much for timing our transit for daylight hours. I should have remembered the first time I transited the portal. I went through at night but woke up during daylight hours. Our bad for wasting time by slowing down.

I felt for Reid. He was next to me.

"Are you awake?" I quietly asked.

"Im taking inventory," he replied.

"That portal sucks," I whispered.

"The alternative is worse."

That was profound. No matter how sore I was or how bad my head was throbbing, it was worse for Bev, Candy, and all of the others. They would die twenty-five thousand seven hundred years in the past.

I removed the flashlight from my pocket, reassembled it, and switched it on. It worked. I aimed it at Reid. He looked tired but managed a smile.

"Charles," I uttered. "What about Charles?"

"Give me a few minutes to get my bearings and we'll go see."

Less than ten minutes later, with Reid behind me, I lightly knocked on his cabin door.

"It's not locked," Jane said.

I could tell from her voice that Charles was alive. For confirmation, I heard him cough.

I opened the door and shined my light inside. Jane looked beat-up but forced a smile. Charles managed another cough. I felt incredibly relieved that he had made it.

Reid motioned for the light. He had the boat's main batteries to reconnect.

I checked on Marta. She was still in her cabin but was awake.

Twenty minutes later, Jane and Marta met me in the salon. They said they were sore and had headaches. Me too, on both counts.

I thought that taking Tylenol in advance would help. It didn't; my head hurt so bad it was pulsating. Jane reported that Charles was worse and insisted our first stop be a hospital.

Reid had finished reconnecting the main batteries and momentarily joined us. Announcing the batteries were really low, he went and started the portable generator. Luckily, there was just enough fuel left in the tank for that. Its rumble made my head throb even harder.

He returned and voiced concern that we were in the dark and drifting. He sent Marta to the helm and told her to keep a lookout.

Moving slowly, Reid got a portable GPS unit working. When he went to plot our coordinates, he cussed the aliens for making us incinerate every chart we had written on.

Fortunately, he found the cruising guide for Puerto Rico. It had a small chart of the entire island. He marked our coordinates.

There were three marinas on the south shore of Puerto Rico. All of them were pretty close, but he decided we should set course for the Pescaderia Marina on the west shore instead.

"Why all the way there when Charles needs a hospital now?" Jane asked. "The marinas at Ponce or Guayama are closer."

Knowing Reid, he had a good reason. I waited for his answer.

"All of us have been to Pescaderia before." Reid smiled, rubbing his temples.

"So?" Jane asked, raising her hands in frustration.

"So three of us don't have identification or passports," he answered. He was right. His, mine, and Charles's IDs and passports were onboard *The Lady Anne*.

Jane lowered her hands. Reid added, "Returning to that marina is our best chance at not being immediately questioned by Puerto Rican immigration."

My earlier thought was right. Reid had a good reason. That marina would have a record of our previous visit. They might even recognize *The Aquaholic's* paint job, unique as it was.

Reid plotted a course for Mayaquez. The Pescaderia Marina was just south of there.

I wanted to rest, at least until daybreak, but Reid insisted we raise the sails, switch on our red and green sidelights and the white stern light, and get underway. His top priority was getting Charles medical attention.

CHAPTER 61

Reid and I sailed through the night, barefoot. Jane and Marta had offered me a pair of shoes, but they didn't fit. Reid tried on Charles's shoes, but they didn't fit either.

We passed a few large vessels. When our batteries were charged, Reid switched off the generator.

I stayed with Reid at the helm but napped on and off. Jane came up to relieve us right after sunup. She told me that Charles wanted to see me when I had a minute.

Reid went to lie down and I went to see Charles. He looked really weak, and his cough sounded even more painful.

"Call Elouise as soon as we dock," he gasped. "Have her bring my wallet, passport, cell phone, and my airplane. Have her bring your stuff too."

I mentally repeated his list. It was pretty basic. I was sure I would remember it long enough to write it down.

"I will," I replied. "Do you happen to know her number?"

He shook his head. Even that motion looked like it hurt. "Call David Goldbloom. He'll have her number."

"Who's David Goldbloom?" I asked.

"The attorney that handled the change of ownership transaction for *The Lady Anne*," Charles replied, shaking a bit.

I vaguely remembered. That seemed an eternity ago—no, a lifetime ago.

"Do you have his number?"

"Look him up. David Goldbloom, attorney. Manhattan."

That helped. I didn't think there could be more than a few attorneys in Manhattan with that name.

Charles added, "Tell him you're calling for me. They'll put you right through." With that he exhaled, coughed, and closed his eyes. I left him to rest.

Later that day we arrived. Reid radioed ahead and told the marina we needed a slip we could sail into. They were eager to accommodate us. They told Reid there were several empty slips facing the marina entrance and to just pick the one we wanted.

Reid and Jane took the helm. Marta and I put the fenders out and got the dock lines ready. Reid furled the jib and then partially furled the mainsail, leaving us only enough power to make way.

Reid directed Jane to sail *The Aquaholic* into the slip while he controlled the mainsail. Marta leapt off the bow and landed on the dock. I didn't jump like Marta but instead stepped onto the dock from the stern. Between the two of us, we kept the boat from ramming the dock. Soon we had her securely tied to the cleats.

Since only Jane and Marta had passports, they went to the marina office. Reid figured they wouldn't have any problems clearing customs. He warned them to avoid any television cameras, reminding them that the CIA monitored all global newscasts.

I hoped that all of our names weren't on some kind of a list since we were the last ones to have seen the missing CIA, NSA, and NORAD agents, not to mention *The USS Fields*.

Jane and Marta got us checked in without any problems. Once I had a gate code, I rushed to the marina's business office and used their complimentary computer. I was barefoot, but nobody said anything.

There were four listings for attorneys named Dave or David Goldbloom in Manhattan. All of their offices were closed so I couldn't call until tomorrow, but I did write the numbers down.

I returned to the flashing lights of an ambulance. I watched as Charles was wheeled down the dock. I could hear him coughing.

Jane and Reid were walking alongside the paramedics. I didn't see Marta.

The ambulance loaded Charles and sped away. Jane rode in the back, but Reid stayed with me.

"Is Charles going to be okay?" I asked.

"They didn't say much, but I've got the name of the hospital where he's being taken," Reid replied, holding up a business card.

Then he added, "Jane bought a prepaid mobile burner phone and charger and said she'd be in touch."

I was curious how since neither Reid nor I had phones.

I followed Reid back to the boat. I asked where Marta was. He said that once the ambulance arrived, she had left to take a shower.

A shower sounded really good. So did food. I was starving, not having had anything to eat but a few pieces of cold fish for an entire day. Reid wanted a shower too, so after he connected the shore power, we gathered what we needed and headed for the marina showers.

We passed Marta on the way back. She looked clean but didn't say anything. I sensed she wasn't very happy. I nudged Reid and shrugged. He didn't comment.

I washed my frightful hair. My body was still sore, but the shower was hot and felt wonderful. I stood there, closed my eyes, and let the water run over me until it started to get cold. I wished Reid could have soaped my back, but he was using the men's side. It would have been nice to have had clean clothes to change into, but I didn't.

I exited the shower room and saw Reid talking to Jane. I was surprised she wasn't at the hospital. I hoped that nothing had happened to Charles. I couldn't think of any other reason why Jane would be back so soon.

Reid motioned me over, saying, "Jane's got a problem."

I tensed and waited.

"Two problems actually," Jane corrected him.

"Is one of them Charles?" I asked, my breathing increasing.

She shook her head. "Charles is in ICU and will likely be there for at least a week."

That wasn't necessarily bad news but didn't explain why Jane had come back so quickly.

As if sensing my confusion, she said, "I spoke with Angie. Pat's got a restraining order against her."

Before I could ask for details, Jane continued, "But that's minor compared to the second problem."

"Which is?" I asked, waiting.

"Oahu is closed," she said.

"What do you mean Oahu is closed?"

Jane lowered her voice and said the entire island was engulfed in fog. The fog had appeared suddenly, covered the entire island, and wasn't burning off during daylight hours as is typical. The scientists interviewed on the news were at a loss to explain the fog's arrival and strange behavior.

She told us that the Honolulu airport was technically open, but the majority of airlines had suspended service. Very few planes, either passenger or freight, were flying into Oahu. There was a backlog of tourists waiting to leave on any available flight out.

Besides interfering with the tourism industry, the island's ports had been closed, disrupting the supply chain of food, fuel, and goods. There were shortages everywhere, and a state of emergency had been declared.

She concluded by saying that Oahu's fog was the major news story on every channel.

My jaw dropped. That had to be Pat's doing. But at least now I knew where to start looking for her.

CHAPTER 62

I was speechless. So was Reid. Jane borrowed my damp towel and my toiletries, saying she'd be back in five minutes, maybe six.

Reid and I waited while she took a shower.

"Fog has to be Pat's doing," I whispered.

"Agreed," he replied. "But I wonder how she managed to get it to cover an entire island?"

I didn't know, but obviously she had figured it out.

Jane finished her shower and we all hustled back to *The Aquaholic*. When Jane commented the shower wasn't very hot, I looked away.

The boat was empty, but Marta had left a note saying she was going to eat and not to wait up or worry.

Her note was puzzling. Why would she eat without us?

Where was she going here that would cause her to be back late? Why would she tell us not to worry? Worry about what?

Maybe she was simply sick and tired of our company. I couldn't really blame her. After all, we'd been in close quarters for months.

Neither Reid nor Jane had anything to say about Marta's note. Reid asked Jane if she would cover dinner if we couldn't charge it to the slip. She quickly said yes.

On the way to eat, Reid and I stopped in the small marina store and each got a new pair of socks and shoes.

At the marina restaurant, I ordered a large salad, a steak, and a glass of Merlot. Reid ordered a burger, a beer, and French fries. Jane ordered a cheese enchilada with chips and mild salsa to share and a virgin strawberry margarita.

We ate quickly, devouring our non-fish meal. I asked Jane what Angie had done to warrant a restraining order.

She didn't have all of the details, but the quick version was that Angie had punched Pat right after Pat activated her alien signaling device, sending *The Aquaholic* back in time.

"Do you remember when we were chasing *The Lady Anne*, trying to outrun the fog?" Reid asked.

I nodded.

"Do you remember when *The Lady Anne* suddenly swerved and slowed?" he continued.

I nodded again.

"I'll bet that's when my daughter punched her," Jane said, laughing. "That's why Pat lost control. Because my daughter was fighting her for control of the helm."

That made sense.

"Angie told me she beat the shit out of Pat after they docked in Hawaii," Jane said, raising her fists and shadow boxing.

"That would certainly explain why Pat got a restraining order," Reid said, smiling as he finished his beer.

And it would mean that Pat was still on Oahu.

We finished eating but didn't discuss the fog. I wanted something sweet for dessert, but my stomach hurt. To the waiter's chagrin, we all passed on the luscious dessert cart he had wheeled over.

Jane charged the drinks and the meal to our slip and we all went back to the boat.

Marta wasn't there. Reid and I didn't wait up. I wasn't sure if Jane did or not. I was suddenly super tired. My head was buzzing from one glass of wine. I felt half sick. I'm sure that was from eating too much too fast after weeks of nothing but fish. I hoped I wouldn't throw up in the middle of the night.

I woke up the next morning. I had slept like a rock and don't think I even moved. Reid and Jane were in the galley with three purchased cups of coffee. It smelled divine and tasted even better.

"Is Marta up yet?" I asked.

Reid answered, "Her cabin is empty."

"I wonder where she went?"

He shrugged.

"Let me clarify," Reid said. "Her cabin is *empty*. Really

empty. The shelves and under berth storage are bare. So is the head she was using."

"She's moved out," Jane stated.

I blinked and glanced around, wondering why she'd leave without even saying goodbye.

I finished my coffee and used Jane's new phone to call New York.

The third David Goldbloom attorney I called was the right one. I told him we were in Puerto Rico and asked for Elouise Ryall's phone number.

He looked it up and then asked if Charles was all right. I grimaced but told him that Charles was in ICU. Reid handed me the card the ambulance had left. I gave him the information.

He thanked me and hung up. We all got the feeling he'd be on the next flight from New York to Puerto Rico.

I called Elouise. She was very relieved to hear from me. She had been worried sick about what had happened to us. When I told her that Charles was in ICU, she began to cry.

I told her Charles, Reid, and I needed our passports, phones, the men's wallets, and my purse from *The Lady Anne*. Jane and Marta were okay since their things had been on board *The Aquaholic* when we were sent back in time.

Elouise said that was a problem due to the mysterious fog that had surrounded the island of Oahu. At present, there was no mail service in or off the island. But she had a solution for the passports, at least.

CHAPTER 63

Elouise said she had extra passport photos for Charles's but would need photos for me and Reid. We used Jane's phone and sent her several head shots of each of us. She said she'd get the three of us duplicate identification and would fly down to Puerto Rico in a New York minute.

I asked if she could also bring us some money for incidentals and perhaps a prepaid credit card or two. She said that wouldn't be a problem. I asked if she knew if Pat was staying at Charles's compound. She said she would check. Before she said goodbye, she got the name of the hospital where Charles was.

Jane suggested we go shopping with her and buy some new clothes. I desperately needed something clean to wear. So did Reid. We found a small clothing shop near the marina.

Reid tried on a hat and said he had a joke. I shook my

head. He was nothing if not consistent. Jane told him to go ahead.

"Why don't sailors like to buy new hats?" he asked, grinning.

"I know," Jane responded excitedly.

I didn't have any idea and waited to see if she was right.

"Fear of cap-sizing," she answered.

Reid high-fived her and told her that was right. I smiled but secretly hoped he wouldn't tell a follow-up joke. Surprisingly, he didn't.

Jane's credit card was declined. She guessed that Angie had reported it lost. Fortunately, she had cash.

We returned to the marina restaurant for a late breakfast. I ordered bacon, scrambled eggs, pancakes, fruit, coffee, and orange juice. Jane smiled and said, "Times two."

Reid made it easy on our server by saying, "Times three." None of us could finish everything we had ordered. I wondered if our stomachs had shrunk.

Next was a trip to the hospital.

We could only see Charles one at a time. His eyes were closed. He looked ghastly. There were tubes stuck everywhere. A machine was breathing for him. It was frightening.

The television in his room was switched to a news channel. The volume was off, but the caption was clear: fog smothering Oahu. A satellite image showed a large patch of gray where Oahu was.

Jane stayed, saying she'd tell him that Reid and I had stopped by.

Back at the boat, Reid and I hosed the salt off the decks. *The Aquaholic* was a charred mess.

"I feel really bad for what we did to Angie's boat," I said.

Reid squeezed my hand and said, "This boat saved our asses. There's nothing here that money and time can't fix."

I changed the subject. "What are we going to do about Pat?"

Reid thought for a moment. "We'll fly to Hawaii, find her, and see what she's up to."

"You're forgetting that Oahu is fog-bound and there are no flights in or out," I said.

My statement didn't faze him. He quickly retorted, "We'll fly into a neighboring island and make our way by boat. When Elouise confirms that Pat is staying at Charles's property, you, Tracy my dear, can show us exactly where that is."

I was curious how we'd navigate a boat in fog that was heavy enough to ground planes, but I let it go for now.

We busied ourselves trying to clean up *The Aquaholic*.

Jane returned from the hospital later that afternoon. She reported that Charles had thanked us for coming by. She had spoken with the doctor. He was slightly annoyed that Charles hadn't been seen sooner, implying that she had been negligent.

Jane laughed at that. "If he only knew," she said. "He confirmed that Charles had pneumonia, double pneumonia actually, but was confident that Charles would recover."

Then Jane asked if we had seen Marta. We both shook our heads. We agreed she might be tired of our company and had simply checked into a hotel. There was no way to verify that one way or the other so nothing further was said.

When Jane returned from the hospital the following morning, she replied that she had met the lawyer David Goldbloom. She only said that he was pleasant enough. I wondered if or when he'd stop by the boat to put a face with a name.

Jane told us she had told her daughter *The Aquaholic* had been through quite an ordeal and might need extensive repairs, including new engines.

I waited to hear Angie's response. I commented that I hoped she wouldn't be mad at me. I said I had no desire to get punched out.

Jane smiled and said, "No worries. Angie was very sorry to hear about Vee but is glad the rest of us are okay."

That was comforting.

Jane continued, "Angie said, 'The boat had been rebuilt once. She could be again.'" Then she smiled and added, "But this time we'll put *The Aquaholic* on a freighter and have her shipped."

I remembered what had happened to Angie and her passengers at the hands of Captain Rick and shuddered. That would have been enough for me to sell *The Aquaholic* at my first opportunity. Adding in our suicide sail around Cape Horn would have sealed my decision. "*The Aquaholic* is either cursed, hexed, or jinxed," I said to myself. "I'd sell her and close that chapter, for good."

But that was me, not Angie.

CHAPTER 64

Attorney David Goldbloom stopped by later that afternoon. He looked like a television attorney—well dressed in a bespoke pin-striped suit, with slicked-back hair, wire-rimmed glasses, and a leather brief case. He looked to be in his early sixties, had a bit of a spare tire, and was pleasant but very soft spoken.

He had come back from the hospital with Jane. They reported that Charles was still in ICU but was responding to the antibiotics.

David gave me his personal cell phone number and said he was staying near the hospital. There was some awkward small talk.

I was sure he'd ask for details about what had happened to make Charles so sick. I was also pretty sure he'd ask why Charles had been out of contact for so long.

Thankfully, he didn't. I wondered if he had already gotten the information he wanted from Jane.

Before leaving, he asked me for the papers Charles had given me. The only way he could have known about them was if Charles had told him.

I retrieved the folded sheets from my cabin and handed them over. Reid tilted his head but didn't say anything.

I was curious about what Charles had written, but had never looked. I suddenly wondered if I should have sneaked a peek while I had the chance. "Oh well," I thought. "It surely doesn't matter now."

Jane escorted attorney David Goldbloom off the boat. When she returned, she said she was tired and was going to take a nap. She asked if someone would wake her in an hour, ninety minutes max.

While we waited for Elouise, Reid outlined his plan for getting to Pat.

The closest island to Oahu was Molokai. The flight time was thirty-six minutes, but with the airports on Oahu closed, our only option was to go by boat.

The Ka'iwi or Molokai channel separated the two islands. It was only about thirty miles across but was known for being very rough. Its nickname was The Channel of Bones.

Crossing The Channel of Bones didn't scare me. Not given our Cape Horn rounding in the winter. However, navigating in fog that was heavy enough to ground airplanes and close ports did sound like it might be a problem. I waited to hear Reid's plan.

Reid suggested we use Charles's plane to get to Molokai. We could detour through Maui or the big island of Hawaii if necessary.

Once on Molokai, we'd rent a boat and cross the channel. We'd use GPS and an accurate chart to land as close to Charles's compound as possible. Then we'd make our way on foot and confront Pat.

"Is this something you and I can do by ourselves?" I asked.

"I plan to have help," he answered.

"What kind of help?"

"Do you remember Tony and Lance, the two men that accompanied us when we took both boats around Puerto Rico?"

I nodded. They were the two ex-military guys that worked for Charles. I didn't know a whole lot about either of them, but they certainly looked the part and were very loyal to Charles. If Reid could get them to meet us in Molokai, and assuming we could rent a suitable boat, then it might just work.

As we discussed his plan, I thought of something that could be a major problem. Two things actually.

"So what about the CIA?" I asked.

Reid shrugged. "What about them?"

"Once our passports are scanned at whichever airport we use between here and Hawaii, the CIA is likely to find out about it."

"If they're looking for us," Reid answered.

"We should assume they are," I replied.

He thought for a moment. "We'll just hope the CIA has bigger fish to fry and we stay under their radar until we can confront Pat. She's the mission, not them."

That seemed reasonable. I asked my second question."What about Marta?"

Reid looked right at me. I could tell that he hadn't thought about her. His jaw tightened. Finally, he leaned closer and said, "I doubt she has access to a private plane and will have to take a commercial flight."

"So?"

"So we might have a couple of days head start." He smiled, relaxed, and leaned back. I thought about it and agreed.

Later that evening, Jane's phone rang. It was Elouise. She had landed in San Juan and was on her way. She also confirmed Pat was indeed on Oahu.

CHAPTER 65

Reid texted back, saying we needed to get to Molokai immediately, if not sooner. He also inquired if Tony and Lance would be available to meet us in Molokai as soon as possible.

It was close to midnight when Elouise arrived at the marina. She had rented a car and driven herself.

Jane had gone back to bed, apologizing for being so wiped out. It was no surprise. She'd nursed Charles 24-7 since he'd taken sick. The surprise was that she wasn't sick too.

Reid and I stayed awake. We were anxious to see Elouise.

Elouise met Reid at the gate and followed him back to *The Aquaholic.* Her eyes betrayed her fatigue, but she seemed really happy to finally be here.

I helped her aboard. She opened her carry-on and handed me a new passport. She had one for Reid and Charles too.

"How did you get this so fast?" I asked, thumbing through it.

"Ashley went to *The Lady Anne* and found all of your passports," she said. "Since there's no mail service in or off the island, we scanned each page of each passport and sent them to a friend of mine, who took the scans and duplicate pictures and then spent the whole day at the passport office."

I was impressed and thanked her and gave her a hug.

"Did you arrive on Charles's plane?" Reid asked.

She shook her head. "His plane is grounded in Hawaii. It was faster to take a commercial flight directly from Newark than to wait for clearance to leave Hawaii."

"So we'll be flying a commercial airline to Hawaii?" I asked.

"You're both booked on the early morning flight from San Juan to Kahului with one stop at Dallas/Fort Worth," she replied, pulling some papers from her bag. "You'll be in Maui before dinnertime tomorrow with ninety minutes to connect to Ho'olehua, Molokai."

She smiled and handed me the papers. "You're booked on that second flight as well. You'll land at seven o'clock p.m. - Aloha Time."

I looked at the papers. They had her handwritten notes. We didn't have boarding passes but we did have confirmation numbers, so that should work. I was astonished she could do all of this between landing in San Juan and arriving here three hours later.

Elouise frowned. "I apologize that you'll be in coach, but that's all that was available. Will that be okay?"

"That's fine," Reid answered. "Thank you very much."

"Yes, thank you for booking all of this," I added.

"Not a problem," she replied, smiling. "I called in a favor from a co-worker in New York. He did all of the heavy lifting. I just wrote down flight times and confirmation numbers."

I was impressed at her resourcefulness and told her so. She was very modest.

I hid my disappointment that we'd be on a commercial flight. If Elouise was able to get last minute seats, then Marta might be able to as well. But how would Marta get from whichever airport she landed at in Hawaii to Oahu? And what about our passports triggering some state department no-fly list? I wasn't as confident as Reid that we were of little interest to the CIA.

"Were you able to contact Tony and Lance?" Reid asked.

"Funny you picked those two," she replied.

Reid looked at her but didn't comment. I was curious why she thought it was funny, but I kept quiet, held my breath, and waited.

"Lance is already on Oahu, staying at Charles's place to watch over everyone."

"And Tony?" Reid asked.

Elouise's answer was fast. "Tony was with me in New York and is on his way to Hawaii as we speak."

I breathed a sigh of relief. Having the two men Reid wanted in place before we arrived would certainly give us an advantage over Marta. I was thankful that lady luck was with us.

"You don't happen to have an extra phone in there do you?" Reid asked.

She grinned and, after a bit of searching, pulled two phones from her bag. She handed us each one and said, "The numbers you'll need have already been added. Charge them while you're waiting in airports."

She then handed me a small paper sack. It contained two bagels. "I thought you might need a snack. Those are fresh from New York."

She asked if we had enough cash for incidentals. We told her we were flat broke and having to borrow from Jane. Elouise smiled and handed us a handful of bills, mostly hundreds.

Reid told her we'd repay her at our earliest convenience. She laughed.

Wow. Elouise was excellent. Whatever her salary was, she was absolutely worth it.

CHAPTER 66

We didn't have any time to waste as it was a two and a half hour drive to the airport. Reid and I packed a few things and then took off. We left Jane a note in case she woke up before Elouise returned.

Elouise never asked what the urgency was, and we didn't volunteer our reasons. She drove, assuring us she was awake. I would have liked to have seen the island from the road, but it was pitch-black.

We had no problems at the San Juan airport. Our new passports worked fine, and we passed through security without a hitch. I scoped out the security line, the concourse, the gate area, and the boarding line as we went. I didn't see Marta. Reid didn't see her either.

We were soon on the plane but not seated together. My

seat was in front, and I kept an eye on everyone boarding. I never did see Marta.

Once in flight, I fell asleep and slept nearly the whole way, even missing the snack cart. I ate Elouise's bagel dry. It was delicious.

When we changed planes in Texas, I thought I saw Marta, but it was a different young woman who just happened to have black hair, muscles, and wore loud spandex. I told myself I was getting paranoid and to chill.

Reid and I weren't able to sit together on that flight either, but like before, I slept most of the way. I guess it was my body's way of telling me I was more tired than I realized.

When we changed planes in Maui, Reid texted Tony to let him know where we were. He got a thumbs-up back.

It was a really short flight to Molokai. Tony was waiting for us. He gave me a lei and welcomed us to "The Friendly Isle." We didn't have to wait for any checked bags and were soon in a taxi on the way to Kaunakakai Harbor.

Molokai was certainly different than the image I had of Hawaiian Islands. There were no traffic lights, no tall buildings, and no luxury resorts that we could see.

Tony explained there were limited boats available for rent here. He thought he might have to buy a boat, but he finally found a local fishing boat captain who would take us across. That's where we were headed now—to meet Captain Fred Miller and *The Ahi Slayer*.

Captain Miller was in his late eighties or maybe even older. His face was weathered and wrinkled. His beard was white. White hair stuck out of his worn captain's hat. His skin was too tan and covered with age spots. He was very slender and shorter than me.

If I Googled images for an "old salt," his picture likely would have come up first.

He told us a small craft warning had been in effect yesterday but was lifted this morning. He said it might be rough in some places but assured us not to be concerned—*The Ahi Slayer* was not a small craft. She was seasoned and completely seaworthy. He also mentioned his first mate had called in sick, so it would just be the four of us. He said that he'd need some assistance getting clear of the slip.

Reid told him he was happy to crew for him. So was I.

The Ahi Slayer was an older boat, forty-eight feet long and surprisingly clean. Pride of ownership was obvious. I wondered if Captain Miller was the original owner.

Like most sport fishing boats I had seen, it had outriggers and a flybridge. There was a small inflatable dinghy on the deck behind the fighting chair. A greasy, white, six-horsepower outboard motor was tied by the transom. There was a portable gas can, three orange life jackets, which we put on, and three small paddles on the deck.

"For getting us ashore in the dinghy?" Reid asked, pointing. Tony nodded.

Before we pushed off, Captain Miller asked point-blank if we were positive we wanted to take that little dinghy through "that danged fog that had paralyzed the entire island."

Reid assured him we knew what we were doing. Captain Miller shook his head. "Okay, your funeral."

Reid and I worked the dock lines and cast us off. Captain Miller was at the flybridge. Once clear of the slip, he invited me to join him, promising the view was better up there. I could smell diesel fumes when we backed up, so I was eager to move.

Reid said he'd handle everything left and to go ahead. I obliged him and climbed up to the flybridge.

We soon cleared the harbor. The engines weren't as loud up here and Captain Miller was right: the view of the coastline was spectacular—lush green forests, steep sea cliffs, and waterfalls that cascaded into the ocean.

He watched as Reid coiled the dock lines and stowed the fenders. He was impressed that Reid knew what to do without being told. Reid also tied a line to the dinghy so it wouldn't accidentally blow away.

Reid asked Captain Miller if he was finished with him. He said he was and he'd holler if he needed him. I thanked Captain Miller for the ride and then left him alone at the helm.

Tony motioned Reid and I inside the salon.

The door leading to the forward cabin was closed. Above it was a crudely lettered sign: Den of Iniquity.

I wondered if the old guy could still get it up. If he couldn't, that sign seemed out of place. Or maybe it was just old, like he was.

I hoped I wouldn't need to use the head, which was

undoubtedly behind that door too. If old Captain Miller really did consider his cabin to be a "Den of Iniquity," I wanted to keep out. I wasn't in the mood to see any graphic or lewd decorations.

There was a chart on the table. Tony pointed to our destination.

"What's your plan for the fog?" Reid asked.

"Lance will be waiting for us at a safe landing spot," Tony replied. "I've got his GPS coordinates. The fog extends about a half a mile out, getting heavier the closer you get to land."

Reid studied the chart. "So Captain Miller will drop us off and we'll take the dinghy through the fog to Lance's coordinates. Is that your plan?"

Tony confirmed that it was.

"How will we find each other in heavy fog?" I asked.

Tony smiled. "Lance and I both have radios." That sounded pretty good.

Tony continued, "Lance will also make sound signals that we can home in on."

That sounded pretty good too. We adjourned the meeting and went out on deck.

CHAPTER 67

The open water was getting rougher, but *The Ahi Slayer* pounded right through the waves, sending sheets of spray all over the bow and the salon windows. Captain Miller slowed for the larger ones and then resumed his desired speed.

Reid was grinning. Tony looked a little uptight. I was glad we had the life jackets on.

I saw a cruise ship, but it wasn't very close. One helicopter flew past in the distance. I couldn't tell if it was military or not. Other than that and some birds, the Molokai Channel was pretty empty.

The engine noise was giving me a headache, so I returned to the salon. The engine still rumbled and vibrated, but the salon was a tad quieter, just a tad. Tony followed me, but Reid climbed up to the flybridge to be with Captain Miller.

There was a GPS display in the salon, so I took a reading

and plotted our position. We were right on course, about halfway there.

I kept watching out the windows. So did Tony. The boat had windshield wipers, but I couldn't find how to switch them on. Neither could Tony, so we just peered through the water droplets.

Tony was really quiet, and besides asking a little about how sick Charles was, didn't have much to say. "At least he's not telling lame sailor jokes," I said to myself, suppressing a grin.

Every so often the boat would smash really hard into a wave. Everything shook. I hoped *The Ahi Slayer* wouldn't start taking on water. My fears were fueled when the automatic bilge pump cycled on. I saw the indicator light and heard it run.

I was ready to go topside when the pump cycled off a few seconds later. "That's probably normal," I said to myself.

I forced myself to stay calm. I was sure that since I had survived a "suicide sail" around Cape Horn, I wasn't going to die in The Channel of Bones in an old sport fishing boat with super senior Captain Miller.

At least I hoped not.

As we inched closer on the chart, I thought about my inevitable confrontation with Pat.

Try as I might, I just couldn't understand what Pat had done with "advanced problem-solving techniques" to warrant the aliens wanting her stopped "permanently and quickly."

Engulfing an entire island in fog could certainly be viewed

as an abuse of power, but the alien's remedy, which implied death, seemed awfully harsh. And even that assumed the fog was Pat's doing, which I suspected it was, but as of now, couldn't prove.

That did not sound at all like the Pat I knew. What she had done to *The USS Fields* was an act of desperation. Her alternative was to be taken prisoner and held as a terrorist. I couldn't blame her for sending the CIA, the NSA, and the Navy destroyer back in time.

I asked myself if I would have done the same thing had I been in her position. I gave myself mixed answers. Sometimes I thought I would. Usually I didn't think so.

As for Pat sending Reid, Vee, me, Dreamgirl, and the others aboard *The Aquaholic* back in time, I chalked that up to her thinking her friends and her lover were tossing her aside, blaming her for what she had done to the Navy.

Creating fog thick enough to engulf and shut down an entire island was a puzzle—and impressive. I wondered if Pat had figured that out on her own or if Mo had helped her.

If Mo had helped her, why was he allowing their fog creation to disrupt so many lives?

I wondered how the plastic magnet was coming along. Even if it was finished and working, the aliens had given me the plans to construct it to clean up our oceans. I didn't think the aliens would be upset with Pat for that.

The more I thought about it, the more I wondered if Pat had done something else besides creating fog.

Her ability to initiate the time portal had been taken away

by the aliens. I seriously doubted Pat was smart enough to have figured out time travel, even with Mo's help.

But if she had, that would certainly be justification for the aliens wanting her stopped. The ability to go back and forth in time would be too great a temptation for the average person not to abuse.

I also thought about Marta. I was sure she would kill Pat if she got the chance. Reid and I were trying to outrun Marta to Hawaii, trying to get to Pat first.

"For what reason?" I asked myself.

Marta would kill Pat because of Vee. We would kill Pat because of the aliens.

Death by Marta or death by us. Yikes! What a choice.

My headache was exacerbated by the combination of a noisy boat and perplexing thoughts. I was sure that Captain Miller had aspirin onboard, but I didn't feel like getting up to go ask him.

I noticed that Tony was staring out the steamy, water-streaked salon window. "See something?" I asked.

"There's fog ahead," he replied, pointing. "That has got to be Oahu."

CHAPTER 68

I wiped the condensation away for a clearer look. Tony was right. Dead ahead, the clouds and blue skies had been replaced with a skyscraper-sized wall of steel-gray fog.

The fog pulsated and oozed mist, like it was alive. It went as far as I could see, hugging the ocean and absorbing the sunlight.

The reality of the fog hit me. To hear about it on the news was one thing. To actually be this close was disconcerting, to say the least.

The sheer height of the thick fog was the perfect backdrop for a fifties sci-fi movie. A small fishing boat approaching a seemingly impenetrable barrier of fog. All that was missing were prehistoric flying creatures . . . and aliens.

Tony moved away from the window. He shook his head

but didn't say anything. I plotted our current position. We had arrived at our coordinates.

The boat slowed. I made my way aft. Tony followed me. Reid was untying the dinghy. Captain Miller came down from the flybridge and looked at his watch. "Right on schedule, even in these conditions," he said. "Am I good or what?"

I smiled. He smiled back.

Reid untied the dinghy. He gave me the bow line, telling me not to let go. He and Tony slid the dinghy over the transom into the water. Reid placed the outboard, gas can, and paddles closer to the stern.

Reid climbed into the dinghy. His weight made it pull harder at its line, so I cleated the bitter end in case it jerked free.

Tony got the motor into position and then, timing the waves, passed it over to Reid. I was concerned he might drop it, but he manhandled it into position. Once it was fastened, Tony sent the gas can, fuel hose, and paddles across. A few minutes later, Reid had the engine running.

Tony went back into the salon and returned with a backpack and the big chart. He passed them over to Reid.

"What's in here?" Reid asked.

"A compass, airhorn, two flashlights, radio, and GPS," Tony replied.

"Then I'd say we're ready," Reid said.

Captain Miller took the line from me and pulled the dinghy in close.

When Reid climbed into the dinghy, he had made it look easy. Now that it was my turn, it looked scary.

The dinghy was rising and falling as *The Ahi Slayer* did, but the dinghy suddenly looked very unstable. Reid must have noticed my trepidation because he moved toward me and offered his hand.

I climbed up on the transom. Tony held my hand and Captain Miller put his hands on my waist. For an ancient mariner, his hands were surprisingly strong.

I stepped down into the dinghy, grabbing Reid's hand on the way. Captain Miller let go. The dinghy tipped under my weight. Tony let go. I immediately sat down and grabbed onto the light line that was strung around the top of the dinghy.

Captain Miller uncleated the bow line and held us manually while Tony came aboard, then he tossed me the bow line. I caught it with one hand, holding on tightly with my other.

Reid applied a little throttle, heading us away from *The Ahi Slayer*.

Captain Miller hollered that he'd wait for one hour. If we didn't return, he'd head back to Molokai. Reid, Tony, and I looked at our watches simultaneously. Reid waved and shouted thank you.

I wondered how Captain Fred Miller would dock *The Ahi Slayer*, but I figured he had most likely done it alone more than once.

Reid was aft, operating the outboard motor. He positioned me and Tony forward, one on each side, saying he needed our weight in the bow. I grinned and told him to watch it. He grinned back.

Reid folded the chart so the section he wanted was on top. Tony passed him the compass and a flashlight. Reid took a compass bearing and slowly turned until the dinghy was facing the fog.

As he did, a wave smashed into the bow, spraying me. The salt water stung my eyes. I tasted saltiness and wiped my lips. The dinghy rose up and down. A little water pooled on the floor. I held on tighter.

Tony kept the radio, the other flashlight, and the GPS unit but handed me the airhorn. He told me to familiarize myself with its operation so that I could use it with my eyes closed. There was only one button so I pushed it. That thing was so loud that I jumped. Tony grinned. So did Reid.

Tony put his paddle behind his legs. It looked like a good idea, so I copied him. Reid pinned his paddle with his foot.

Reid gave a thumbs-up. I returned it. So did Tony.

Reid accelerated toward the fog, checking the compass and adjusting his course. Tony radioed Lance, telling him we were only a few hundred yards from penetrating the fog and to stand by.

Lance acknowledged. Reid kept the power steady. The dinghy bounced over the waves, heading right at the looming fog.

Even without a small craft warning in place, this suddenly seemed like a really bad idea.

CHAPTER 69

The fog swallowed us whole. In the span of a few seconds, our visibility was zero. Reid slowed down. Without any visual reference, I got scared. This was too much like the time portal.

Tony radioed Lance, telling him we were in the fog. Lance acknowledged. It was an odd feeling being able to hear a conversation but not see anything but a blanket of gray.

"Can you see the compass?" I asked.

"Barely," Reid replied. "Even with the light. Tony, it's up to you. Tell me you can read the GPS."

"Barely," Tony replied. "But yes."

"How are we doing?" Reid asked.

"Angle just a bit to the left."

"Aye, aye," Reid responded.

I felt us change direction but still couldn't see anything.

"Call out direction changes and distance," Reid said.

"Fourteen hundred yards, hold your course," Tony replied.

When we were one thousand yards out, Tony radioed Lance that we were going to blow our airhorn. Lance said okay. I pushed the button three times, signaling three long blasts.

It seemed even louder in the fog. I hoped Lance heard it.

"Did you hear that?" Tony radioed.

"Negative," Lance replied.

Reid was surprised at that answer. He guessed the moist fog was obscuring the sound. At seven hundred yards, I tried again.

This time the response was yes.

Lance radioed it was his turn. We all listened intently. All any of us could hear was the motor.

Reid stopped the engine. I hoped he wouldn't have to try and start it again in basically zero visibility.

Tony radioed Lance to try again. We heard one long blast. It sounded a long way away, but at least we heard it.

Tony confirmed we could hear him and instructed Lance to signal at thirty second intervals.

"Paddle toward the sound, but keep an eye on the GPS," Reid told us.

Paddling in zero visibility was challenging at best. I couldn't see where we were headed and I couldn't even see Reid or Tony paddling.

Tony called out his strokes, and I matched him. Reid steered. Lance's signal was getting closer. Then I heard another sound: breaking waves.

I was sure our puny little dinghy would get flipped or we'd smash into a rock and capsize.

Tony and I stopped paddling long enough for him to consult the GPS. "Two hundred yards," he stated.

Lance's signal sounded closer than that. I wondered if Lance was standing right at the water's edge. If he was standing back very far, I feared we would run aground prematurely.

I tried to remember if the chart had indicated any reefs. Climbing out of a stuck dingy onto a sharp reef would be dangerous.

I sounded my airhorn again—three short blasts. Tony said that I needed to warn him before blasting away. He said I had startled him so much that he nearly dropped his paddle. I think he was joking, but I apologized anyway.

Lance signaled back with the same pattern. He was close.

I could feel the waves propelling us forward. I heard them hitting the beach. Reid said he was tilting the motor up and to paddle harder. I sat the airhorn down and then dug in, pulling with all of my strength on my paddle. I hoped it wouldn't snap.

I felt my paddle scrape the bottom. The back of the dinghy hit something and suddenly stopped. The little dinghy began to turn sideways. I was sure the next wave would flip us.

I felt Reid climb out and heard him splash into the water.

A second later, Tony hollered for Lance and then jumped out too.

"What's happening?" I asked, wondering if I was supposed to climb out with them.

"It's not very deep," Reid answered. "Climb out and help us."

I gingerly slid over the side. The water was cool. The receding wave tried to drag my feet backwards. I tried steading myself against the dinghy, but it simply pushed away.

I heard splashing coming right at us.

"Lance, is that you?" Tony asked.

It was. Reid directed Tony and Lance to the other side. The plan was to hoist the dinghy on the count of three and carry/drag it ashore.

The next wave tried to knock me over, but I remained standing. The dinghy bounced all around, but I held onto the little rope.

Reid counted to three and we lifted the boat and headed ashore. I stumbled a few times but did my best to keep up with the guys.

As we cleared the water, the sand was wet and tried to suck my shoes off. The dinghy was suddenly heavier, but we kept going. Finally, the ground felt firm.

There was no visibility ashore either. I hoped I wouldn't kick any rocks or walk into a palm tree. We finally put the dinghy down. I wondered how we'd find it in the fog if we needed it again.

"Aloha," Lance said, his booming voice startling me. "Welcome to Oahu."

CHAPTER 70

Tony and Lance both marked our current location in their respective GPS units.

"Is the whole island covered in fog?" I asked.

"There are three places on the island over three thousand feet elevation," Lance answered. "Those are your best bets to get above the fog."

"Is it heavy like this everywhere?" Reid asked.

"It's like this near the coast," Lance said. "But sometimes it's lighter inland, toward the center."

My mind reeled. Most of an entire island covered in thick fog below three thousand feet. If Pat was responsible, how did she manage it? I suddenly had an important question.

"How are we going to find Charles's compound?"

Lance answered. "I just came from there and marked my

route in my GPS. There's a road about a quarter of a mile from here. We'll use the GPS to find the road."

"Then what?" Reid asked.

"Then we walk."

"How far?" I asked.

"Two point two miles," Lance replied. "Charles's compound lies in an area between two bases, one Air Force, one Marine. This was the most strategic landing spot."

I wondered if Reid would say anything about wanting to see the Marine base, since he used to be a Marine. He didn't.

I was secretly glad we were only about two miles away. Going that far, by foot, in heavy fog would be challenging enough. Any farther might take too long as I was still worried about Marta.

"I've got a length of rope," Lance announced. "I want you three to grab on to it. I'll take point. Tony can bring up the rear."

I envisioned a line of young school kids, holding onto a rope and following their teacher on a field trip. It seemed childish yet, given the circumstances, incredibly practical.

We got lined up and when the rope pulled, I started walking. It felt like we were still on sand. I couldn't see Reid, who was only a few feet ahead of me. I just went slow and hoped I wouldn't trip.

Lance called out there were rocks ahead. I felt for them with one foot before moving the other, taking small, hesitant steps. He said he was stopping and to join him.

Reid and I caught up to Lance. Tony caught up to me.

Lance aimed his flashlight at the ground just ahead. Tony aimed his light forward as well. The lights were bright, but the fog absorbed most of it. However, some rocks were slightly visible.

They were large, low, and pretty flat. Lance stepped up on the first on. The rest of us followed. We kept going, nice and slow.

Once we cleared the rocks, we reached a paved road. We moved to the center. Lance checked his GPS and then we proceeded, holding onto the rope and following the yellow line as best we could. I hoped we wouldn't get hit by a car.

After about ten minutes of walking in silence, I asked Reid if he knew any fog jokes.

"As a matter of fact," Reid replied, "I do."

I waited, wondering if I'd regret my question.

"What happens when the fog lifts over Los Angeles?"

"I don't know," I replied.

"UCLA." I didn't get it until he spelled it out. Then I groaned.

"Quiet, you two," Lance scolded. "We need to stay quiet and listen for vehicles. Did you forget that we're walking down the center of a road?"

"Sorry," I said sheepishly. After Lance's chastising, Reid and I remained quiet.

We walked for about an hour. Thankfully, we didn't see or hear any vehicles. I couldn't imagine anyone intentionally driving in this stuff.

Without a flashlight, visibility was less than three inches. If

I touched my nose with the palm of my hand or put my watch almost against my eye, I could see it. Any farther away than that, forget it.

Lance signaled we would be turning onto another street. I just followed the rope. We walked another thirty minutes and then turned again.

If it hadn't been for the GPS and Lance knowing where he was going, we might as well have been wandering around in the dark.

I followed Lance another twenty minutes before he turned again. Five minutes later, in a falsetto voice, he announced, "We have arrived at our destination. The route guidance is finished."

CHAPTER 71

I remembered that Charles's compound was in a gated community. I didn't remember the gate code but was sure Lance did.

"You can get us through the gate, right?" I asked.

"Yes, ma'am," he replied. "Through the gate and past security."

"What security?" I knew there was a main gate. I didn't remember anything else.

"There are roving security patrols," Lance said.

"Because of the fog?" I asked, not sure why the gate wouldn't be sufficient.

"Because of the looting," he calmly responded.

"What looting?" Reid asked.

"The fog has made some people a little crazy. Crime is up,

especially in the business districts, poor areas, and wealthier neighborhoods."

"I didn't hear anything about looting on the news," I said.

"To be expected," Lance answered. "Reports of street crime and looting would discourage tourists from ever returning."

That made sense. I was disappointed that people would freak out and resort to criminal activity just because of unexplained fog.

It suddenly occurred to me that the aliens would be observing all human behavior occurring around Pat's location. I was sorry they would be seeing some of us at our worst.

"Can't the local police or Hawaii Five-O or the National Guard keep people calm?" I asked.

"The fog has greatly increased response times. Those that can afford it have taken measures into their own hands."

We waited while Lance located a small personnel gate. He opened it and then, still holding the rope, we followed him through.

A patch of light was visible ahead. As we got closer, I could see a small canopy bathed in floodlights.

"That's the primary security checkpoint," Lance informed us. "We need to check in immediately."

There were two clean-cut, uniformed young men under the canopy. They were both armed with pistols. One had a rifle. They knew Lance but had the rest of us write our names and the reason for our visit on a clipboard.

We were issued visitor badges, which I didn't expect.

"Don't lose these," the first guard said. His tone indicated he was serious.

The other guard radioed there were four authorized persons proceeding to the Williams' compound—one female and three males. His transmission was acknowledged with "Roger that."

Lance picked up a sheet of paper. It was a diagram of the entire community. I knew where Charles's compound was and pointed it out to Reid.

We were told that bright-colored lights had been placed within sight of each other. We were to follow the proper color light until we found our location. The diagram indicated there was a green-white-green-white light right in front of Charles's place.

Reid asked if he could have a diagram. The guard nodded and gave us each one. I folded mine and put it in my pocket.

I noticed some lengths of rope coiled on the end of the table. It was the same kind of rope Lance had. Now I knew why he had it and where he had gotten it.

Lance said he'd take point again and handed out his rope. The guard advised us to stay together and follow the green lights. It was spooky. Outside of the canopy it was very dark.

We left the brightness of the canopy and followed the main road. Just as the canopy's lights faded, I could see red, yellow, green, and blue lights ahead. They were visible, but just barely.

Lance told us to head for the green light. That seemed pretty easy.

When we reached it, the next green light was visible. We headed for that one. On the way I thought of something.

"Who's staying here at Charles's place?" I asked.

"Ashley, Donna, and I are staying in the main house," Lance replied. "I was staying in the mother-in-law suite attached to the garage, but Pat took that whole building over and kicked me out."

"Anyone else on the property?" Reid asked.

"The cook and groundskeeper were excused right after the fog smothered the island," Lance replied.

We reached the next green light. Across and a little past it was one green and one yellow light. A solitary green light was barely visible in the distance. That single green light became our new direction.

"You, Ashley, Donna, and Pat are four," I stated. "Where are the others?"

Lance delayed before answering. I wondered why. I was about to repeat the question when he finally answered. "Angie and Gert are staying in one of Charles's condos on the north shore."

When he didn't say anything else, I asked, "Is Mo with Gert?"

Lance didn't answer right away. It didn't seem like all that difficult of a question.

After an especially long delay, Reid asked, "Is there something you're not at liberty to tell us about Mo?"

Another slice of silence. Then, instead of Lance responding

to that, Tony chimed in, "You should speak with Gert about Mo."

Oh my, that was evasive. I wondered why. Was Mo sick? Had he and Gert broken up? Filed for divorce? Had he been caught cheating? Run afoul of looters? What had happened that Lance was basically refusing to discuss?

We continued onward in the fog in silence. We passed two more green lights, and then found the double green, double white lights we were looking for.

CHAPTER 72

"Okay, we're here," I said. "Now what?"

Reid responded. "Let's go talk to Pat."

Lance said that clothesline had been strung from a pole near the lights to the front door. That was handy. Reid found the clothesline and we followed it.

The front porch was well lit, which was good. Before we got there, Reid stopped us, saying he had something important to say. I gathered close, wanting to see his face. I was very curious.

"Pat has crossed some very powerful people," he said, keeping his voice low. "Tracy and I have been sent here to stop her."

I wasn't expecting him to tell Tony and Lance that. However, knowing Reid as well as I did, he must have a reason. I waited to see how much information he was going to divulge.

"In the event that Tracy and/or I are unsuccessful, have an accident, meet an untimely death, or mysteriously disappear, one or both of you need to finish the mission."

Reid's voice was devoid of emotion. That surprised me considering Pat was his ex-finance. I wondered if Pat's and my roles had been reversed, would Reid have spoken the same way about me?

Lance cleared his throat and said, "Interesting that you mention 'an untimely death.'"

"What do you mean?" Reid asked.

"I'm not at liberty to say, but now you definitely need all of the details about Mo," Lance answered.

"Can you give me a hint?" I asked, smiling big. I knew he couldn't see my face but hoped he could hear the sweetness in my voice.

"I've said enough." Lance didn't sound like he was smiling. Reid didn't comment.

Now I was even more intrigued. What in the hell had happened with or to Mo? Had he been killed? By Pat? Intentionally? Perhaps he had tried, unsuccessfully, to stop her from making fog shut down the island. Maybe Mo had been detained by the CIA and Pat had made the fog as a bargaining chip. My head reeled with possible scenarios.

Pat had proven capable of sending countless numbers of innocent people back in time, including me and Reid, who were in her inner circle. She was likely responsible for generating fog thick enough to close an entire island. What else had she done, or might she be planning to do?

"What exactly does 'stop her' mean?" Tony asked, interrupting my crazy, out-of-control, negative thoughts about Pat Taylor.

"It means take her life," Reid answered. He showed no emotion. He could have used the same tone and said "wash the car" or "takeout the trash."

I was shocked.

"Stop her, as in take her life." Those words echoed in my head, shaking my very soul. I knew that was what the aliens wanted us to do. Could I actually do it?

If Reid and I didn't, Marta surely would. Now Reid was telling Tony and Lance what had to be done. If Reid or I failed, he was taking out an insurance policy.

Death by one of us or by Marta. There had to be another option. I couldn't immediately think of one, but for Pat's sake, I needed to.

Wow. What an unforeseen consequence of letting Pat communicate with the aliens. I felt myself shaking. I was suddenly thankful for the fog. None of the others could see me cry.

Reid told me to follow him. He said it was time to get on with business. He instructed Lance and Tony to hang back in the shadows.

Before we left them, Tony said, "I understand, but I'm sorry. I know she is your friend." He switched off his flashlight and blended into the darkness. Lance vanished with him.

Neither had asked for an explanation for Reid's order. It made me realize there was more to what Pat had done than I imagined. I shed another tear.

Reid walked up to the porch. I wiped my eyes, sniffled softly, and followed him. I glanced back. Neither Tony nor Lance were visible. Reid rang the doorbell.

I heard a dog bark. It had to be Buster. I had missed him terribly. I wondered if he'd remember me.

Ashley opened the door. Her dark brown hair was a little longer than I remembered. She looked surprised to see us. Buster darted past, barked a friendly bark, and jumped up on Reid's legs. Buster's tail was wagging a mile a minute. Reid bent down and scratched Buster's head. Buster pressed against him, still barking and wagging.

Then Buster saw me. He started cavorting in circles and his bark went up a whole octave. He wagged his tail so hard his entire body was shaking. I was sure he was going to pee all over the porch.

I knelt down and let Buster climb on me and lick my face. He definitely remembered me. I spoke to him, telling him he was a good dog. As if understanding, he lay down on his back —an invitation to scratch his belly. After only a few scratches, he jumped up and started baying, then yelping, then barking in high *C* again. The whole time his tail was whipping side to side.

As Reid stood, Ashley hugged him so hard he nearly toppled back over. Donna appeared at the door to see why Buster was going crazy.

Donna was her usual slender self. Her hair was still a wild, fuchsia color but looked coarse and ratty. I chalked that up to chemical overprocessing.

I thought about how Candy, Bev, and Dreamgirl's hair would look after a prolonged spell in the past with no salon facilities. I questioned if the Navy personnel would still find them attractive when their dark roots showed through, but then figured any lonely man would find those three attractive, fancy hair or not.

Donna recognized us. A big smile appeared on her face. She lifted her hands high. Buster got between Donna and me and raised up on his hind legs. I picked him up. He was a little heavier than I remembered.

Holding Buster with one hand, I exchanged hugs with Donna and then Ashley. Buster squirmed so hard I thought I might drop him, so I gently put him down.

"May we come in?" Reid asked.

They ushered us in. Buster stayed right on my heels, nearly tripping me. Ashley quickly closed, then locked, the door. That seemed odd until I remembered reports of looting and the security guards patrolling the premises.

"How did you get here?" Ashley asked, smiling, obviously happy to see us.

"Where is Charles?" Donna asked, looking back toward the door.

"Is Jane with you?" Ashley wanted to know, raising her voice. "How about Elouise? How did you get here through the fog?"

"What about the rest of the crew Charles hired?" Donna asked, louder still. "Are they with you?"

Their questions were coming right and left. Donna and Ashley were talking over each other, trying to outshout the other. It reminded me of reporters trying to be picked at a press conference.

Reid held up his hands. I did too. We needed for both of them to stop talking and just listen.

Ashley and Donna exchanged glances but, thankfully, quit talking.

"Where's Pat?" Reid asked.

Before either of them could answer, I shot my hand high. A question was burning in my brain. I knew that Pat was our priority, but I needed to know something else, and I needed to know it now.

"Did something happen to Mo?" I asked.

CHAPTER 73

The way that Ashley and Donna looked at each other made me cringe. Though they hadn't said a word, their body language was unmistakable. I feared their answer.

I waited. They both looked down. I looked at Reid. His face reflected his concern.

Finally, Ashley looked up at me and swallowed. I waited, my breathing increasing.

"Mo had a heart attack," Ashley said.

"Is he alright?" Reid asked.

Ashley shook her head. "He's no longer with us," she said softly.

My energy drained. It felt like I had been hit in the stomach by a sledgehammer. Tears started to form.

Ashley moved closer and said, "I'm so sorry."

"What happened?" Reid asked softly.

Donna moved close and took one of Reid's and one of my hands. She squeezed and said, "He fell over in the shop. Pat applied CPR until the ambulance arrived, but it was too late."

"What shop?" I asked. I had stayed here before but didn't remember seeing any shop.

"That's what Pat calls part of the garage she took over," Ashley answered. There was a trace of sarcasm in her voice. Or perhaps it was resentment. I wasn't sure.

"That's where she and Mo spent most of their time," Donna confirmed. "Working."

"Working on what?" I asked. My pangs of sorrow were replaced by curiosity. Donna let go of our hands and moved back slightly.

Ashley spoke up. "Something about cell phones."

"Cell phones?" I asked.

Before I could ask any more, Donna cut me off. "They were working on your plastic magnet too," Donna said.

"Until they ran out of money," Ashley added, finishing Donna's sentence.

"Out of money?" Reid asked. "I thought Charles was funding construction of the plastic magnet."

That was my understanding as well. I waited to hear more.

Ashley cleared her throat. "Charles allocated four hundred thousand dollars to design, build, and test a prototype."

"And?" I asked. Nearly a half million dollars seemed more than sufficient to make a working device, based on the drawings I had provided, compliments of the aliens. I wondered how they had managed to spend that much and not be finished.

"They fabricated one unit but ran out of money just prior to testing," Ashley said.

Donna took over speaking. "But Charles wasn't available to allocate any more money to the next phase of the project. According to Angie, Mo, and Gert, Charles, you two, and the rest of those onboard *The Aquaholic* had been sent back in time."

"That's where we were," Reid confirmed. "Courtesy of Pat."

"We heard all the details from Angie about what Pat did. We couldn't believe it at first. We're so sorry," Donna said.

"Donna and I are really glad you got back safely," Ashley added. "Would you like to sit down? Can I get you something to eat or drink? How did you get here with the fog shutting everything down?"

Reid and I followed them to the sitting area. I said a bottle of water would be fine. So did Reid. Buster jumped up on my lap, his tail still wagging fifty miles per hour.

In between getting my face licked, I told them we had taken a fishing boat from Molokai and rendezvoused with Lance, who guided us here. Donna asked if he was outside somewhere. I nodded. I didn't mention Tony was with him.

Donna asked again about Charles. I told her that he had caught pneumonia on the journey and was in a hospital in Puerto Rico. I mentioned that Jane was with him but didn't mention he was in the ICU. She expressed sympathy but didn't press for any details.

After we had been served two cold bottles of water, Reid said, "I have some questions."

"Go ahead," Donna replied, making eye contact. "I'll try my best to answer."

"How did the ambulance get here for Mo with all of the fog?"

"Oh, that happened weeks before the fog arrived," Donna answered.

That was interesting. I pictured Mo having a heart attack. I pictured the fog arriving. I was sure Pat was responsible for creating the fog. I wondered if the time lapse between Mo's death and Pat's fog was of any significance. I remained silent. I was curious to hear what else Reid had on his mind.

"Was Mo alone with Pat when he died, or was anyone else present?"

"I'm pretty sure they were alone," Donna answered. "Gert was here with Ashley, me, and Buster. I don't remember where Angie was exactly, but I think at the condo. Lance comes and goes as he pleases, running errands and providing security, so I don't remember where he was either."

"Where is Gert now?"

"She's staying with Angie across the island. They haven't been back since the fog arrived. We think they are commiserating over their losses."

I suddenly thought of something and interrupted Reid's

next question. "Excuse me," I said. "But why did Pat get a restraining order against Angie?"

"Angie threatened to beat her up every day that her mom, Jane, remained lost back in time," Donna answered.

"Did she?" Reid asked. "Did Angie ever hit Pat?"

"Twice that I saw. The first time, she punched her pretty hard, giving her a bloody nose." Donna continued, "After the second incident, Pat called the police and pressed charges."

Donna didn't seem concerned by our questions. Ashley hung back, letting Donna answer.

"What were they working on with cell phones?" I asked.

"Something about jamming them I think," Donna replied, glancing at Ashley, who shrugged.

Reid didn't ask anything else. I wondered if he had run out of questions. Maybe he had, but I had at least two more. "How are you able to go shopping with all of this fog?"

Donna and Ashley exchanged an odd glance. I wondered what part of my question deserved the look they gave each other.

"Pat had a backup generator installed the week before the fog hit." Ashley answered this time.

"Why did she get a generator?" Reid asked, leaning forward.

"In case we lost power," Ashley replied. "She also bought shelving, refrigerators, and freezers."

"Why did Pat need shelving, refrigerators, and freezers?" I asked. "What does that have to do with jamming cell phones?"

"She got them for our emergency provisions," Ashley replied.

"We are very lucky she did that," Donna chirped. "The fog and the looting have disrupted most of the shopping on the island."

"What emergency provisions?" I asked, barely keeping up.

"Pat nearly cleaned out Costco," Donna answered next. "We've got enough food for weeks. She transformed Charles's four car garage into a warehouse. You won't recognize it."

I shook my head, hoping the pieces of what I had just heard would magically fall into place.

Reid looked right at Donna and asked, "Did Pat buy those things and go to Costco before or after the fog hit?"

"Before I think," Donna answered hesitantly.

"Definitely before the fog," Ashley said, sounding confident. "Actually, she went to Costco two days before the fog first arrived. We made fun of her when she came back driving a rental truck. But we're not laughing now."

Donna added, "Ashley and I set up shelving as fast as Pat and Lance could unload the truck. It was a serious workout."

Reid looked at me. I could tell we were thinking the same thing. Pat's preparations could only mean that she was responsible for creating the fog.

"Where is Pat now?" Reid asked.

"Probably in the garage," Donna answered.

"She's in there nearly all the time," Ashley added. "There's a small apartment adjoining the garage. We hardly see her anymore unless we need food or stuff."

Reid and I thanked them for the water and excused ourselves to another room to talk. Buster followed me, like a shadow.

"I know where that garage apartment is," I said. "I'm sure I can find it, even in this fog."

CHAPTER 74

"Before we confront Pat," Reid said, moving close and lowering his voice, "we need to agree on a plan."

I knew what the aliens expected of us—stop her permanently. When I told Reid that, he shook his head.

"I owe it to Pat to hear her side of the story," he said.

"What story?" I asked, forcing myself to talk quietly.

"I'd like to know what set her off course so severely that she sent you and me to what very well may have been our deaths."

I looked at him, trying to decide if talking or attacking first was the better option.

As if reading my mind, Reid said, "I'd also like to hear what happened to Mo, because it seems she was with him when he died."

That seemed fair enough, maybe. But Reid wasn't finished.

"We also need to know how to stop the fog, if indeed Pat is responsible for creating it."

That was a good point. It would be tragic for the island if the fog didn't dissipate after Pat was stopped. "Tragic or ironic?" I asked myself.

"So we're going to waltz up to the front door, ring the bell, and ask her about Mo's death and the fog?" I asked, tilting my head.

"More or less," Reid answered. "We'll just play it by ear."

I followed Reid back to Donna and Ashley. I hoped that talking to Pat wouldn't cause any problems between the three of them.

Buster barked when I told him to stay. If Reid and I were going to confront Pat, I didn't want the dog in the way. I wondered why Buster was here and not with Pat. After all, she knew him better than Ashley or Donna.

I told the women where we were going and to please stay until we got back.

Reid followed me out the front door. I heard it lock behind us. We hadn't gone very far when Tony stepped out of nowhere, startling me. I didn't see Lance but figured he must be close by too.

Reid told Tony we were going to talk to Pat. He wanted Tony and Lance to give us two hours. Then they were to reevaluate the situation.

Reid made Tony promise that if Reid and I didn't come back, or mysteriously disappeared, or worse, Tony and Lance needed to stop Pat. Tony nodded. The three of us looked at our watches.

We followed Tony toward the garage building, his flashlight's feeble beam leading the way.

I debated asking Tony if he or Lance had a gun I could borrow. Reid and I were unarmed. Pat had been provoked enough by both of us to send us back in time. What if she still felt that way? How would she react upon seeing me and Reid suddenly appear from the fog?

I was still royally pissed at her for sending me on a "suicide sail." Was I angry enough to shoot her when she opened the door? Murder her in cold blood? What would be the cost to satisfy the aliens? Being sentenced to life in prison? Pleading insanity and being committed to a mental hospital? Have eternal nightmares about watching her brains splatter when I pulled the trigger? Had I reached a line I couldn't cross? I dismissed the idea of asking about a gun.

I saw bright lights ahead. They were the lights on either side of the garage doors. Tony stopped and wished us success. I still didn't see Lance.

There was a regular door next to the big garage doors. Reid knocked on it. I had rehearsed in my mind what I would say to Pat, but I was suddenly drawing a blank.

The door opened. Pat looked at Reid, then at me. My heart beat faster. What would I do if she closed the door in our faces?

"Tracy? Reid?" she gasped, stepping back. She looked

stunned, our presence having caught her completely by surprise.

There was awkward silence. I wanted to cuss her out for sending us back in time . . . to die. I wasn't exactly sure how Reid felt. He should have been as livid as I was, but he was better at concealing his feelings.

Pat came outside and looked past me. "Are those sailing floozies with you?"

Her earlier look of surprise was gone. She glared right through me, waiting for my answer.

Reid shook his head and answered for me. "No floozies, just us."

Pat's glare changed to a smirk. "What took you so long to convince the aliens to return you to this time?"

Reid asked if we could come in. Pat's look changed again. Now she looked pissed.

She pointed her hand at the open door. It wasn't a welcoming gesture, but it did seem like she was inviting us in.

Reid went first. Pat turned sharply and followed him, cutting me off. I sped up and stayed right behind her. I had no desire to get locked out.

I passed her and followed Reid into the garage area. The cars had been removed. In their place were rows of industrial metal shelving.

I heard Pat slam the door behind us. Reid gave me a quizzical look. My heart rate increased. I turned slightly to look at Pat. She was shaking her head, muttering and fuming. Her face was turning red.

She stormed by and led us past the shelving. She strode

with purpose. She was headed toward the living quarters. Reid and I quickened our pace to keep up.

We passed row after row of shelving stuffed full of cases of food and supplies. There were enough supplies to outfit an expedition. I did see two workbenches which I didn't remember being there. I also counted at least four large, white freezers.

Reid and I exchanged glances. Pat was certainly prepared for an extended stay here. I wondered how long the fog was going to last. Weeks? Months? Longer?

I had another thought. What if the looters found out what was in here? Would those security guards be a sufficient deterrent against an angry mob?

We entered the living quarters and followed Pat to the kitchen area. There were more cases of food stacked in here as well. I spied cases of Spam. I wished we would have had them aboard *The Aquaholic*. Heck, if we'd have had half of the food in the garage, our passage back would have been much less stressful food-wise.

She roughly cleared some spiral notebooks from the kitchen table, leaving two calculators, a cup full of pencils, and a well-worn pink eraser.

I thought she was going to say something, but she clenched her teeth and pointed at the chairs. Reid and I took a seat. She remained standing. Her face was bright red and her hands were trembling.

"The airports are still closed. How did you get here?"

I glanced at Reid, hoping he'd answer. She looked on the

verge of losing control. I told myself to remain calm and not get provoked.

"We boated across the channel from Molokai." Reid's answer was calm and controlled.

Pat's face contorted with rage. "Why did you pick now to show up?"

Her tone was harsh.

I had a moment of clarity. The creature standing over me might have looked like the old Pat, but the Pat I knew, the one who had been my best friend, was gone. The new Pat broke my heart. I looked down and away.

"It took many months to get returned. The aliens didn't make it easy. We had to sail thousands of miles around Cape Horn, in the winter. We were only returned once we reached the Bermuda Triangle."

Reid's voice was calm. So calm it seemed out of place. But I didn't feel calm. I was alarmed by the undertone in Pat's simple question.

"Looks like you made it okay." Her tone changed from vicious to sarcastic.

I responded before Reid could. "Only some of us made it. Vee was killed."

"Oh," Pat said.

One word. That's all the response that Vee's death elicited from Pat. One word.

I was quick to reply. "Charles is in ICU in Puerto Rico, fighting double pneumonia. Jane is with him. Making the treacherous voyage through the Southern Ocean, in the winter, without suitable clothing nearly killed us all."

I took a breath. My voice shook, but I didn't really care.

"And Bev, Candy, and Dreamgirl are still stuck in the past." I spat the words at her.

Pat didn't respond. Her face showed no hint of remorse. I was frustrated. Talking to her was like talking to a rock. My hands began trembling. Her attitude was pissing me off.

Pat looked directly at me. "Did Marta die with Vee or is she with you two? Keeping out of sight? Hiding in the fog perhaps?"

You two. That's what Reid and I were now. Two persons generically. I wasn't her best friend. Reid wasn't her ex-lover. The three of us weren't the ones who got sent back in time by aliens and then returned. She had arbitrarily divided what I thought was a tightly bonded trio into "her" and "us." I felt my breathing increase. My heart began pounding its own drum solo.

I wanted to scream at her, but instead I kept my voice low. "Marta blames you for Vee's death. When she finds you, she'll likely take revenge for the suicide sail you sent us on."

I stopped, outburst over. I didn't feel better, but I was glad I had said it.

Pat looked around the kitchen. "Thanks for the heads-up. I'll be ready."

Ready. How in the hell would Pat be ready for a trained killer like Marta? The Pat I used to know overanalyzed everything. By the time Pat decided what the best move was, the funeral would be over and Marta would be defecating on Pat's grave.

I raised my hands. I was exasperated by Pat's change. I shook my head. The new Pat sucked. Was this another nightmare? I wanted to wake up—now.

Reid took my hand, squeezing it lightly. He looked at Pat. "Can I ask you a question?"

She hesitated, then nodded.

"Was the CIA waiting for you when *The Lady Anne* docked?"

My first question would have been why she sent us back in time without ever giving Reid a chance to decide who he was going to stay with—her or me. Or it might have been was she responsible for the fog surrounding the island? Reid asked something unexpected.

"Not initially. But they showed up here two days later."

Her response was so fast and so short, it felt like she had things to do and we were bothering her. I was dying to know what had happened. When Pat didn't volunteer any details, Reid asked her to continue.

"CIA and NSA agents arrived here and demanded to know what had happened to Agents Hill and Washington and *The USS Fields*."

"What did you tell them?" Reid sounded very curious and was still speaking calmly.

"I told them that I didn't know, but I wanted a complete investigation as my friends aboard *The Aquaholic* were missing as well."

I blinked, wondering where she was going with that logic. I was also surprised that she referred to us as "my friends." The irony was almost laughable.

I told her I needed a drink—a strong one. She reached into a nearby box and handed me a bottle of vodka. I took a swig, not even bothering to wait for a glass.

She continued. "The guy from the CIA said he had read the file and seen the satellite imagery. He knew I was directly involved with aliens in time travel, somehow."

I waited. I was still shaking. My heart was still pounding.

"I told them that if time travel was possible, not that I was admitting it was, why in the world would my friends go back in time when their boat was nearly out of food and fuel, not having provisioned since Panama."

Reid asked how they responded to that.

"They grumbled a little but couldn't answer me as to why *The Aquaholic* would choose to go back in time when it could have fully refueled and reprovisioned in a day or two."

"And?" Reid asked, raising an eyebrow.

"And they left. Oh sure, they kept surveillance on this place for a few weeks, but not any longer."

The way she emphasized "not any longer" was scary.

It was now crystal clear there was more to this than Pat Taylor was sharing.

"So what are you doing with cell phones?" Reid asked, abruptly changing the subject.

I hadn't forgotten about Pat sending us back in time. I couldn't imagine why Reid wasn't asking about that. I told myself to give him one or two more questions and then ask her point-blank why she did what she did—sending us on a suicide sail to die in the past.

She jerked her head around so fast I thought I heard a little pop. The way she looked at Reid, and then me, was frightening. Pat's eyes showed rage, the look of a vicious predator. I tensed up. Reid's simple question had certainly hit a nerve.

Pat exhaled, looked around the kitchen again, and then leaned back in her chair. The maniacal look in her eyes was gone.

"Have you talked to the CIA?" Her voice was calm, but her eyes were narrowed and focused.

Reid shook his head.

"Were you tailed from Molokai?"

I shook my head. "Not unless they followed our fishing boat in a submarine."

She leaned forward, put her elbow on the table, and rested her chin on her hand. "What did you hear about cell phones?"

"Only a vague reference that you and Mo were working on something about jamming cell phones," Reid answered.

Pat raised her head. Her face tightened for a second. "Clearly you've spoken with Donna and Ashley."

"They told us you were here," I answered.

"What else did they tell you?" Her eyes twitched, and her posture stiffened. Pat's anger was building. Reid saw it too.

"Never mind them," Reid said quietly. "Tell me about your work with cell phones."

Pat exhaled, leaned back in her chair, and closed her eyes. She didn't say anything. I waited. She was taking deep breaths. She remained silent, obviously thinking about how to answer Reid's question.

Two or three minutes went by. The kitchen was quiet. I turned my head slowly and faced Reid. I opened my mouth but didn't speak. I raised my fingers. I didn't know what to do. I didn't know how long we should wait before saying something. I knew the clock was ticking on our backup plan with Tony and Lance.

I jumped a little when Pat finally spoke.

"Oahu gets about a half a million tourists a month." Her voice was calm. She had suppressed whatever anger she displayed earlier.

Everyone knew Hawaii was a popular tourist destination. I loved it here. What did that have to do with cell phones?

I waited for her to continue.

"Tourists are so addicted to their cell phones, they have become unacceptably rude."

She took a quick breath and continued. "Everywhere you go, people are either talking or texting. In restaurants, in shops, on the beach, fucking everywhere."

I had to agree with her. Once I nearly hit a pedestrian who was talking on his phone and walked right in front of my car without even looking. What really frosted me about that guy was that he had the balls to flip me off, as if it was somehow my fault that I squealed to a stop a few inches from hitting him.

"Do you remember the device I constructed to activate the alien's time portal?" she continued.

Reid nodded. So did I. I would never forget her aiming that thing with the three radios with their foil antennas at *The USS Fields* and sending it back in time. She had also used it on us.

"I was sure I could improve on those crude foil antennas to concentrate a signal that would interfere with a cell phone's operation."

"You mean jam them?" Reid asked.

"Exactly." Pat smiled.

I kept listening.

"It took two eighty-hour weeks to design and another month to build, but Mo and I succeeded. We developed a tool that not only jammed cell phones, it rendered them inoperable, useless, non-repairable, kaput."

She smiled again. "I can't tell you how many phones we destroyed in the testing phase, but as they say, you can't make an omelet without breaking a few eggs."

She now seemed lighthearted, like the old Pat. But if she had aimed a signal at my phone and broke it, I'd have been mad as hell.

CHAPTER 77

Pat continued. "We tested it, perfected it, miniaturized it, concealed it in my purse, and put it to use."

It was easy to see that Pat was proud of what she and Mo had accomplished. I had a bad feeling her "cell phone killer" story was going to end poorly.

Reid leaned forward. "What do you do with your device?" His tone was stern.

"I stop people from being disruptive with their phone in public." There was no emotion in her voice or on her face.

Her choice of words made me cringe. Was "stop people" different than rendering a cell phone inoperable?

"When I see a family at dinner on vacation and they are all texting but not talking to each other, I aim my purse at them, push a secret button, and watch as they try and figure out why all of their phones suddenly quit working."

The way she said it was almost humorous. I could envision what she so accurately described actually happening. But destruction of another's private property wasn't humorous. It was wrong. And expensive.

It was not Pat's place to decide how a vacationing family spent their dinnertime. Just because texting was wrong to her didn't make it wrong for that family.

"So you disable cell phones?" Reid asked. "That's it?"

I wondered about that too. Disabling a cell phone didn't seem enough abuse of "advanced alien problem-solving techniques" to warrant the aliens wanting her "stopped permanently." I was positive there was more.

All I could think of was her creation of the fog. That didn't seem bad enough to warrant her death either. I was puzzled.

I watched Pat closely and waited. Waited to see if she had anything else to say. Reid watched closely too.

As Pat shifted her gaze between us, she wiped a bead of sweat from her brow. Was it the heat? Or was it something else?

After a few minutes of silence, I was ready to change the subject. I figured it was time to know why she sent *The Aquaholic* back in time. I thought about how to phrase my question so as not to make her angry.

Pat looked down and suddenly began to cry. It was so unexpected, Reid and I stared. "I didn't mean to kill him. It was an accident." Pat was babbling so much she was hard to understand.

"Kill who?" Reid asked, reaching for Pat's hand.

I moved closer and, using my most soothing voice, asked, "Pat, did you kill a tourist?"

She looked at me, then Reid, then back at me. In between sobs she managed to blurt out, "I killed Mo."

I froze. I must have heard Pat wrong. I distinctly remembered Ashley saying that Mo had died of a heart attack. One of them was wrong.

Reid went and got the box of tissues from the counter. Pat wiped her eyes and then blew her nose.

After a few minutes, she stopped crying. She hung her head.

"I thought Mo had a heart attack." Reid's voice was very kind and brimming with compassion.

"He did." Pat took another tissue and blew her nose again.

"Then you didn't kill him." I tried hard to sound positive. Secretly I hoped that was true. Deep down, I wasn't sure.

"I made a modification to our signal disruption machine." Pat coughed and then cleared her throat. She paused and eyed another tissue but didn't take one.

"When I increased the power, the signal did more than overload circuitry." She paused, took a breath, and then continued. "The signal stopped the heart of whoever was in the path of the frequency beams."

"And Mo somehow got caught in the beam?" Reid's tone was soft and calming. "Assuming everything you said is true, Mo's death was an accident."

"I should have foreseen the more powerful signal might cause collateral damage." Pat sniffled. "I blame myself."

She used her hands and then another tissue to wipe her eyes. I waited for her to compose herself. I needed to hear the whole story.

"I called 911 and tried to revive him, but it was no use. The paramedics pronounced him dead at the scene."

The three of us sat there, not speaking. Except for Pat's occasional sniffling, it was strangely quiet.

I tried to remember what she had said earlier. They had increased the power but Mo got in the way. Now he was dead. Was labeling his death "collateral damage" a way to lessen her responsibility for what had happened?

Mo was one of the smartest people I knew. He deserved much more than dying because of a science experiment gone terribly wrong. I bowed my head. I was both crestfallen and speechless.

Then I looked at Reid. I had a pesky thought that I tried to dismiss but couldn't. I wondered if Gert knew the truth.

CHAPTER 78

Seeing her cry, I almost felt bad for Pat. But my pity was short-lived. It was time to ask the question.

"Why did you send *The Aquaholic* back in time?" I tried hard to sound sincere and not convey the lividness that was boiling inside me.

She leaned away. The look she gave me was strange. Surely she must have anticipated either me or Reid asking that question. Why the strange look?

She picked up her used tissues. After depositing them in a nearby wastebasket, she went over to a cupboard and got three glasses. She returned to the table, picked up the vodka bottle, and poured three shots.

Reid and Pat downed theirs, but I waited. I wanted a clear head to hear what she had to say. Depending on her reasons, I knew I could drink later.

She reached for the bottle but Reid moved it out of her reach. "I'd really like to hear why you did what you did."

He sounded so sweet. Much sweeter than I was feeling. Pat had nearly killed all of us. What could she possibly say to make either of us forgive her? My short answer was nothing.

Pat looked into Reid's eyes. "I knew that you were going to sail away with Tracy and those other women to escape the CIA."

I figured Reid would respond to that. I was very curious what his answer would be. I didn't remember that he had ever said one way or the other whether he wanted to go with me or stay with her.

During sex, he sometimes told me he loved me. Now was his chance to prove it. All he had to do was tell her that he had chosen me. That was it. I watched them watching each other, waiting for Reid's answer.

Reid stayed quiet, his gaze never straying from hers.

Pat broke the silence. "I didn't want you to go with those other women. I don't mind sharing you with Tracy, but I can't compete with Dreamgirl, let alone Candy, Bev, Vee, and maybe even Marta."

Reid didn't speak. He just listened. I hoped he was formulating a response. I hoped it was coming soon. After all, the clock was ticking.

Pat looked at me and then back at Reid. Her face was changing. Her eyes were narrowing. Whatever sweetness she had exuded when gazing into her ex-lover's eyes was quickly being replaced by something else. Something less sweet.

Then she blew up. "I couldn't bear the thought of not having you with me, so I decided that if I couldn't have you, you could die with those skanks."

Reid quickly glanced at me. Then he looked back at Pat. "You guessed that I was going to choose them over you and that infuriated you so much that you turned the time portal on us?"

"I figured that Tracy would immediately explain what had happened and ask the aliens to return you." Pat looked and sounded sincere.

"I did," I said. "They wouldn't."

She looked at me. "When you didn't come back right away, I figured that out," she said dryly. "Tell me, why did they require you to sail all the way to the Bermuda Triangle?"

I had a ready answer. "They wanted us to reflect on the consequences of your actions."

"What?" Pat's tone indicated surprise at the speed and substance of my answer.

"The aliens who returned us told us you were abusing the 'problem-solving techniques' they showed you," I said. "Do you think that jamming cell phones was what they meant?"

She slowly looked around the kitchen. Nothing had changed. I wondered what she was looking for or expecting to see. A few seconds later, an odd look appeared on her face. She was holding something back. I knew there was more about to be revealed. I swallowed and braced myself.

"Mo's death, as unfortunate as it was, gave me the ability

to right a flaw in this country's criminal justice system." Her tone was level and unemotional.

I glanced at Reid again. Where did that come from? Now I was really confused. And intrigued.

"Did you know that out of one thousand armed robberies, less than twenty-five of the perpetrators will be incarcerated?"

I shook my head.

"And out of the same number of sexual assaults, fewer than five of the rapists will ever see the inside of a prison cell."

I didn't know that either, but I kept listening, waiting to see where she was headed with her facts.

"Of those sex offenders unlucky enough to serve hard time, the average sentence is less than ten years and the actual time a convicted rapist spends behind bars is less than half that."

"What's your point?" Reid asked.

"The victim will need therapy and have nightmares for the rest of her life, but the bad guy spends less than sixty months in jail and while he's in there, gets three meals a day and better medical care than any of the homeless veterans who fought for their country."

I wasn't sure what to say. This was the first time I had ever heard any of this. I was surprised she even knew those numbers. That sounded more like something Jane would have learned to compete on *Jeopardy*.

"If the aliens think I'm abusing something, it's not because I accidentally gave Mo a fatal heart attack." Her voice was strong, her statement powerful. She knew she had my and Reid's attention.

"It's because I've taken it upon myself to administer justice. The verdict that happens in court doesn't accurately reflect the viciousness that happened at the crime scene."

"Pat, what are you talking about?" I couldn't have masked my anxiousness even if I wanted to.

She looked right at me. "Tracy, you were in and out of consciousness the night Pincus kidnapped us, and I don't have to remind you that we were minutes away from being raped and murdered." Her voice was building with anger.

I knew all too well the hell we had nearly gone through. What I didn't remember firsthand, I had been told many times.

I had closed that chapter. Apparently Pat hadn't.

"And it wasn't just Pincus that wanted to violate us. Do you remember Captain Rick?"

I vividly remembered that. Pat and I had avoided getting abused by that maniac, but our compassion that led us to release him on a deserted island caused the passengers of the next boat, *The Aquaholic*, to suffer terrible acts, including multiple murders and repeated violent rapes.

I wondered why she was dredging all of this up. As far I as I was concerned, it was ancient history. Captain Rick had been decapitated and Captain Pincus had been transported back through time. Their names no longer deserved any mentioning. None.

When Pat announced she had a new use for her signaling device, my thoughts were jolted back to the present.

Reid and I listened while she explained that Hawaii had detailed public records of sex offenders. With an internet connection and minimal effort, anyone could find the names, addresses, and even pictures of convicted rapists and child molesters.

She stopped talking for a second. I waited, watching her intently.

Pat stood up, taking command. "Vee's four thousand carat diamond heist from dead bad guys is not the only perfect crime. I'm sure the police are baffled by thirty-one convicted sexual predators suffering fatal heart attacks."

"You've killed thirty-one people?" I exclaimed, not wanting to believe what I just heard.

"I've tried to kill more than that," she corrected me. Then she smiled and added, "Not all of the heart attacks were fatal."

I just stared at her. Pat Taylor had crossed a line. Flawed or not, our criminal justice system was what separated us from lawless societies, vigilante or "Old West" justice. Regardless of the victim's suffering, I didn't think Pat had the right to hand out death sentences in the form of heart attacks.

No wonder the aliens wanted her stopped.

CHAPTER 79

Reid didn't comment on her boastful admission about taking the law into her own hands. He asked her to be seated. Then he asked if the fog was her doing.

I'm not sure I would have changed subjects, but it was a good question. I looked at her and waited.

"Mo and I made fog in a terrarium in eight days."

"Why?" was all I could think to ask.

She gave me a quizzical look. "To see if we could progress from theoretical to actual."

That sounded like something the old Pat would say. But I feared the old Pat was history. The new Pat was a vengeful murderess.

Pat narrowed her eyes and looked me up and down. "Before you judge me about giving convicted rapists heart attacks, let's talk about the fog."

"What about it?"

"A little fog rolls in for a few weeks and society completely breaks down. There are riots, looting, violence, and widespread mayhem. Hell, we've got armed guards right here in Charles's gated, upscale community."

Reid raised his hand and spoke. "I wouldn't classify enough fog to shut down an entire island as 'a little fog.'"

I nodded my agreement. What I had seen from *The Ahi Slayer* and then paddled and walked through was hardly "a little fog."

"My fog has served two purposes."

"What purposes?" Reid asked.

"Mo and I took the creation of fog from a theory on paper to a working model in a terrarium." She looked quite smug.

"I took the next step. I proved that woman-made fog was possible outside of the controlled environment of a laboratory."

I wondered if she could make her fog cover a larger area than the island of Oahu. If so, and assuming the same lawlessness ensued, simple fog could become a terrorist weapon.

I glanced at Reid. He didn't notice but asked what the second purpose was.

"Convicted sex offenders weren't the only casualty of my signal disruption machine." Pat said.

Her casual statement made my eye involuntarily twitch.

She raised her hands and said, rather proudly, "There are no more governments agents keeping me under surveillance."

Oh no. Now she was giving heart attacks to innocent

people who were just doing their job. I was surprised the aliens hadn't stopped her themselves. In the time it took *The Aqua-holic* to sail from Hawaiian waters to the Bermuda Triangle, more than thirty-one deaths could have been prevented.

But then I remembered that the aliens were only here to observe, not to interfere with us and the consequences of our choices.

"How does somebody make fog?" As soon as I asked it, I realized to Pat it must seem a stupid question, but I needed time for my brain to process what she had done. And to try to understand how a woman I had known so well could now casually talk about committing murder.

Pat turned and looked at me. She paused briefly and then said, "Didn't you go to the science fair when you were a kid?"

I shook my head.

"Pour some hot water into a glass bottle, plug the hole with a bag of ice cubes, and voila—fog." Her response was terse.

"Won't the glass crack?"

"Use Pyrex." She sounded as if she was lecturing someone who hadn't read the assigned homework.

"But making fog in a bottle is a lot different than covering an entire island," Reid said.

"Only if you think small," Pat retorted.

Reid spoke again, keeping me from saying something I might regret. "So if Hawaii represents the hot water and the air is the air in the bottle, what represents the bag of ice cubes?"

I tried to picture what he had just described. All I could think of was that Pat had somehow managed to vacuum cold air from the upper atmosphere down, closer to the ground. I knew that wasn't right, but that's all I could think of.

"What is cold?" Pat asked, not changing her "smartest person in the room" attitude.

When neither of us responded, she told us. "It's the absence of heat."

That was profound. I wanted to say something about having an engineering degree to figure that out but I held my tongue.

"How do you get the heat out of the air when the sun is shining?" Reid asked. He was certainly following her easier than I was.

Pat smiled really big. I guessed that what she was about to say had come from using "advanced problem-solving techniques."

"Mo and I discovered an unusual frequency that absorbs the heat from the air as it passes through it." She paused a second, allowing us to comprehend what she had just described.

"We hand-built a generator that emitted that frequency. Once working, we tested it in the terrarium in the garage. The test was successful."

"How did you transmit that signal all over the island?" Reid asked.

"I made the generator larger and piggy-backed that

frequency on the existing cell phone tower infrastructure." She was still smiling, obviously very proud of her accomplishment.

"So Mo was okay with you covering the entire island of Oahu in fog?" I kept my voice steady and free of emotion.

Her eyes bored a hole through me. "He absolutely wouldn't have allowed it. But Mo's not with us anymore." Mentioning Mo's death earlier had choked her up. This time it didn't. The change was frightening.

I needed to get away. I needed to digest everything I had heard. I gulped my shot of vodka. It burned my throat. I excused myself to use the bathroom.

CHAPTER 80

I closed and locked the door behind me and looked at my watch. We still had plenty of time before Tony would follow Reid's orders. Seeing my watch made me think of Mo. He had bought it for me—a practical gift that didn't need a battery. My eyes began to tear up.

I leaned my head against the door.

I had really liked that man. He was smart, kind, and generous. He was so happy with Gert. I felt terrible that his time with her had been so brief. I closed my eyes and promised myself that Gert would not hear the true cause of Mo's heart attack. Not from me. Neither would Ashley or Donna. My lips were sealed.

I thought about Pat's lack of concern when I told her Marta was coming after her. Pat's lethal weapon—and that's exactly what her cell phone destroying, signal jamming, heart attack causing device was—would drop Marta in her tracks. I needed to warn Marta that confronting Pat was a very bad idea.

I remembered Pat's restraining order against Angie. Perhaps that was fortuitous for Angie. If Angie had continued to smack her around every day that her mom was gone, it was easy to guess who Pat would strike down next.

How would Reid and I stop Pat? The alien's message was clear as to action but vague as to method. Slit her throat with a knife? Bash in her skull with a big can of soup? Find a gun and execute her without warning?

If we gave her warning, would she cause us to have heart attacks? I felt a headache coming on.

I flushed the toilet to signal I was coming out. On the way back to the kitchen, I could hear Reid and Pat talking.

I didn't hear Reid's question, but I heard Pat tell him that she was going to stop the fog in a few days and then leave the island with thousands of others.

I heard Reid ask, "Where are you going to go?"

"I'll take the first flight out to any major US city."

"And then what?"

"And then I'll check out that city's sex offender registry."

I couldn't see her face, but I now knew that Pat had a method to her madness. She had a plan. It was both dastardly and brilliant.

When her shroud of fog lifted, there would be a crazy scramble out of Hawaii. She would blend in with the others and be gone. If the CIA was watching the airport, it was unlikely they'd spot her.

But what about later? Just because she had caused heart attacks in agents that she discovered watching her didn't really eliminate the problem. Stopping agents was simply a Band-aid. Her name would be on CIA and NSA lists, I was sure of it. I rejoined them in the kitchen.

"How do you propose to keep your identity hidden?" I asked. "You could change your name, but how would you live? You can't apply for work anywhere without—"

I stopped. The look on her face made the answer obvious.

"The gold on board *The Lady Anne*," I said. "You've taken it, haven't you?"

She smiled. "Of course I took it. No one but the three of us here in this room know about Charles's cache of gold—no one else except Charles, that is." She waved a hand. "Might have been a problem, you coming back before I could make my escape, but Charles getting sick enough to be hospitalized was a stroke of luck."

"You're that sure we won't stop you?" Reid asked.

"You could try," was her smug response. "Short of killing me, I can't see how you'd accomplish that."

I stared at her. She had no idea we were prepared to do just that—kill her.

Still, she'd never get her purse weapon through security, though Pat had already thought of that, I was sure. I guessed she'd just check it in her luggage. And if it did get confiscated, I had no doubts that the spiral notebooks she had hastily cleared from the kitchen table contained her notes detailing how to build a new one.

I envisioned a vengeful Pat Taylor with unlimited resources, at large in a country full of men she believed needed to die, with a weapon that left a victim with a perfectly natural, explainable cause of death. I was speechless.

Reid had been quiet for the last few minutes, no doubt thinking the same things I was. He glanced at me, and I expected him to ask Pat when she was going to stop the fog. He didn't. He asked something else.

"Pat, would you like to know what I was planning to do when Tracy asked me to sail away with her and the others?"

Reid's voice had softened. His expression had too.

"I had decided to ask Charles to put crews aboard *The Lady Anne* and *The Aquaholic* and use them as a diversion. While those boats led the Navy on a wild goose chase, the rest of us, all of us—you, me, Tracy, and the other five women— would make our escape on the Clarriage ninety-five that Vee knew about."

I could hear the love in Reid's voice. The way he emphasized the three of us—he, Pat and I—sealed the deal. Reid Adams was cursed with loving two women at the same time. It was deep, romantic love. I hoped Pat heard it too.

Reid continued, "Since *The Lady Anne* was under satellite surveillance, we would simply have stayed out of sight somewhere, likely on a large fishing or pleasure boat, until Charles could arrange for the Clarriage ninety-five in Vancouver to be purchased, outfitted, and delivered."

"You would still want me after what I did to *The USS Fields*?"

I didn't stick around for his answer. I retreated again to the safety of the bathroom and locked the door. I sat on the counter, leaned up against the wall, closed my eyes, and relaxed. I had an idea.

"This is Tracy calling the aliens." I projected that thought, focused on it, and repeated it.

We are listening, Tracy.

I could hear them in my head. I had made contact.

I chose my next thoughts carefully. "Pat believes that her behavior is justified. I am not defending her actions, but I believe there is an alternative to going into the next room and killing her."

I didn't have to wait long for the alien's response.

What do you propose?

That was the question I wanted but, honestly, hadn't expected so quickly. I was sure the aliens would demand Pat's immediate execution. Now she had a chance. Pat Taylor's future depended on my next thought.

"Exile her back in time. Her weapon and her problem-solving knowledge will die with her. She won't hurt anyone else. And Reid and I won't have to slay our friend and live with those consequences."

I had barely finished my thoughts when the aliens responded.

Pat Taylor may not accept your proposed solution.

"Leave that to me," I thought quickly. "If she doesn't, I will see that she is stopped before she hurts anyone else."

I waited. Would my proposal be accepted? It seemed sound. If it wasn't, could I simply stroll back into the kitchen and kill Pat? In cold blood? Without warning? I'd have to. Then what? Serve time in prison for first-degree murder? For what? To save a bunch of convicted rapists that I didn't even know or had ever heard of from having heart attacks. How would I feel when Reid was called on the stand to testify against me?

Tracy Palmer. You have seventy-two Earth hours.

"To do what?" I concentrated on projecting that thought.

To have Pat Taylor on board her vessel, stopped, fifteen nautical miles offshore. Then contact us again.

I felt the connection terminate. My thoughts were my own. In case the aliens might still be watching or listening, I looked up and said, "Thank you."

CHAPTER 81

I was proud of my proposed solution. Sacrificing *The Lady Anne* seemed a small price to pay for Pat's life.

True, Pat would be stuck back in time, alone, with no possibility of being returned, but at least she would be alive. I noted the time. I had seventy-two hours.

Now, what if Pat didn't go along with it? If it were me, would I willingly sail back in time to a certain, eventual death? Or would I resist? Knowing Pat, it was highly likely that she would resist.

I wasn't exactly sure what I was going to say or do, but I figured I had been in the bathroom long enough to raise suspicions. I got down from the counter, flushed the toilet, ran the faucet as if washing my hands, and then returned to the kitchen.

Pat and Reid weren't there. I made my way to the garage. I

heard talking and followed the voices to the far end. Pat and Reid were looking at a fish tank that was sitting on a workbench.

He saw me and asked if I was alright. I nodded and then made a face. "Sorry, but that took longer than I expected. You might not want to go in there for a few minutes."

Both Pat and Reid rolled their eyes. I immediately noticed Pat had a purse slung across her shoulder. Was that the infamous killer purse? I had to assume it was.

I wondered why she had it. I was positive she hadn't had it when she answered the door or when we were in the kitchen.

Reid spoke, jolting my thoughts back to the present. "You should check this out."

I glanced at the fish tank. It was full of fog. So this was the terrarium where Pat and Mo had made fog in eight days. I took a closer look.

The inside was cloudy and opaque. Tiny droplets of moisture were running down the inside of the glass. There was a length of flexible silver pipe sticking through a neat hole in the glass near the top of one side. It looked like the vent duct hose on a dryer, only much smaller. The hole appeared to be perfectly round. I wondered how they had managed that. I didn't know how to drill a hole through glass.

The duct hose went to a short metal rack holding electrical equipment. The pointers on two meters indicated something was switched on and working. There were also some green indicator lights and several various knobs and switches.

Another piece of a somewhat larger duct hose exited the

terrarium on the opposite side. It went straight into the lower part of a large metal bucket that was sitting atop two cinder blocks.

I peeked inside the bucket. It was about two-thirds full of what looked like coarse black sand. Pat warned me not to touch it. She explained that's where the heat from the displaced frequency waves bisecting the air spilled its energy. I could feel the heat coming from the bucket.

I wondered if the aliens had used a similar technology to make the heat hole behind the boats where we incinerated our records of having been sent back in time. Maybe.

Reid congratulated her on making fog, then he asked her how to stop it.

Pat gave him a stern look. "Why do you want to know?"

He didn't reply right away, looking at me instead. I shrugged.

Pat moved around to the other side of the workbench. She stared at Reid. He stared back. I watched them watching each other. I wondered what he had told her.

Nonchalantly, Pat took her purse in her hands and spoke. "If the aliens returned you to stop me for abusing their technology, what's next?" She didn't sound scared or intimidated, just curious. I, on the other hand, was laser focused on her purse.

"How do you stop the fog?" Reid repeated his question, his voice and demeanor curious and nonthreatening.

Pat hesitated. I could see in her eyes that she was analyzing his question. Knowing Pat, overanalyzing it.

"Are you concerned that if you stop me before I stop the fog, Oahu will be cursed in fog—forever and eternity?"

Reid chuckled. "That sounds comically terrifying."

Pat's expression softened a little. I waited.

"Your experiment was a complete success," Reid said. "There is no reason to prolong the suffering."

After a long silence, Pat sighed. "The equipment and transmission antenna array is on the roof. Flip the breaker."

That was it? Just turn off a circuit breaker? I figured it would be more complicated than that.

Then she laughed. "You know the governor could have stopped the fog the same day it began."

Reid tilted his head. "How?"

"All he had to do was have the phone companies turn off the power to their cell towers."

CHAPTER 82

That made sense. If her signal was piggybacking on the phone company's equipment, shutting down that equipment would have orphaned her signal. I was surprised that nobody on the island had figured out the fog was manmade, or in this case woman-made, and not a natural phenomenon or a biblical plague.

Pat's fidgeting with her purse brought my focus back to her. "So back to the question of the day. How are you two supposed to stop me?"

Clearly Reid had noticed Pat's purse. Hopefully he had made the connection to it being *the* purse.

"Are you going to point that thing at me and give me a heart attack?" Reid asked.

Pat's response was quick. "Are you going to shoot me? I don't see a gun."

I wondered if I had made a mistake not asking Tony to borrow a weapon. When Reid reached behind his back and produced a pistol, my jaw dropped. Although I had decided against asking to borrow a gun, obviously Reid hadn't.

I had no idea he had it. I couldn't believe what was happening.

I watched Pat closely. She didn't aim her purse at him, or at me, but she did keep focused on Reid.

If she suddenly pointed her purse at him, could she give him a heart attack before he could shoot? Maybe. But maybe he'd have time to fire. If he extended the gun, as close as they were to each other, there'd be no way he could miss.

The term "Mexican standoff" came to mind. Neither could act without losing.

My mind raced. "Do something, Tracy," I said to myself. "Or you're going to witness the unthinkable."

"The aliens have provided me with an alternative solution."

My heart was pounding. I kept my voice as calm as I could manage. They both glanced at me. I had their attention.

"Pat, put your purse down. And Reid, put the gun down." I watched, not sure what I would say if they didn't comply.

Reid acted first. He put his gun on the workbench and slid it off to the side. It was still within his reach, but it was far enough away that Pat could now give him a heart attack before he could grab the gun, point, and shoot.

I watched Pat. Had I made a grave mistake? Would she comply with my instruction like Reid had? She didn't move. I could see she was thinking. I motioned with my head. She looked at Reid, smiled, and set her purse down across from the gun.

Then she looked at me. "What's your solution?"

Her question should have calmed me, but it didn't. My heart was still pounding, thumping like crazy. What if she didn't accept it? Could she grab her purse again before Reid or I could grab the gun? What if I got the gun first and it went off in my hands? What if I accidentally shot myself, or Reid? I needed to get both weapons out of play. I glanced around the area.

"I want both of you to back away nice and slow. There are two stools at the other workbench. Would both of you please go and be seated?"

Reid went first. He didn't seemed concerned about getting away from his gun. Maybe he had another one. TV cops carried backup weapons. Maybe he had one too. Or maybe he trusted Pat to do the right thing. Trusted her with his life.

Reid took a seat and patted the other stool. Pat hesitated, took another look at her purse, and then joined him. I moved in between them and the weapons. My palms were sweaty and my heart was still pounding so loudly I was sure they could hear it.

Pat cleared her throat. "You were saying something about an alien-provided solution." She looked up and then back at me. "Please elaborate."

I told how the aliens had agreed to send her and *The Lady Anne* back in time. She could keep her life, but she would live out the rest of her days exploring twenty-five thousand seven hundred years in the past. I waited, watching closely for her reaction.

While she was thinking, Reid spoke. "That's a generous offer. You should take the deal."

"You should," I said. "You have seventy-two hours. If it were up to me, I would have put you on *The Lady Anne* and sent you back within an hour of you opening the door. Maybe I'd have let you buy some diesel and maybe you could have taken a few loads of stuff from the garage with you, but you'd have been out of here and back in time with more preparation than you gave me, Reid, and *The Aquaholic*."

Pat looked momentarily stunned by my outburst. She took one deep breath and then exhaled slowly.

"As I see it, I've got some options." That sounded like the old Pat.

"Why do you think you have options?" I asked. "Don't get a sheet of paper and starting numbering it. Just tell us what's going through your mind. And don't make a career out of it."

"Try and relax, Tracy. I'm not going to give you or Reid a heart attack, and you're obviously not going to shoot me."

Reid tilted his head. "How can you be so certain?" he asked.

"Because you would have blasted me full of lead the instant I opened the door."

Was she saying we were weak and she was strong? Was she going to bolt for her purse? She said she wasn't going to give me a heart attack, but could I trust her with my life, and with Reid's too?

I spotted another metal bucket underneath the work-bench. It was empty. With both of them watching me, I picked up the bucket, gently put her purse inside, and then even more gently put Reid's gun in with it.

I placed the bucket on the floor over by the shelving. After that, I returned to let Pat continue.

Reid looked pleased with my temporary solution to the weapon's problem. Pat looked surprised.

"Let's say I refuse the deal," she said after a moment. "Since I'm one hundred percent certain that neither of you will kill me in cold blood, the aliens will most assuredly send someone else to stop me. Someone reliable. Pincus for instance. You two won't shoot. I can't count on being that lucky with your replacement."

I didn't expect to hear that bastard's name. If the aliens offered to return Pincus to this time in exchange for him killing Pat, he'd accept without hesitation and act without mercy.

Pat continued, "Instead of your deal of a lifetime of soli-tary confinement on sixty-eight feet of Clarriage, I could just turn myself in. Between the CIA, the NSA, NORAD, the Navy destroyer, and jumping to conclusions about Reid's deci-sion to possibly leave me alone, I was distraught."

Distraught? I could hear an insanity plea coming from a mile away.

"Between the ability to easily create fog and the deadliness of my cell phone signal disruption machine, I was corrupted and seduced by the power."

"Would you surrender your purse and the fog machine as evidence?" Reid asked. "Along with your notes?"

When Pat nodded, Reid said what I was thinking, "I don't believe the aliens would want their technology handed off to someone else. They want it destroyed. That's why we're here."

Pat hesitated. I waited.

"How about this. I willingly go back in time and bring Bev, Penelope, and Candy back. I admit I overreacted. I'm sorry for sending those women back in time. If the aliens agree, I can go fetch them from the past. If the same return route around Cape Horn is part of the deal, then I'll accept those terms. *The Aquaholic* made it. I'm sure *The Lady Anne* would too."

It took a moment to register that Penelope was Dreamgirl's real name. Pat offering to bring the others back was unexpected. Her admission of overreacting seemed an oversimplification of her losing complete control.

Pat looked directly at me. "Tracy, will you please go talk with the aliens? Tell them what I propose. Remind them they allowed me, Reid, and Mo to conduct a rescue mission once before to save Elouise and Marta from their abductors."

She looked and sounded like she was finished. Reid's silence implied he agreed with her. Would the aliens agree to her fetching the other women from the past? They had allowed it once. Might they again?

I nodded and headed back to the bathroom. I hoped the aliens would communicate with me.

The connection was established right away. I explained Pat's rescue counteroffer.

The aliens' response was immediate. Their earlier offer was firm. There would be no changes or negotiations. They reminded me of the time remaining.

I sensed that arguing would be pointless. If I did press them, would they cancel the deal? Maybe. If the deal got cancelled because I wouldn't take no for an answer, how would Pat react? I couldn't risk any of it.

I thanked the aliens for their time and opened my eyes, terminating the connection.

Pat and Reid hadn't moved from the workbench. They watched me return. I told them the aliens' original offer was not subject to modification. The unmistakable look of disappointment registered in Pat's eyes.

"So what are you going to do?" Reid asked.

My heart had resumed pounding. This was worse than waiting for the dealer to turn over the last poker card.

I tried to relax and not "what if" this to death.

Finally Pat spoke. "I'll take the original offer to go back in time alone. Sixty-eight feet of Clarriage with unlimited sky is far superior to a six-by-eight foot prison cell without. I won't cause any trouble for you. No one else the aliens would send would be half as compassionate. I won't ask for any leniency. My revenge on sexual predators came with consequences. I will accept whatever fate awaits me. You and the aliens have been more kind than I deserve."

It was quite a moving speech, loaded with apparent sincerity.

"You're doing the right thing." Reid took her hand. "If you want, I'll help you get ready."

She smiled at him, wiping at the tears that were cascading down her cheeks. Reid was obviously convinced that she was sincere. I hoped he was right and that Pat wasn't just telling us what we wanted to hear.

I was extremely thankful there hadn't been a mad dash for the weapons. I added the stipulation about needing to be fifteen nautical miles offshore in seventy-two hours. Reid and Pat both looked at me. Then they looked at their watches.

Reid stood. "Let's go turn off the fog machine."

Pat wiped her eyes and we followed her to the circuit breaker panel. She opened it and flipped a single breaker. "What's here now will burn off, and then the fog will be gone." She sounded a little disappointed. I knew what was next.

I took the bucket back to the workbench. Reid took his gun.

I picked up the purse and handed it to her. "Destroy it."

I was immediately bombarded with second thoughts. Would she suddenly change her mind and use it on us? Was I taking a huge gamble, trusting a serial killer? Or would she comply, not wanting the aliens to send Pincus to finish the job I may have just botched?

"Her purse weapon is really a directed energy weapon and it has numerous military applications," Reid said. "So does her invention to create fog. Maybe we should discuss alternatives to flat-out destroying them."

I whirled around. "You can't be serious. Everything needs to be destroyed. You must know that. Don't be smitten by the power of alien technology. You know the consequences."

Reid looked at me. I was expecting an argument, but Pat opened her purse. I watched intently. Did she have to open her purse to activate her weapon? If Pat had decided to fight, it made sense that she would attack Reid first. He was armed; I wasn't. If she pointed her purse at Reid, would I be able to do anything? Had I just blown it? I could feel my heartbeat increasing.

Pat slowly slid out a long, thin, black, plastic case, encircled by three snake-like coils of wire. The case was connected to wires that went back inside the purse. I figured that was the switch. She carefully pried off the lid and removed some short, squatty batteries. She smiled, disconnected the switch wires, and said it was disarmed and now safe to handle. She placed the case on the workbench and handed me a large hammer and some safety glasses.

I bashed that case until pieces had flown everywhere. That thing was history. They both helped sweep up. The hammer and I made sure that anything larger than a quarter was smashed.

I thanked Pat for cooperating. "Is there still a grill outside?"

When she nodded, I told her to get all of her notes except the notes for the plastic magnet. We went back to the kitchen and she did as asked.

Reid mentioned "military applications" again, but I put my finger over my lips, signaling him to stop talking. I left the spiral notebook containing my original drawings and the file folders labeled "Plastic Magnet" on the table and took the rest outside.

The fog hadn't lifted, but we found the grill and Reid lit it for me. I placed all of the notebooks inside and closed the lid.

Destroying the fog machine attached to the terrarium was pretty easy. A vice and a hacksaw made appetizer-sized pieces out of the duct tubing. The hammer smashed the circuit boards and everything else that looked suspicious. I had Reid put these pieces, and the scrap from her purse weapon, in multiple plastic bags.

"We will dispose of these separately and in different locations," I said. "I don't want some clever CIA agents finding the broken components in a dumpster and putting 'Humpty Dumpty' back together again." Both Pat and Reid agreed.

Pat explained the fog machine on the roof was larger and would be harder to get rid of. I shot Reid "the look" so he wouldn't bring up military applications again. He got the hint and remained silent.

When Pat confirmed the device on the roof would fit aboard *The Lady Anne*, I told them we would get rid of it fifteen nautical miles offshore. She begrudgingly nodded.

I turned to look at the shelving. "You can provision the

boat with the food and supplies that are already here." Reid nodded.

Pat thought for a second. "I can use some of this, but I will want to go to Kauai for everything else, including fuel. Thanks to the looters and all of the closed businesses, provisioning locally on Oahu will be problematic in the seventy-two hours I've been granted."

Reid argued that Molokai was much closer and she could get what she needed there. She pleaded that she needed a Costco and repeated the looting had affected Oahu's Costcos. Not counting Oahu, the closest Costco was on Kauai. I double-checked on her computer. She was right.

"Sailing to Kauai and then warp-speed provisioning is going to be a lot of work for three people," I remarked.

"Not if we have help," Reid answered, grinning.

While Pat and Reid strolled past the shelving, making notes and setting things aside, I took Reid's gun and went outside to find Tony.

He found me actually and asked if things were okay or if the clock was still ticking. I told him it was, but in a different way. I handed him the gun, which turned out to belong to Lance, and told him that our plans had changed.

He looked concerned.

I explained *The Lady Anne* would be headed for Kauai for extensive reprovisioning. We wanted him and Lance to accompany us.

"No problem, ma'am. When are we leaving?" I was

expecting questions or an argument. His instant agreement caught me a bit off guard.

"As soon as possible," I stammered.

"I'll go get Lance." With that short response, he hustled out of sight into the fog.

I took a moment to turn off the gas to the grill. When I lifted the lid, the escaping heat forced me to back away. All that remained of Pat's notebooks were clumps of ashes and blackened, twisted pieces of the wire bindings.

Back in the garage, I looked around for a safe. I didn't see one. When I asked Pat if the gold was here, she started grinning. "I borrowed a page from Charles about the best hiding place being in plain sight."

I remembered that's what he had said about keeping rolls of gold coins in *The Lady Anne's* grab rails. I looked up. There weren't any railings or pipes on the ceiling.

"You've both walked right past it. Several times actually."

Reid and I looked around some more. We didn't see any gold or likely hiding spots. "Remember that I'm an engineer and a general contractor," she said, egging us on.

Reid gave up and pointed at his watch. "Where is it?"

She beckoned us to the kitchen window. I didn't see anything unusual or suspicious.

She pressed a section of the wall and it opened out. Tightly stacked in the space between the studs were coin rolls. Lots of them.

There was also a stack of one-hundred-dollar-bill bundles, about two feet high. Each bundle contained ten thousand dollars. She confirmed she had previously sold some of the gold coins.

"Help yourself," she smiled and said.

I took one bundle, Reid took two, Pat took ten. To our amazed looks, she replied, "Ten is my lucky number."

I remembered that a ten was the card she had won the poker game with. How could I ever forget? That card had changed a lot of things. In less than seventy-two hours, Pat Taylor was about to experience another change. A big one, epic even. Permanently.

I ruffled the edges. My hundreds were new, crisp, sticking together, and numbered sequentially. I was pretty sure it wouldn't cost anywhere near one hundred thirty thousand dollars to reprovision *The Lady Anne*. I was also fairly certain that we couldn't spend that much in less than seventy-two hours. I didn't say anything.

Pat beamed. "I rebuilt that wall with two by eight inch studs instead of two by fours. I also replaced the drywall with plywood and then textured and painted it to match. I know how to use invisible hinges." She put the panel back. It clicked into place.

Even knowing where the seams were, I couldn't spot them. Neither could Reid. I made a mental note to remember exactly where the panel was. Exactly.

CHAPTER 84

While waiting for the fog to lift, Pat and Reid gathered what she wanted from the garage and carried it outside. I told Ashley and Donna that Pat would be leaving on *The Lady Anne* and asked for their help for a few days.

Unlike Tony, they did not quickly consent.

They reminded me that after their ordeal on *The Aquaholic*, neither of them wanted to get back on a boat again, ever.

I remembered and sympathized but explained the purpose, the timeframe, and the crew. Just as I was ready to beg, they exchanged glances and agreed to help.

Thankfully, their only question was what we were going to do about Buster.

"Take him with us," I replied. "He loves being aboard."

The fog lifted later, thinning first and then disappearing completely. The sun's warmth was a welcome relief.

There were three vehicles at Charles's place: two luxury cars and a minivan.

Tony removed the rear seats from the minivan and packed it full of boxes of canned food. Pat had several duffle bags. They all fit in the larger trunk.

The rest of us put one bag each in the other trunk. I wondered if Lance's bag contained his gun or if he was concealing it, like Reid had.

Donna carried a small bag of dog food. Buster kept prancing between her and me. His wagging tail signaled he knew we were going somewhere.

The men had taken the fog machine down from the roof, but we didn't have room for it. Tony said he and Lance would come right back. The plan was to destroy it once out at sea.

We promptly caravanned to *The Lady Anne*. There wasn't much traffic.

The boat was berthed in a gated marina which had been undiscovered by the looters. A feeling of melancholy washed over me when I saw her. I had already been sentenced once to life in the past aboard her. The aliens had changed their mind and returned me. Would Pat be as fortunate? I doubted it.

We unloaded the vehicles, starting with the minivan. As soon as it was empty, Tony drove it back for the fog machine. Reid went with him. After he had gone, I kicked myself for not going with them.

Reid knew the fog machine had definite military

applications. Now he had an opportunity to abscond with a working prototype. Had I misjudged him? All I could do was cart bags and boxes down to the boat and not worry about what Reid might or might not be up to.

My fears vanished when Reid and Tony returned with the fog machine. The guys wheeled it down the dock and used *The Lady Anne's* crane to get it aboard. Nobody questioned what it was or why we were bringing it along.

When Reid saw all of the garage boxes taking over the salon, he tried convincing Pat that sailing all the way to Kauai just so she could shop at Costco was a waste of her limited, precious time.

He argued that if all of us went shopping, a scavenger hunt so to speak, she could get what she needed, including fuel, right here on Oahu.

His reasoning fell on deaf ears. Pat's mind was made up.

Tony asked for two drivers to help him return the cars. Lance volunteered. So did I. I retrieved my purse from the owner's suite where I had left it months ago and followed them back to Charles's place. The drive provided me with some much needed alone time.

I was still pissed at Pat for sending me back in time with minimal provisions and not enough fuel, while she had the luxury of being properly outfitted. It didn't seem fair she had three days to get ready when she hadn't afforded us the same opportunity. Adding to my frustration was Reid helping her. He had already gone through what awaited her. His knowledge was priceless.

Tony put the seats back in and drove us back to the marina. There still wasn't much traffic. I spotted an over-flowing dumpster. I had him circle back so I could dispose of a bag of Pat's busted purse weapon.

The seven of us, plus Buster, sailed straight to Kauai. I calculated it would take fourteen hours.

While underway, Reid tolled *The Lady Anne's* brass bell. He explained he was mourning the passing of two sailors, Captain Veronica Kline and Morrie Mordechai Morris. Afterwards, he got his trumpet and played "Taps." Tony and Lance saluted.

I wondered who would toll the bell for Pat when her time came.

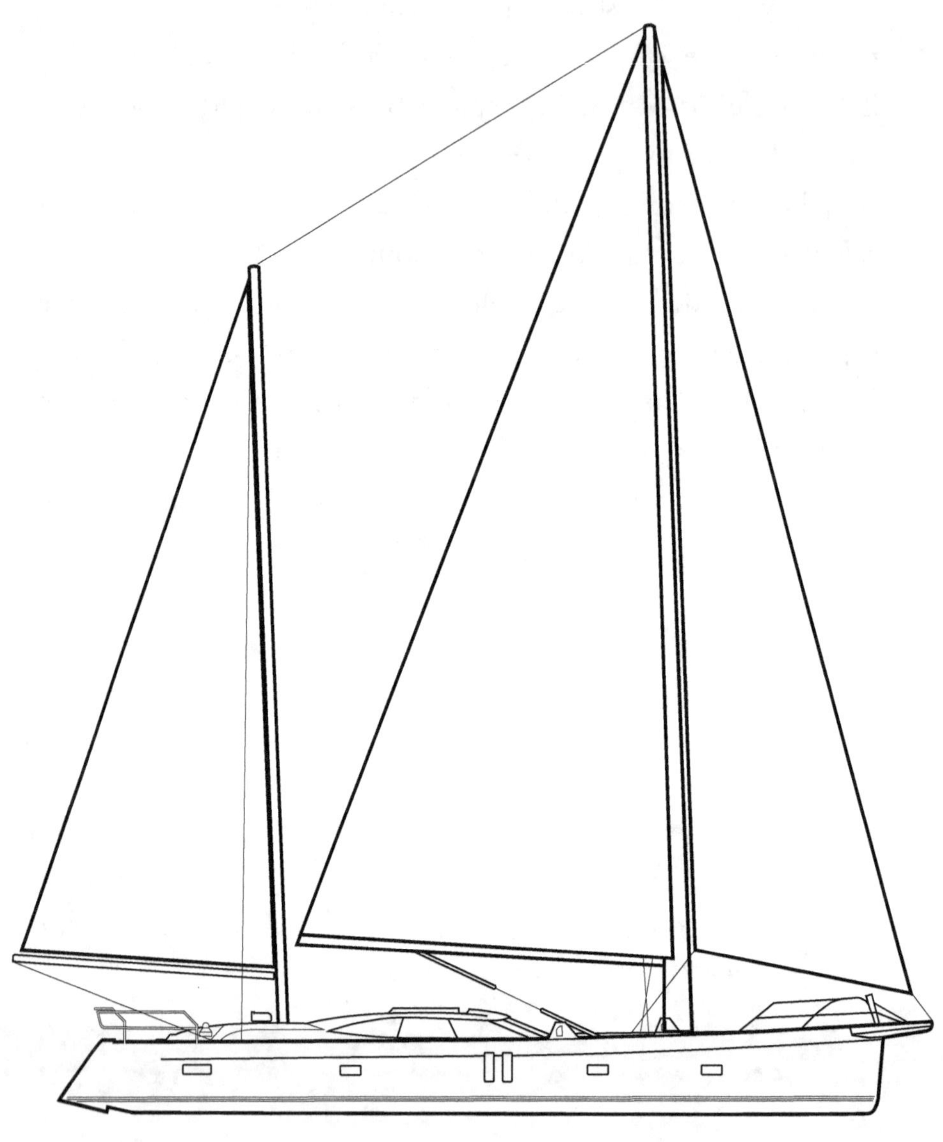

THE LADY ANNE
VESSEL OVERVIEW
NOT TO SCALE

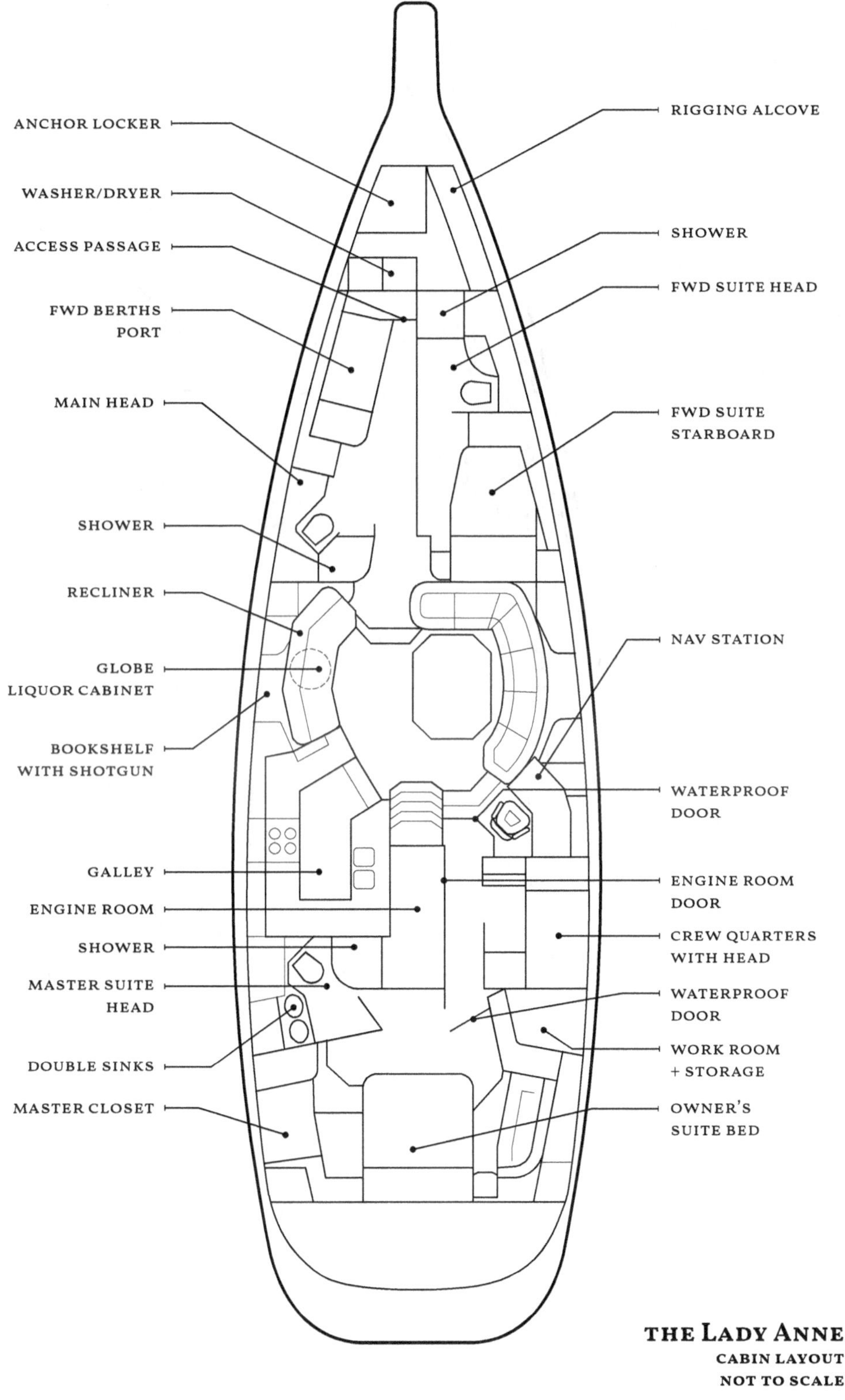

ANCHOR LOCKER
WASHER/DRYER
ACCESS PASSAGE
FWD BERTHS PORT
MAIN HEAD
SHOWER
RECLINER
GLOBE LIQUOR CABINET
BOOKSHELF WITH SHOTGUN
GALLEY
ENGINE ROOM
SHOWER
MASTER SUITE HEAD
DOUBLE SINKS
MASTER CLOSET
RIGGING ALCOVE
SHOWER
FWD SUITE HEAD
FWD SUITE STARBOARD
NAV STATION
WATERPROOF DOOR
ENGINE ROOM DOOR
CREW QUARTERS WITH HEAD
WATERPROOF DOOR
WORK ROOM + STORAGE
OWNER'S SUITE BED
THE LADY ANNE
CABIN LAYOUT
NOT TO SCALE

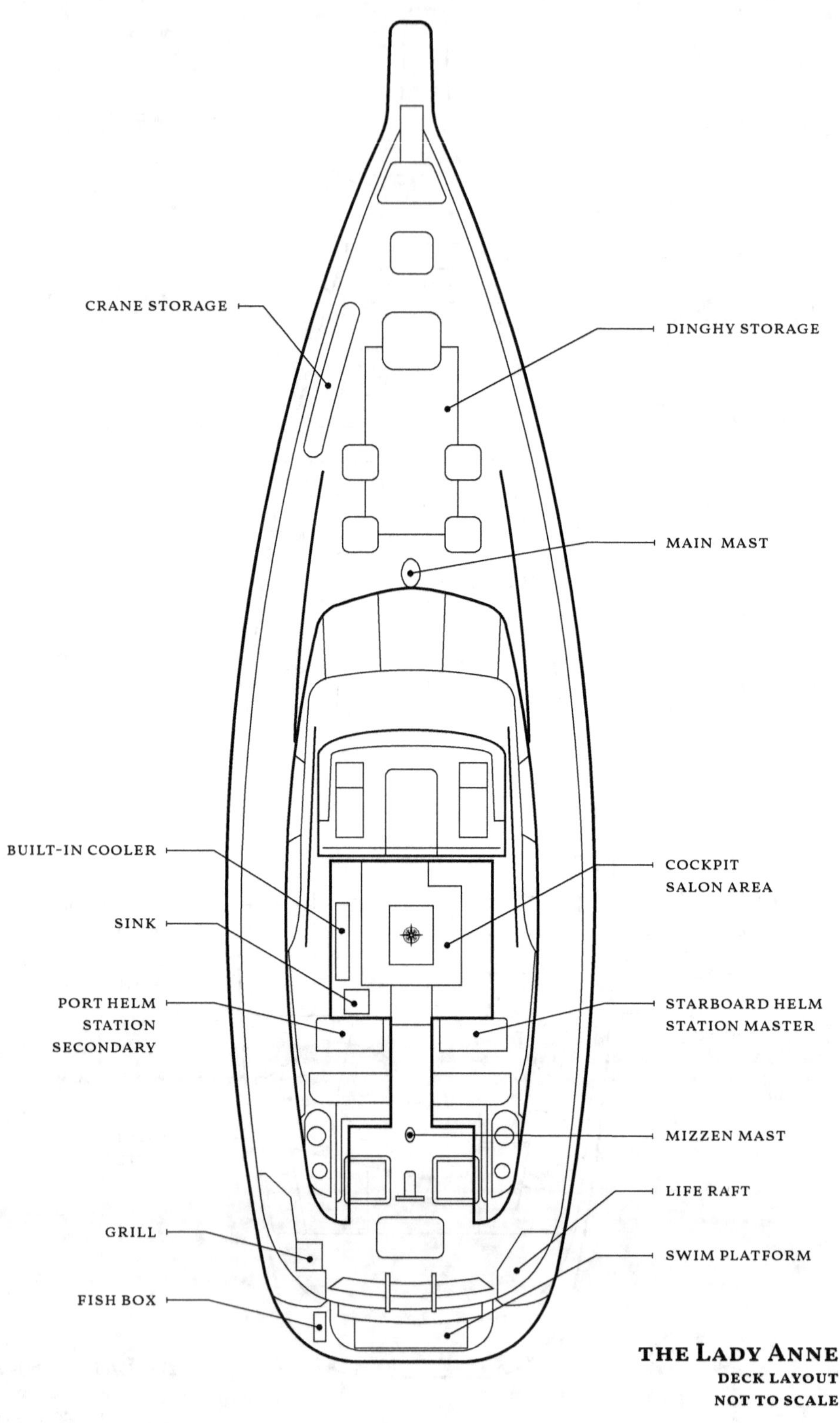

CRANE STORAGE
DINGHY STORAGE
MAIN MAST
BUILT-IN COOLER
COCKPIT SALON AREA
SINK
PORT HELM STATION SECONDARY
STARBOARD HELM STATION MASTER
MIZZEN MAST
LIFE RAFT
GRILL
SWIM PLATFORM
FISH BOX
THE LADY ANNE
DECK LAYOUT
NOT TO SCALE

CHAPTER 85

The ocean was strangely empty. I expected a flotilla of cargo ships rushing to Oahu to restock the entire island. When I consulted the chart, I saw that the major shipping lane was on the other side of the Kauai channel.

Reid and Pat took her fog machine apart and discarded the pieces every few miles. I emptied the remaining plastic bags as well. I hated littering the sea floor but understood this was the safest way to get rid of the evidence, smashed or not.

When the machine's last piece went over the side, I felt easier in my mind that her machine was now rusting at the bottom of the Kauai Channel, strewn over twenty or thirty nautical miles.

Ashley and Donna relieved me at the helm, giving me a break. Tony and Lance joined them. I told them to yell if they needed anything.

I found Reid and Pat below at the salon table. She motioned me to join them.

"What's up?" I asked.

"Pat's been thinking about her future," Reid said. His face reflected concern.

"And?" I looked right at her. She looked tired.

"I can't live aboard *The Lady Anne* long-term."

That was an unexpected statement. "Why not?" I asked, suddenly curious.

"Logistics." Her reply was short and succinct.

"What about them?"

"Shelf life. Every can, box, and package in here has an expiration date. At best I'll have a year or two's worth of supplies."

She was right. Unless she could survive on a total fish diet, eventually she would open the last can or box. Mo and Gert barely made it six months alone on their island. Even if she doubled or tripled that, her life sentence in the past would only be a few years.

Was I supposed to feel sorry for Pat? She had killed dozens with heart attacks, including Mo. She was also directly responsible for all of the mayhem her fog had caused.

I stood. "I better go topside and check on Donna and Ashley," I said. I suddenly wanted some distance.

Reid put his hand on my shoulder and said, "Pat, tell her your plan."

I sat back down, glanced at my watch, and then faced Pat. "You've got five minutes."

"Five minutes is plenty," Pat said. She drew a breath. "Unless I'm able to negotiate a return trip back via the Southern Ocean like you did, in order to last more than a few years, I will be forced to live ashore. Since I intend to live longer than that, living ashore it is. That requires a source of fresh water, food, and shelter.

"If I want more stability than wandering around chasing fish, birds, and reptiles, I'll have no choice but to grow my own food."

I stared at her. "How will you get plants or seeds through the alien's sterilization field?"

"I have three ideas. As long as one of them works, I'll be good for the rest of my natural life."

Pat turned away and didn't elaborate.

Reid and I glanced at each other.

We reached our destination. Reid got us a slip at a marina near the Costco. There was a motel a couple of blocks away, so I walked over and reserved some rooms. On my way back to the marina, I wondered how we would get back to Oahu after Pat left us. Then I remembered the stack of bills in my pocket, smiled, and the worry was gone.

There wasn't much time to sleep or eat. Pat had compiled several lists, and the aliens' clock was running.

The first order of business was to refuel, which we did with no problems. There may have been a fuel shortage on Oahu, but things on the island of Kauai seemed normal.

Once the tanks were topped off, I stayed aboard with Buster. The others each took a list and went shopping, armed with a handful of crisp one-hundred-dollar bills. Between waiting for deliveries or for someone to drop off their purchases, I had plenty of stuff from the garage to inventory and put away.

Slowly but surely *The Lady Anne* filled up. There was a cute guy on a yellow and white, go-fast cigarette boat in the next slip. He was very smooth and quite talkative. I suspected he was as fast as his boat. He smiled and offered me a ride, or even help with the dock carts. Both offers were tempting, but I declined.

Six tall, oversized propane tanks were delivered. They looked really heavy. Despite my offer of a nice tip, the driver wouldn't bring them any further than his dolly could wheel them.

The driver had instructions to pick up all of our existing propane tanks and make sure they were full. However, he wouldn't help me disconnect or move them to the dock.

Thankfully, Jack, the cute guy, saw my predicament and offered his services. Jack disconnected and then carried all of our propane tanks to where the driver would take them.

He then helped with the new tanks. Between Jack's muscles and *The Lady Anne's* crane, the two of us soon had those oversized propane tanks aboard along with a box of hoses and various fittings.

Tony and Ashley delivered a bunch of plastic fuel tanks. I was expecting heavy, steel, fifty-five gallon fuel drums, but Ashley explained Pat had insisted on plastic tanks that were easy to secure, wouldn't rust, and could be cleaned and repurposed for water storage. Tony handed me a package of ratchet straps for securing the tanks, and then he and Ashley left to conquer another item on their list.

I debated motoring back to the fuel dock to fill them. I would have needed to use my credit card or a big chunk of the hundreds. I finally decided that Reid or Pat could go fill them.

Pat and Reid carted a huge load of boxes from Costco down the dock. Instead of helping me get them below, they left me staring at their mountain of purchases and went to get more. Thankfully, Jack once again came over and helped me carry everything below, stacking them wherever there was room. He looked liked he had a million questions about what kind of trip required this much provisioning.

"*The Lady Anne* is sailing around the world," I said before he asked. "Trying for a record, so the more she can carry with her, the fewer stops she has to make."

His eyebrows rose, but he only shrugged and went back topside for another load.

Lance and Donna returned from Home Depot. Donna gently handed me a moving box. She told me to put it somewhere safe. I glanced inside. It was full of seed packets.

Lance carried a bag of dirt below, asking me to leave it and three more just like it accessible, Pat's orders. Cart by cart, items kept coming. There were shovels, picks, hoes, axes, and saws. There were battery-operated power tools, rolls of chicken wire, orange buckets containing nails, screws, bug spray, ant killer, fertilizer, boxes of canning jars, and even bags of concrete and mortar mix.

"Did you get all of this in one cab?" I asked, wiping my forehead after taking a super-heavy bag of concrete mix below.

"Nope," Lance smiled. "We rented a truck."

The next load was purchases from an army surplus store. Tony and Donna had tarps, solar showers, cookware, sleeping bags, tents, cots, wool blankets, lanterns, candles, and various other pieces of camping, survival, and military surplus equipment.

Tony handed me two metal ammunition boxes and said to put them somewhere where they would be readily available. His tone conveyed their importance. I put them by the seeds and the dirt.

Tony took a case of shotgun shells below. I asked if guns were next. He shook his head. Next, he carried below a bow and a quiver full of arrows. I moved out of his way.

The rude driver returned with our propane tanks. Tony helped get them aboard this time.

Pat and Reid returned from visiting the local marine supply store. They had fishing gear, boat parts, and lots of charts and chart books. By this time there was hardly room to move about below, but stuff kept coming.

Donna returned and handed me a thick, blue apron. She grinned when I nearly dropped it. It was way heavier than it looked. "What the hell is this?"

She smiled. "A shielded apron from a dentist's office."

"What for?"

She smiled again. "Ask Pat, but I've got one more coming, so she must have a reason."

I wasn't keeping track of receipts, but Pat was spending a great deal of money. I was envious, wishing *The Aquaholic* would have had half of this stuff. When I remembered this was all that Pat would have to live on, my envy quickly subsided—a little.

Pat and Reid brought several bags from Walmart and Goodwill aboard. Walmart purchases were expected. Going to Goodwill seemed weird. "Why are you shopping at Goodwill?" I asked.

Reid answered. "I've taught skiing to lots of vacationers from Hawaii. I remembered some of them telling me they bought new gear every season and rather than store their old, slightly used gear, they'd just donate it back home."

Pat continued. "We checked the local Goodwill and sure enough, they had a whole section of ski gear and winter clothing."

I took the bags. "Why do you need winter clothing? Won't you just sail somewhere where it's warm?"

Pat answered. "In case I'm able to negotiate the same deal you did. Sail around Cape Horn to the Bermuda Triangle and get returned to this time."

I didn't think that was even a remote possibility but didn't comment.

Reid then motioned for Lance and Tony to follow him. When they returned, each carrying a stack of used encyclopedias, I realized that Reid just needed their muscles.

"A little light reading?" I joked.

Pat answered that she'd have plenty of time to read. I

would have picked thrillers over encyclopedias. "Only an engineer would bring the equivalent of a textbook," I joked to myself.

I had seen a few other books but hadn't seen a Bible. Looking back at what she had done, that's the one book she really needed. I didn't say anything.

Reid suggested that since everyone was here, this would be a good time to take a break and get something to eat and drink. He then excused himself, saying he had some errands to run and he'd be back.

CHAPTER 87

Donna and Ashley found a place to sit. They looked worn out from power shopping. Tony and Lance went for takeout and returned with more sandwiches than the seven of us could possibly eat.

Pat and I each took a dock cart of her clothing purchases over to the marina's laundry room. Sure enough, she had some winter gear that looked brand-new.

All four washing machines were available, so Pat sorted the loads and I got a roll of quarters. While the machines were running, Pat said she had a theory. I put down my sandwich and listened.

"Do you remember when you told me that the women in your bloodline all died from a rare ovarian cancer before age fifty?"

That stung. I had tried to put that thought out of my

mind and only think about it on my birthday. Why in the world had she brought that up? I nodded.

She smiled. "You would need extensive medical testing to confirm this, but I believe the alien's sterilization process has likely changed your future."

"You don't think the cancer is hereditary and will show up when it's ready?"

"I don't believe that cancer, or numerous other ailments, would make it through the portal. Those cells would be sterilized along with anything else that could compromise the past if it lived and multiplied."

If she was right, which could be verified with testing, that was the best news I had ever heard. Well, maybe the second best news. Passing the aliens' test of "selflessness" and getting returned from the past had to be the best news. I needed time to process the implications for my future based on her theory.

However, it raised another question, one that had been percolating since she mentioned she had three ideas to beat the aliens' sterilization field.

"So if nothing that could compromise the past is going to survive the alien's sterilization process, what's your plan for the seeds?"

She nodded a few times as if approving her response before she said it aloud.

"I'm going to evenly divide the seeds into three groups. The first batch will go into the ammo cans, which I will lower over the side just as the fog appears. I'm hoping that fifty feet of salt water will protect the seeds from getting sterilized."

I never would have thought of that. But when the aliens kept me back in time before, the thought of eventually living ashore never crossed my mind. Plus, I didn't have any seeds, so growing food wasn't an option.

"Are you using the bags of dirt to hide the second batch?"

"Sort of." She winked. "Those are decoys."

She noticed my puzzled look. "The aliens would surely sterilize all of the twenty-first-century microbes in the dirt. In fact, I'm betting on it. What I'm hoping they won't care about are bags and buckets of concrete and mortar mix. That's where I'll conceal seed batch number two."

"Why take concrete and mortar?"

"How many cases of cans are onboard?"

I thought for a moment. "Forty or fifty I suppose. Why?"

"That's over a thousand cans."

She could tell from my expression that I wasn't making the connection.

"An empty can, filled with rock or sand, is basically a round brick. Empty cans are trash. Repurposed cans are building materials."

My brain just didn't work that way, but I forgot that Pat was a contractor. Nowadays, lots of things were used to build shelters—old tires, for instance—so why not bricks made out of cans? Ingenious, really. I grudgingly had to give her credit.

"And batch number three?" I said. "What are your plans for that one?"

"Did you see the protective aprons from the dental office?"

I nodded.

"Those are specifically designed and manufactured to block stray X-ray radiation. Batch number three will be wrapped and secured inside the folds of those aprons."

"Will they stop the aliens' scan from sterilizing the seeds?"

"I surely hope so."

"Are you going to try and smuggle some plants too?"

"Plants would be challenging to conceal, but I might get some small citrus fruit through."

She paused. I could tell she had something else on her mind. At last, she said, "Tracy, I really am sorry for what's happened. I made some stupid choices. I keep thinking about the sailors aboard that ship and what their families are going through. I wish I could take it all back."

"Has the Navy come out with a cover story?" I asked.

She shook her head. "I haven't heard of one."

I turned away. I wasn't ready yet to accept her apology.

I left her to wait for the laundry. I needed time to think about not dying of cancer in less than sixteen years. If that was true, I might have to consider making changes to several aspects of my life. The first would have something to do with not drinking so much.

The six of us had all the laundry washed, folded, and stowed before Reid returned from his shopping excursion. He had a bunch of perishable food and two more large Pelican coolers. He also brought a few more duffel bags aboard, explaining he had found Pat some more clothing she might need.

She offered to de-tag and wash everything, but he said she should take a break and he'd do it for her later.

He sent Lance and Ashley to get blocks of ice for the coolers. Donna went with them. When the food was packed, he sent me for some bags of crushed ice to top off the coolers.

We spent the rest of the day rechecking her lists and trying to secure everything for the trip through the portal.

Buster had no problem moving freely between the stacks of supplies. He sniffed each and every item he could reach. Pat said she hoped he wouldn't lift his leg. I forced myself not to laugh at the thought of Buster marking his territory. The rest of us could barely maneuver. There was hardly room to breathe. About the only clear space was the bed in the owner's cabin.

We all agreed it was time to eat, so I let Buster go topside and then we all went out to dinner.

After eating, Reid and Pat said they'd motor over to the fuel dock and fill all the fuel tanks. Tony and Lance agreed to go along and help. Donna and Ashley went back to the motel.

Reid pulled me aside and quietly asked if I'd mind if he spent the night with Pat.

I was a little surprised but appreciated his asking. I said I didn't mind and went back to the motel.

Besides, I refused to be jealous of a soon-to-be memory.

CHAPTER 88

Our last full day was busy. Reid and Pat went over the old lists and made new ones. As crowded as it was, Reid did his best to check every inch of *The Lady Anne*, looking for anything that needed backup, repair, or replacement.

I was surprised when Pat said she wanted a sea kayak. Vee's accidental death was caused by a sea kayak coming loose, But I didn't say anything about that to Pat. I didn't want to hex Pat by mentioning something where the chance was one in a million it might happen again.

I found a gently used one for sale at the marina and the staff even carried it back for me. Reid and Pat lashed it to the dinghy, not against the lifelines the way we had on *The Aquaholic*.

The Lady Anne's topsides were crowded but less than I originally envisioned. Besides the fuel tanks, propane tanks, kayak, and new coolers, her decks were fairly clear. With her sails removed, she looked naked.

I noticed a powerboat tied to the swim platform. That was unexpected. There was no way that powerboat would survive the time portal without ripping loose. When I asked about it, Reid said he had rented it so he and I would have a way to get back after *The Lady Anne* was taken by the fog.

He had put a chart onboard and some bottles of water. There was also a receipt and the phone number in case we were going to be late returning it.

While topside was relatively clear, below deck was another story. It looked like a warehouse or long-term storage locker. Reid had draped cargo netting over everything. He wanted every item secure for when the boat heeled or got pounded in a storm.

The Lady Anne certainly was well provisioned. It still rankled that we hadn't had a chance to prepare like this, but I couldn't really blame Pat for taking advantage of the seventy-two hour window she had been gifted.

Pat produced Buster's leash. He immediately started barking, excited to go for a walk. I was a little surprised when Pat asked if I'd go with her. She looked as if she had something on her mind. Since it was her last night in civilization, I humored her and agreed.

"I know you're still ticked at what I did, but I need to clear the air."

She sounded sincere, but I doubted another apology was going to change anything.

"I can count all of my lovers on one hand," she said, stopping so Buster could sniff the ground.

"Is this where you call me promiscuous again?" I asked, wondering what her point could possibly be.

"Not at all. This is where I tell you that I have no idea what in the universe I was thinking when I called Charles's risqué poker bet."

"You wanted a chance to win a luxury yacht and you wagered your inhibitions." I had expected Pat to apologize, not bring up the event that began our unbelievable alien encounter and subsequent life-changing events.

"Charles suggested the wager, you were drinking and agreed, and against my better judgement, some kind of 'gambling fever' made me call. I knew that not folding was stupid, but I couldn't walk away."

I wasn't sure what point she was making. None of this sounded like an apology. I waited.

"When I overheard Vee ask you and Reid directly if you were going to 'ditch the bitch' and sail away with them, I was overcome not with gambling fever this time, but rage. I knew that banishing all of you back in time was totally irresponsible, but having the aliens' technology so readily available was too great a temptation."

She was tearing up.

"It was the same with the fog. Mo and I made fog in a fish tank to see if we could. The rush of success went to my head. I repeated the experiment on a larger scale. I expected more fog, not looting and chaos. I should have stopped my fog machine, but I couldn't. The power of controlling nature was too addicting to relinquish."

Buster saw another dog and began barking. We resumed walking.

"Depression and grief haunted me shortly after Mo's heart attack. I was ready to destroy my device when I had a revelation."

"What kind of revelation?" I asked.

"I saw a way my signal disruption machine could bring an end to my recurring Pincus nightmares." Pat's voice changed from somber to intense.

"Mo's heart attack proved my device could exact revenge against sexual demons. There would be no murder weapon, no ballistics, no toxicology reports showing poisons—no clues whatsoever. There wouldn't even be a crime scene. Without an eyewitness, the bad guy's body would just be classified as death by natural causes."

"I'm still not condoning what you did," I said. "Two wrongs don't make a right."

"I'm not asking for your approval. You were unconscious most of the time Pincus held us prisoner. You didn't experience the helplessness, the fear I felt when I thought he was going to rape me. I hope you never do. I'm only asking that you understand when I say that dispensing my method of justice became so satisfying that I couldn't stop. What I did was wrong, but in my heart, I was trying to save anyone else from being a victim."

We stopped walking. Pat lowered her voice and looked right at me. I tensed and waited.

"Please know that I'm very sorry for what I did to you and Reid. You are my best friend, and I hurt you deeply when I didn't give you a chance to talk to me, when I didn't give Reid a chance to choose. I think deep down I figured the aliens would send you right back. I kept *The Lady Anne* in the vicinity where you disappeared for days, waiting. Finally, I had to accept what I had done. But believe me when I tell you I know it will haunt me for the rest of my life."

She paused a moment, then continued. "But there will be plenty of time for self-reflection when I sail away on *The Lady Anne* tomorrow, won't there?"

How right she was. A life sentence of being alone, of talking to yourself about what you should have done differently, suddenly seemed a suitable punishment.

CHAPTER 89

I spent another night alone in the motel room. I was disappointed Reid chose to be with her, but I understood. Besides, there would be plenty of time for us to be together. A lifetime.

I couldn't sleep thinking about all the things Pat had said. For always being so precise and logical, when Pat finally gave into her emotions, the repercussions had almost proved disastrous for Reid and me. At least she had admitted her mistakes. That was a small amount of progress. Unfortunately, for Mo and the others, it was too little too late.

After tossing and turning for hours, I decided to forgive Pat for what she had done. I accepted that holding a grudge was pointless. Her deeds were done and couldn't be undone. Her talk with me last night had been a cry for help. She needed my forgiveness for closure before her exile.

Maybe I did too.

Thoughts of Pat's bleak future nagged at me. Did she deserve to suffer? Yes. But I couldn't imagine what it would be like for her facing her future, but I had to admire how bravely she was approaching it.

I dozed in and out until the sun woke me. I got cleaned up and met the others at the dock.

After a few last minute items, including more ice and a case of pineapples, it was time for her to go.

Ashley, Donna, Lance, and Tony said their goodbyes and wished Pat luck. She thanked them for all of their help. She told Buster goodbye too. He wanted to come with us on board, but Donna held his leash.

I heard Tony ask Reid if he wanted him to come along. Reid shook his head. Tony said they'd be waiting for me and Reid back at the motel. I waved as we motored out of the slip. Buster was barking. I knew I'd be back, but Pat was getting her last look at civilization.

As we motored out of sight, I asked Reid to take the helm and motioned Pat below.

I took her hands. "I wasn't ready for this last night, but I am now. I forgive you. You have my love and my prayers as you pilot *The Lady Anne* across uncharted waters."

When we hugged, it felt good.

We returned topside, both wiping away tears. If Reid wondered what had been said, he didn't ask.

Motoring fifteen nautical miles offshore without the benefit of the mainsail for stability was rough. Being severely overloaded, *The Lady Anne* labored like a pig in quicksand. But the sails had to be secured below so they would survive the portal unscorched.

Nobody said much on the way out. We all knew the future that awaited Pat.

We finally reached our desired coordinates. I had concerns the rolling, pitching, heaving slog would make us late, but we were actually a little early.

While we waited, Pat tied fifty feet of line to each ammo can. They contained plastic bags of assorted seeds, oranges, lemons, grapefruit, and even a few small red onions.

She duct-taped the containers shut, ensuring a watertight seal. Reid double-checked her knots. When satisfied, he lowered the cans into the water. He then double-checked that the kayak and dinghy were secure too.

I helped Pat cover the fuel tanks, propane tanks, and solar panels with heavy canvas drop cloths. I also helped her drain the melted ice water from the coolers.

Reid went below and disconnected the batteries. I couldn't envision how he had room to access them, but he returned shortly, reporting the job was done.

He reminded her to tighten the shipping screws on the two helm compasses. She nodded.

He also reminded her to retrieve the ammo cans as soon as the sterilization scan ended. She nodded again.

The aliens' fog hadn't yet appeared, but Reid and I said our goodbyes to Pat. She told me again that she was sorry, and I hugged her for the last time. Reid told her she would be okay. They shared one final kiss.

Reid started the powerboat while I cast us off. Pat stood at the stern rail and wished us a safe trip back to Kauai and then to Oahu. She thanked us for all of our help and wiped her eyes as she waved goodbye.

Reid motored out about fifty yards, and then we waited. Exactly fifteen minutes before the seventy-two hours ticked away, he reached under the seat and handed me a large mailing envelope.

I hesitated, not sure what was happening.

He leaned close and said, "You'll know when it's time to open this." He put the envelope in my hands. I just looked at him. What the hell was he doing?

He stood up and hollered over to Pat, "Request permission to come aboard."

"Permission denied," Pat yelled back. "You don't have much time, and I'm as ready as I'll ever be."

Reid faced me. "Please know that I love you very much. Also understand that I can't let Pat face her consequences alone."

Before I could muster a response, Reid dove in, clothes and all, and swam toward *The Lady Anne*.

I motored alongside as he swam. I asked him repeatedly to change his mind. He ignored my pleadings. When he reached the swim platform, I had no choice but to veer away or risk a collision.

Any fantasies I entertained that he would swim back and

return with me vanished when the fog appeared. I looked at my watch. It was seventy-two hours exactly.

I shifted into forward and steered away. Reid waved at me. Pat was hugging him. I increased my speed. For a split second, I wondered if I should join them. We'd done it once-the three of us.

I glanced back. Reid and Pat weren't looking at me, just each other. They didn't look unhappy or worried. They looked content. I gunned the engine and continued on course. Right now, the only thing that mattered was putting distance between me and them.

I glanced back once more. The fog was engulfing *The Lady Anne*. I started crying and wished them fair winds and following seas.

As I sped back to Kauai, the punchline from one of Reid's old jokes popped unexpectedly into my head. I smiled in spite of myself. "Good luck in your new location," I whispered.

CHAPTER 90

One week later, I was finishing dinner at Charles's compound with Ashley, Donna, Angie, and Gert. Buster was close by, watching for scraps.

None of them mentioned Reid or Pat or *The Lady Anne*. I had already told them what happened. There was no reason to bring it up again. Thinking of Reid diving into the water only made me want to cry.

I wondered how long Reid had known that he would be going back in time with her. I imagined the bags he said contained extra clothes for Pat contained spare clothing for him. I figured he had returned to Walmart and Goodwill and bought what he thought he'd need. After all, he had a wad of cash—courtesy of Pat.

I never suspected Reid of plotting to return with Pat. That was a one-way ticket. I don't believe that Pat knew his plans either. At least not until he jumped in the water. I vacillated between being angry with him and impressed with his sacrifice. None of that mattered now. He was gone.

I still didn't fully understand why Reid chose Pat and left me alone. I consoled myself by saying that Pat needed him more than I did. But it was small consolation. I missed him.

I also wondered if the aliens were surprised when *The Lady Anne* transited the time portal with two persons aboard instead of just Pat.

Had Reid passed some kind of test? Would the aliens be impressed with his "act of selflessness?" Impressed enough to forgive Pat's misuse of "advanced problem-solving techniques" and give them a chance to return to this time?

Deep down I knew the answer was no.

Jane called earlier to say Charles had been discharged from the hospital. They would be resting for several days in Puerto Rico before returning to the compound in Hawaii.

I told her that Pat and Reid were taking *The Lady Anne* on a long sea voyage and would be out of contact for sometime. I didn't volunteer any details but said I'd tell her more when we were together. In case the CIA was eavesdropping, I didn't want to say anything incriminating.

I had already asked Angie not to tell her mom either but to stick to the long sea voyage story. She understood and promised to be very careful on the phone, in texts, or in emails.

Charles took the phone to let me know that he was happy to contribute additional funding to the plastic magnet project.

He was confident the testing phase would be successful and eager to get it started.

I had originally decided to call it the "Palmer Polymer Magnet" and sell licenses for one dollar so as not to profit from the aliens' technology. Now that Mo and Pat, the two people responsible for turning my drawings into a working prototype, were no longer with us, I was rethinking the name. So far nothing sounded right.

If the plastic magnet did actually work and was able to remove the plastic debris from the ocean, I'd start with the waters around Oahu. I figured I owed the islanders that as a partial payment for the problems Pat's fog had created.

Charles also mentioned that he had agreed to buy the Clarriage ninety-five that was in Canada after all. He said he would have it professionally delivered to Hawaii.

Before dinner, I filled everyone in on the conversation.

Angie had made a giant oatmeal raisin cookie for dessert that smelled delicious. She wanted to celebrate the news that *The Aquaholic's* engines could be rebuilt and didn't have to be replaced.

She still wanted to move her charter business to Hawaii. She planned to have her boat shipped this time. When the Clarriage ninety-five arrived, she and her mom would run their charter business out of the marina in Kailua where *The Lady Anne* had been berthed.

Angie had planned on Reid and me helping with her business. I wasn't ready for that, but my decision didn't deter them. She would simply interview and hire captains and professional crews. Angie and her mom would personally manage the behind-the-scenes operations.

I asked Angie if the new Clarriage was going to get razzle-dazzle paint to match *The Aquaholic*. She smiled and said that was a brilliant idea.

Gert was going to work for them, flying to boat and travel shows promoting their new company. She was very excited at the prospect of getting paid to travel and talk about charter sailing vacations. She talked occasionally about missing Mo. When she did, she teared up. I could relate.

Tony and Lance would continue to provide security but would also shuttle charter guests back and forth to the airport.

Ashley and Donna were going to continue to manage Pat's and Reid's affairs stateside from here while they were away. They knew that was likely indefinitely, or until someone had them declared legally missing, presumed dead.

They also kept busy working with Elouise, reviewing some of Charles's insurance coverages. They loved it on Charles's estate and planned to stay as long as that was an option.

None of us had heard from Bonnie. I debated telling her what had happened but decided that she didn't need to know.

We all wondered if we were under CIA surveillance. I never saw anyone suspicious but didn't say or write anything that I'd regret. I told myself I wasn't really paranoid, just cautious.

After dinner, I broke off a big piece of cookie and excused myself to the garage apartment where I was now staying. Buster followed me.

On the way, I thought about Marta. She had arrived at Charles's compound an hour after Ashley, Donna, Tony, Lance, and I got back from Kauai. Jack had brought the five of us back to Oahu in his boat. It was fast and fun. He didn't want any gas money but didn't refuse when I shoved a wad of cash into his pocket.

Marta demanded to know where Pat was. I told her the whole story.

She didn't believe me at first but eventually decided I was telling the truth. She confided that she felt cheated out of her revenge. She was sorry I had lost Reid. She was going to miss him as well. She wasn't sure what was next for her.

I had her talk to Elouise about getting a job providing security for Charles. She liked the idea of working with Lance and Tony but wasn't sure. Elouise was eager to hire her.

Marta left, saying she needed some time alone to think about her future. I told her she was always welcome. Deep down, I wasn't sure if I'd ever see her again.

I took a bite of cookie and resumed my online search for cruises that included the Galapagos Islands, Komodo, and Easter Island. Seeing those places still interested me. So far I had only found one cruise that encompassed that itinerary, but it catered to older couples, not younger singles. I was sure there were other cruises. They just weren't coming up.

There was a noise, and then Buster started barking. I peeked out the window and recognized Donna's fuchsia hair. She was excited and insisted I immediately switch on the local news.

There were a few reports that life on the island was slowly returning to normal. Those were followed by the weather forecast. Then the evening's top story repeated.

After a large meteor crashed into the Antarctic ice, a group of scientists visited the impact site. Inside the massive crater, they discovered a strange object encased in a block of ice. Using precision lasers, they extracted a bell. The bell is made of brass and is perfectly preserved. It has been positively identified as the ship's bell from The Lady Anne, a luxury Clarriage sailing yacht with a mysterious past. The Lady Anne was reported missing near the Bahamas in the Bermuda Triangle, only to reappear some time later in Bermuda. It was later reported berthed at a marina on Oahu, Hawaii, but had recently left and hasn't been reported anywhere since. The ice surrounding the bell has been dated to be between twenty thousand and thirty thousand years old. There is no logical explanation as to how this could be possible. Either this is an elaborate hoax or this will give the followers of ancient alien stories enough material to last for years.

There was a picture of the bell and a close-up of the engraving. It was indeed *The Lady Anne's*.

Donna took the remote and switched off the television. She took my hand. "Finding the ship's bell doesn't mean *The Lady Anne* was lost with all aboard," she said.

She released my hand and then walked away. I locked the door behind her.

Satisfied I was alone, I went into the kitchen and opened the panel concealing the gold.

On top of the coins was the folder that Gert had secretly

given me. It contained Mo's duplicate notes for the fog generator and the cell phone jamming device. She had entrusted his notes to me. No one else knew they existed.

I moved that folder aside and removed the envelope that Reid had given me. Hearing the news story suggested this was the right time to open it. I wasn't sure why *The Lady Anne* would have sailed to Antartica. I knew Donna's words were meant to comfort me, and maybe Reid and Pat had successfully negotiated a return trip, but more realistically, this time it really had been a suicide sail.

I shrugged and opened the envelope.

Inside was Reid's will. It left his strip mall and everything else he owned to me.

There was also a handwritten note.

Dearest Tracy. If you're reading this, I won't restate the obvious. There is room in my heart to love two women. Please have room in yours to forgive me for leaving with Pat and not staying with you.

I left you alone once but I didn't have a choice. This time I did. I give you permission to move forward with your life.

My parents left me their commercial property. I am now leaving that legacy to you. When you cash the monthly rent checks, think of me and all the great times we had. Please don't grieve. I died like Cookie Cook did—a sailor's death at sea. Fair winds and following seas. With all my love - Reid.

There was a PS.

I'll leave you with my favorite knock-knock joke. You start it.

I glanced at Buster and said, "Knock knock."

I looked back at Reid's note. A few spaces below was written *Who's there?*

I didn't know. Then I got it. Asking someone to finish a knock-knock joke they hadn't started was funny. Despite the fact that I was crying a river, his last joke, another lame one of course, made me chuckle.

I refolded the will and the note, placed them back in their envelope, and put it back in the wall. I took off my pendant and put that away too. I closed the panel. The seams were still perfect. The treasure was safely hidden.

As I wiped my eyes, the last line from *Sea Fever* came to mind. *And quiet sleep and a sweet dream when the long trick's over.*

The End

NAUTICAL GLOSSARY

Nautical Glossary

Abeam	The area at a right angle to the vessel.
Aboard	On a vessel, or to go onto a vessel.
Adjustable keel	The ballasted structure on the bottom of the vessel's hull that can be raised or lowered to suit conditions.
Adrift	Moving on the water but not under power or control. (See also drifting.)
Aft	At or toward the stern.
Aground	Stuck on the ground in shallow water.
Ahoy	1. A nautical greeting. 2. A shout used to attract attention.
Alarm tone	A loud tone that sounds when the diesel engine is first started, indicating low oil pressure. Once the oil begins pumping and lubricating the engine, the tone stops.
Amidships	Area in the middle of the vessel, either front to back or side to side.
Anchor	A device, usually deployed from the bow, used to secure the vessel to the bottom to keep the vessel from moving away. Anchors come in different shapes and sizes to optimize holding in different bottom compositions (mud, sand, rock, etc.).

Anchor alarm function	A device using GPS to monitor the vessel's position and sound an alarm if the vessel moves outside of a preset boundary.
Anchor light	One or more white lights shown at night when a vessel is at anchor. Sailboats often have this light atop the mast.
Anchor station	Topside area where the anchor is kept.
Anchor storage compartment / Anchor locker	A compartment where the anchor and associated tackle are kept. On a dinghy, this is often in the bow. On some vessels, there are provisions for a freshwater rinse of the anchor and its chain/line.
Anchor windlass	See windlass.
Anchoring	A process of deploying or retrieving the anchor.
Anemometer	An instrument for measuring wind speed.
Astern	The area behind the stern (back) of the boat.
Autopilot	A device of various designs to automatically keep the vessel on a preset course.
Backstay	A support, often made of cable or rod, that leads downward and aft from the upper part of the mast. It is used to support the mast and to control sail trim.
Baja-ha-ha race	An annual fall sailboat rally that begins in San Diego, CA, and ends in Cabo San Lucas, Baja, Mexico. It is not officially a race, but there is a lot of informal competition.

Bare poles	Not having any sails deployed. The masts are "bare."
Bareboat charter company	Companies that allow sailors to charter (rent) sailboats/yachts with or without any crew for a few days or a few weeks. Those persons chartering the boat will need to prove they are qualified to sail and operate the size boat they are chartering.
Bareboat Chartering class	Instruction to take the Bareboat Chartering test, an advanced-intermediate level of certification to be able to charter (rent) sailboats, between 30 - 50 feet in length, for sailing in moderate wind and sea conditions, within sight of land, during daylight hours. The prerequisite is usually the Coastal Cruising certification or equivalent. There is normally textbook, classroom, and on-the-water instruction, including an overnight sail.
Basic Keelboat class	Instruction to take the Basic Keelboat test, a beginning level of certification that demonstrates the ability to prepare the sailboat to sail, get away from the dock, raise sail, preform basic sailing maneuvers such as tacking and jibing, and get the boat safely back to the dock. There is usually no prerequisite as this is a beginning level course. There is normally textbook, classroom, and on-the-water instruction, including learning several knots.
Battery selector switch	A mechanical switch to select which battery (house or starter) to use (charge or discharge). It usually can be switched to either battery, both, or neither.

Beam	The widest part of the boat.
Beam reach	A point of sail where the wind is coming over the side of the vessel at roughly the 3:00 or 9:00 position.
Becalmed	A condition that exists for a sailboat when there is no wind whatsoever.
Belay that	A command to cancel the previous order.
Below	The area beneath the deck.
Bermuda Triangle	An area loosely bordered by points in Florida, Puerto Rico, and Bermuda where dozens of ships and planes have disappeared, some under mysterious or unexplained circumstances.
Berth	1. A sleeping space aboard a vessel. 2. A vessel's allotted space at a dock.
Bilge	1. The lowest, deepest part of a vessel where the bottom curves up to meet the sides. 2. The water (often dirty and smelly) that collects in the bilge.
Bimini top	A temporary cover that can be deployed for shade or protection from the elements over the open cockpit of a boat. They are often made of a treated material to resist fading and are usually collapsible.
Bitter end	1. The inboard end of the anchor line, hopefully secured to the vessel. 2. The end of a line that is not attached to anything.
Blip	See radar blip.

Board/Boarding/Boarded	To get on, to be getting on, or to have gotten on a boat.
Boarding ladder	Temporary steps allowing people access to a vessel from the water. Boarding ladders are usually near the stern and often fold for storage.
Boat	A small vessel propelled by oar, paddle, sail, pole, or an engine. Rule of thumb: a boat will fit on the deck of a ship, but a ship will not fit on the deck of a boat.
Boatmeal	1. The punchline to Reid's joke about what sailors eat for breakfast. 2. What Tracy calls oatmeal.
Boat hook	A long pole, sometime telescoping, with a hook on one end used for grabbing or pushing something.
Boom	1. A long spar of various materials, protruding out from the mast, holding the foot (bottom edge) of the sail. The boom can be released (eased) to swing from side to side. 2. The last sound you hear when you are unexpectedly hit in the head by the boom. This can be very dangerous, even fatal.
Bow	The front of the vessel, also called the pointy end.
Bow line	A dock line used to secure the front of the boat to the dock.

Bow pulpit	A railing, usually metal, at the bow of the vessel. It sometimes extends forward past the deck. On some larger vessels, it may hold the anchor.
Bow wake	A wave that forms at the bow of a vessel as it moves through the water.
Bowline knot	A temporary, nonslipping loop. The bowline can be untied easily, even when wet, as long as there is no load (tension) on the line. (Pronounced like "colon," with a B.)
Bowsprit	A spar or pole, protruding forward from the bow, to which sails or rigging can be attached.
Brass bell	The ship's bell, made of brass or bronze, used to signal the time or produce required sound signals. They are normally engraved with the vessel's name and can be quite ornate.
Bridge	The dedicated area of a ship, usually with a good view or immediate access to such a view, from where the ship is commanded.
Broad reach	A point of sail where the wind is coming over the rear quarter of the vessel at roughly the 5:00 or 7:00 position.
Broadside	The side of a ship above the waterline.
Bulb-keel	A specific type of keel, ballast filled and usually teardrop shaped.
Bulkhead	A support or dividing wall between compartments to strengthen the vessel.

Buoy	An anchored float, normally used as an aid to navigation or to display warnings or mark dangerous areas.
Cabin	An enclosed area on a vessel that may or may not be tall enough to stand up in. The nautical equivalent of a room.
Canadian-flagged boat	A boat displaying the Canadian flag.
Capsize	To turn over or upside down in the water.
Captain	The person in charge of the vessel and responsible for its safe operation and the safety of the crew and passengers.
Cat	Abbreviation for catamaran.
Catalina 470	A 47-foot long American sailboat, first built in 1998. They were built by Catalina Yachts but are no longer in production.
Catamaran	A vessel with twin hulls running parallel to each other.
Celestial navigation	The process of finding one's way by observing the positions of celestial bodies (the sun, the moon, and/or the stars).
Channel	1. A navigable length of water, often marked with buoys or other aids to navigation, connecting two other, often larger bodies of water. 2. A specific band of frequencies used in radio or television.

Channel 16	A specific VHF radio frequency primarily designated for international distress and safety calls.
Chart	A nautical map, paper or electronic, used for navigation. It usually shows the water depth, land features, markers (buoys), traffic lanes, distances between islands, the method to convert magnetic to true north, etc. Charts are marked in degrees latitude and longitude. The depth can be shown in feet, meters, or fathoms (6 feet in a fathom).
Charter boat	A vessel for rent or hire, normally located in island or coastal destinations.
Cigarette boat	A small, often quite expensive boat (usually between thirty and fifty feet long) with a long, narrow body (thought by some to resemble a cigarette) and a hull designed to go fast. They were originally called "rum runners" and used to transport illegal alcohol during prohibition. They were much faster than the patrol boats chasing them.
Circumnavigation	The process of sailing (or traveling) all the way around something, often the world.
Clarriage 68 / Clarriage 95	A fictional luxury sailing yacht, 68/95 feet in length, designed to cross oceans and be lived aboard for extended periods in complete comfort.
Clarriage Yachts	A line of fictional luxury sailing yachts designed to cross oceans and be lived aboard for extended periods in complete comfort.

Cleat	A normally metal object upon which a line can be fastened.
Cleat hitch knot	A type of knot, resembling a figure eight, used to secure a line around a cleat.
Cleating / Cleated	The process of securing a line to a cleat.
Clipped in	Attached to the boat by various methods so as not to fall overboard.
CO2 cartridge	Some PFDs are inflated using a compressed gas (carbon dioxide) cylinder that contains enough gas for one inflation.
Coastal Cruising class	Instruction to take the Coastal Cruising test, an intermediate level of certification that adds to the Basic Keelboat instruction. Advanced topics include reefing, anchoring, heaving to, docking under power, and additional proficiency with knots. The prerequisite is usually the Basic Keelboat certification or equivalent. There is normally textbook, classroom, and on-the-water instruction.
Cockpit	The location of the controls on a vessel, normally outside the pilothouse/deckhouse and often recessed slightly into the deck. There may be a separate helm station on some designs.
Cockpit curtains	Side and aft curtains, often with a see-through panel, used to enclose and protect the occupants from the elements. Usually used in conjunction with some type of roof structure or Bimini top. The curtains are often made from a water-resistant material.

Cockpit table	A table, usually in the cockpit of a boat. They can be of several designs, including pedestal, drop-leaf, fold-down, adjustable height, etc. and can be made of various materials (various species of wood, plastics, fiberglass, acrylics, metal, composites, etc.) with varying degrees of resistance to the harsh marine environment.
Compass	An instrument to determine directions that contains an easily rotating magnetized pointer (needle) which shows the direction of magnetic north and bearings from it.
Compass needle	The magnetized pointer in a compass.
Compass rose	1. A circular reference tool on a nautical chart displaying true north, magnetic north, and indicating adjustments for compass variation. 2. A decorative figure displaying north, south, east, and west and perhaps points in between.
Compass variation	The angle or difference between magnetic north (on a compass point) and true north (on the meridian toward geographic north). Variation changes in amount and direction, based on location and year.
Crew	The person or persons who assist in the operation of the vessel.
Crew's quarters	A spartan but efficient living space to offer the crew some privacy. Somewhat self-contained and may or may not have minimal galley facilities.

Crewed charter boat	A boat for charter (rent) that comes fully equipped (food, drinks, dishes, linens, towels, fuel, captain, cook, crew, etc.) so all the guests have to do is bring personal items and relax.
Cruisers	1. Those that sail from place to place, living aboard for extended periods, for pleasure. 2. Vessels designed specifically for cruisers. 3. Those persons who repair their boats in exotic locations.
Cruising	What cruisers do—sail from place to place and fix their boat in exotic locations.
Cruising guide	A publication, either hardcopy or electronic, dedicated to a specific area, giving various levels of information and details about the area. May include information such as marina locations, yacht clubs, approach/departure routes, monitored radio frequencies, facilities, lodging, shopping, marine repair, sightseeing, dining, fishing, customs information, etc. May also include chart excerpts for specific locations.
Current	The movement of water usually caused by tides, winds, or flow.
Current position	Accurately obtaining the vessel's location by electronic or other means. Caveat: If the vessel is moving, the position you obtained and noted may be several minutes old.
Cutlass	A short, broad sword sharpened on the cutting edge. They could be straight or curved and were a common weapon during the age of sail.

Davits	See dinghy davits.
Deck	A floor-like surface, permanently covering one or more level(s) of a hull or compartment and serving to strengthen the hull.
Depth finder	A device, usually electrical or electronic, used to measure the depth of the water.
Diesel engine	The most common engine in sailboats over 25 feet long. Compared to gasoline fuel powered engines, diesel fuel powered engines offer higher torque, higher available horsepower, lower maintenance costs, no carbon monoxide production, and less sensitivity to moisture. But, diesel engines are heavier, noisier, and more expensive, initially.
Diesel fuel	Just as gasoline has different octane ratings, diesel fuel is available in different grades.
Diesel generator	An additional mechanical device to provide electricity other than using a diesel engine. Diesel fuel is safer to store than gasoline because diesel fuel doesn't vaporize as easily and is less combustible.
Dinghy	A small open boat, often carried on or towed behind a larger vessel. A dinghy can be used as a tender (transport), for recreation, or even as a lifeboat. Dinghies can be rowed, sailed, or motor driven. Their hull can be inflatable or rigid.
Dinghy davits	A crane-type mechanical device used to raise, lower, or support the vessel's dinghy.

Distance Speed Time formula	A formula (D = S x T) used by navigators to calculate distance, speed, or time when only two of the three values are known.
Distress signal	1. Any of various internationally recognized indicators (either visual or audible) signifying a vessel is in danger. 2. A request for assistance.
Divider	An instrument used by navigators to measure and transfer distances on a nautical chart using the latitude scale.
Dock cart	A wheeled, wagon-type carrier used for moving supplies to or from the vessel when docked. Some dock carts fold for compact storage aboard.
Dock line	A specialty line used to secure the vessel to the dock. Dock lines often have a factory spliced loop at one end, are water and fade resistant, and provide some stretch. They vary in size, load rating, and length, depending on application.
Dock(s)	Manmade walkway(s) in the water from which to access boats. Many docks are floating to allow for tides or fluctuating water levels.
Docking	The act of bringing the vessel in to the dock and securing it.
Docking Certification class	Additional instruction to practice safely and efficiently maneuvering and docking an engine-powered sailboat.
Dogged	To close something (watertight door, porthole, hatch, etc.) and securely latch it closed.

Dorado	The Caribbean name for the dolphinfish, a species of fish with its dorsal fin running the length its body. Also called mahi-mahi in Hawaiian waters.
Downwind	The direction the wind is blowing.
Draw	The depth of water necessary to operate the vessel without grounding (running aground).
Drifting	At the mercy of the wind or current, having no means of directing the motion of the vessel.
Drogue	An external device attached to the vessel's bow or stern that is used to slow the vessel down in a storm. They are designed to keep the hull perpendicular to the waves. Also called a sea anchor.
Duffel bag	A type of bag, traditionally cylindrical in shape and closed by a drawstring or zipper. The bag got its name from Duffel, a town in Belgium where the cloth was first made. Duffel bags are preferred by sailors because, unlike a suitcase, they can be collapsed when emptied, thus saving precious space.
Ease	To slacken, let out, decrease tension, or pay out slightly.
Electronic chart overlay	Using GPS and an electronic chart, an electronic method to synchronize the vessel's autopilot to keep the vessel on a predetermined course.
Emergency Locator Beacon	See EPIRB

Engine compartment	A usually limited space to access the vessel's engine. On sailboats, the engine compartment is often located behind the ladder (steps) leading belowdecks. The ladder is removed to access the front of the engine and then additional panels can be removed to access the remainder of the engine.
Engine room	A specific compartment or large area dedicated to housing the vessel's engine(s). There is usually comfortable and well-lit access to all sides of the engine for inspection or maintenance purposes. The engine room is normally well insulated to reduce the engine's noise.
Engine throttle back	To manually slow the engine down, usually by pulling backwards on the throttle handle or lever.
EPIRB	An Emergency Position Indicating Radio Beacon (EPIRB for short) is a distress beacon used by mariners worldwide to alert (using satellite technology) search and rescue forces that the mariner/their vessel is in distress.
Eye of the wind	The direction where the wind is coming from.
Fair winds	1. A nautical blessing for a safe journey. 2. A favorable wind blowing in a desirable direction of travel for the mariner.
Fall off	To turn the sailboat away from the direction of the wind.
Falling tide	A movement of a tidal current away from a shore or down a tidal river or estuary.

Fender	A bumper placed outside the hull, used to prevent damage to the vessel. Fenders are often deployed when docking or rafting two or more vessels together. Fenders can protect both the vessel(s) and the dock.
Ferry	A specially designed boat or ship to carry passengers, vehicles, and/or limited cargo across a normally small body of water at regular intervals.
Fighting belt	A fishing accessory designed for use when fishing standing up. The belt straps around the fisherman's waist and has a receptacle that mates to the end of the fishing rod. The belt spreads the load across the fisherman's thighs and provides a mechanical advantage when fighting large gamefish.
Fighting chair	A specially designed chair for reeling in large game fish. The chairs angle, rock, and swivel. They include a footrest and a rod holder(s). Some models have a built-in harness and armrests.
Fillet knife	A specialty knife designed for filleting. It typically has a very sharp, flexible blade to allow the blade to easily cut underneath the fish's skin, just above the backbone.
Fish box	A container, built-in or freestanding, in which to keep the fish you have caught fresher, longer. A fish box should offer good insulation, a smooth interior finish, and adequate drainage to keep ice and the day's catch colder and speed the cleanup process at the end of the day.

Fittings	Mechanical devices to connect various components together, i.e., sailing hardware.
Fix	1. See position. 2. Repair.
Floorboards	The floor of the vessel, also called the sole. It is often made of long pieces of a species of wood that is resistant to water damage, such as teak. Some floorboards are removable to access the space(s) beneath them, such as the bilge.
Flybridge	The flybridge is a small, often open area situated high on the vessel (usually larger fishing boats), offering duplicate controls, where the vessel can be steered. The flybridge usually offers greater visibility due to unobstructed views of the fore, aft, and sides of the vessel.
Flying the spinnaker	Having deployed the spinnaker sail. (See also spinnaker.)
Following sea	Waves coming from behind the vessel.
Fore	See forward.
Foredeck	1. The deck at the forward part of a vessel. 2. The forward part of a vessel's main deck.
Forepeak	The farthest forward area/compartment in the vessel's hull.
Forestay	A support, often made of cable or rod, that leads downward and forward from the upper part of the mast. It is used to support the mast and the headsails. (See also standing rigging.)
Forward	At or toward the bow.

Fuel dock	A fixed or floating structure (dock) used to dispense (sell) fuel (gasoline or diesel) to boats while in the water. Fuel prices at marina fuel docks are often considerably higher than traditional, land-based gas stations.
Full sail	When all of a sailboat's sails are set, raised, hauled out, unfurled, or deployed.
Furl/Furled	To roll a sail over itself by using the roller furling mechanism. Opposite of hauled out.
Gaff	A handheld hook, often attached to a rigid handle of various lengths, used for holding or lifting heavy fish. The hook can be barbed or not and is often fairly sharp and pointy.
Gale	A strong, sustained wind. A gale at sea is accompanied by large waves and regular whitecaps. There may be blowing foam or churning seas. It is stronger than a breeze but weaker than a tropical storm.
Galley	The kitchen area aboard a boat or ship.
Gangplank	A portable walkway or bridge used for boarding or leaving a ship.
Gated pier	A locking gate, often made of metal, across the entrance to a pier or dock, controlling access.
Genoa	A sail set near the bow that extends aft of the main mast. A genoa is larger than a jib.
Gimbaled rod butt	A fitting mounted into or onto the butt of a saltwater fishing rod that fits inside a mating fixture that is attached to a fighting belt or a fighting chair.

Ginger ale	A carbonated soft drink, flavored with ginger. Ginger is thought by many boaters to help reduce vomiting, a typical result of being seasick.
Give way vessel	As per the navigation rules, the vessel that is required to keep out of the way of another vessel.
Glassing	To scan one's surroundings with binoculars.
Gnomon pointer	The part of a sundial that casts a shadow.
GPS	A satellite navigation system (Global Positioning System) used to determine the ground position of an object. The GPS receiver uses multiple signals from orbiting satellites to calculate a fairly accurate position using the process of triangulation.
Grab rail	A safety device, often in the shape of a railing or bar, used to provide the sailor with a strong and convenient handhold while moving about the vessel.
Gulf Stream	A warm ocean current flowing north from the Gulf of Mexico, along the east coast of the United States to an area off the south-east coast of Newfoundland where it becomes the western terminus of the north Atlantic current and flows towards Europe.
Hail	An attempt to establish contact by various methods, including a radio call, to see if anyone is listening.
Halyard	A line that raises a sail (or flag) up or down.

Hand bearing compass	A handheld magnetic compass, capable of one-handed use.
Handed off the helm	1. Literally, to not let go of the wheel or tiller until your replacement has a hold of it. 2. To relinquish control of the helm to a replacement.
Harbor	A place on the coast where vessels may find shelter. Harbors are usually protected from rough water by land, piers, jetties, sea walls, or other artificial structures.
Hatch	1. An opening in the deck leading to a lower level through which cargo, personnel, and even air can be passed. 2. A covering for such an opening.
Hatchway	A passage or opening leading to or from a compartment. (See also hatch.)
Hauled out	To deploy a sail that has roller furling by pulling it out by the clew (one of the corners on a triangular sail). Also called unfurling the sail.
Head	1. The bathroom on a vessel. 2. The top corner of a triangular sail.
Heading	A direction or course to steer.
Headsail	Any sail set forward of the most forward mast.
Heave to	A technique for (nearly) stopping a sailboat by positioning the sails to counteract each other. The vessel will oscillate slowly from one direction to another and then back again, over and over and over.

Heavy weather	Strong winds and large waves. May or may not be accompanied by rain, thunder, and/or lighting.
Heel/Heeling	The angle the boat sails at. The more the boat is heeled, the steeper the angle.
Helm	1. The tiller or the wheel that controls the angle of the rudder. 2. The area of a sailboat from which the boat is steered.
Helmsman / Helmswoman	The person who steers/drives the vessel.
Holding tank	A container, usually metal or plastic, in which wastewater is temporarily held prior to its proper disposal.
Horseshoe	A throwable cushion used for lifesaving. It is usually mounted on the stern rail at the rear of the vessel. Larger vessels may have them placed at strategic locations.
House battery	The battery that provides power to run the vessel's lights and electrical equipment but is not used to start the engine.
Hove to	Past tense of heave to. A sailboat that has "heaved to."
Hull	The main body of a vessel, including the bottom and the sides.
J/44	A 44-foot long American sailboat, designed as both a racer and a cruiser, first built in 1989. They were built by J Boats but are no longer in production.

Jackline	A temporary line, webbing strap, or wire, strung tightly from the bow to the stern to which a safety harness tether can be attached, allowing a crew member to safely move about the deck when there is a risk of falling or being swept overboard.
Jeanneau 45	A 45-foot long French production sailboat designed with lots of space for cruising in comfort, first built in 2007. They were built by Jeanneau Yachts but are no longer in production.
Jib	A sail set near the bow that does not extend aft of the main mast. A jib is smaller than a genoa.
Jibe/Jibing	A maneuver to bring the stern of the boat through the eye of the wind.
Jibe ho	A command issued (normally by the helmsman) while jibing, just prior to the boom swinging across to the other side.
Keel	An extension of the hull that goes deep(er) into the water and provides stability from heel and sideways resistance to the wind.
Ketch	A type of sailboat having two masts. The aft (rear) mast (the mizzen mast) is generally shorter than the forward mast (the main mast).
Knot	1. A measurement of speed at sea equal to one nautical mile per hour. 2. Used to fasten (tie) a line to itself or another object.

Knot meter	An instrument, normally electric or electronic, that measures the vessel's speed through the water.
Ladder	What steps on a ship (not a cruise ship) are often referred to, due to their steepness.
Land ho	An expression shouted by the vessel's watch to inform the crew that land has been spotted. After long passages at sea, "Land ho" is very comforting to hear.
Latitude	The angular distance, measured in degrees, minutes, and seconds, running north or south of the equator.
Lazarette	A small compartment or locker used for storage.
Lee cloth	A sheet of canvas, or other fabric, attached to the open side of a berth. It can provide an illusion of privacy but is primarily used to keep a sleeping person from falling out of bed when the vessel heels during sailing or rough weather.
Lee shore	A nearby shore that is downwind from your present position. They are particularly dangerous to mariners because with the wind blowing toward them, it is very difficult to get away from it against the oncoming waves.
Leech	The back edge of a triangular shaped sail.
Leeward	1. On or toward the side sheltered from the wind. 2. The side sheltered or away from the wind. (The side opposite windward.) (Pronounced loo ward, like "steward" with an L.)

Life jacket/Life vest	A flotation device designed to keep the wearer afloat in the water. They are available in different styles and are designed for various purposes and sea conditions.
Life raft	A smaller boat used in emergencies, often inflatable. Some life rafts provide a cover that can be used as shade. Some life rafts are designed to be difficult to sink or flip in rough seas.
Lifeline(s)	A wire or cable that runs along the outside of the deck, designed to help restrain passengers (or crew) from falling overboard.
Lifeline gate	A section of the lifeline that can be unhooked/unfastened to allow easy access on or off the boat without having to step over the lifeline.
Light air	Wind with a very low speed.
Light stick	A self-contained, short-term source of light. It consists of two plastic tubes containing chemicals that, when mixed together, begin glowing. They are available in different colors and intensities, although usually the brighter the glow, the shorter the time they last. (Also called a glow stick.)
Line	Rope or other forms of cordage that have come onboard a vessel. Lines with specific uses may be called by other names.
List or listing	When the vessel heels (tips) with no outside forces being applied.

Log	1. A book in which all matters concerning the vessel are notated. 2. To make a notation of an event worth recording. (Similar to an entry in a journal.)
Long tack	A sailing vessel being on the same tack (point of sail) for a long period of time.
Longitude	The angular distance, measured in degrees, minutes, and seconds, running east or west of the prime meridian running through Greenwich, England.
Loose-footed mainsail	A method of attaching the mainsail to the boom using only the two lower corners of the sail as attachment points.
Luff	1. The leading edge of a triangular-shaped sail. 2. A sail fluttering or flapping in the wind.
Macerate	The act of using a machine to grind solids (including sewage and food waste) in wastewater into small pieces so they can be discharged directly into the sea (normally when a minimum of 12 nautical miles offshore).
Magnetic north	A compass bearing relating to the magnetic poles rather than the true north and south poles.
Main mast	The primary, usually the tallest, mast aboard a sailboat.
Main salon	The primary indoor guest area on a vessel.

Mainsail	The primary source of power for a sailboat. The mainsail is attached to the main mast and the boom.
Mainsheet	The line that controls the mainsail, bringing it in or letting it out, from side to side.
Making way	A vessel moving through the water.
Man overboard drill	Various techniques used to retrieve a person who has fallen overboard. The method used will depend on the type of vessel, the prevailing sea conditions, and whether the victim is conscious or not.
Marina	A normally sheltered or protected commercial area where yachts and small vessels can dock, refuel, and get repairs and supplies.
Marlin spike	A pointy tool used in marine rope work. It may be a separate tool or one item on a specialty pocketknife.
Mast	A tall, upright spar of various materials and designs, erected vertically, generally along the centerline of the vessel. On a sailboat, the mast(s) carry the sail(s).
Mayday	The international distress signal that a vessel uses to declare they have a life-threatening emergency.
Messenger line	A light line used to haul a heavier line between vessels or to the shore.

Mizzen mast	The mizzen mast is aft of (behind) the main mast. It is usually shorter than the main mast. (See also ketch.)
Mizzen sail	A sail affixed to the mizzen mast. The mizzen sail is usually smaller than the mainsail.
Mizzen sheet	The line that controls the mizzen sail, bringing it in or letting it out, from side to side.
Monkey-fist knot	1. A knot in the category of heaving knots tied to the end of a line serving as a weight, making it easier to throw. 2. An ornamental knot. (It is so named because it resembles a bunched fist or paw.)
Monohull	A vessel with a single hull.
Motion sickness pills	A medication, in pill form, used to relieve the symptoms of travel or motion sickness.
Motorsailing	The act of a sailboat using engine power while keeping the mainsail up (for stability).
Multihull	A vessel with two, three, or more hulls, running parallel to each other. (All catamarans are multihulls but not all multihulls are catamarans.)
Multihull Certification class	Additional instruction to learn how to safely sail a catamaran. This class is for those that already have experience sailing monohulls.
Multi-tool	A versatile hand tool that combines several individual functions (screwdriver, knife, pliers, etc.) into a single unit.

Nautical almanac	A publication providing detailed information about various celestial bodies to aid navigators in determining their position at sea using celestial navigation.
Nautical mile	A unit used for measuring distances at sea. Historically it was equal to 1 minute of 1 degree of latitude. Now it is equal to 1,852 meters, 6,076 feet, or approximately 1.151 statute (regular) miles. It is abbreviated "nm."
Nautical uniform/ Nautical white	A clothing style borrowing from naval officers' designs. Uniform will be white in color, not blue. Shirts will have epaulet straps. Epaulets (an ornamental shoulder piece) may be plain or striped, with or without an insignia. Pants are often a solid color and may be pleated. Belt may have nautical themed designs, possibly signal flags, and the buckle may have an insignia. Hats are captain's style, with or without gold striping, insignias, and/or scrambled eggs (leaf-shaped embellishments) on the visor.
Navigation light(s)	A source of illumination on a vessel that give information on the vessel's type, position, heading, and status. Also called running lights.
Navigation station	A dedicated area of a vessel that houses the navigation tools and equipment. On a sailboat, it is usually below deck, often near the radio and the electrical circuit breaker/switches. Also called the Nav station.

Newport-Ensenada race	An international sailing yacht race first run in 1948. It begins in Newport Beach, CA, and ends 125 nautical miles later in Ensenada, Baja, Mexico. It is an annual event with numerous classes of competitors. It is often abbreviated N2E.
Night watch	A lookout during the night or a person(s) keeping such a lookout.
Noon sun shot	A navigational method to give a close approximation of your current latitude. It requires a sextant, an accurate timepiece, and a current copy of a Nautical Almanac. The calculation is fairly straightforward if the sighting is at LAN (local area noon). A close approximation of longitude can be determined in this manner as well.
Ocean crossing	1. The passage of passengers (and/or cargo) across an ocean. 2. An ocean crossing vessel is designed to handle rough seas and long passages.
Offshore	1. At sea, often out of sight of land. 2. A wind that is blowing away from the land.

Offshore Passage Making class	Instruction to take the Offshore Passage Making test, an advanced level of certification. It is a weeklong (or longer) live-aboard class, consisting of nearly nonstop sailing for a minimum of 600 miles, 250 of which are at least 50 miles from shore. The prerequisites are usually the Bareboat Chartering certification and the successful completion of a Coastal Navigation course and possibly a Celestial Navigation course, or equivalent. This is a capstone class for those wanting serious sailing instruction in real-world conditions. Instructors for this class will be highly qualified.
Offshore rain gear	Foul weather gear designed for consecutive days or weeks of use in extreme conditions. It must be durable, waterproof, highly breathable, and made of heavy-duty, high-quality fabrics, components, and construction.
Out of step	An often hazardous condition that exists when a multihull vessel gets its hulls in a different wave. Large enough waves can literally rip the hulls apart.
Outboard motor	A small internal combustion engine with a propeller integrally attached for mounting at the stern of a small boat.
Outhaul	A sail control line that allows adjustments to tension the sail.

Outrigger	A pair of long poles, fitted on both sides of a fishing boat, designed to hold fishing lines apart from each other and away from the boat. They are often used for trolling multiple fishing lines.
Overhead hatch	A hatch leading to the space above. They can be used for ventilation, light, or, if they are large enough, as an emergency exit for personnel.
Overtaking	To come up (on another vessel) from behind.
Owner's suite	Normally the most luxurious accommodation/cabin aboard in terms of size, comfort, location, and features.
Pan-pan	The international urgency signal that a vessel uses to declare they have an urgent situation, but for the time being, the situation is not life-threatening or posing an immediate threat to the vessel itself.
Paper chart	A nautical chart printed on paper. They are often laminated or a heavy-duty, smudge-resistant paper. (See also chart.)
Paracord	A lightweight nylon rope originally used in the suspension lines of parachutes but now used as a general-purpose utility cord.

Parallel rules	A drafting instrument used by navigators to draw parallel lines on charts. It consists of two straight edges joined by two arms, which allows the edges to move closer or farther away from each other, while always remaining parallel.
Passage	A voyage between points that entails a large number (hundreds or thousands) of miles of boating/sailing in the open ocean.
Passageway	An internal corridor allowing access (horizontally) to different areas or compartments onboard a ship. (The nautical equivalent of a hallway.)
Pelican cooler	A brand of deluxe coolers, heavily insulated and rated for extreme temperatures. They are made of sturdy plastic, have freezer-grade gaskets, and are leakproof.
PFD	Abbreviation for a Personal Flotation Device. (See also life jacket.)
Pier	A manmade structure that protrudes from the shore.
Pilot boat	A vessel dedicated to transferring a skilled helmsman/helmswoman (pilot) from a harbor (or river mouth) to a ship that requires steering or guidance (piloting) into the harbor, and vice versa.

Pilot chart atlas	An aid to navigation that depicts historical averages of winds, wave heights, currents, barometric pressure, and other weather conditions broken out per month, per ocean.
Pilothouse	An enclosed structure on a vessel from which the vessel can be steered and navigated by the helmsman. Also called a deckhouse.
Piracy	The practice of attacking, robbing, stealing from, or committing illegal violence against vessels at sea.
Pirate	One who engages in piracy.
Pirate flag	A flag, sometimes displaying a white skull and white crossbones on a black background, originally flown to indicate a pirate ship. The first recorded use of a flag displaying such symbols dates to the seventeenth century. Other pirate flags featured a skeleton and could be black or red. The pirate flag was usually only flown when the pirates wanted to announce their presence, i.e., just before a raid or battle. Now they are displayed for fun.
Pitching	An up and down movement of the bow and stern of a vessel at sea.
Pitchpoling	To turn upside down in the water by flipping the stern over the bow.
Plot a course	Basically drawing a line between two points on a chart, calculating the distance between them, and determining the compass heading. (Having dividers and parallel rules makes this easier.)

Point of sail	The angle of the sailboat related to the direction from which the wind is blowing. Sailing very close to the wind is called "close hauled" or "beating." Sailing with the wind directly behind you is called "running." The points in between those two are "close reach," "beam reach," and "broad reach." Sails are trimmed (adjusted) to be more or less efficient depending on where the wind is coming from.
Polarized sunglasses	While ordinary sunglasses can reduce the total amount of light reaching your eyes, they don't eliminate much glare. Polarized lenses filter out most of the glare and block nearly all the damaging UVA and UVB (ultraviolet) rays.
Port	1. The left side of the vessel when aboard and facing forward. 2. Where vessels come in to dock.
Porthole	A round, window-like opening with a hinged, watertight glass cover in the side of a vessel for admitting light and/or air.
Position	Also called a fix, it is the determination of the vessel's location, arrived at by various methods, usually expressed as precise coordinates, in degrees, minutes, and seconds of latitude and longitude.
Powerboat	1. A boat propelled by an engine. 2. A fast boat used in racing.

Primary helm station/ Master helm station	When there are steering wheels on both sides of the boat, the side where the engine controls are located.
Propeller	A rounded blade that rotates in a circle and moves the vessel forward (or backward) through the water. Can be called "prop" for short.
Propane/Propane tanks	Liquid Propane Gas (LPG) is a flammable fuel, usually used for heating or cooking, that is stored in pressurized tanks.
Propane locker	A vapor-tight compartment enclosing propane (LPG) tanks and some of their associated connections, separated from the interior of the vessel or outside of the vessel in a location where leaking gas will not drain to the interior of the vessel.
Quarter berth	A sleeping space (bed) aboard a vessel, often a single bunk, and sometimes placed where there is minimal space.
Radar	Equipment to, or a means of, sending out radio waves to detect objects in the distance that may be obscured by weather, darkness, are simply out of sight, or difficult to see.
Radar blip	A generic term for a radar echo or radar response from an object displayed on the radar screen or other type of display.

Radar reflector	A device designed to reflect radar waves in order to make the vessel more highly visible on radar screens. The radar reflector should be sized for the vessel it will be used on and mounted as high as is practical. Radar reflectors are often lightweight and modular for ease in storage. When assembled, they usually contain at least three intersecting planes and are often, but not always, circular.
Raft	1. Buoyant materials fastened together to make a floating platform. 2. To tie two (or more) boats together, side by side, while in the water, away from a dock, to assist in easily moving between them. 3. Two or more boats tied side by side are said to be "rafted."
Railing	See stern rail. See lifeline.
Raise sail	The act of hoisting, hauling out, unfurling, or otherwise deploying the sail(s).
Reaching	A point of sail where the wind is coming from a direction approximately between 2-5:00 or 7-10:00.

Red and green lights	A type of navigation light used at night by vessels at sea. They are called sidelights or combination lights. One of them will be visible to another vessel approaching, or being approached from the side. Both of them will be visible on a vessel that is approaching/overtaking your vessel from behind. The red light indicates the port side of a vessel while the green light indicates the starboard side of the vessel. However, when either color is used in conjunction with one or more white lights, it may mean something else entirely.
Reef	1. To decrease sail area (make the sail smaller). 2. A ridge of jagged rock, coral, or sand just above or below the surface of the water/sea.
Reefing	The act of making the sail smaller.
Regatta	A rowing, powerboat, or sailing race or a series of such races.
Registration papers	Written documentation providing evidence of vessel ownership.
Repel boarders	Any action used to keep people from coming aboard a vessel uninvited or unwelcomed.
Replacement canvas	Another name for spare sails, even if the sails aren't made of canvas but another material instead.
RIB	Abbreviation for a Rigid Inflatable Boat. A lightweight but high performance, high-capacity boat constructed of a solid and an inflatable hull.

Rigging	1. Standing rigging are the cables, shrouds, and stays that support the mast(s). 2. Running rigging are the sheets, halyards, and lines that control the sail(s) or parts of the sail(s).
Rigging knife	A specially designed knife used to cut heavy lines. It may have a serrated edge for sawing through the line. It may have an extra-heavy blade, suitable for pounding with a mallet, to drive the blade through the line. The folding models often come equipped with a marlinspike for convenience. (See also marlinspike.)
Rigging station/ Rigging alcove	A dedicated area in a vessel containing rigging equipment, specialized tools, and supplies, often including an assortment of lines and fittings and perhaps even extra sails.
Right-of-way	As per the navigation rules, the vessel that has the legal authority to stay on (hold) its course.
Roaring forties	Winds that consistently blow from west to east in the Southern Hemisphere, located in the area between forty and fifty degrees south latitude.
Roller furling	A mechanism to furl (roll) a sail in or out. It is also used when reefing (making the sail smaller) by furling it in partway.
Round turn with two half hitches knot	A two-part knot commonly used to secure a vessel to a dock post. The first part (the round turn) passes the line around the object, encircling it, while the second part (the two half hitches) secures the end of the line to itself.

Rudder	An underwater appendage that controls the direction of the vessel when moving through the water.
Run aground	The act of getting the vessel stuck (on the bottom) in shallow water. (See also aground.)
Running	Point of sail where the wind is coming from directly behind you at roughly the 6:00 position.
Running lights	See navigation light(s).
Running rigging	The sheets, halyards, and lines that control the sail(s) or parts of the sail(s). (See also rigging.)
Sail	Material (often a specialty fabric) used on a vessel that uses wind for power to propel the vessel.
Sail loft	An area (often a large room) where the manufacturing (making) of sails takes place.
Sail slugs	A fitting on the sail that allows it to attach to the mast by fitting into a slot.
Sailboat	A vessel that uses wind power to propel it forward through the water.
Sailing certifications	A certification, issued by various sailing organizations, stating the individual has completed progressively advancing levels of training. Proof of certification, including presenting a sailing resume, is often a requirement to charter a sailboat, especially the larger ones. There are also various levels of certifications for sailing instructors.

Sailing gloves	Gloves designed to protect the hands from abrasion and blisters that often occur when handling lines. They are available in different styles, fabrics, and colors, depending on the expected usage.
Sailing shoes	Comfortable, casual shoes usually made of canvas, suede, or leather, with non-marking rubber soles designed for use on slippery surfaces. (Also known as boat or deck shoes.)
Salon table	The primary dining table in the salon of a vessel. Some salon tables can convert into a berth for sleeping.
Sargasso Sea	A region of the north Atlantic Ocean bounded entirely by ocean currents. It is the only sea without a land boundary. Unlike most of the Atlantic Ocean, the Sargasso Sea has characteristic brown Sargassum seaweed and calm blue water.
Satellite phone	A telephone that transmits and receives voice (and possibly short messages) from orbiting satellites providing coverage around the world.

SCUBA certification	A diving certification, issued by various dive organizations, stating the individual has completed required levels of training, normally consisting of coursework, pool work, and open water experience. Proof of certification, including presenting a logbook with recent dives, is a requirement to have dive tanks refilled (with air). There are also various levels of certifications for diving instructors. (SCUBA stands for Self-Contained Underwater Breathing Apparatus.)
Sculling	To move the boat forward by rapidly swinging the rudder back and forth.
Scuttle/scuttling	To deliberately sink a vessel, often by making holes in the side or bottom of it.
Sea anchor	See drogue.
Secondary helm station	When there are steering wheels on both sides of the boat, the side that doesn't have the engine controls.
Sextant	A precision astronomical instrument used to determine latitude and longitude by measuring the angular distances, especially the altitude, of the sun, the moon, and/or the stars.
Shakedown cruise	Time on the water to test a vessel's performance. Usually used for new vessels or those having undergone substantial repairs.
Sheet bend knot	A type of knot used to tie together two lines of unequal diameter.

Sheet-in	To tighten, bring in, or increase tension on the sail for sailing closer (higher) to the wind.
Sheet(s)	A control line(s) for a sail. Sheets control the sails side to side.
Shellback	A sailor who has crossed the equator.
Ship	A large vessel. Rule of thumb: a boat will fit on the deck of a ship, but a ship will not fit on the deck of a boat.
Shipshape	A desirable condition aboard a vessel where everything is clean, neat, tidy, organized, and in good working order or condition.
Shipwreck	1. An accident in which a vessel is destroyed, lost, or sunk, especially by hitting a reef or running aground. 2. The skeletal structure of such an unfortunate vessel.
Shipwrecked	Those persons affected by a shipwreck.
Shoal	A shallow area of rock or coral.
Shore power	The provision of shoreside electrical power to a vessel at berth while its main and auxiliary engines (or generators) are shut down.
Shroud	A wire or cable supporting the mast. (See also standing rigging.)
Sidelights	See red and green lights.

Signal flags	1. Various flags, used internationally, by vessels at sea to spell out short messages. When used in certain combinations, they may have special meanings. 2. Signal flags were used in military operations to communicate while maintaining radio silence.
Signal flag halyard	A line specifically used to display a signal flag.
Single-handed	To pilot or sail the vessel alone or without help.
Skiff	Any type of shallow, flat-bottomed, open boat with a sharp bow and square stern. (See also dinghy or tender.)
Skipper	See captain. Skipper is a less formal title.
Slip	1. The area of water that is between docks, piers, or wharves where vessels can be moored. (A space to park/secure your vessel that has shore access. See berth def. #2) 2. To fall or lose one's balance.
Slip fee	A fee paid to keep your vessel in its slip/berth/allotted space at a dock.
Solar panels	A device used to convert the sun's energy into electricity (or heat).
Solar shower	A device originally designed for campers, it consists of a container that absorbs the sun's direct heat to raise the temperature of the inside water. It will have a hose and showerhead with a valve to regulate the flow and normally a hole or hook from which to hang it.

Sock	See spinnaker sleeve.
Sole	See floorboards.
Spar	A long, cylindrical object made of wood, metal, or composite material, such as the mast, boom, or bowsprit.
Spinnaker	A large, usually colorful, three-cornered sail, typically bulging when full (of wind), set near the bow, used when running (sailing downwind).
Spinnaker pole	A spar used to help support and control the spinnaker. It can also be used with other headsails when sailing downwind without the spinnaker.
Spinnaker sleeve	A device used to make deploying and retrieving the spinnaker sail much easier. Also called a "dousing sock" or simply a "sock."
Spreader	A horizontal support for the shrouds that sticks out from the mast.
Squall	A sudden, strong wind gust, often lasting only a few minutes, and usually blowing in excess of 16 knots.
Stacked berths	A bed on a vessel, stacked one above the other, like bunk beds.
Stanchion	A vertical metal support along the outside of the deck supporting the lifelines.

Stand on vessel	As per the navigation rules, the vessel that has the right-of-way and should hold its course.
Standing rigging	Cables that support the mast, usually braided wire. These have specific names depending on location. The cable in the front of the mast is the forestay, the cable on the side(s) of the mast is a shroud, and the cable at the back of the mast is the backstay. (See also rigging.)
Starboard	The right side of the vessel when aboard and facing forward.
Starter / Starting battery	The battery that provides power to start the engine.
Statute mile	A unit of measurement equal to 5,280 feet. (See also nautical mile.)
Steerage	Having enough speed through the water to be able to steer/control the vessel's direction.
Stern	The aftermost part of the vessel.
Stern light	Part of the navigation lights. They are white and often located at or near the stern (rear) of the vessel so they are visible from behind or from nearly behind the vessel.
Stern line	A dock line used to secure the rear of the boat to the dock.

Stern rail	A railing, often metal, at or near the stern of a vessel designed to help restrain passengers (or crew) from falling overboard. It is usually more substantial than a lifeline. May also be called the "stern pulpit."
Stiff breeze	Vague term for a moderate wind with a speed of 10-15 knots.
Stow	To put something away on a boat.
Support	See stanchion
Surface clutter	Unwanted echoes (blips) in the radar system causing sometimes serious performance issues. Such echoes can be returned from ground, sea, rain, atmospheric turbulence, etc. Sometimes the "clutter" can be eliminated by adjusting the radar's sensitivity controls.
Swells	Big waves that travel over long distances in the open ocean.
Swim platform	A structure on the stern of a boat designed to make getting into or out of the water easier.
Tack/tacking	1. A maneuver to bring the bow (front) of the boat through the eye of the wind. 2. The direction the boat is sailing as it moves through the wind.
Tall ship	Although not strictly defined, it refers to any large, traditionally rigged sailing vessel. Tall ships usually have more than one mast and often have square sails.
Tankage	The capacity and/or contents of a tank.

Teak	The wood from a teak tree. It is strong, durable, resistant to insects and warping, and is frequently used in ship building.
Tender	A small boat used to ferry crew to and from a larger vessel. (See also dinghy.)
Tether	A short lead for a safety harness.
Tethered	The process of connecting your safety tether to something secure.
Thru-hull fitting	An intentional hole through the hull, fitted with a metal or plastic device, through which fluids can flow in either direction. Thru-hull fittings used below the waterline are equipped with a shut-off valve.
Thru-hull plug	A tapered or cone-shaped stopper, often made of teak, that can be used to temporarily plug a leaking thru-hull fitting.
Tommy Kraft	A fictional person with a fictional line of marine supply stores.
Topside	On or toward the upper deck of a vessel.
Tower	An elevated structure on some deep-sea fishing boats used as an aid in spotting certain species of fish.
Transom	A structural reinforcement to strengthen the stern of the vessel.
Traveler	A track which allows for side-to-side adjustments of the mainsail (or mizzen sail).

Trim	1. To adjust the sails to be more or less efficient. 2. To pull in or let out a sheet.
Trucker's hitches knot	A type of knot, used like a block and tackle, to increase the amount of tension on a line.
True north	North according to the earth's axis, not magnetic north (according to a compass).
UFO	Any unidentified flying object, often associated with sightings of alien ships.
Underway	Moving through the water.
Unfurl/Unfurled (the sails)	See hauled out.
United States Coast Guard	A branch of the United States' armed forces, responsible for the enforcement of maritime law and for the protection of life and property at sea.
Vented locker	A storage compartment utilizing vents to offer increased or maximum ventilation and airflow.
Vessel	Any boat, ship, yacht, or watercraft.
VHF radio	A common type of radio used in marine applications. VHF (very high frequency) refers to the marine frequency range of 156 to 174 MHz, inclusive. Channel 16 (156.8 MHz) is the international calling and distress channel.
Wake	The waves caused by the motion of the vessel through the water. The wake from a large vessel, like a cruise ship, can be dangerous to small craft getting caught in it.

Wastewater	The product contained by the vessel's sewage system. Numerous laws and rules govern where and when wastewater can be discharged overboard. It is normally referred to as "greywater" when without fecal contamination, such as that from sinks, baths, showers, or dishwashers. It is normally referred to as "blackwater" when having fecal contamination (from toilets).
Wastewater pump-out station	A specific area with specialized equipment to remove wastewater from the vessel's holding tanks. Your nose will usually alert you to the proximity of where such an area is located.
Water maker	A device used to obtain potable (drinkable) water from seawater by the process of reverse osmosis. Also called a "desalinator".
Waterline	1. A line that marks the level of the surface of water on something, usually the vessel's hull but often the shoreline as well. 2. A line marked on the outside of a vessel that corresponds to the water's surface when the vessel is afloat.
Watertight door	A special type of door, found on vessels, designed to prevent the ingress of water from one compartment to another during flooding or accidents.
Wave trough	The low point in the cycle of a wave.
Weather fax	A facsimile machine designed to receive and print high-quality, high-definition weather charts and satellite images.
Weigh anchor	To retrieve the anchor when ready to get underway.

Wheel	Used to steer the sailboat by controlling the rudder. Some wheels fold to save space when not in use.
White light	A type of navigation light used at night by vessels at sea.
Winch	A mechanical, drum-shaped device, using gears and a handle (or electric operation) to increase the tension on a line.
Wind rose	A circular graphic that represents the speed and direction of the wind over a period of time for a particular area.
Windlass	A machine (usually powered by electricity) used to feed or retract the anchor chain (or line). Essentially a winch for the anchor.
Windward	1. Facing the wind or the side facing the wind. 2. The side or direction from which the wind is blowing. (The side opposite leeward.)
Wire cable	See standing rigging
Workroom	A room (or compartment) containing specialized tools, parts, supplies, and/or equipment for making repairs or building needed things.
Yacht	Any sail or power vessel used for pleasure, cruising, or racing. Conventionally, any watercraft over 40 feet in length will likely qualify as a yacht, but the minimum length to be considered a yacht is debatable. And the category of "mega" or "super" yacht is also very subjective.
Yacht club	A club organized for the enjoyment of sailing (and boating).

ABOUT THE AUTHORS

Jim Schoendaller

Jim Schoendaller is a Certified Sailing Instructor, ironically teaching in the landlocked state of Colorado. He is a retired public-sector employee who is enjoying writing novels instead of contracts. He is an avid traveler, having visited 5 continents so far, and is an accomplished Ballroom dancer.

Jeanne C. Stein

Jeanne C. Stein is the national bestselling author of the Urban Fantasy series, The Anna Strong Vampire Chronicles and most recently, The Fallen Siren Series written as S. J. Harper. There are nine books in the Anna Strong series and two books and two novellas in a series written with Samantha Sommersby under the S. J. Harper pseudonym. She also has more that a dozen short story credits, including the novella, Blood Debt, from the New York Times bestselling anthology, Hexed and The NYT bestselling anthology, Dead But Not Forgotten edited by Charlaine Harris. Her short stories have been published in collections here in the US and the UK. Her latest, an Anna Strong novel titled Paradox, was released in November 2019.